The EROTICA BOOK CLUB
for Nice Ladies

CONNIE SPITTLER

Connie Spittler 4/27/15
For the joy of reading

Fiction Junction
an imprint of River Junction Press LLC

The Erotica Book Club for Nice Ladies is a work of fiction, and names, characters, places, and incidents are fictional. Any resemblance to actual events, locales, or persons living or dead is entirely coincidental. Although the poisonous potions are imaginary, the herbs used within them are dangerous and should not be used in any way. The herb "lively" is fictional. Other listed herbs should not be regarded as consumable and no herbal uses contained in this novel are intended to constitute, nor should be considered as medical advice or serve as a substitute for the advice of a physician or other qualified health care provider.

Copyright © 2015 by Connie Spittler
All rights reserved.

Published in the United States by Fiction Junction, an imprint of River Junction Press LLC, Omaha, NE.
www.riverjunctionpress.com
Trade paper May 1, 2015

Book Design by Jamison Design

Publisher's Cataloging-In-Publication Data
(Prepared by The Donohue Group, Inc.)

Spittler, Connie.
  The Erotica Book Club for Nice Ladies / Connie Spittler.
   pages ; cm
  Issued also in various ebook formats.
  ISBN: 978-0-9914093-6-5
  1. Librarians--California--Fiction. 2. Book clubs (Discussion groups)--California--Fiction. 3. Rare books--Fiction. 4. Murder--California--Fiction. 5. Erotic literature--Fiction. 6. Mystery fiction. I. Title.

PS3619.P588 E76 2015
813/.6

ALSO BY CONNIE SPITTLER

The Desert Eternal

The Legend of Brook Hollow

Lincoln & the Gettysburg Address

Powerball 33

Analysis of a Novel, Powerball 33

Cowboys & Wild, Wild Things

PROLOGUE: 1500 A.D.

The wrinkled hand of Duchess Jardin trembled as she dipped her quill in the pot of blood-red ink. *Foxglove. Monkshood. Belladonna.* She scrolled each scarlet letter with care, spelling out herbal names that dripped with poison, dangerous herbs used by Z, the gypsy healer, in his experimental treatments. Her goose feather pen marked down each remedy, listing the exact ingredients and instructions.

She straightened her gold-brocade sleeves, then stared out the window of the high tower, thinking back to the arrival of the quiet traveler. He'd requested permission to enter the iron gate of their Alsatian chateau, then told her of his experimental cures. As head of the estate, she'd offered him the storage cave for his work. After a few days, she began to pluck herbs from the bouquets drying in the scullery for him to use in his recipes. Then she began to assist him, crushing and pounding mixtures in the hope of healing her own aches and pains. When signs appeared from others that his curatives had healing powers, she tried small sips, but found no relief from illnesses that ravaged her worn body.

Sparrow song outside the window brought her back to the writing. She began again, this time listing the five ingredients for Z's strange tea, a brew flowery with the fragrance of erotic scents. *Dragoncello. Mint. Lovage. Yarrow. Lively.* It was his only recipe using herbs safe to ingest. When Z declared this brew not only reversed the signs of aging, but increased the appetite for love, she noticed those who drank it regularly appeared younger and more vital.

Unable to contain her curiosity, one day she tried the elixir.

Reeling from its effects, she crept off to bed to dream of bronzed men who satisfied her in every way. The next day, she walked for hours in the garden, recalling the pleasures that had overtaken her aging body and mind. Returning to the chateau, she worried about ways the tea might affect the lives of castle estate dwellers. When death took some extremely ill patients who'd taken Z's cures, she sent the healer away.

But for the duchess, the question remained: had the sick and old died as nature intended, or from the healer's potions? Like the gypsy, she believed that earth's green things could heal. Now, sensing she had little time left to live, she recorded his herbal cures for the future, a time when the validity and safety of such plants could be studied and applied to dreaded diseases of all kinds.

After the Duchess finished writing, she folded the pages of cures and placed them in the placket she'd attached to the end-papers of her book of gardening and herbals cures. She lit the candle and applied two red seals, one for the inside pocket that held Z's remedies, the other to seal the cover of her book. The Duchess gathered her strength and wrote a short note to her son.

> *My beloved Gozbert,*
>
> *You have shown great promise since your father died. My time to pass is near and now you must guide the workings of our beloved Jardin Estate. I ask one thing of you, to lock my book of herbal cures safely away from curious eyes. It contains no personal family secrets, just my drawings and listings of our garden plants and peasant cures, but it also includes the gypsy healer's potions for dropsy, growths and romantic aging. Keep the book safe in the storage cave until an appropriate time. There is no way to foresee if one day, my record of curatives might be thought valuable by truly learned persons and used for serious illnesses that befall others.*
>
> *Your loving mother, the Duchess Jardin*

She placed her note on the scarlet cover of the *Book of Cures* and tied a gold ribbon around it. Weak and weary, she blew out the candle and let her hand rest on a sprig of lovage picked from her garden. She waited for the shadow of death to visit, its lingering weight pressing down on her body. When a breeze sailed by, the frail spirit of the Duchess was gone, an old soul catching a ride on the wing of a sparrow.

A butterfly strayed through the opening of the chateau cupola and lit on the manuscript. Orange and black wings swung back and forth. No sound issued from the steady movement. But the air moved and the flutter of its mosaic tapestry continued as the air received the invisible tapping of fragile beating. The movement increased and expanded. It filled the tower space and beyond, joining the gathering wind that rushed over the sun-burst design of the garden, traveling past the eerie cloud of war and disease that hovered over the Alsatian countryside.

Later, sparrows nested in the blossoming plum trees and whistled to herbal seedlings that sprouted from loamy depths.

Later still, bees congregated in the greening fields, called by the scent of lovage, clover, and wild carrot that enriched the country air.

And the silent song of rhythmic orange wings swept on through time and weather.

CHAPTER 1

As the earth spun in the universe, plagues and disasters came and went, but the Jardin family survived in their rugged stone castle, set amidst the rolling Alsatian landscape. The Jardin family invested in Pinot Blanc grape vines, and their emphasis moved from gilded chateau life to that of a vineyard famed for its excellent product, a smoky Klevner. Surrounded by fields of intertwining grapevines, the same vegetables and unusual herbs still grew in the garden that gave the Jardin Estate vintages their name.

The heaviness of centuries turned over, and the *Book of Cures* remained hidden from the world in the estate storage cave, until a scarlet marketing tool sent its herbal message tumbling into the 21st century. By 2015, Jardin wine was selling well enough, but the elderly Duke Quincy wanted more financial return. He hired a marketing firm to expand international sales and the company proposed a red, attention-getting direct mail leaflet. Not only did the flyer promote the estate wine, it enticed the curious by mentioning the hidden family book.

———

Alsatian Heirloom Seeds for Sale
Poisonous and Nonpoisonous
For Decorative Use Only
From the Medieval Garden of the Jardin Estates
Home of the hidden, sealed Book of Cures
Jardin Wine & Herbal Seed Prices Inside

———

According to the marketing man, seeds were the key to herbal life. Seeds enhanced by ancient and dangerous mystique were not easily available. Where would one buy such an unconventional collection? From the Jardin Estates, of course, an Alsatian vineyard known for its excellent Klevner.

In a computerized selection, the first global area chosen for distribution of the leaflet was the United States, a country known for its deep pockets and generous spirit. After additional research, the first state selected to test the use of mysterious seeds to sell wine, was California.

CHAPTER 2

The salty fragrance of a seaside morning washed over the stucco of the mission style building in Groverly, California. Inside, Assistant Director Lily McFae worked in her standard cubicle at the Main Branch Library, sorting real mail from junk. She let her mind wander over her hopeless, loveless life. Now in her early forties, she longed again for a man to love, for kisses and embraces, that special touch of romance. Someone she'd yet to meet. Someone somewhere waiting for her. She shivered. It was now so unlikely.

Accompanied by the music of Mozart from her iPhone, she propped open a book on origami destined to be removed from the library shelves because of its low checkout number. Nose to page, she reached for a scarlet flyer, the top piece on the throw-away mail pile. Her fingers followed the detailed illustration. Valley folds. Mountain folds. Multiple folds. A paper butterfly emerged out of a pleated cocoon. In a flippant mood, the librarian sent her handiwork fluttering over the top of the partition.

An annoyed voice came from the other side. "What on earth was that?"

Peering around the wall, Lily saw her origami masterpiece lodged in the upswept hairdo of her stern boss, Library Director Trummel.

"Whoops," Lily said, "sorry about that."

"Playtime's over." Ms. Trummel flicked the paper insect to the floor. "Have you found a replacement exhibit for the baseball cards? They gave us such a short cancellation notice."

"Nothing yet, but I'll find something."

"Try to find a replacement soon, will you?" Director Trummel handed over an official envelope. "This is for you from the Groverly City Employment Services."

Tearing open the flap, Lily pulled out and unfolded a single piece of paper.

> *Dear Ms. McFae:*
> *Due to unfortunate cutbacks, the position of Assistant*
> *Director will expire in two months. Please consider this*
> *your official termination notice.*

Her mind stumbled and stopped. No words formed and a throbbing swept through her body. She closed her eyes. Her job of watching over precious, old volumes in the Special Collections Room would be gone. A wave of disbelief engulfed her.

Ms. Trummel adjusted the crisp cuffs of her business suit. "Unfortunately, you're the first to go, but the library's financial problems are real and there must be sacrifices."

Lily counted. "It took twenty-four words to officially strike down my life as I know it. Is my head the only one on the guillotine?"

"Yes, but consider this, the blade's not falling for a while. You must have heard the budget rumors and talk of cutbacks." Ms. Trummel looked around, examining Lily's cubicle. "That letter is the reason I've assigned you a speaking engagement, a small road trip so you can get away from here. I received a request from a woman named Piper Valerian in Nolan. Since her town has no library, she needs help starting a community book club. I thought you'd like to get out of the building to consider your options."

Lily bent to pick up the paper butterfly and set it aside. "I'm not the best public speaker. Perhaps someone else should go."

"No one else is available. Think of this as your last chance to shine."

"I don't feel like shining. Maybe reflecting." She considered her recent run-in with Director Trummel, the argument over removing classics and other selections from the shelves. As Assistant Director, she'd protested the new library edict: Due to lack of shelf space, any book not checked out within the last two years would be sent to a state warehouse and retrieved only by special request. The elaborate protest she'd staged had failed. Maybe that recent maneuver figured in her dismissal.

Ms. Trummel examined the tall stack of books on Lily's desk. *Tap, tap*, the perfectly manicured finger sounded on the top book cover. "These are classics you've checked out because they were in trouble, right? You do skate near the edge, don't you?"

"You know I've been a dedicated librarian and reliable worker in the system for years." Bitterness sounded in Lily's voice as she crumpled the letter and stuffed it in her pocket. "I take exception to my dismissal. I really must." Her raised tone carried out into other cubicles.

"Your bad attitude is showing, Lily. Nothing is permanent in today's business world. Let me know when you find the exhibit replacement. By the way, you're on call in half an hour for the Readers' Advisory Desk." The Director's heels clipped down the hall.

Dragging her feet, Lily followed a few steps behind to find consolation in library books she loved. Her willowy frame in a wrinkled, loose linen dress and her unruly auburn hair, were in marked contrast to the high style figure of her boss.

But head high, Lily strode the stacks like a duchess in her garden, walking through the rows, choosing selections for the start-up book club as she remembered favored fiction. The plot of Willa Cather's *Death Comes for the Archbishop*. The characters in *Middlemarch* by George Eliot. The lilting phrases and passages of Virginia Woolf's *The Waves*. Rather than best sellers for the new reading group, she gravitated to beloved classics. An additional factor in her choices was the absence of checkout dates. She pulled an assortment of books in trouble, those that had inspired readers for ages, but not recently. Later at her desk, she'd decide on a varied assortment of reading to present to the club.

Back in her cubbyhole, Lily's hands moved slowly through the pieces of junk mail and one by one, dropped them into the wastebasket, until her desk was almost clear. She unfolded the origami butterfly made from the scarlet flyer and smoothed the creases. As she studied the ad copy about seeds for sale from the Jardin Estate in Europe, her heart leapt.

Alsatian Heirloom Seeds for Sale
Poisonous and Nonpoisonous
For Decorative Use Only
From the Medieval Garden of the Jardin Estates
Home of the hidden, sealed Book of Cures
Jardin Wine & Herbal Seed Prices Inside

Immediately, her mind jumped to a certain volume in the Special Collections Room, *Unexplained Ancient Mysteries, Volume II*, a rare encyclopedia that was her favorite browsing book. The only such volume known to exist, she found it a mixed delight of history, mystery and unraveled puzzles. She was certain the flyer tied into an article in that encyclopedia.

She rushed off to the library's inner haven of collectibles and donned the compulsory white gloves. Standing still, she let the printer's ink of ancient writers enfold her. The subtle aura of antique fonts on deepened pigskin replaced the unexpected words of her termination letter. She breathed in the perfume of old books, catching a whiff of Egyptian marble paper and the scent of elephant folios.

After a few minutes, the sense of grace, wit, beauty, and intelligence persisting on pages for hundreds of years eased her troubled mind. And the tension in her shoulders disappeared.

Lifting her favorite encyclopedic reference from its assigned place, her gloved finger trailed down the index to find the article on page 102.

> *Accounts occasionally surface about the existence of a hidden manuscript, called the* Book of Cures, *hidden away by the Jardin family in Alsace. The story revolves around the book of the Duchess Jardin, her garden, and a healing gypsy. The family maintains the book was discovered during World War I when battles came near the Jardin Estate, and the storage vault was cleared for a*

shelter. Interviews with family members indicated they believed the book might contain information about herbal experiments conducted in the 1500's, perhaps using unsafe garden herbs. It's rumored that possibilities include remedies for dropsy, tremors, growths and confusion that might relate to cancer, heart disease and Alzheimer's. Herbalists find the mention of an anti-aging tea with sexually stimulating side effects particularly interesting.

Her mind flitted off course when she read the phrase "sexually stimulating side effects." She removed her glasses and rubbed her eyes. Regarding romantic prospects, things were different now. Since her surgery, she'd turned to the library bookshelves, letting classic lovers remind her of past encounters. The rough weave of herringbone. A loosened collar. The feel of a man's whiskers on a tanned face. Soft mouths together. Hardness pressed against her. Lily jerked back to the present, put on her glasses and read on.

None of these healing remedies have been studied or assessed since the family keeps the book sealed and hidden away. Jardin family members refuse to be responsible for serious medical problems that might occur from trials of mentioned cures in their family book. Herbalists speculate about the use of dangerous plants cultivated in the seven herbal beds of the circular garden, although poisonous herbs like belladonna, foxglove and monkshood, are cultivated separately from safer plants like yarrow, lovage, and dragoncello.

She checked the flyer. The winery order form matched the description of both safe and deadly herbs. She slipped *Volume II* back on the shelf, and smoothed her curly wisps of flyaway hair, leaving unanswered questions dancing in the air, like motes in the sunlight.

At her desk, she sent off an emailed seed order with instructions for rush delivery. This day, she needed the assurance of seeds; tiny, changing bits of life that moved from dark to light and flourished. She picked up the discarded scarlet flyer and followed the folds to reclaim the butterfly once more. The origami insect fluttered through the air for a brief moment before it nosedived.

In Strasbourg, France, the Global Antiquarian Society chose twenty of their rarest books to take on tour to the United States.

In a small town in California, heirloom plants of unusual strengths and aromas thrived in a secluded gypsy garden.

CHAPTER 3

The sun shone down on the clover, alfalfa, and lavender fields that surrounded the Verkie goat farm outside Nolan, California. White-tailed animals scrambled to nibble their oats and groats, nudging against Aggie Verkie as she poured grain into the trough. When the old woman finished her chores, she roamed the garden.

Lost in memories, she thought back to her husband, Camlo. Years ago, driving in their horse-drawn gypsy wagon, they'd slowed down at the first whisper of divine scent and watched bees cluster in fields of lavender, poppies, and wild carrot. When they came upon the abandoned goat farm, with the stream running through it, Camlo tied up their horse and parked their vardo near the dilapidated garage. In welcome, monarch butterflies sent silent, semaphore messages with their wings. The minute the two looked in each other's eyes, they gave up their wandering, turned into land dwellers, and drew even closer. They whitewashed the gabled house, the weathered barn, sheds, and drive-through garage. Camlo built a railroad tie garden and Aggie planted it, providing food for their table and green nourishment for their souls.

Now, the sight of bright, growing things nagged at Aggie like a loose tooth. The candle she called the California sun burned high in the sky, and she pulled her hand knit, brown sweater close to her body. The vigor of the garden pained her and contrasted to the last days of her dear Camlo. Sick and weakened, he'd died in slow motion from a decay she could not heal despite her constant tending. No gypsy remedies or blessings, no healing incantations, no potions or rich broth helped. Even doctors from the Groverly Hospital worked no magic. Although his body left her several months ago, her grief with its bone-chilling loss, still lingered on. After fifty years together, she could not let him go. Even with the rising temperature of the days, she stayed cold. Her salvation was his long dark cape that kept her warm.

Through the months since he'd been gone, she'd watched the circular garden of seven beds flourish. Overlooked by a stand of tall milkweed, the seasonal wheel turned as her gypsy herbs and vegetables swayed in the sun. Parsnip tops and rutabaga peered from rich dirt. Garlic shoots curled in loop-de-loops. Rosemary and periwinkle bristled with bees. In special rows, lovage and dragoncello tumbled, matching the vigor of yarrow and verbena, while gypsywort rambled along the garden edge that bordered the stream. Stalks of foxglove, monkshood and belladonna hid in the corner by the thorn apple, separated from other growing things because of their deadly juices. Only the old plum tree bowed and lost its leaves in respect for Camlo's leaving. The wrinkles on Aggie's face deepened. She rubbed pained, arthritic hands over her gray, braided hair.

Griffo, her tall, muscular nephew, hurried down the stairs from his room over the garage. He wore his red embroidered vest and Homburg hat. "I'm headed over to the Emporium. I got a job picketing from Boris, the new owner."

"Deliver the goat milk in town first. Then go build your fences."

Griffo waved a stick with a placard that read, "Save Our Town from XXX Movies!" He smirked. "Not fencing, I'm paid to walk back and forth in front of the place with this sign, so I don't have time to deliver milk today. I wonder if he'd consider carrying your goat milk."

Aggie knelt to touch a leaf of agrimony tinged with decay. "So will your important job bring you home for supper?"

"Probably. I get paid by the hour, come and go as I please."

"Then explain why you don't have time to deliver the milk." She yanked out the wilting plant, wincing from the twinge in her fingers. "Never mind, be on your way. I'll take the milk to town."

"Maybe you can get some new customers at the town meeting in the Used Stuff Store," Griffo said, "but you're probably afraid to ask anyone, since you're the local old gypsy hermit."

"Well, I just might go to the meeting." Aggie stood and brushed off her knees. She clacked her tongue and lifted the corners of her paisley apron. The beat of a zither played in her mind as she moved toward the kitchen. "I might just do that."

On her way to the porch, she snatched one sprig of yarrow to add a touch of bitterness to the sundown beet salad.

Piper Valerian, twenty-eight years old and the prettiest blonde in Nolan, tidied her Cut & Curl Salon, the only beauty/barber shop in town. The white exterior, with its candy-striped awnings, pots of pink geraniums, and plastic flamingos, invited local citizens in need of personal beautification. With time to spare before the book club meeting, she sterilized combs, swept the floor, polished the long wall mirror and threw towels in the salon's washing machine. Noticing the stack of old magazines with their torn corners, she pitched them one at a time into the trash bucket. Her hand brushed away the pink streak of hair that fell across her cheek and set her apart from other women in town. Her petite figure, turning this way and that in front of the mirror, was perfect. She sat down to study her face for blemishes, then trimmed potential split ends from her hair, and deepened her rosy lips. Finally, she let her hand touch her breast and felt softly, softly, then more firmly.

The revolving chair swung back and forth as Piper worried about her marriage with its set of new problems, Freddie wanting a baby for one thing, coupled with the other agonizing, secret worry. They had a perfect marriage with no discussions, ignoring any trouble that came near. She wondered if that was the reason their life sailed along so smoothly. Most of her high school girlfriends had married and moved away. Her mother lived in another state and serious phone conversations were impossible for both of them. With no one available for advice, she needed to figure things out alone. Through recent sleepless nights, flat on her back, feeling the lump, she came up with a solution: stop having sex with Freddie. The thought of him finding it, touching it, fondling the poison within her made her tremble.

She hoped for something to replace love making, like drowning herself in books of the romantic kind she'd always been curious about, books that told stories about the how, where and how often of other couples. What better place to find out this kind of intriguing stuff than in…not dirty books exactly, but novels called "hairotica" or something like that. If she could find exciting enough books to read, it might shake her mind away from her worries. That was the reason she'd requested a woman speaker from the Groverly Main Branch Library to help start a book club for the residents of Nolan. As soon as she was able, she'd find a way to fix things with Freddie.

Piper intended to pull the speaker aside after the talk and get some tips on that more delicious, provocative kind of reading. Librarians knew about such things, and the woman could point her toward titles filled with fantasy and fondling. She thought about Freddie's fingers, stroking her skin, roaming her body and her mouth tightened. Fiddling with the tweezers, she plucked a new arch for her eyebrows and looked around for more cleaning to keep busy, but the salon gleamed. She switched her pink work smock for a pastel plaid jacket and squaring her shoulders, strolled past two buildings to the Used Stuff Store. Chosen for size and seat selection, it was the only site possible for the Nolan town meeting about a book club.

Filled with regret over her confrontation with the library director, Lily drove past eucalyptus stands in Groverly toward her Nolan assignment. The miles of Monterey County ticked by as fields of grape vines softened the landscape, their heart-shaped leaves catching the light. She passed by the billboard that announced "Salad Bowl of the World." Soon, fields of pale green lettuce stretched into the horizon, followed by rows of strawberry plants offering occasional glimpses of plump, red berries.

A clammy feeling swept over her as she neared her destination. Nervous about her speech, she practiced by addressing the steering wheel. "How wonderful for all assembled here to discover the joys of creating a book club. I am sorry your town has no library.

(Here, smile sympathetically.) When I was informed of your wish, I was delighted. It will be an energizing experience to choose the first volume for your discussion. I bring a boxful of excellent possibilities. (Now hold up first book.) For example, *Wuthering Heights,* a classic, romantic novel written by Emily Bronte."

Informing the windshield, Lily condensed the plot and described the characters, but carefully, did not give away the ending. As the scenery sped by, she talked knowledgeably about the other selections in the box, chosen to represent literary diversity. "I sincerely thank you for this opportunity. (Perhaps nod.) I leave these examples for consideration by you, the new Nolan Book Club members. Perhaps you recall from *Tatler* that Joseph Addison and Richard Steele told us, 'Reading is to the mind what exercise is to the body.' With that to ponder, my very best to you all. Happy reading and hearty exercising." (Smile. Give a little farewell wave.)

Her foot pressed harder on the gas pedal, edging past the speed limit. She sighed, thinking about how one anxiety had replaced another, the practice session distracting her from the rumpled dismissal letter in the pocket of her dress.

The car flew past the straight green rows of the countryside. A sharp turn brought The Emporium in sight, an old wooden building a couple miles outside Nolan that she knew well from previous visits. But she'd never driven into the town proper. Nestled in a lush valley, the town was a picture-perfect California town. She slowed down and studied the residences that rolled by. Live oak trees hovered over brick and clapboard Victorian houses. Porches, rows of porches furnished with old rockers, beckoned the weary. Zinnia beds, stands of hollyhocks, and grape arbors thrived in side yards, with front yards abloom with butterfly gardens of asters, lantana, and milkweed. The traditional town square showed heavy plantings of flowers, shrubby pine, and tall eucalyptus. One bench in the little park was provided for anyone who cared to sit and watch the activities on Main Street.

She continued down the thoroughfare, passing by a gas station, post office, grocery, feed store, and hardware. She noticed the Cut & Curl, next to a bar called The Hopper. At the end of the street, stood the Used Stuff Store, the place chosen by Piper

Valerian as the location for a town meeting about a book club.

She blanched when she saw about thirty townsfolk settled in chairs of mixed pedigree, each with a tag marked "available for sale." The room hummed with the murmur of an expectant audience as she hauled her small box of books to the front.

A voluptuous, blonde woman behind a painted desk flipped her pink streak of hair and waved. She pointed to a chair in the first row. "Welcome, a big welcome to our guest speaker. Come and sit down." The young woman's enthusiastic voice filled the room. "Wow, so many of you interested in starting a book club. Thanks to the Used Stuff twins, Sax Morton, who moved lots of bureaus and tables to make room for the seating, and Maxine Morton, for allowing us to meet here."

Maxine stood up to small applause. Her wavy brown hair framed a full face and her sturdy form showed off lacy white finery. "Sax and I are both readers, but it seems Sax is busy elsewhere at the moment."

Piper forged on. "This is how it came to be. The other day, I called the Main Library in Groverly and just like that, they sent us an expert." She pointed at Lily, perched primly in an overstuffed chair. "So at this time, I give you our smart lady, Ms. McFae." Piper slipped into the chair next to the still seated speaker and leaned over. "I need to talk to you, afterward. Will you stay?"

Lily nodded. She smoothed her hair and her loose beige shift, clasped and unclasped her hands, pursed and re-pursed her mouth. She sat, waiting for some unknown energy to move her, then felt a strong nudge from Piper.

The librarian adjusted her glasses, picked up her book box and followed her loose knees to the makeshift podium. She heard her breath weave in and out of her lungs' soft tissue. Like a moth swimming through thick, red wine, the sensation of flapping wings moved through her bloodstream. When the pulsating creature reached her heart, she'd explode. She knew it.

A prisoner in the Used Stuff Store, she faced that form of civilized torture accepted by polite society described as public speaking. She worked to reclaim the words chosen on her drive from the city.

"Thank you, uh, all assembled here."

The eyes of the audience bored through her and judged her, a dreary woman from the city.

She looked around the store, overburdened with leftovers from closets and basements, from attics and hideaways. She was the perfect addition, one more remnant.

"I was informed that you have no library in town and wish to…" The eggbeater in her mind revolved to a standstill and she cleared her throat. Waiting for inspiration, she looked down at the box of books she'd brought from the library. Her hand sought the top of a familiar volume, *Wuthering Heights*. With the cover cool to her palm, she lifted the classic book to display to the group. "…wish to read. Perhaps, a romance."

Lily reached into the box again, her hand seeking the next book exterior. "I brought different genres for your consideration, like science fiction. This is Bradbury's *Fahrenheit 451*." She quickly grabbed other books. "A biography of *John Quincy Adams*. An anthology of women's stories called *Our Spirit, Our Reality*. Or poetry, like *Favorite Verse Through the Ages*. These books are lent from the Groverly Library so you can …" Lily put the books down to push her glasses closer to her eyebrows. "…can read. Select one. Contact the library for multiple copies. Everyone reads the same title. Then you discuss. Remember, reading is brain food. On that note, happy exercising."

Polite clapping filled the store, and the audience filed out in silence. The front door of the store beckoned its escape hatch, and Lily followed the crowd, moving toward the outside air.

✥

Piper hurried to the desk to study the literary assortment. The stack of library books brought only one other person to the front. Aggie, in her multi-colored patchwork skirt, gradually inched forward against the shuffle of leaving attendees. When the owner of the goat farm reached the pile of books, she hung back to give Piper first choice of the selections.

"What an exit that lady made," Piper whispered. "And she loses points for a bad hairdo. Admit it, she's an odd bird."

"Maybe a person to figure out," Aggie moved closer. "Case of jippety nerves, I expect."

"I'll take the romance, for sure." Piper grabbed *Wuthering Heights*.

Aggie took the poetry book, then set it down. "She didn't talk long. I liked that about her."

"You know, a trim at my shop would fix up her straggles in one sitting. I asked her to stay afterward, but she took off like a bat."

"Maybe she's waiting outside," Aggie said.

"Of course." Piper rushed toward the last of the audience emptying into the street. She found Lily gazing at the gathering clouds of the wheezy afternoon.

She touched the librarian's arm. "Thank you so much for coming. I thought more people would stay and I did hope for a few spicier selections. Come back in. For a minute. Please?"

"I guess so." Lily followed Piper, and they returned to Aggie and the books.

"Two people would be enough for a club, don't you think, in a little town the size of ours?" Piper reached for the science fiction.

"You can have as many or as few as you like," Lily said. "I don't see a problem."

Aggie blinked. "I'm not sure I belong in any club. I came to deliver goat milk to Used Stuff, then stayed to listen to the meeting. It was free entertainment."

"Please join. It will be fun and easy too." Piper picked up the poetry anthology.

"If one person likes the book, you pass it on to the other person," suggested Lily. "Then get together and discuss the parts you liked or didn't like."

"I don't have much time left after the goats." Aggie looked down at her gnarled hands. "And I've never…discussed."

"I know I never drove out to your farm for milk and you never came into my shop, but this way, we'll get to know each other. We'll chat. Here, take this one. It looks like it has lots of different writers inside." Piper thrust the volume of poetry into Aggie's hands.

"I don't know." Aggie paged through the book.

"Tell you what, if Ms. McFae comes back to lead our first meeting and helps us get the hang of it, we'll do it." She gave Lily a pleading look.

The librarian gazed at the classics on the desk, and then at the faces of the women. "I suppose I could."

"I'll take three books, if you don't mind." Piper tucked away the thick anthology of women's writing. She handed Aggie the last volume. "You take the biography of J. Q. Adams. He's an important person, but a dead one and I already heard about him in high school."

"So if I read and you read, that makes a club?" Aggie put the books in her milk carryall.

"Seems like it." Piper took Lily's arm and whispered in her ear. "Do you know any books called, uh, her-otica? You know, X-Rated?"

"I do," Lily said. "They even exist in libraries, available to check out."

"I'd be interested in some of those titles."

Lily smiled at the request. "I'll see what I can do."

⚜

The smell of dusty furniture blessed the beginning of a book club.

⚜

One by one, Boris Ratchov released his antique daggers, imbedding sharply honed points deep into the cork lined wall of the Emporium office. Afterward, he smoked a joint and shined his ancient swords.

⚜

Near Groverly, research herbalists from Neubland Pharmaceutical composed experimental formulas from plants with medieval backgrounds. They started with monkshood, measuring roots and leaves, oils and essences, weighing drops and grams, tinkering with its poison and potential.

CHAPTER 4

One lone butterfly dipped down from the sky fluttering past the neon tubes of the Emporium marquee. The sign blinked at Piper as she drove into the vacant parking lot. She noticed the picketer walking back and forth with a sign that read "Ban Erotic DVDs. Every Single Sexy Scene!" When she recognized Griffo, she was glad she'd worn sunglasses and a big hat to protect against the bright sun. After he turned to go the other direction, she hurried into the store on her private errand. Inside, wind-up metallic birds perched in little brass cages, filling the room with melodies of mechanical notes. She wrinkled her nose at the unusual smell and moved past the bins of old herbs to look around for a clerk. Voices drifted from behind a purple satin drape that covered a side room of the store. She considered leaving, but curiosity trumped caution, and she tiptoed toward the curtain.

"Hey, who's out there?" A strong male voice made her jump.

She cleared her throat. "Just a customer. I'll browse until you're free, or I can come back another time."

"Hell, if it's okay with my client, come on in and take a look at my tattoo work."

A weak voice stammered, "I...I...I guess so."

"Permission granted, lady. Enter and view the art show."

Piper took a deep breath and couldn't resist pulling the drape open to see what was inside. Huge posters of tattoos emblazoned on body parts filled the walls of the little enclosure. Elaborate griffons and vampires and bats and snakes decorated arms, legs, chests, stomachs, backs, and behinds. She gasped when she saw the markings nuzzled against male and female genitalia and closed her eyes against the pointed pen-like tattoo needles hanging on the wall.

A broad-chested muscular man in green medical scrubs turned toward her. "I'm Boris Ratchov, owner of the Emporium. Sit down and watch it happen. Right in front of your eyes." A faint scar running along one cheek showed against his tan. Her eyes lingered on his arms decorated with rainbow colored tattoos. The drill buzzed to announce his return to work as he deliberately and permanently marked the pale, inner flesh of Sax Morton's forearm.

"Oh, Piper, it's you." Sax's voice was soft as wilted lettuce. "If you talk to me, it might keep me from watching and wincing."

Eyes wide, she gazed at the rows of colored inks waiting to be infused into thick silvery needles. "I'll try."

"What can I do for you, pink lady?"

She stared at Boris. "I'm Piper from the Cut & Curl Salon in town. You know, with the pink awnings. I, uh, came in for some potpourri. Definitely not a tattoo."

"Not even pink flowers to match your hair and awnings?" Boris winked.

"Not today." Piper studied the marks imprinted on Sax's skin. "Does it hurt much?"

He managed a weak smile. "Not as bad as you think."

Fascinated, Piper watched the tattoo artist scroll the design on the ivory backdrop of Sax's forearm. He looked pale and insecure, but she understood. Her own stomach churned, seeing the tiny rivulets of red seep from the row of needles. The blood masked a strange flower erupting from a bulbous beginning.

"Why'd you decide to get a tat?" she said. "Does Maxine have one?"

"Maxine's too busy being Queen of Used Stuff to pay attention to other things. It was the mystery and power of tattoo that intrigued me."

Boris mopped around the penetrated skin.

Sax cringed. "Don't get any blood on my new mauve shirt."

"Next time, you'll change," Boris said. "There are robes in the dressing room."

Piper looked away. "Say, how's business over at Used Stuff these days? Mine's pretty steady."

Sax lowered his head. "Okay, I guess, but my recommendation? Never go into partnership with a relative, especially if she's bossy and insists on controlling every damn thing. Max makes the decisions. I do the grunt work." He peeked up at her. "No offense to women in business, okay?"

"Yeah, yeah. Just take her on, Sax." Piper kept her face turned away from the blood. "But your store's a partnership, right?"

"My folks set it up for us to share, even the upstairs apartment, but somehow she never got the idea of a partnership. Just bulldozes right over me."

Boris grinned. "Well, today gives you the balls to start fresh. You're the one with the tattoo."

"I just want a place where I can get some sleep. She's an insomniac. Wants me to stay up nights playing chess. I need a life and a good night's rest."

"Man, why not get your own apartment?" Boris said.

"I dunno. Not many available around town."

Piper wrinkled her nose. "Get a room at the motel."

"That won't work. I've got too much stuff."

Boris pointed in the direction of the storage room. "Dump some of it here until later. The storage room's not full. I'll rent it out cheap, now that you're a customer."

"You know what? I might take you up on that."

Boris changed needles and resumed the work. "You look a little peaked. How you doing?"

Sax winced. "First time's kind of a surprise."

"When you walked in, I never thought you'd be the type for a tattoo." Boris dabbed at the red bubbles.

Sax gazed at the blood threading its way through the design. "Actually, I do feel a little sick."

"Think about moving out of Used Stuff," Boris said. "Get a hobby."

Sax let out a groan. "I guess that's enough design work for today. When I bring over some of my things, you can finish."

He watched the last swabbing of the strange bulb and floral design, followed by a sweep of stinging alcohol and a bandage.

He stood and got his bearings before unfolding his shirt sleeve. "And I do have a hobby. I play chess. With Maxine. Teaches a person how to plan ahead. She's really good at that. Me, not so much, but I can do better."

A car rumbled into the front parking stall of the Emporium. A door slammed. The store bell announced a visitor.

In a few quick moves, Boris put away the tattoo paraphernalia, tubes and tips, grips and transfers. "Come by for your second tattoo session, Sax, and afterward, we might try chess. Or even a more dangerous game."

Backing out through the shiny curtain, Piper looked at the store entrance and saw a heavyset man in a rumpled suit leaning against Griffo.

His slurred voice made her jump. "Hello. Hello there, honey. Greetings and slalutations. Anyone else here?"

"I'm just looking for some potpourri." Piper scurried away and buried her face in a bouquet of eucalyptus leaves.

"Gimme a minute," Boris called out. "I'm cleaning brushes."

"No hurry. It's Llewellyn Blanding, the new Neu guy, otherwise known as your Neubland Pharmathermical...Pharmaceutical rep. Holy shit, look at those movie titles." He nudged Griffo, still at his elbow. "No wonder this guy's picketing, but he kindly showed me in."

"I thought he was a tipsy customer." Griffo put down his sign.

"I don't believe I've bought anything from your company." Boris marched up to the counter, Sax trailing behind.

"Well, hell, the previous Ratchov did." The salesman pulled down his wrinkled jacket. "Account's still set up. Waitin' for that next order. Call me Llewellyn."

"But no one shops on the herbal side of the store anymore."

The salesman gestured toward Piper. "What about her?"

Boris shrugged. "With you in a minute, Miss."

"No hurry," she said, content to eavesdrop.

Boris held up a DVD. "Most customers choose a mildly exotic or madly erotic selection. These badly lit movies keep me and the place afloat."

The salesman leaned against the "Hottest of Hot" display. "You're saying that herbs can't compete, huh? Where d'ya keep your medicinal bottles and jars?"

Boris pointed down two short aisles past the open bins.

Llewellyn stumbled and Griffo caught his arm. "Careful there, mister."

As the salesman moved closer, Piper slid over to the display of singing metal birds. She watched him pick up various items, then toss them aside.

Boris followed behind, placing the items in their proper slots. "Yup, my herb business is dying out."

The salesman pitched his voice to the end of the store. "Lookee this dwindling display of salves and tins. Fella, your inventory's gone to pot." He inched closer to Boris's face. "But I'm loaded with bargains."

Boris stepped back. "Right. Loaded. Look, I don't need anything today." He rubbed at a dark streak of tattoo ink that marked his forefinger.

"Wait. Wait. Just one minute." Llewellyn rummaged inside his case "Our Sweet Sleep Pills are on special. Puts the restless down for the night. Smoother than a vodka tonic."

"Unique sales pitch, I admit." Boris's thumb stroked the ink on his finger.

"Do not be testy, sir." Llewellyn pulled out a tiny tin. "I get enough of that from my brother. But I'm the one with the million dollar ideas." The salesman struggled with the lid until it snapped open. He waved it under Boris's nose. "You buy half a case of our Sweet Sleep Pills, I throw in this sample of Calendula Cream. It will erase all your black ink marks. Try it."

Piper peered from the next aisle to watch Boris apply salve to his finger. The stain faded away. "Amazing," she whispered.

"I'll be damned," Boris said.

Griffo and Sax stepped closer to examine the finger.

Llewellyn nodded. "What'd I say? Look, I know what's what and I plan to rock Elcott's boat. My idea takes on the big stuff. A cure for cancer. Heart disease. Alz...heimies. Sales'll explode for Neubland when I'm done." He shuffled papers in his case and pulled out an order form.

Piper took a few steps closer. "You really mean you have a cure for cancer?"

"Shoot, the cures aren't on the market yet, lady. Look, our company is working on drugs from medieval plants. The poison ones. But so far, they haven't found a damn thing. I'm betting I can get the cures before the lab. We'll see what ole Elcott thinks of me then."

"And Elcott is …" Boris leaned forward.

Llewelyn sighed. "Told you, my brother, President of Neubland. I'll come up with healing herb remedies from some poisons."

"Well, morphine and codeine come from a poppy connection." Boris rubbed his thumb over his clean finger.

Griffo let out a whoop. "And you're the guy who'll discover the cures?"

Llewellyn bristled. "Not exactly what I said. Elcott showed me a flyer he got in the mail. From over in Europe, Jar Done, Jar Deen, something. It was there in black and red. About a book of old cures."

"You mean Verdun?" Boris rubbed his scar.

"No, sir. Jar done."

"Never heard of the place."

"Elcott neither, but you can read about it at the Groverly Library. Elcott heard it from an herb guy. Over in Europe, there's this cure book kept hidden away for years." He leaned against a counter. "Family is worried about lawsuits. But if we get the cures, we got corporate insurance."

"Why do you need the book if your lab's working on the cures?" Boris said.

"Because the lab's not come up with a damn thing. Might take 'em forever."

Sax rolled his eyes. "And exactly, what's your plan?"

"Just go to Jardon. Get the book." The salesman stumbled and barely caught himself. "Hey, your floor's crooked, fella."

Boris nodded. "Yeah, drinking makes it that way."

The Neubland salesman pointed to the half empty herbal shelves. "You gotta get with the times." His eyes swept around the store and landed on Piper. "Right, lady?"

All heads swiveled to look at Piper, who flipped her pink locks. "Yes, indeed, definitely go with the times."

"So how about that order for sleep pills?"

Boris nodded. "I'll consider half a case."

Llewellyn closed his display case with a thump. "I'll put it on your tab." He leaned against the window for support. "Whoa."

Griffo reached for him. "I gotcha."

"Say, picketing guy, you still here? Thought the town was dead set against the DVDs."

Boris cocked his head. "Well, I'm an idea man too. I hired him for advertising. Gets the attention of the citizenry. They think he's picketing, and they rent a DVD to see what the fuss is about. When they talk about it, other folks rent it. Called the human condition. The quest for knowledge."

Piper wrinkled her brow in surprise. She stared at Boris and shook her head.

"My friend, we got things in common." Llewellyn wobbled a bit. "Not many customers understand that kinda thing."

Boris put a hand on the salesman's shoulder. "Look, there's vodka in the office. Want a short one for the road?"

"Never been known to turn down a drink."

"Griffo, wait on the lady. Sax, see you later." Boris led Llewellyn past Piper into the office. The faint clink of glassware escaped through the open door.

Piper looked at Griffo, who held up his hand, motioning for her to wait. Then he slid forward to eavesdrop on Boris's conversation with Llewellyn. Sax joined him, and Piper moved closer too.

Loud, booming voices carried out into the store from the office.

"Yeah, Mr. Emplorium, a million. I plan to sell that book for a million to Elcott. Soon as I work out a plan. No one's been able to talk that family into selling it, but I'm one helluva convincing guy."

Boris's enthusiastic voice carried into the store. "Terrific idea. And the book's really worth a million to Neubland?"

"Means billions in sales, fella. Cancer, remember. Heart disease. That other one. Hey, bottoms up. Gotta get going."

Piper moved out of Sax's way as he brushed by her to dash for his car. Griffo trotted to the register and a minute later, Boris led Llewellyn to the door.

Piper waited near the herbs until Griffo left with his sign. Then, she wandered up to Boris. "Did you know your place has the local gossips buzzing?"

"Good indication that picketing works." He sorted through returned DVDs. "I'd appreciate you not passing the word around about who hired Griffo."

"Sure thing. I just wondered what kind of X-rated stuff you carried here."

"Ma'am, shelves and shelves of sexy movies, for rent or purchase. To any and all discriminating viewers."

"But not much good without a DVD player. What I'm looking for are books that might cover the same subjects. You know, 'Hairotica'?"

"If you crave titillation, better buy yourself a machine, lady. I don't carry any books. And the word you're looking for is 'erotica.'"

"That's what I said. 'Airotica.'"

"Just look around, lady. You see any books?"

In the tattoo room, Boris took a last puff of weed before refining the lizard tattoo on his knee. Ideas dark as smoke billowed from his mind. About how to beat a tipsy Neubland salesman out of a million bucks.

Wildly waving his sign, Griffo stepped along, mulling over the information he'd overheard. His feet beat a tempo to the tune of stealing an old book. Force might be necessary, but no scheme involving a fortune was impossible for a clever gypsy.

After nearby sales calls for Neubland, Llewellyn dropped by the Groverly Library. He concentrated on the *Book of Cures*. About taking a leave of absence. Posing as a collector or journalist. Or breaking in and stealing the damn thing.

Sax emptied trash into the dumpster. He grabbed the red flyer about to tumble in the bin's open mouth, then analyzed ways to steal the *Book of Cures*, but came up empty. Putting aside his pride, he approached Maxine.

"Hey sis, I need your devious mind. This guy was talking about a book worth a million dollars. If I'm clever enough, I could cash in on his scheme."

She listened, then scoffed. "You're a sucker, if you think you could get in on that. It's way too complicated and seriously criminal. Frankly, you don't have the balls."

After store hours, Sax slipped away to visit the library in Groverly. To his surprise, he found Maxine in the Special Collections Room, reading the article in the encyclopedia. She looked up. "Like I said, very complicated."

The lone butterfly skirted the black cloud rising from the machinations of four men and one woman, all intent on possessing a hidden book of unbelievable possibilities.

CHAPTER 5

The next morning's sunlight turned the window shade to glowing parchment. Piper woke with her husband's fingers roaming gently across the back of her rose-colored nightie, then slipping toward her breast. She sat up with a start and ran her fingertips through her glinting golden ringlets. "Wow, Freddie, it must be late."

Fred checked the clock by the bedside. "Nope, it's early. Plenty of time for some sweet affection before the alarm goes off."

"Thing is, I didn't get much sleep last night." She slipped out of bed. "Too excited about the book club."

"How about a relaxing back rub?"

"Great idea, but I've got truckloads of stuff to do at the shop." She grabbed an outfit from the closet. "I'll let the dog out."

"You know, Piper, you been givin' me the cold shoulder lately and you've never been like that before. You give up on sex or just me?"

"Oh Freddie." Her feet padded to the doorway.

"What did I do?" he said, "let me in on it, will you?"

She called from the hall bathroom. "You didn't do anything, honest. It's me. Please, honey, just let it wait till later."

In fifteen minutes, she poked her head in the bedroom door. "Sorry to rush off. Love ya." On her way out of the house, she grabbed her book club selections and walked the short distance to Cut & Curl.

After she entered, she relocked the salon door. Pulse pounding, she opened *Wuthering Heights*. She flipped through the romance on loan from the library, and scoured the chapters for torrid scenes. The language fell far short of her expectations. What kind of folks named their son, Heathcliff, anyway? She turned to the last page of the book to see how the story ended and grimaced. No haunting sex scene. No final sensuous embrace. She put the book down and opened the anthology to read the first memoir, then went on to the next and the next, but found no spine tingling scenes. No rapturous caresses. No heavy breathing, gasping, and heaving. She grabbed the science fiction, but the intrigue of Ray Bradbury only intensified her unsettled feelings.

She spun in the chrome-armed chair until she was dizzy, worrying about the lump and the possibility of getting pregnant. It didn't help that Freddie's beliefs prohibited the pill. She just knew she shouldn't think about having a baby. She stared into the salon mirror and picked up the phone book. In a few minutes, she made an appointment with a new doctor in Groverly, to get his opinion of her plight and a secret prescription for birth control pills. If she hid them and took them, that might be a solution.

Until then…she made a spur of the moment decision and rushed off to the house to move her clothes into the spare room. Before she left home, she went to the storage cupboard and found their high school yearbook. She wrote a few lines and put it on the bedside table in the master bedroom.

Then, she dashed off a note and tacked it to the fridge. It said, "We'll talk." She knew discussing serious matters was something married people were supposed to do, but she and Freddie didn't. Never had. Who wants to share sad or bad things? She decided if she could find the right time and place, she'd try. The move to the spare room, the note in the kitchen might force her into a serious talk with her husband. It shouldn't be so hard to talk to someone you loved, but fear and panic kept her mind muddled and her mouth shut. If she said the words to him, her whole life might fall apart.

Pushing wisps of hair from her forehead, Lily sat at the Readers' Advisory Desk, wondering why she was given the responsibility of this desk so often, keeping her away from the books she loved in the Special Collections room. She'd struggled to keep her composure since receiving the job loss notice, often fighting back tears that might mark her as an overly emotional employee. With no patrons in sight, she searched Google and read about the Jardin Estates and the winery mentioned in the flyer. It took only a few sentences to drown herself in the account, myth or true, of an old Duchess who died in the 1500's. And a son who found her next to her *Book of Cures* with a request to hide it. Lily imagined the young duke wrapping the book in a simple cloth and storing it in the castle storage cave. Her mind whirled, thinking of the ancient pages stashed under a mountain of objects, worn linens, used tablecloths, dented tea pots, folded tapestries, unmatched candlesticks, and stringless lutes. There it waited for centuries to be released. And waited still. She crossed her arms over her flat chest and smiled. It was the first time in quite a while.

The smile turned into a positive feeling about the future, enough to pick up the *Library Weekly* to browse for employment opportunities in other facilities.

"Aha!" Her sudden cry jolted the air around her as she read the small headline at the bottom of the page: *Antiquarian Books from Europe to Tour U.S. Libraries.* Not a job ad, but an exhibit opportunity. The last line of the article indicated one short-term slot left at the beginning of the itinerary.

She clicked away at the computer to contact the sponsoring Global Antiquarian Society in Strasbourg. In her quick email, she offered the organization the time vacated by the baseball card exhibit. "Assignment accomplished, I hope."

Aggie pushed open the door of the Used Stuff Store, hauling in her goat milk carrier. She waved at Sax who was admiring the tattoo on his upper arm.

"Look at you," Aggie crowed, and he rolled down his sleeve.

"It's not finished yet, but I'll get it done."

"I like it so far," she said and walked on to find Maxine, sitting upright at the office desk, reading a book on business success.

"Morning, Maxine. Bringing the milk delivery."

"Today, if you don't mind, take it to the extra fridge in back. I need to talk to my brother and give him his chores."

It took Aggie only a few minutes to put the milk away and weave her way through the furniture toward the front of the store.

Nose to nose, Sax and Max stood next to the register.

Sax's voice penetrated the sales room. "Damn it, Maxine, I'm through being your follower. I'm moving out."

Aggie trudged past breakfronts and bedposts to head for the front door.

Maxine's voice pitched higher. "You might want to think twice about that."

Aggie's hand found the knob and twisted it.

"The front door opens and closes," Maxine yelled. "Either of us is free to do as we please. Just tell me if you intend to keep working here. There's a schedule to keep."

Sax shouted back. "Damn right, I'll keep working. I own half the store, even if it doesn't seem like it to you. I'll be back for my things."

Aggie slipped out with the sound of Sax's boots close behind her.

"Guess you heard us fighting." He came up to her. "She's a bitch. Always has been."

"Families are like that, made up of all kinds of folks."

"We're together too much. But no more holding back for me. I've been too unhappy."

"You do what you do in this world." Aggie fitted the milk carrier into the makeshift stand on the moped.

The front door of Used Stuff opened. "Hey, Sax, we might be twins, but we each have our talents. It's always been like that. I make the plans, find ways to make the money. You help me."

"Go to hell," Sax hollered.

"By the way, you're a lousy chess player." Maxine slammed the door.

Aggie climbed on the moped. The engine sputtered, then caught. "Twice as much joy. Twice as much trouble," she called to Sax. "My gypsy grandma used to say that about twins."

She headed for her last stop, The Emporium. The old, wooden building looked the same as the last time she'd been there, except for the addition of a glowing neon sign. She hadn't visited the shop since the last owner died. Still sad over losing a friend, she stepped inside to take in the changes. The rows of DVD displays were new. A purple satin drape now covered the alcove once reserved for reading *The Groverly Gazette*. From a row of cages, metal birds twittered their tinny songs. She caught her breath at the smell of smoking and faded herbs.

"Can I help you? I'm Boris Ratchov."

She noted his vivid arm sleeve tattoos. "I'm Aggie Verkie from the local goat farm. I, uh, I wondered if you'd like to carry goat milk for your customers again. A few places in Nolan do. It seems to sell and it's a nice addition for your herb customers."

"The herbs, for your information, don't sell at all. And it wouldn't work anyway. The cooler went out." He shrugged. "Anyway, who knows how long I'll stay. I'm a globetrotting tattoo artist, who makes a few bucks selling the occasional collectible. When I'm bored, I try something different, like a rental department of X-rated DVDs."

"I knew your uncle and am very sorry he passed on."

"Yeah, when I heard my uncle died, I thought I'd take a break and crawl inside his hidey-hole."

"He was such a nice man."

"I suppose so. Take a look around. You might find something to buy."

Sax Morton stumbled in and threw himself down into one of the viewing chair by the DVDs. He looked over at Aggie. "Oh, hello again. I've almost recovered after that fuss with Maxine." He sighed. "Boris, I told my sister I'm moving out and I just got a room at the motel. Paid for six months."

"Aren't you the one?" Boris said. "Hell, why don't we throw a few sharps to celebrate?"

"I heard about your knives. I was hoping you'd offer some time. C'mon, Aggie."

"Sure, come on," Boris moved into the office.

Aggie followed and stood in the back. She silently admired the shiny relics he'd collected, ancient swords displayed along one wall and small daggers attached to hooks on a knotted, gold rope. A heavy-duty nail secured each end of the cord that stretched from window to window across the thick cork wall.

Boris walked near his treasures, pointing to each one. "Scimitar from Turkey. Claymore from the Scottish highlands. Egyptian ritual knife. Japanese Samurai. Purchased during my worldly travels." He glanced at Aggie. "Sax and I are going to throw daggers. You want to watch or are you planning to join in?"

Aggie shook her head. "You two go first, while I think about it."

Boris took a dagger from the wall and handed it to Sax. "Here you go."

Sax grinned and accepted the knife. "I'm more than ready to try."

Boris undid his own favorite dagger. "This is how to do it right. Grip the handle, so. Angle it and swing it forward to release. Not like throwing a ball, but like this." His dagger dug into the edge of the target center.

"Here goes nothing." In a wicked frenzy, Sax threw his knife and it fell to the floor.

"Not so rushed. Relax and focus. Grip. Angle. Release. Try again."

The two men set about flinging the sharp and shiny objects at a target on the cork.

Sax concentrated, flicking knife after knife with no luck. "Not doing so good, huh?"

"Remember, a weapon in hand bolsters confidence," Boris said. "You'll improve with practice. Believe in your power to do it. Want to give it a shot, missus?"

Aggie stepped forward and took the dagger. She held it lightly and stared at the target, then flipped the knife in an arc. The golden point hit the bullseye, digging deep into the cork.

"Wow," Sax said.

"We can quit now." Boris collected the daggers and connected them back on the rope. "What's your deal, lady?"

"I'm a gypsy, you know. Traveling the countryside, a person finds many gifts in the woods. Thank you for including me today, but now it's time to feed the goats."

Driving home, the first meeting with her husband cut like a flying dagger through her heart. She remembered the bands of gypsies gathered in a faraway forest for an afternoon of raucous stories and dancing to the strands of zither music. When she took a break from the lively songs, she noticed a group of men who'd pinned chicken feet to the thick trunk of a tree. Laughing and yelling oaths, they took turns, aiming their knives at their target, with extra points for slicing off any of the toes. One tan and slender young man outshone them all, Camlo. As he aimed, his knife caught the sun shafts and glittered. When she moved closer to watch, he smiled at her each time his weapon flew through the air, hitting a tiny toe dead on. His dagger, his accurate throws repeated over and over sent her quivering inside. That night, he proved his point and afterward, they were never apart.

Sax prowled the Used Stuff Store, grabbing old suitcases and hanging bags. He packed his clothes, dropped off items to keep in the Emporium storeroom and returned to his room at Motel 5.

Annoyed, Maxine tapped her pencil on the distressed oak desk top. Finally, she realized the appeal of the new situation, the run of both apartment and store in off-hours. Indeed, she was as free of her twin brother as he was of her.

Aggie unlocked the closet door in her bedroom. She took down the samovar and removed the Mason jar. "To seeds of love planted in wild nights," she cried. Cold to the bone, she wrapped herself in the black cape from the dresser. When it enfolded her, his spirit haunted her, holding her close. Clutching the jar to her bosom, she danced in circles around the room until she was exhausted. Then she lay down, the cape covering her, a dark, rounded blanket of passion remembered.

CHAPTER 6

Lily checked the new shipment of best sellers and sorted the library mail. To keep a lid on her emotions, she avoided the Head Librarian whenever she could, keeping to her cubicle, concentrating on repairing books and updating the catalog. Midmorning, she checked her email and found a reply from overseas.

> *Ms. McFae:*
>
> *The Global Antiquarian Society accepts the offer of the Groverly Main Branch Library to participate in the upcoming tour of ancient books. Fill out the enclosed forms and specific information will follow. The itinerary is now complete. Your facility will be the first stop.*

Lily completed the application and sent it back immediately. She sighed, knowing she'd be gone from the library by the time the tour arrived. She emailed a press release to local newspapers, TV and radio stations, then forwarded all the information to Library Director Trummel.

On her way to the lunchroom, a husky patron marched toward her. "Well, if it isn't Ms. McFae. Imagine running into you." He hesitated. "I've missed you at the Emporium."

"I didn't recognize you, Boris." She blushed. "That particular chapter of my life is over."

"I'm looking for some information you keep in a special room."

"We have a Special Collections Room. Follow me." Lily ushered him into the rarified atmosphere, closing the door to erase the murmur of outside sounds.

"I'm interested in a European estate called Jar Don. Jar Deen?"

"I know exactly what you mean. The Jardin Estate in Alsace. There's an article about it in one of our reference books. Sign in at the reading desk, please."

"Of course."

Lily opened the log book and turned a new page for him. "You've made an interesting choice. Looks like others have looked at this book as well."

"Mark me down as another one of them." He flipped back the page and squinted at the signatures, then turned the page to scrawl his name and required information.

"I'll get the book for you." She pointed to a batch of white gloves. "You wear them while handling the book. After your research, toss them in the basket."

The chair squeaked as Boris positioned himself at the reader's table near the door. He set his cap on the table, opened his black briefcase and brought out notepad and pen before he pulled on the flimsy cotton protectors.

She laid the volume on the table. "One of our most interesting books. I do have other duties. Do you know how long you'll be?"

"Not long at all, but go ahead with your work. Come back later."

The humidifier whispered, adjusting the moisture in the air.

"Someone always stays with the patron. I'll be working in the back stack."

Boris found the article on the *Book of Cures* and skimmed through it. After glancing over his shoulder, he pulled out a tiny knife. He coughed softly as the knife edge skimmed along the inside of the page.

"Are you all right?" Lily peered around the corner, then sailed toward him.

Boris slid the knife under his cap.

"We do appreciate no coughing on the pages. I'll get you a tissue."

"Just a mild allergy. I'll almost done." He waited for her to leave, but she stayed close. Hunched over the book, he made extensive notes, then filed them in his black case.

"All finished, Ms. McFae." He closed the volume, coughed

again and rose from the chair.

He reached for his hat and slipped the knife into his pocket. "Thank you."

She tidied up and stopped by her office to carry another armload of rescued books to the non-fiction stacks. "Here you go. Home again," she whispered and placed a volume into its rightful position. Her palm swept lightly over the spines in their orderly presentation. It gave her joy, the side by side gifts of biography, essay, travel and reference waiting for readers. Numbered. Filed. Ready to reveal the breadth of history and tangle of civilization to anyone who presented a library card.

Library Board President Humphrey rounded the corner, followed by Ms. Trummel, who wore one of her immaculately tailored business suits, this one in a rich bronze tone.

The old gentleman tapped his cane and nodded at Lily. "Hard at it, I see, even in light of the regrettable recent budget decision."

"I suppose." She straightened her shoulders.

"Ms. McFae, since I study so many reports and business journals, I have a question. What's your suggestion for a reading change of pace?"

She handed him the book in her hand. "You might try *The Chaos Theory* by Edward Lorenz."

Director Trummel stepped into the conversation. "That's one idea, but I have several other recommendations. I'll make a list."

"Not necessary. This looks interesting. I've heard about it often enough. What's it about?"

Ms. Trummel pounced. "Well, very well known, of course, and discussed by many authorities. A theory that's been around for years. A treatise on…on…."

"Random influences offering limitless possibilities." Lily's smile was smug. "The most quoted example, a butterfly waves its wings and later, perhaps thousands of miles away, that waft becomes a wind and then, that wind, a tornado. I think of it as long distance cause and effect. Something like that. Change evolving from a small, simple thing. The shape of a sand dune. A falling leaf."

"Lily, please, Mr. Humphrey doesn't have time for your convoluted explanations of nature." Ms. Trummel looked grim.

"No, go on, I'm interested," he said.

The director turned her back to adjust her perfect lapels as Lily continued, "In a way, the library functions as a literary chaos theory, words wending off in different directions, stimulating the ideas and imagination of others, the printed page verifying cause and effect, sometimes exploding with infinite ramifications."

"Sold," he said.

The director glared at Lily, then marched off with the president holding the book to his chest.

In another minute, Ms. Trummel poked her head around the corner. "Lily, I need you to fill in for the readers' advisor again. She's leaving early."

Lily continued to unload her armful of books.

Director Trummel scowled. "And stop cozying up to the board president. The budget and your attitude determined your bad fortune. Besides, I can't believe you accepted that rare book tour without consulting me. Not a smart move."

Lily shrugged. "You told me to find something as soon as possible."

"Yes, but there are rules, which you chose to ignore. I should have been notified first. It's already on the radio. Because of your cavalier attitude, do not expect a recommendation from me."

Lily adjusted her glasses and massaged her temples. "This discussion has given me a sincere headache. I can't fill in for the advisor. I'm going home to rest and figure out what's next for me and my sad little life."

The director held up her hand. "Stop right there. You'll put me in a bind at the advisor's desk. I order you not to leave the premises."

"Sorry, but my head hurts. I'm going home. 'How much of life is lost in waiting?' Ralph Waldo Emerson."

"A very literary way to continue your insubordination." Ms. Trummel glowered. "I'm done playing games with you. If you leave now, don't bother to come back."

"Then fare thee well, I guess."

Lily strode off to her office, grabbed the red butterfly flyer, shoved it in her purse, and hurried toward the arched exit. She slammed her palm against the carved Spanish door. Her flat heels clapped against the pavement on the way to her old Plymouth.

On the way home, she stopped at a nearby drive-in, trying to regain control of herself. "Two soft tacos, extra hot sauce," she murmured into the microphone. Her knuckles were white as she clutched the steering wheel. Like falling dominos, she thought, one circumstance striking another, finally knocking her down. Her surgery. Her disagreements with the library director over classic books. The unexpected envelope of dismissal. A roomful of people in Nolan who'd scared her silly because they wanted to read. She ate her tacos. One slight headache followed by her quick words of defiance. She didn't know how to turn back.

She squeezed the last taco bite. Minced lettuce coated with Tabasco squished out. How perfect, she thought. All I have to show for my library career is hot sauce dribbled down my front.

Nerves jangling, she blew through a stop sign on the way home. A trucker honked and threw her the finger. Swerving to avoid a collision, she smacked her car into a temporary concrete barrier. The front of the car folded. "Yikes," she yelled. "Not fair. Oh, dammit."

She coaxed the Plymouth to an off-road position and her examination revealed a dented fender, broken headlight and crushed grillwork. When the engine wouldn't start, she clomped home to her cottage, called for a tow, and the favor of a quick estimate from the service station man she'd used for years.

That evening, he called with the bad news. "Damage versus cost of repair equals a totaled vehicle. I'm sorry, Ms. McFae."

"I don't believe it," she mumbled. "Everything's in shambles, but thanks for letting me know." She hung up, sat down, and closed her eyes against the real world.

In the goat barn, Aggie put the billie goat on the milk stand. Her swollen fingers cradled a hoof pick to clean the muck from his toes. The billie jerked away at first, then settled down to allow her to trim the sides of each hoof, slicing off the hard edges. She scrubbed the hooves down with a little toothbrush and finally, planed off the bottoms. When she turned the goat free, he galloped off and she started on the next one.

Eventually, her energy flagged and she flopped into the disintegrating, wicker porch rocker, soaking her skin in sunshine to ease her perpetual goose bumps. Opening the anthology of poetry she'd taken from the club meeting, she decided to give a gent called Alfred Lord Tennyson the chance to break through her misery.

> *"Tis a morning pure and sweet,*
> *And a dewy splendour falls …"*

But Tennyson's "Maud" couldn't crack the ice that gripped Aggie's every move. Mornings were not sweet. The dew no longer splendid. Her stiff fingers crumbled a fresh basil leaf in her apron pocket and she lifted it to her nose. No juicy green scent erupted from the pulp. Plum dumplings no longer tasted plummy. Tap water didn't run hot. She shuddered. Life without her beloved only meant a samovar kept locked in the closet. A ghost haunting her. And a cold heart.

"Taking a nice lazy break, Auntie?" Griffo ambled down the stairs of the garage, then down the driveway to the mailbox.

Aggie watched him return, waving a bright red piece of paper.

"Halleluiah," he cried. "It's from the Jardin Estate."

"What does that mean?"

"It means a damn lucky break for me." He tucked the paper in his pocket and got into his roadster. "I'm off to check something out at the library in Groverly. A chance to get rich."

When the dust settled, Aggie picked up the book to try again.

In her salon, Piper finished two cuts and a perm. She needed a break, but faint marks on the mirror bothered her. She started at one end of the salon glass and worked her way down, spraying, wiping, spraying, wiping. Halfway there, she breathed on a difficult smudge.

Her hand shook when she saw Freddie's reflection in the glass, his long strides aiming for the shop, coming through the door, standing close behind her. She rubbed against an imperceptible spot with a towel and felt his warmth invade the back of her neck.

"Look at me, Piper. I went home for lunch and found your note. I want to know what the hell's going on?"

She spoke to his mirror image. "If you give me a little time, I promise we'll talk about it."

"You're acting squirrely."

"Maybe I am. Maybe I have a reason. There are things."

"At least tell me why you moved out of our bedroom."

Her back muscles tightened. "Because I needed some time to figure something out."

"Tell me what's wrong?" His voice was loud and angry. "Jeez, is it another guy? Who the hell is he?"

"It's no one. Please, go back to work. Give me a few days."

His hands reached out to grab her shoulders, but she stepped aside to evade him. "My next appointment will come in a minute, so we can't get into it now. I've got something to figure out, Freddie. Some time, that's all I'm asking."

"It had better not be another guy. I don't understand, but if that's the way you want it." His heel marked a black streak on the linoleum when he swiveled to leave.

She collapsed into her revolving chair and let the tears fall. Back and forth, around and around, she rocked.

Lily took two aspirins, changed into sweats and pulled herself together before browsing the newspaper employment want ads. No job opportunities tempted her, but a full page announcement of a big auto auction caught her eye. The special box with information about a certain vehicle lifted her spirits a notch. A bookmobile.

It took only ten minutes in the Groverly Library for the man in drab brown to gather his information. Sauntering down the hallway, he stopped at the long glass case that displayed local kids' drawings of polka dot snakes, green cows and purple fish. He looked behind the safely locked cabinet to see the screw tops that held the storage piece together. Near the back exit, he saw the stairs that led to the basement, then tried the door near the restrooms and successfully located the utility closet. He left the building.

CHAPTER 7

Lily stood on her sidewalk, looking at her mailbox. A symbol of expectation and dread, she thought, and wondered if the mail would contain ads or bills. Instead, she found the manila envelope from the Jardin Estates.

She struggled with the tape, finally tearing a ragged edge to get to the contents. Envelopes of yarrow. Dragoncello. Lovage. Lively. She counted out the order, opened the corners of the packets and peered inside. Pods of monkshood. Seeds of belladonna and foxglove. She felt the infused magic of her Alsatian mystery living in these envelopes, in the embryonic bits of herbal life.

Gently, she poured seeds of lively into her palm. An errant breeze arrived from distant shores and a few flecks, dark as pepper spilled onto the grass. Cupping her hand, she emptied the remaining seedlets back into the packet and retreated to her backyard, to the small, unused pots that leaned against the side of her garage. Hands deep in potting soil, she couldn't shake a limping kind of aching as she planted, then dribbled fresh water over the dried bits. She stared at the clay containers, visualizing colorless pods opening underground, uncurling, transforming from the wet warmth she provided, green needles piercing through darkness, ready to unfold twisted leaves and flower buds. To Lily, the seeds were a symbol of a shadowed figure in an Alsatian garden, plucking herbs to create a remedy for loneliness, a potion, a tea of romance. Many years had passed since the days of the old Duchess, but perhaps the cure would be found in time to help a librarian in need.

Hosing off her hands, she ended her daydream, checked her watch, and changed into an indigo blue pant suit. She sat at her desk and rushed through the morning newspaper, stopping to read the small announcement about the Global Antiquarian Society Book Tour scheduled to visit the Groverly Main Branch Library. She folded the paper and left to grab the city bus that routinely passed her street corner. As she rode through the stops and starts, headed to the auto auction, she wondered about the price and size of the offered vehicle. Would it be one of the smaller vans or one of the huge ones? Clutching her purse, she stepped out at a downtown stop and walked the few blocks to her destination.

At the lot, she stood near the back of the crowd, listening to the auctioneer babble on.

"What'll you give? C'mon people, loosen those purse strings. This station wagon's a steal at ten thousand. C'mon, mister." The auctioneer cajoled the man who'd offered the next-to-last bid. "Okay then, if you're all through, that's once, twice, and the gentleman in the red tie's got it at nine-nine."

She clutched her checkbook and eyed the orange vehicle next in line, with BOOKMOBILE spelled out on both sides. It was a size she thought she could handle.

"Okay. Next up. Who will give me an opening bid on this fine, old van? C'mon. C'mon, people. Word is that this vintage piece of machinery was used in the next county as a bookmobile. Seventeen feet long. Comes with a six month warranty on the reconditioned engine. Back and front entryways with one little step. A few small windows here and there for light. Filled with shelves, shelves, and more shelves. Not much rust. Little storage closet near the back entry And hey, a built-in seating nook. You could use this van as a ...." He stopped and gestured wildly toward it.

"Place to read." A voice came from the front and the crowd tittered.

"Why not? But it has other uses. Gimme an opening bid, someone. Anyone? Eight thousand dollars for this orange beauty ready to streak down the road."

Lily looked around. Not one bid. She opened her mouth.

And the auctioneer continued. "How about seven…six…five…four thousand? Put it in the backyard. Store your tools. Make a playhouse for the kids."

People in the crowd shook their heads.

"Thirty-five hundred? Anyone, anyone? A doghouse for huge pets? A storage closet for your light bulbs? Your knitting needles? Your dirty books?"

A chuckle ran through the crowd.

The auctioneer's eyes swept the crowd. "I hate to pull this one off the market. Anyone?"

"Thirty-five hundred dollars," Lily said.

"Now we're on a roll. Who will up the ante? C'mon, this is a steal. Anyone? Hate to let this orange delight go for such a bargain basement price." The auctioneer hesitated. "Okay, then. Going once, twice. All yours, lady. But you gotta tell us. What are you gonna do with it?"

"I thought I'd use it as a bookmobile."

"Hell of an idea. Pay the man in back."

The cashier handed her a series of papers to fill out, and her pen wobbled as she wrote.

"Where you planning to park this bookmobile? Maybe I can get you some customers, if you peddle a few of those porno pages the guy mentioned." He smirked. "Loads of interest in that kind of stuff these days. Hell, any day."

Lily kept her eyes on the small print of the contract. "My plan is to offer intelligent material to those who hunger for reading. From my diverse and personal selection."

"Diverse, huh? So that's what they call it nowadays."

Her chin went up. "They call it literature, and if my place of employment no longer wants me to offer it from their hallowed halls, I'll start my own damn library."

"Yeah," he said. "To hell with 'em."

Dipping into her savings, she paid the tab.

"Sign this last one and you're on your way."

Her hands firm on the unfamiliar wheel, she lurched the bookmobile down the road toward home. Gears jumping. Brakes squealing. Vroom. Vroom.

Llewellyn leaned back from his desk in a corner of the pharmaceutical sales room. He answered his cell phone. "Blanding here. Who's this?"

A low voice answered, "A friend, wondering how your big plan's going? Getting that *Book of Cures.*"

Llewellyn frowned. "Sometimes I get loaded and shoot off my mouth. Who's this?"

"Never mind that. It's an offer to buy that book from me, not the family. When I have it in my possession, I sell it to Neubland for a million dollars. Or to a higher bidder. I need to know if your company is interested in such a purchase."

Llewellyn gulped. "Absolutely, but I need time to get the money together. Don't contact anyone else."

"Fine. You'll hear from me when I have it."

At the window of the goat farm, the curtains flapped to and fro, a dance of forlorn netting that matched Aggie's gypsy shawl. Her spoon beat the bowl of batter in a cycle of circles, while Griffo drank coffee at the weather-beaten table, reading a newspaper.

She stopped stirring. "Better close the window or the draft'll blow us both away." She set the bowl down. "Are the accounts ready?"

He put down the paper and pushed up from the surface of the table to stand at the screenless window. "Not yet. My back's out of whack. Sitting on that damn kitchen chair did it." He shoved down hard and the window shut. "Ow! That hurt. I thought you called me for breakfast, not bookkeeping."

"I worry about you dipping into the farm money for your own dealings."

"Look, I help with the chores and the accounting, whenever I can."

"And you get free room and board." She poured molasses into a bowl.

"I'm busy picketing. And a new gem business." He slumped back down to the table. "Besides, other opportunities arise."

"More gamboozles. Griffo, you bring dishonor to our family."Agitation dripped like syrup from Aggie's bent spoon. "What jobs have you had? Illegal cab driver. Tricky card dealer. Old books sold as valuables. All your plots hold the promise of jail time. Are your jewels fake or real?"

"They're called synthetics and customers can't tell the difference. Now this one's real. Worth several hundred bucks wholesale." His pinkie finger wiggled and flashed, then scratched his chin. "Purple is an unusual shade for a sapphire. Worth big money."

"And how do you fund this grandness?"

"I deal. Sometimes I steal. Whatever is necessary to succeed. And you, dear Auntie, live in the past, hoarding and pinching. Scraping the bottom of every bowl. Stirring up recipes old as the book they come from. But speaking of recipes, my skin allergies have been kicking up lately. I could use one of your salves."

"I offer goat milk at an honest price. And seeds and herbs for an amount that's fair."

"Bingo. Bango. You hit it. Honest and fair don't hack it. That's dinky piddles."

"Goats are my income. Dinky though it be."

Griffo gave her a hard look. "You're getting old. And frail. Maybe you should sell the goats. And the farm. I'll handle the sale. Save you the trouble. We divvy up the proceeds."

"Not to worry about my health yet, Griffo. Do you want me to look for a remedy for your skin?" She pulled out the green family book.

"Now here's a real idea. You translate all the gypsy recipes and I'll sell them. Folk remedies are the rage these days." He reached for the volume.

Aggie hugged the book close. "Listen to me. The remedies are never to be sold, but to be passed on, generation to generation. That's why I learned words of the languages from my family, so I could read the recipes not translated." She stared at him. "Nothing from it ever sold."

"Gotcha."

"I meant to ask, have you stopped selling those old books in the garage? How much would each book be worth?"

"Different books, different prices. I'd have to go through the stacks. Why?" He juggled three brown onions from a basket on the counter, moving around the kitchen to demonstrate his skill.

"If there were any spicy ones, could I borrow them? Or maybe trade for the herbal salve."

An onion dropped and bounced. "Holy goats, Auntie, you're a stitch. Spicy, huh? Go ahead and take a look at the books. Call me when it's time to eat."

Her crooked finger wagged. "I see your back is better. While the batter rests, the small barn needs cleaning. Food on the table after you finish your chores."

He grabbed his musty, dusty Homburg from the hook. "Some-day you'll find out that life is more than goat droppings, Auntie."

"How would you know?" Aggie shook her head.

He tilted the hat on his head. "One day soon, I'll be out of your hair for good." He crammed the hat down around his ears, a crumpled end to the conversation. "The world awaits me."

The screen door slammed. His worn boots plowed a path through the gravel. Aggie saw the wind grab his hat and knock it flippety-loop. Griffo scrambled to catch it.

The sky fed sunbursts to the goat farm garden. After break-fast, sitting in the front porch rocker, Aggie saw only gray. A car pulled up the farm lane and parked. She rocked on, eying the woman who got out from the driver's seat and ambled over to the porch. Thoroughly covered, she wore a lavender long-sleeved shirt and slacks. Big sunglasses covered her eyes and a matching cowboy hat hid her hair.

She reached into her pocket. "I'm looking for herbs for my university study." Her voice was soft. "Here's my list. Mint. Lovage. Would you have belladonna and monkshood?"

They moved to the garden and Aggie pointed to some nearby plants with her arthritic hand. "Yes to mint and lovage." She picked a few handfuls of leaves. "Not many requests for the other two."

"I heard monkshood was used to kill wolves. Though, if you're worried, I don't plan to kill any." The woman kept her head down while she walked past the rows.

"Long ago, soldiers put it in the drinking water of enemies. Armies tipped their arrows with it. But I don't sell dangerous seeds or plants from my garden. I grow them only for family tradition."

"I desperately need a few samples for my research project. If you'll do a one-time only sale, I'll pay double and I always wear gloves when handling dangerous herbs. I promise not to kill any army personnel either." She smiled.

Aggie paused. "I'm sorry, but I never sell the ones that are dangerous."

"Then, I'll take the mint leaves and sprigs of lovage." The woman paid cash.

A sliver of a chill slipped down Aggie's back as the buyer left. No one had ever asked to buy poisonous herbs before.

After the sound of the visitor's car engine faded away, she went to the raggedy dark green book she kept in the kitchen drawer. Willed to her by her Mama Nanninski, it was filled with secrets handed down through the centuries, messages poured out in a language sweet as violin notes. Her stiff fingers slowly untied the twine that kept the treasure together, pages that condensed her family history of gypsy life into remedies and recipes in German and French. Written by ancestors as they traveled through Europe, many recipes now had English translations, but not all. She browsed through the musical language of her family's past cooking. Schnitzels and dumples, oxtail soup, parsnip stew, yarrow salad, dill sandwiches, flower biscuits and pippin pielets.

The next section listed herbal remedies for sore throat, flu, achy bones, constipation, nausea, palpitations, toothache, fevers, skin eruptions, nose troubles, and skinned elbows and knees.

Toward the back, faint handwriting listed poisonous herbs, borrowed from the gardens of others or pulled from roadsides: Monkshood. Belladonna. Foxglove.

She closed the book. Each syllable paid tribute to a time not many understood, the passages in her book as rhythmic as patched skirts swaying on a frayed clothesline.

Even Griffo, from Camlo's side of the family, was not allowed to read it. Though he helped out at the farm, Aggie did not trust him. He was seldom around anyway, sneaking off into the unknown with his schemes.

After she changed the bedding straw in the barn, she collapsed in the porch rocker and picked up the poetry anthology again. This time she decided to give Christina Rossetti a chance.

Remember me when I am gone away,
Gone far away into the silent land;
When you can no more hold me by the hand,

She felt words of sadness slip over her like the worn cotton case on her goose down pillow. Tear stains darkened the page as she wept for her lost love, part of him gone to his own silent land, yet leaving his soul hidden in the closet. Gypsies held their secrets tight to their hearts and their ghosts did not let go easily. Years of the world's misunderstanding kept them walking in a land of silence. Flashes of forgotten desire closed over her. Lost lightning. Romantic thunder now too distant.

She dried her eyes on a corner of her apron. She should eat, but she was too tired. Temptation flared. Should she open up the family book? Unfold her ancestors' recipe for the lively tea of love? But if she did that, she'd spend a sleepless night wishing and yearning for the lost ingredient. There had been too many nights like that. She settled instead on warming up boiled parsnips mashed with fresh rosemary butter.

Toward midnight, Aggie woke and looked out the window to see the light of Griffo's lantern. The vardo cast a huge shadow against the garage. She watched her nephew attach the wagon to his green and yellow roadster. Then she heard the wheels of the decorated caravan thump down the driveway, bumpido, bumpido, onto the country lane. Apparently, Griffo was off and away again to find his fortune.

After a cup of morning tea, she fed the goats. At the feeding troughs, the animals nuzzled their noses in oat bran and made noises of approval. Plodding back to the house, the empty garage loomed lonely in the early light. Oh, good riddance, she thought, without him to frazzle her, life might turn as easy as flapjacks. He was a gypsy in the wind. Unstoppable. Untrackable. Unreachable.

℞

The man clicked away on the Internet until he located the overseas phone number. The call went through from the United States to the Jardin Estates in Alsace.

The static cleared. "Duke Quincy here."

"Your Grace," he began. "I represent the Global Antiquarian Society. As you may know, ours is a prestigious organization, dedicated to the preservation of volumes of the past."

"I see."

"At this time, we are assembling a tour of fine old volumes for display in specially selected libraries in the United States of America. You may have heard of this tour of antique books."

"I don't think so."

"I'm calling to see if you would consider adding a book in your possession to our prestigious book tour. I believe your volume concerns ancient cures."

"I'm sorry, that is impossible," the duke said.

"I understand your reluctance." The low voice continued calmly, "My research tells me its contents are a mystery sought by many, but I'd like you to consider another possibility that does not include anyone looking inside the book. I am a scholar overseeing a study on ancient bookbinding techniques, and we would like to mention your manuscript. All I need to do is view it, describe it and give measurements. I would come to you."

"Our book cannot be touched."

"It can be measured using new technology, so not one finger would light on its valuable cover."

"Our book is sealed."

"As I said, I'd only view the binding exterior and its condition." He heard the muted sound of a distant bell. "In addition, if you agree to my visit, our organization would make an exceptionally large donation to your winery."

"How much would that be?"

"Because of the mystique surrounding your book, we'd be willing to offer five thousand euros."

"And exactly how would this information be used?"

"It's for historic purposes only. The information in our archive is only available to qualified scholars. It is kept under lock and key in our own vault. I would come to the Jardin Estate for a private viewing. You would be present for the inspection of the exterior. That's it. Except for our donation of appreciation."

"Well now, this might work. Information in the study done for your prestigious archive might help sell our wine. I will allow it.

I see no harm in one brief visit as long as you don't publicize it beforehand. I'm always here. Let me know when you'll arrive."

"Excellent. One visit. No touching of the book. No publicity."

"Forgive me, the bell for teatime calls. I must go. Dill and cucumber sandwiches await."

❧

Dipping an old sea sponge into a pail, Lily scrubbed down the used bookmobile to chase away her dark images, the thoughts of an ended career and a loveless, friendless existence. If she stayed in town, she foresaw a life of suffocation in her rooms, re-reading poetry and passionate passages, breathing air heavy with disappointment.

Soapsuds trickled from her elbows, splashed on her jeans and melted on the cement. The one chance she had was her traveling machine. She could flee the cottage and the city and head into a world of promise.

Freed from layers of dust, her escape vehicle glowed, a behemoth mirroring the vibrant color of the setting sun. Inside, the van was gray, with empty shelves for books, a nook with frayed seating for three, a little fold-up table and a small storage closet. She threw a few striped scarves over the drab seating to liven it up. She sprayed citrus scent up and down the center aisle.

Back and forth, forth and back, she trekked carrying stacks of books from the house to the bookmobile, literary classics she'd acquired through the years. *Moby Dick. Last of the Mohicans. The Scarlet Letter.* Several works by Dickens. She worked until she'd emptied the main shelves of her cottage. After she remembered Piper's request, she climbed up to the attic to look for books from college reading explorations of erotica. Her armload of classics stretched along the illusive borderline between erotica and pornography, debated by scholars and judges for years. Boxed up in the corner, she found the faded, brown leather collectibles she'd bought in used bookstores bordering the edge of the campus. She lugged them out to the bookmobile: *Villette. The Decameron. Candide.* Casanova's *The Story of My Life.* After some thought, she put the books from the erotica category on the shelves in the small storage closet.

A vague future lay ahead. The six month guarantee on the van engine provided a deadline for her traveling experiment. Shoved from the dim safety of the Special Collection Room, she was about to enter the direct sunlight of other people's lives. She closed her eyes, then opened them slowly. After the time was up, if another library position did not surface, if the bookmobile did not give her a life worth table salt....

Picking up a few smooth stones from the driveway, she dwelled on the final solution found by Virginia Woolf. Saddened by life, with rocks in her pocket, that author had walked to the bottom of the river. Emulating Virginia, she slipped a few pebbles into her jeans, then rested her damp hand on her engraved chest. Her hidden away, intricate tattoos surfaced, exposing a pattern through the threads of her damp, thin T-shirt. No man except the tattoo artist had seen her chest since her surgery. She didn't have the courage to survive another episode.

She changed clothes and drove away in the bookmobile to scour the city's new and used bookstores for classic erotica. For hours, she let herself fall under the spell of books again, pulling out favorites and sitting on readers' stools to browse literary memories. In the end, she pulled into her driveway with a few boxfuls of delight: *The London Journals of Boswell. Venus in India. The Lustful Memoirs of a Young and Passionate Girl. Marcella. The Spy in the House of Love.* She also bought works by Colette, Virginia Woolf, George Sand, Jean Rhys and Gertrude Stein. She assembled a short list of other qualified classic erotic authors: George Eliot. Dorothy Parker, Dorothy Wordsworth. Edna O'Brien. And why not Elizabeth Barrett Browning?

In her bedroom, birds chirped outside her window and her mind strayed to the erotic possibilities before her in the books she'd brought home. She opened up a tattered book of love poems she'd found in a budget bin and fell head first into Elizabeth Browning.

> *We paled with love, we shook with love,*
> *We kissed so close we could not vow;*

She skimmed the poem, haunted by images of past pleasure.

And through his words the nightingales
Drove straight and full their long clear call,
Like arrows through heroic mails,
And love was awful in it all.
The nightingales, the nightingales!

She remembered a night spent in the mountains with a man she loved in college. They'd walked hand in hand through the woods, listening to the rustling of creatures around them. Suddenly, he stopped and turned her toward him. In a black night with no moon or stars, he kissed her until she trembled. And a bird sang loud and clear.

She sighed and took her time, browsing the stack of sensuous reading she'd purchased. Eventually, the books found their place on a special shelf in the closet of the bookmobile. There was room for more. Always room for more books, she thought.

The next morning, she showered, splashing warm water over her body to remove any last bit of uncertainty, then toweled herself dry. She carried out two packed suitcases and stowed them by the main back door entry. Early fragments from the east streamed onto the bookmobile, her perfect getaway ride for a librarian on the loose. She picked up the tray of potted straggly herbs and deposited them next to her baggage.

At her desk, she wrote checks for two utility statements and filled out the official post office form for held mail. She left the end date blank and signed it. Then, the urge to amplify made her write a few words along the bottom of the card for her postman:

If you wonder why I left, it's because people should care
more about books. Now, I do what I can. If others ask
where I've gone, tell them destination unknown.

Sincerely, L. M.

In a final gesture, she dialed the phone company. "Please temporarily cut off my service. I'll call if I decide to make it permanent." When she put the receiver down, she felt disconnected from the city she'd known for years.

She picked up the folded newspaper on the edge of the desk. A disturbing photo caught her eye, part of an article about monarch butterflies. More than 200 million butterflies had rained down from their roosts in the towering fir trees of a Mexican forest. She visualized the monumental amount of flapping wings now stilled and melancholy enveloped her. As she read the article at the bottom of the page about the antique book tour coming to Groverly, the gloom lingered. It was only a squib written from the press release she'd sent out, but it represented one of her last duties at the library she loved. She marked it with a red pen and underlined the headline three times. Then, she circled the article on lost butterflies. The newspaper remained on her desk, a red inked commentary on leaving.

Lily took the utility payment envelopes and post office notice to her mailbox and flipped up the red flag. Gas tank full, engine revving, the wheels of the bookmobile met the pavement. Her literary flight stretched out before her. After a quick stop in Nolan, she'd fly down the road again to find adventure.

With DVD sales stalled at the Emporium, Boris was bored with the flinging of knives. Regular store hours, shelf stocking, and bookwork rubbed against his action mentality. Finally, his wild and restless spirit triumphed and he closed up shop, turning the sign to "Temporarily Closed." With that one gesture, he could hide in the back apartment and no one would bother him, while he worked on whatever plan the fates suggested for him next.

At three a.m., a car coasted down the country road and parked. A man glided down the goat farm driveway and invaded the garden. After picking leaves of certain plants, the figure crept back to the car and drove on.

The next morning, Aggie stood outside the Used Stuff door, looking at a sign that read "Closed." Although it meant she couldn't deliver goat milk to Maxine and Sax, she didn't fret. She understood the value of such announcements. Signs like this popped up often on local shopkeepers' doors in Nolan. Owners had the right to come and go, and customers dealt with it.

Zooming down the highway, Lily worked to stay optimistic as the macadam's yellow line led her toward an unsuspecting reading public. She would work to find people she didn't know, who yearned for books they didn't realize they wanted to read. Random influence with limitless possibilities, she thought.

In her quick exit, Lily left a paper trail of information that would follow her, mile after mile.

If a butterfly flaps his wings ....

CHAPTER 8

It was his bullet-point plan. The man studied it and nodded. After detailed investigation and the proper amount of money, he'd obtained a fake passport. Next, he'd constructed an ID card with his new name and identification as an American representative of the Global Antiquarian Society. Then, he'd acquired the proper herbs.

Rows of wilting plants and seeds lay in a line on a small table. "Lovage. Yarrow," he mumbled as he double-checked the ingredients. "Foxglove. Monkshood. Belladonna." He knew which herbs killed, but needed more information on amounts, so fired up his laptop. When he was satisfied, he minced fresh leaves and maneuvered a rolling pin over seeds. He poured boiling water over smidgeons of pounded ingredients. With a careful hand, he added yarrow and lovage for a bright spiciness and honey to provide a touch of sweetness for any who imbibed. After he was satisfied, he hid the completed vials in the closet and drove several miles to buy small laboratory animals.

Back at his quarters, he took out his mixtures. One at a time, he invited the purchased lab creatures to his perilous tea party. After each experiment, he logged the result. When the winning subject showed little apparent pain and transformed quickly from furry mammal into stiff body, he adapted the recipe for human consumption, according to his Internet research. Finally, he wrapped the small corpse in a towel and placed it in the corner with the other misfortunates. After dark, he set the remaining live animals free in a nearby field and buried the dead. Everything went off without a hitch. He emptied all the liquid from his vials, and put the correct amounts of pounded herbs in a well taped envelope.

Another glance at his plan and he moved on to finishing his preparations for leaving town.

The call to the airlines was short. "Book me on the first available flight to Strasbourg."

In his travel kit, he placed the sealed plastic oblong of restaurant honey in the bag with his toiletries. The small empty flask found a place under the folded clothes in his suitcase.

He sighed and sat down. With everything perfect, he placed the call to Alsace. "We finally will meet as planned." He gave time and date to the duke.

"I will expect you," the duke said. "I am looking forward to it, although the family doesn't know."

Once the duke clicked off the phone line, the countdown started.

The next day, dressed in a navy business suit, false ID in place, the man stood in line at the airport security checkpoint. The sealed envelope of herbs was in his shirt pocket. The plastic bin containing his wallet, belt, keys, ring and shoes inched ahead on the conveyor belt. His luggage and briefcase crept through the machine and stopped for screening.

The TSA man pulled him aside. "Place your luggage and case on this table. We need to open them for inspection."

Startled, he complied. "Certainly." The wand zoomed up, down and around his body.

The TSA worker rummaged through his brief case, then flipped open the suitcase for the standard fabric rumple. He shook the empty flask and took the lid off, then unzipped the travel kit. "This looks like trouble."

The man flinched, but did not speak.

"Look here, your shampoo bottle is too big. I need to confiscate it."

"Sorry, I didn't realize."

The TSA man jammed all the clothing into the suitcase. "Thank you for your cooperation. On your way."

The man moved on, troubled over his new problem: getting the *Book of Cures* through customs on the way back from

Alsace. The examination of his suitcase had been thorough. The simple plan of hiding the stolen object in his suitcase had been naive. If his case was opened, even a disguised book would be discovered, particularly if police bulletins were flashing out to all the airports. Luckily, he had a long overseas flight to come up with a new way to get the book to America.

※

Aggie discovered folds of money missing from the farm cash box. Food, some herbs and other supplies were gone from the kitchen. In the garden, it looked like some of the most dangerous plants leaves had been picked and a couple of the safe ones too. She swore a few gypsy oaths, wishing Griffo everything he deserved. She flipped to the back of her green family book to see if the recipe for lively tea was still there. It was. Through the years, she'd kept the crumbly paper secure in its unsealed envelope. Five ingredients spelled out a magical tea of romance her family had received from a wandering gypsy hundreds of years ago. The old ones told of ways the recipe was passed down for generations until now, it rested in Aggie's family book. Early in her life, relatives had whispered the tale of a healer and his mysterious tea. Often, like vapors through moon fires, the thought of the tantalizing drink tripped through her mind. Her mama made her promise on an oath of gypsy blood not to stir up the remedy until a sign appeared from above. The sign never came, because the most important ingredient, the lively plant, was never found. The drawing in her book showed its shape, different from other plants, with leaves shaped like elf ears. She hung the other ingredients in bunches, waiting in the garage, sending out earthy aromas to tempt her with possibilities.

All her life, like countless gypsies before her, she'd been pulled into the shadows of a gloomy premonition about this special drink that made a person feel good, a tea of love and fulfillment. In the old country, relatives before her had gathered all the ingredients and re-created the drink, but they had not waited for a sign from above. Family lore said that afterward, storms of locusts fell from the heavens upon them. Toes and earlobes turned to twisted sticks. Minds emptied like wine jugs.

So Aggie waited and waited some more. By her seventieth decade, she'd never tried to mix up the recipe because she'd never found the strange elf-eared plant. No gypsy she knew had ever seen or been visited by the sign.

"Oh, live a little," she murmured, "to celebrate the book club." Aggie traipsed out to the garage and plucked bits of the four available herbs. In the kitchen, she donned an old apron bequeathed to her from her mama, put the kettle on, and measured the ingredients. Even though she was unable to create the actual forbidden drink of five ingredients, she could mix the other four herbs in a mason jar for a batch of "almost feel good" tea. She heated water to boiling and poured it into a flowered tea pot. Slowly she added the herb mixture and waited for the mystical liquid to steep.

After time infused the hot water with flavor and fragrance, she poured the tea into a crackled cup. She took a spoon and raised the tiniest drop to her lips for a taste. Even without the missing herb, she felt almost better. She touched her ear, no twisted lobe. She looked out the window. Gratefully, no influx of locusts had descended. After she downed the contents of the tea pot, she danced around the kitchen, baking a batch of flower cookies. Then, she decorated the platter with chive blossoms from the garden, petals of edible monarda from the patch by the porch, and slivers of dandelions greens. She assembled other items to take to the club meeting. "Next time, I'll make a batch of this tea for the others."

Dressed in her crazy quilt skirt, she drove to Cut & Curl for book club.

❧

Piper stood with the salon door wide open, letting the sunshine pour in. "Welcome, dear book club lady."

"I'm ready to get started." Aggie carried in two brown paper bags, with a carry-all of bottled milk slung over her shoulder. "Goat milk to drink, farm cheese, oat and seed flower cookies."

"Great idea. I wasn't expecting refreshments." Piper took the bags from her and set them on the salon counter. Aggie unloaded the food, while Piper went to the window to look up the street.

"I expect she'll be here soon," Aggie said.

An orange bookmobile crept down Main Street and parked. Lily slowly opened the door and got out.

Piper ran out the door to meet her. "It's Ms. McFae, isn't it? You look different. Must be the great jeans. How about a free haircut, for making the trip to help us?"

Lily pursed her mouth. "Oh...kay."

"I had something to ask you before we start. About personal reading for me, maybe stimulating...suggestive..."

"What a magical traveling orange-mobile." Aggie stood at the door.

"Oh, never mind, let's go in," Piper said.

A circle of three folding chairs waited. The library volumes left behind for consideration by the book club lay on a little table.

"I'm not much for chitchat," Lily said, "but I do talk books." She brought out notes and one at a time, picked up the selections. "Any others coming?"

"No, we're all here." Piper waved to the librarian. "Go for it."

"I believe you had a question, Piper."

"Talk to you about that later."

The librarian pushed her glasses to the bridge of her nose. "I'm not disappointed there are only two of you. I'm sure you are kindred literary spirits."

"Well, we needed you to come," Piper said, "to jump-start the club."

"Mostly, we don't know what we're doing, that's why we asked," Aggie added. She put the cookie platter near their chairs, poured little paper cups of milk, and handed out tidbits of cheese. "Made at my farm."

Lily took a bite, then tried a sip of milk. "I never sampled goat milk before. It's good. The cheese is excellent." She picked up the poetry book. "I am incredibly happy you love books enough to nourish the beginning of a book club. As a way to begin, let me find a passage to share."

"Is that the way to start each time?" Piper got up to grab a pencil and paper from a drawer. "I'll write that down."

"Only if you want to do it. This maxim comes to me: 'We read to train the mind, to fill the mind, to rest the mind, to recreate the mind, or to escape the mind.' Holbrook Jackson said that."

"That makes reading sound pretty serious." Piper put down the pencil and reached for a cookie. "I'm not all that dedicated to training or recreating or even resting. But definitely escaping. Something snappy would do it."

Lily closed the poetry book. "An understandable approach. Reading does not have to be serious."

"Good. I've had enough of that. A few years ago, my mom skipped out to Vegas and left me her beauty shop. In this town, I'm young to own a business, and I'm grateful she left it to me. Even though it's a big obligation, I took it on. I've always jumped into things. 'Leap before you look,' I say."

Lily sat still, looking thoughtful, then smiled. "Is leaping into books why you started the club? It's as good a reason as any."

"Yup, I thought a book club might be fun and an escape from more serious things."

"Doesn't your mama give you advice on running the shop? Gypsies talk rings around things like that."

"Oh, we never talked much in our family. And never about advice or problems." Piper reached for a cheese cube. "So that's why I'm here. You're next, Aggie."

"For me, reading is something to do when the work is done, when I can sit. And the club doesn't cost money." Her voice dropped. "Not many dollars left over for entertainments when a gypsy runs a goat farm." She sighed.

"So that's the story on us." Piper pointed to Lily. "What about you?"

Lily reached for a book and looked away. "Me? Gracious, I'm not personally interesting at all, but I care for the special books at the library. The beautiful volumes are important, not me. And I keep busy dusting their spines. Breathing their fumes. Arranging cloth-cased folders and elegant calfskin and Japanned oxhide. Every time I touched those books, it was with reverence and white gloves." She gazed out the window. "'O would I were where I would be! Then should I be where I am not. But where I am, there I must be, and where I would be I cannot.'"

A puzzled look flitted over Piper's face. "What on earth does that mean?"

"I am where I am, I guess, not where I might choose to...."

The women's eyes shifted away.

"Oh, don't misunderstand." Lily's shoulders dropped. "It's not that I don't want to be with you, but right now my job is… changing in a way. But here I am to talk about the adventures of reading. How it can sweep you away. Make you laugh. Throw you off cliffs."

"Not too much throwing and falling, I hope. My arthritis." Aggie curled her crooked fingers. "But the laughing part, I like. Not much laughter at the farm nowadays."

"That's the great part about book clubs. You read whatever you like. Books of humor, for example. Or adventurous subjects."

"Now you're talking." Piper leaned forward. "Like how adventurous?"

Lily studied the alert expressions on the two women's faces. "As far as you want to go. An infinite number of possibilities dwells in books: exploring for diamonds in caves, skimming past mountains on feathery gliders, swinging on vines in the jungle. You can conquer the world while remaining safe in your chair."

"I used to explore and skim and swing." Aggie sighed. "Not so much, any more."

"Then lose yourself in novels of other people's lives. Or in mysteries. No one gets hurt during the reading process," said Lily.

"I can tell you're pretty jazzed up about books." Piper brushed crumbs from her lap. "You have the perfect job."

"Actually, there was a disappointment in that regard, due to my own temperament." Lily clutched the book against her breast. "Anyway, let's forget that."

"I understand about disappointment." Aggie looked way. "And trying not to remember."

"Hey, I'd like to forget a few things too," Piper said.

Lily put the book back on the table. "For a while now, I've looked for different things to brighten my life. I pierced my ears on my thirty-fifth birthday and every birthday after that, I pushed myself into something new. Tasted the local calamari. Attempted to surf. Drank corn coffee. Last year, something private, but this year, I turned forty and I'm driving my splurge, an orange bookmobile." Lily took a big breath. "And that is more than enough about me."

The women regarded their hands, folded neatly in their laps.

"Then on to something new," Piper said.

Aggie folded her hands over her faded patchwork skirt and cleared her throat. "New things are not always good. Illness. Sadness. Grief. Not many people in town know, but a while back, I lost my husband, Cim."

Lily leaned forward. "My condolences."

Piper gave Aggie an odd look. "But what about Camlo?"

"Whenever possible, gypsies do not say the name aloud of a departed one. So I do not say his name, except in my inner thoughts. Cim is the name I use for him now."

Piper reached over and patted Aggie's hand. "I didn't know. Ever so often, I saw you and your husband around town. Not for a while, I guess. I didn't realize he died."

"I'm not certain if you want to go ahead with book club today. We've gotten personal rather quickly." Lily's face flushed. "Although I've heard sometimes it's easier to talk to people who don't know you. What do you want to do?"

"If Aggie agrees, I say we keep going," Piper glanced over at the old woman. "Maybe reading will give us some sort of escape from our dark times."

Aggie nodded.

Lily pointed to the library books on the table. "Looking at the selections I brought, which book reached you enough to want to discuss it?"

"I did like Rossetti," Aggie said, "but she made me weep."

Piper's back straightened up. "Oh, let's not do sad. We don't need that. We need something to liven us up."

"It's your club." Lily pointed to the science fiction on the table. "What comes to mind? Sci Fi or spy novels?"

Piper's cheeks flushed as she stood up and moved to the barber chair. "Since it looks like we're getting along pretty good here, I'll throw out a suggestion. Just a thought, but how about something romantic? I mean very, very romantic. I mean books with sexy scenes. I love the real thing, but heck, reading about it might be worth something. We could have kind of a risqué book club."

Aggie gave her a blank stare. The room was quiet enough to hear the calls of small children playing in a far yard. The slam of a car door in the next block. The chirping of a sparrow on the outskirts of town.

Piper returned to her seat. "I mean my life's not so sexy right now for whatever reason, and I'm curious, like most women. That kind of reading might be a substitute for..." Her hand lingered next to her mouth. "Things. To forget certain things. I don't mean a dirty book club, exactly, but one about...airotica."

Lily thought of the books in the bookmobile closet. "An Erotica Book Club is absolutely possible."

Aggie and Piper perched like birds, waiting for Lily to feed them mysterious seeds.

The librarian smiled. "There are classics in a genre called erotica."

"Exactly how's that spelled?" asked Piper.

"E-r-o-t-i-c-a, erotica."

Piper nodded. "Oh, yeah."

Lily leaned back in the chair. "In the beginning, you might want to broaden the term for your club. Think about the desire and hunger for pleasure as well as passion. Remember though, you don't have to choose erotica. You could choose another book, one about –"

"Pleasure that feels like waves of a wild hairdo. With moving and swirling." Piper shook her head to let her curls fly.

"Pleasure rolling in like an enormous sunburst, warming my body." Aggie stretched out her arms. "I think what we want to read is ...."

Aggie and Piper shouted together, "Erotica."

Piper jumped up. "We could call ourselves The Erotica Book Club for Nice Ladies. And not tell anyone. I'm not sure how that name would go over in town."

Aggie wrinkled her brow. "And I'm not sure exactly what it is."

Lily stacked the library books. "Erotica has many meanings. It's studied by scholars and historians. Even religious figures."

"Let's not do history. Or religion," Piper said. "What about reading for the curious woman?"

Aggie massaged her thumbs. "Maybe start with slow and short. I'm not the most up-to-date lady. It was pleasure that sounded right. My gypsy family understood and yearned for pleasure."

"The material doesn't have to be explicit. Sometimes pleasure can be derived from being tantalized." Lily held up a square of cheese. "For example, a craving for this creamy morsel. Or a voluptuous pear. Juicy. Tempting. The anticipation of tasting it."

"Nibbling food to substitute for ears. Or other parts." Piper tilted her head. "I can see that."

Aggie mumbled to herself. "Yes, a strong man with a gentle mouth is to be wished for."

Piper's eyes widened. "You, Aggie, get right to the point."

Lily paged through the poetry book. "Perhaps something acceptable to most people. Like Algernon Charles Swinburne. This is called "A Match." From the last stanza,

> *If you were queen of pleasure,*
> *And I were king of pain,*
> *We'd hunt down love together,*
> *Pluck out his flying-feather,*
> *And teach his feet a measure,*
> *And find his mouth a rein;*

Piper frowned. "King of pain. Like whips and stuff?"

"We could talk about whether that's what the poet meant," Lily said.

"Or talk about plucking feathers. I know more about that from the farm."

Piper nodded. "And sexy feet, I wonder how that works."

"So with only a few words, you've run off in different directions. That's good." Lily closed the book.

"Leave that book of poetry for Piper, so she can figure out the sexy feet." Aggie chuckled. "Although I'd really like to take it home first, to read the thoughts of different poets."

"You go ahead. Give it to me when you're finished," Piper said.

Lily took off her glasses and handed the book to Aggie. "Next time, maybe try Emily Dickinson. The poetry book includes her small poem about wild nights. It's filled with meaning and promise. I'll write out another copy right now." She took a sheet out of her notebook and began to write. "Read it. Study it. At your next meeting, discuss the writer's intentions and the feelings her words engender in you, the reader. Decide if you feel the same or differently about the poem. There's no right or wrong. I can send information about the author, if you're interested. She was quite a woman."

"Gee, Emily Dickinson was an assignment in high school, but I must not have been paying attention, 'cause I don't think they taught erotica in my English class." Piper wiggled the pencil back and forth.

"Where do we find these writers of erotica?" Aggie said.

"In bookstores, the library, on the Internet. There is something for everyone. Several famous authors raised the temperature of writing. Anais Nin. Vita Sackville-West. For an even higher degrees of intensity, Sappho and the Marquis de Sade. But if you prefer mild romantic fare, there are well-known authors, like Jane Austen. Actually, some fan fiction writers today have sensed an underlying heat in her classic novels and they've re-written certain scenes more explicitly, for example from *Pride and Prejudice*. I doubt any author of old would accept such revisions."

"But which one should we start with?"

"There's *Mrs. Dalloway* by Virginia Woolf. Or *Jane Eyre* by Charlotte Bronte." Lily gestured outside toward her bookmobile. "I have examples in my van. Want to come take a look?"

"We could do that, but I'm not sure about taking one home today." Piper shrugged. "I need to decide where to keep it. Maybe hide it under the kitchen sink at home with the cleaning stuff. Freddie's a bit of a prude about some things. And if it's in the salon, some customer might pick it up. Maybe when you come back through town, we'll be ready."

Aggie pursed her lips. "Looks like we both need time to think about how to go about this before we start reading."

"I can send a list of a few books with a theme line, so you can decide if the contents might appeal to you. When you're ready, the library could mail them."

"Books in brown wrappers, coming through our post office to our mailboxes. Not a good idea," Piper said. "We'll figure something out. But send the list." She ran her hands through her pink streak of hair.

Aggie started packing up the leftovers. "Maybe there's some erotica in the farm garage. Griffo has piles of books there. He sold old books for a time."

Piper stood up. "Then, it looks like we're set. A great start for the first meeting of The Erotica Book Club."

"For Nice Ladies." Aggie put the cookie platter in a paper bag. "That's the part I like, being thought of as a nice lady."

Lily handed Piper a copy of the Dickinson poem. "Now you each have one."

Piper filed the poem in her bookkeeping ledger. "Before I forget, I heard something really interesting about a book when I was at the Emporium."

Aggie turned her head in surprise. "I wouldn't have guessed you shop there. It's an unusual place, at least for Nolan."

"I was there on an errand, and these guys were talking about a book worth a million dollars. Is that possible?"

Lily nodded. "Certainly, if it's scarce or historical. Maybe a first edition, or signed by an important author. A copy of Audubon's *Birds of America* sold for 11 million and a *Gutenberg Bible* went for over four."

"Wow." Piper folded up chairs. "I wished I remembered exactly what they said. Mostly about a drug company wanting to buy some old book."

"I don't know any book about drugs worth a million, but could be," Lily said. "Not many people participate in investments like that. Certainly not me."

"I'm partial to simple things," Aggie said. "By necessity, but more than that."

Lily stacked up the unwanted volumes from the library. "And I'm the same way. I'll leave these library books, just in case." She took a deep breath. "Can anyone stay to talk? I don't have to be anywhere. We could chat about anything. Doesn't have to be erotic. Or even personal."

Piper carried the chairs to the back storage closet. "Darn, I have a wash and set in a few minutes." She came back and shook out a plastic cape. "I put off the appointment because of our meeting."

"And goat hooves wait for trimming at the farm. I didn't finish my work."

Lily held out a card. "Here's my cell phone number, in case you have questions. Goodbye and good luck."

Piper put the card on the counter. "Thanks for your help and sorry we didn't get to that haircut." She turned to Aggie. "Let's meet same time tomorrow to get this thing rolling."

Aggie smiled. "I'll be here."

Piper watched the women leave, then wandered back to the storage room. Talking about her mom brought memories of the unopened boxes stacked in the back closet. Each one was marked "personal" and Piper stood staring at them, until her customer arrived.

Lily drove the bookmobile to the town square and parked. Like a smoking combination of chemicals, she'd felt connected to these women. There was an ease to their conversation about books, and after that, the personal sharing. They'd twisted together, then sprung apart, yet sent out rarified fumes of friendliness in her direction.

Then, just like that, it was over and the camaraderie dried up and blew away. For a few brief moments, she thought she'd found friendship with two clubwomen curious about erotica. But it didn't happen.

The door of the bookmobile opened and a mother with three noisy kids tumbled in.

"This bunch needs distraction." The woman's eyes looked tired. "A reason to sit down and be quiet."

"Sorry, I don't have much reading for kids." Lily pulled out several books and spread them on the table. "This is it. Available to check out or purchase."

The mother looked inside at the prices, then drew out a wad of money. "I'll buy them. My kids are pretty hard on books."

Lily pocketed the money and locked the door when the group left. At the drive-in, she ordered a double mocha shake and thought again about the book club women. Their quick dismissal of her hurt. Loneliness settled in when she realized she wasn't headed home to Groverly. She checked into a room at Motel 5 on the outskirts of Nolan. Collapsing on the twin bed, she wrote out the short list of possible erotica she'd promised to the nice ladies.

❧

Lady Chatterley's Lover. 1928 novel by D. H. Lawrence about the mind and the body. Well known and controversial. Main characters: an English lady, her paralyzed husband, and a young gamekeeper. With explicit sexual passages and four letter words that couldn't be printed back in the 1920's.

❧

Canadian author Margaret Atwood's *The Handmaid's Tale.* A dystopian or futuristic novel with strangely erotic overtones. Women in assigned and subjugated roles, some kept for reproductive purposes.

❧

Crossed out, *Aurora Leigh* by Elizabeth Barrett Browning, the story of a woman who gradually realizes she loves her cousin.

❧

In an Alsatian hotel room, dried leaves and hot, hot tap water swirled into a brew. The result was poured into a silver flask.

❧

In her room, Piper read,

> *Were I with thee*
> *Wild nights should be*
> *Our luxury!*

And Aggie read,

> *Might I but moor – tonight –*
> *In thee!*

CHAPTER 9

The businessman rented a car in Strasbourg and studied the map for routes to and from the Global Antiquarian Society. He looked in the trunk of the vehicle and made one stop at a hardware store. Then he drove to the city's outskirts, down a long lane to check out the lay of the land. After his baggage inspection at the airport, he'd formulated another way to get the book home. It was more complicated with some tricky parts, but he thought he could manage it.

Back at the hotel, he unpacked and made a call.

"Global Antiquarian Society."

"Can you give me information about your tour of ancient books? It starts soon and I want to make sure of the dates. Our family is going to the States, and we plan to visit your exhibit while there. A special treat for our family of dedicated readers."

He listened as the cheery-voiced receptionist read the itinerary.

"Perfect. I'm ready to make our airline reservations, and I had a terrific idea. Perhaps the books and my family could leave the country at the same time and cross the ocean in tandem. I'd impress my kids and grandkids no end with my literary dedication."

"I've never heard of anything like that, but it's a unique idea. I like it."

"I'm one of the society's most devoted fans. So can you tell me when we should depart? It would make an exceptional memory for us all."

The receptionist laughed. "It's not a secret. We even plan some publicity at the airport." She told him the day and time the exhibit was scheduled to leave the building and the name of the airport.

He hung up, went to the hotel restaurant and ordered jambon en croute. Afterward, he called the duke, reviewed his plan, then set off driving through the Alsatian hills to the Jardin Estate.

The sound of jet planes streaked through the sky, breaking the meditative silence of the chateau setting. The man pulled himself together, then rang the bell on the gate.

Soon, an old gentleman strolled to the entryway. " I am Duke Quincy, head of the Jardin Estate. Welcome to our winery. I assume you are the society representative. Please follow me to the vault." He checked his timepiece, then ushered his visitor toward a rustic doorway built into a hillside. "Our evening meal begins soon. Do you think we'll be finished before the bell rings in an hour?"

"This won't take much time. I realize you're breaking precedent."

The door creaked on heavy, rusted hinges and they went down a set of stairs.

"Do not think me rude if I ask to see your credentials."

"Of course, here they are." The visitor displayed the ID card from his wallet.

"Centuries ago, workers dug this vault into the hillside." The duke stopped by a long, oak table. A battery lamp burned, revealing the vacant mouth of an open vault. A black velvet placemat decorated the table.

"I see you are ready for me. Is your seed business doing well?"

"Yes, we're pleasantly surprised at the volume of orders, because the herbs are only to be used decoratively."

The man placed his bulky briefcase on the table. "Your flyer excited our officers, an opportunity to authenticate the existence of your manuscript and include it in our bookbinding study."

"For years, we've tried to avoid attention to the book, but interest remains. It's a new world and our marketer recommends we join in, if we intend the winery to prosper. I admit the intrigue about the book has increased wine sales, and we've turned down several offers to sell it."

The duke disappeared into the dark enclosure. When he reappeared, his gloved hands cradled an old manuscript. "The stone and mortar of this cave have provided a secure home for our book for hundreds of years."

"It's not too late to include it on our book tour. The volumes leave soon for their first library showing, and I could take the book with me. Make all the arrangements."

"The answer is still no. I've thought long and hard over whether to show you the exterior of the manuscript."

"Know that the society members are grateful for this viewing."

"All I provide is a look at the exterior." The elderly duke placed the scarlet-covered book on the dark velvet. The faded cover gave off a soft radiance. "Is this worth your trip?"

"It is. After centuries of rumors, it validates an existing volume no one has seen, except your family. It's said the book holds information about unique herbal combinations. What do you say?"

"I have nothing to reveal, since I've seen nothing of its contents. We've kept it sealed."

"Amazing." The visitor took out a notebook and ruler. "I see a touch of worn gilding on the cover. See, without touching, this laser ruler can measure the dimensions. I hold it just so, to get the precise height and length." The ruler hovered over the cover, then the man marked down the calculations.

"Careful. Don't get too close."

"Quite right. One quick photo and I'm done." The visitor reached into the briefcase for his iPhone and a flask. "We have a tradition at our headquarters that honors each rare book we uncover. We toast with a special tea of yarrow and lovage, often served at room temperature to enjoy its rare flavors. I thought it appropriate to bring some, so we could celebrate together."

The duke moved the placemat aside. "Yes, here at the estate, we often use herbal tea for different occasions."

"Think of it. After all this time, information about your manuscript will hold a place of honor in our archival study." Tiny cups appeared from the depths of the briefcase and the visitor poured the amber liquid. "We drink to good fortune."

The duke raised his cup. "To the healing properties of yarrow and lovage. I've been troubled by ill health of late."

"May you soon escape that burden." The visitor lifted his cup. He did not sip, only watched the old man drink his tea.

The old duke whispered, "The yarrow we grow is not so pungent, the lovage not so bitter." He gasped, struggling to speak again, to breathe. He grabbed the book and stumbled against the table, but the volume fell free as his body crashed to the ground. The outer seal quivered when the book hit the floor. He stretched out his fingers to reclaim it. Only one inch away. Yet a canyon of space separated him from the manuscript. "Help me," he whispered. His face drained to a salt-white color.

"I apologize for the flavor. Perhaps you taste the presence of monkshood behind the flavor of lovage. The dab of honey should have balanced that hint of poison."

The victim's weary eyes met the visitor's. "Why?"

"My good man, so your book can travel to the States, after all," the man answered.

The duke's violent cough left one splot of blood on the worn tile. His lids closed in his pale face.

Drop by drop, the remaining cup of untouched tea was poured back into the flask. The gloves were stripped from the dead man's fingers and used by the man to wrap the book in a soft covering, before placing it in the briefcase. He grabbed a bottle of wine and nudged the vault's metal door closed until the lock caught. With a quick swipe of his handkerchief, he wiped the blood from the tile, and set the bottle near the duke's hand. As he snapped off the lamp, the dinner bell rang out. "Sleep in peace, old fella," he whispered to the motionless figure.

Nearby sparrows huddled in their nests as blackness pushed against the silhouette that scuttled away from the winery.

After dinner, the family checked the elderly duke's bedroom to see why he'd missed the meal he most enjoyed. They found his bed made up, everything in place, except the duke. Within minutes, they'd organized a tour of the château, up and down staircases, floor by floor, room by room. But they didn't find him.

They grabbed flashlights and scattered to search the edges of the courtyard, the rows of the vineyard, the garden spaces. When they reassembled and checked off the points searched, they realized no one had visited the wine storage vault.

They found him. His still body looked at peace, his hand outstretched toward a bottle of wine. Everything appeared in order. The table, clean. The vault, closed. The lamp, extinguished. Except for death's swift visit, the place looked as cool and tranquil as always.

The visit from their family physician determined that the duke had succumbed to a heart attack while getting a bottle of wine. His skin color was off, but his health complaints of late had been many. He was an old gentleman, after all.

All through the night, the outside gate of the chateau swung back and forth from a breeze that chilled the garden. The odor of lovage mixed with the scent of blossoming plum trees, fanning a rare perfume into the air.

Aggie clutched her worn sweater close to her body. She slumped in the porch rocker, a rounded monolith, holding the heaviness of years in her folded hands. Suddenly she sighed, went inside and yanked open a warped drawer. With a black marker, she slowly penned "Room for Rent" on a piece of cardboard. She walked to the mailbox and attached the sign to the metal with strips of duct tape. Griffo's room was officially available.

A clear and perfect dawn arrived on schedule at Motel 5. Comfy in old gray sweats, Lily checked out and started on her trip, with Aggie and Piper prominent in her mind. It was the closest she'd come to friendship in a long time. She drove for an hour into the next county. Bumps in the road shook the bookmobile and rattled her spirits. At a three-way junction, she braked to let a band of bright-winged monarchs float across the road. As she watched them, she felt her thoughts lift with happiness. She turned the bookmobile around and followed the butterflies back to Nolan.

CHAPTER 10

The two women of the book club sat across from each other at Cut & Curl, library books stacked in front of them on the table. Piper held up the notes she'd taken. "Are we ready?"

Aggie nodded.

"Okay, here we go. The Erotica Book Club for Nice Ladies will begin," she announced.

They sat for a minute. Piper looked at her notes, while Aggie kneaded her thumbs.

"Go ahead," Aggie said. "The poem."

"The title is "Wild Nights." But the words are printed twice and there's an exclamation point at the end. That's probably important."

They looked at each other.

"Later, it says things about nights and luxury. What do you think, Aggie?"

"I'll say this, I asked Lily for short. We got short."

"But what do you think it means?" Piper asked. "Our luxury."

Aggie shook her head. "I only know that goat farms don't have any."

"And neither do salons, but to tell the truth, Freddie and I sure had some wild evenings."

"Even this old gypsy lady had her share of rowdy nights."

The women stared into their laps.

"I guess we're done for now." Piper stood up. "We'll try the second verse next time. Maybe we should meet more often to get used to discussing. What do you say?"

"I don't mind coming to town," Aggie said. "The change of scene perks me up."

The door opened. Lily stood in the entryway with a tote bag. "I thought I'd stop by one more time. In case you had questions."

Piper rushed toward Lily and hugged her. "You're here. We're here."

"Your club is waiting." Aggie patted Lily's arm.

Piper pointed to the barber chair. "Hop up and I'll trim your hair while we talk." She wrapped the plastic cape around Lily's shoulders. "We didn't get very far on our own. Maybe we're hopeless."

"Of course, you're not. Maybe just a word or two about getting organized," Lily said.

"Our meeting was shorter than the poem." Aggie twisted her long, gray braid.

Piper held up strands of Lily's hair and started cutting. "We need to know more about erotica. The questions to ask each other."

"Well, first decide what type of books you want to read. As I indicated, the kind of writing called erotica covers a blanket of subjects. Desire, consummation, frustration, danger, voyeurism, sin. Even self-love. You'll think of others."

Piper snipped away. "What about romance?"

"A definite oversight," Lily said.

"Fantasy." Aggie strolled over to the window. "And taboo?"

"Absolutely. Erotica is different from culture to culture, place to place, moment to moment, from beating heart to living speck. If you want to talk about men and women, you might consider certain books that include sexual acts, orgasms, orgies and the like. There is controversy about some of them. Henry Miller's *Tropic of Cancer* was banned for twenty-seven years in this country. Decide if that kind of reading would interest you."

"Maybe I'm not quite ready for that yet," Aggie said.

"How about a classic tale of adultery and the town's reaction to it? That's the plot of *The Scarlet Letter*."

"Maybe just more about a man and a woman. Forget what other people think." Piper lifted and trimmed strands of hair. "Just two people in love, with problems. Who don't know how to talk to each other."

"Are the words in these books shocking or sweet or what?" Aggie tugged at her collar.

"There are plenty of romantic tales with euphemisms for love making. Bursting bosoms. Unbuttoned trousers. Flower of womanhood. Stalk of manhood. Are you up to reading and talking about that?"

"This may be more complicated than I thought." Piper's scissors worked their way around Lily's crown.

"It's odd, looking inside a writer's mind and trying to understand what the words mean. Sex is everywhere on the farm, but we talk about animals in a different way."

"Well then, nature is an excellent place to begin," Lily said. "Fifty thousand endangered turtles crawled ashore on a small stretch of coastal land in India to lay eggs in their annual migration. A night that possibly saved their species. Imagine that beach. An orgy of turtle sex."

"Yeah, I see that." Piper ruffled and shaped the haircut. "The old story about the birds and bees."

"Gypsies know things about such matters. When the male zebra finch is ready to mate, he does not seek out his love bird until it rains."

Piper giggled. "So does the female finch spend her time praying for rain clouds?"

With her auburn locks strewn over the linoleum floor, suddenly Lily felt lightheaded. "Since we've talked of birds and turtles, sex and orgies, why not give the spinster, Ms. Dickinson, another try. In her poem, she writes about rowing and two lines later suggests mooring. What do you think Ms. Dickinson meant by that?"

Piper trimmed around Lily's ear. "Knowing she was a spinster, it could mean she liked boating, but I'm pretty sure that's not it."

"Now you've got it. Look behind the words for other meanings," Lily said. "How did the poem make you feel? Did the poem give you yearnings? Memories? Sensations? "

Aggie clasped her swollen hands. "I'm thinking, just not saying. Maybe I could save it for next time. The 'wild nights' part anyway."

"What if, in our club we read the books you suggest, but didn't talk about them." Piper whipped off Lily's cape.

"That wouldn't exactly be a book club, but it's your call. If you don't want to discuss, stay inside your minds. It's a private place that belongs to each person alone," Lily said. "And speaking of privacy, maybe Dickinson meant private moments between two people, a close affection that lasted through the night, like a boat snug in a harbor. Two people with the luxury of time to spend together."

"I see." Piper whisked Lily's shoulders with a little broom. She went to the closet and pulled out another folding chair. "Let's sit down and think about that."

As a silence heavy with romance drifted into the room, the women remembered and fell into rich, inner thoughts, long as tunnels, deep as caverns, dark as the secrets of their own inner hearts. For a long while, they did not speak.

And Lily didn't expect them to. She sat quietly until a bicycle zoomed past the window, the ching of its bell singing a pure Zen note. "Okay. Forget erotica for today. Talk about something else. Anything come to mind?"

Piper rose and paced around the circle. "But what I'm thinking about is not happy. When I can't talk or I start worrying, I get busy. I know I should learn to talk about things." She stopped. "And I need to tell you something."

"Well, here we are," Aggie said.

"I moved into the spare room, so in a way, Freddie and I are separated. There are reasons I can't deal with now, but I thought a book club, if we read erotica might chase away the blues, until I sorted things out." She dropped back into her chair. "There, I've said it and now that I've said it aloud, I feel better. Maybe since I don't know either one of you very well, you won't judge me."

Lily bit her lip. "No judgments at all, Piper. Is there anything we can do?"

"You listened," Piper said. "That's all I wanted."

"It will work out for you. This gypsy feels that." Aggie stood up, gripping her hands together. "And I have something to ask Piper. Do I belong in this club? In this town? Romas have a troubled past. To the townsfolk, I wonder if I'm a suspicion. Do they think I'll steal their silver? I worry about that all the time."

"Oh, Aggie, they are wary of Griffo, but not you," Piper said.

"When Cim and I traveled, I yearned for our gypsy wheels to stop, to have a home and a garden rooted firmly in the ground. Now, with him gone, I don't know if that was wise."

"Well, I'm glad you're here in this town and in my shop and in the club right now. So there."

Lily sighed. "Looks like you two have formed a club."

Aggie nodded and dropped to her seat. 'I hope so. If I can figure out how to understand what the writer means."

Lily lifted her chin. "They do say that sharing lightens the load. So, here goes." She took a breath. "What I didn't tell you, was that I was fired by the library."

"Oh no," Piper said.

"Oh dear." Aggie's finger traced the design in one of her skirt patches.

"In one moment, my temper flared. I lost all those books at the Main Branch and worse, those in the Special Collections Room." Lily made two fists and touched them together. "I snapped, even though I'm usually a calm, patient person." She lifted the book of poetry on the table. "Through the years, books were my passion. Not just the words, but even the white spaces between someone's thoughts. The expanse of the author's mind." She leafed through the pages. "I mean the whole package. The paper. Fonts. Edges. Glue." She closed the book. "Although I'll always have reading, I no longer have an endless supply of literature surrounding me, a multiplying supply of volumes at my fingertips."

Aggie reached over and took Lily's hand. "But now you're free to do anything you choose."

Piper jumped up. "And you're here with us. We barely know each other, but we've found a place to talk about our troubles. Who'd have thought we all have secrets." She grabbed a broom and swept hair from under the barber chair into a dustpan. "Telling one of mine made me feel lots better."

"At your next meeting, you may decide to read some erotica and discuss it," Lily said. "Or not. You could change the name of your club to make things simpler."

"No, I love the name," Piper said, "although Fred might object, if he knew what it was called. He's against porno."

"But pornography is different from erotica, if not in subject matter, then in style. There are subtle and not so subtle differences. A matter of taste and hard to explain. Anyway, good luck." Lily picked up the poetry anthology Aggie had brought back to the meeting. "Look inside and try *Ah! Why, Because the Dazzling Sun* by Emily Bronte. I'll bet you get the idea of what she's saying."

She pulled out a book from her tote bag. "Piper, give *The New Atalantis* a whirl. It may get you started."

On her way to the door, Lily tipped her head this way and that in the mirror. "Thank you for the fringy haircut. It makes me look different." She stared at her image.

"Sexy. With a definite come-hither look," Piper said. "The sweat suit makes you look younger too. Not so sexy, but you never know what might turn a guy on."

"Are you rushing back to the city today?" Aggie asked.

Lily pulled her fingers through her new coiffure. "No, I'm not going back. The lavender fields up the road are calling to me. I closed my house in Groverly and turned into a rover with a traveling bookmobile."

Aggie grabbed Lily's arm. "Then lucky I have an extra room. If you're a gypsy, that makes you a kindred soul. Follow me to the farm in your magical, orange-colored bookbus."

A friendly ember flared inside Lily. "I could do that."

Out of sight, the man waited near the loading zone at the Global Antiquarian Society. The delivery van pulled up and the uniformed driver entered the building. Casual and quiet, the man bent down to fumble with the truck's rear tire on the driver's side. Then, he hurried back to his hidden vehicle to wait and watch the loading of a wooden crate into the back of the van.

As the truck moved down the lonely lane toward the main artery into Strasbourg, he followed a distance behind. When the van pulled over and the driver inspected his flat, the man pulled up behind and jumped out of his car. "Need some help, mate?"

"No, thanks. I called and help will arrive in less than an hour." The driver bent over and fiddled with the tire.

It took only a few quick steps before the tire iron grazed the back of the driver's head, and he crumpled like a puppet. Another snappy move and his billfold disappeared into the intruder's pocket.

He swung the back truck doors open to locate the crate. With a state-of-the-art screwdriver, he pried open the top, undid some of the packing material, and slipped in an envelope containing the sealed manuscript. Next to the packing list was a small, separate sheet about the addition of the *Book of Cures*. He screwed the crate shut, removed the money from the driver's wallet before pitching it into the ditch.

At the airport, he breezed through his baggage inspection and reviewed his plan: The serviceman who came to fix the tire would call the authorities. When the driver was roused, he'd describe "a man who pulled up behind." The freight company would verify that all packages and crates remained secure. With a new driver at the wheel, the van would speed off to the airport.

Snug in the cool freight section, the crate flew across the ocean on its long voyage, carrying ancient remedies written in the hand of a sixteenth century duchess. Her simple garden book nestled next to illustrious, collectible manuscripts saved by antiquarians, whose work documented the history of books and the way they'd evolved through the ages.

From the large plane that landed in the States, the crate was transferred to a smaller airline, then loaded onto a delivery truck. The crate moved toward the first tour stop, a small library added at the last minute.

Without a butterfly whisper. Without one note of melancholy birdsong, the secrets of the ancient book moved to the sounds and fumes of the diesel truck engine. After hundreds of years, the fragile old pages edged closer to the light.

CHAPTER 11

Lily grabbed a book of poetry and her small overnight case from the bookmobile, then followed Aggie into the garage. Above the uneven stacks of Griffo's used book supply, herbal bundles hung from an old rope tacked to the wall. She walked by them, breathing in the smell of lovage and rosemary, mint, dill and basil. The scents of the earth carried up the narrow staircase that hugged the side of the building and led to a small room on top.

Aggie opened the door and pointed at the depression age furniture. "Bed, chest, rocker, desk. Sink, hot plate, and small refrigerator. Plumbing's over there. Not fancy, but useful."

Lily gravitated to the rocker by the open window. Cottonwood leaves grazed the pane. A jasmine vine twined up the drainpipe toward the roof. "It's perfect. The smell of growing greenery above me, the scent of drying herbal bunches and stacks of saved old books beneath."

Aggie puttered around, tidying up. "I hope you find it comfy."

"How much is the rent for a night or two?" Lily looked out the large window toward the goats rambling in the field.

Aggie paused. "The room is empty. Friends stay free, but only if you promise to nudge Piper and me, squeaking and creaking, into our book club for foolish women."

"I can manage a push or two. Thank you, Aggie."

"I'll call Piper and tell her. You can drive the bookmobile into town and back, or you can ride with me."

"Or I can walk. It's only a couple miles and I liked walking to the library when the sun was shining and I was in the mood."

"If you miss your library books, try Griffo's downstairs, or visit the Used Stuff Store. They have a few shelves of old books there." She moved to the stairs. "I'll leave you to settle in and later, put a plate of cheese and fruit outside your door. If you are still hungry, stop by the kitchen."

Lily heard Aggie's footsteps retreat down the stairs. She knew the Global Antiquarian Society Book Tour was arriving at the library. She thought about the unpacking of the wooden crate. A tour representative would supervise Director Trummel as she unlocked the glass case and positioned the books. When the display was perfect, the lights would be set to highlight the old manuscripts. Then, the case would be locked and the alarm set. Everyone would leave.

Depressed, Lily stared out the window. She'd missed out on arranging the most beautiful book display ever to visit the Groverly Main Library. Beyond the main house porch, grew Aggie's garden, with its odd mix of beds. Farther on, a stream flowed and fields undulated like unwound bolts of green silk. The ghost of Virginia Woolf slipped into the room as Lily thought of running through the wild grass outside, finding rocks, rocks next to water. With enough rocks and deep enough water, she could plunge into its cold wet cave and disappear.

She got up to pick up the books scattered around the room and randomly immersed herself in a tattered copy of Mary Shelley's *Frankenstein*. She thought she heard a sound and when she peeked outside, found the plate of food. She ate a few bites, then pulled the red flyer butterfly from her purse, and undid the folds. Its bright color under the bed lamp cheered the dim setting. After she unpacked, she pulled on a soft, white nightshirt and climbed into bed. She couldn't keep a dark loneliness from wrapping itself around her. She couldn't forget her surgery. Or forget the firing. Losing her job and her books, with only an uncertain future ahead. Would traveling give even a modicum of pleasure? And if not?

She shivered. With her head flat on the mattress, she tried to relax, but the bedsprings creaked with every move. She whispered an old Zen phrase, "Be like a damp stone." She repeated it over and over, then edited it. "Be like a stone. Be like. Be like.

Be." Be like Virginia. The haunting by Virginia Woolf surfaced again, the tortured writer with stones in her pocket, walking into the water to die. "Be. Be. Be." Lily pushed thoughts of the author aside. She burrowed into the comforter and got through the night the best way she could. A toss. A turn. A warm pillow flipped to the cool side.

⚜

At the Craft Market in Groverly, Griffo waited for customers to visit the vividly painted gypsy vardo. He'd parked near the road to catch the eye of any passerby, certain his place would be hard to miss, with its wild-eyed griffins, gargoyles and dragons. Each morning, he rolled up the yellow awning and flipped down the back counter. He expected his hand-lettered sign *"Griffo's Rare Gems & Jewels"* would draw in the crowds. Each day, he counted change and pulled out his credit card machine in preparation for rich customers. His sales pitch sold a couple bracelets for a couple dollars, but the place was dead. Finally, he locked up the vardo and drove to the Emporium in his roadster.

"Looks like you could use some picketing today," he said.

Boris shook his head. "Sorry, the picketing stunt's worn out. Care to sample the latest DVD trailers?" He hit the play button.

When Sax walked in the door, Boris beckoned to the two men. "Tell you what, things are slow. Why don't you guys join me with the ritual polishing of the knives?"

They grinned and followed Boris to the office. It took only a few minutes for him to release the large ancient swords from the wall. "Watch carefully, the rubbing is like a caress." He held the soft cloth and swabbed the blades with metal cleaner.

The men worked with care and tenderness, shining each sword until it gleamed. Boris removed the delicate daggers from the gold cord, and the three cleaned the intricate crevices and designs of each handle.

"Now we throw. My weapons are light, balanced, and deadly sharp." Boris whipped a knife through the air with perfect aim. "Sax knows."

"Sometimes, Boris lets me throw a few." Sax let his dagger loose with a slow and deliberate thrust. It almost stuck to the outer rim of the target.

Boris thumped him on the back. "Much better."

Griffo laughed and threw his knife with savage intensity. It fell to the ground.

"You need practice to do it right," Boris said. "When we throw together, it forms a bond." He touched his fingertip with the blade and waited for a small drop of blood to form, then placed his finger on the counter, marking it with a perfect imprint. He offered the dagger to Sax, who followed suit and pushed down hard on the counter to create a blob.

"Gypsies don't believe in leaving fingerprints." But Griffo poked his finger and put his light bloody print next to the other two.

After the goats bedded down in their straw nests, Aggie found the Bronte poem.

> *Thought followed thought – star followed star*
> *Through boundless regions on,*
> *While one sweet influence, near and far,*
> *Thrilled through and proved us one.*

The corners of her mouth raised. She was quite sure she got it.

In the spare room, Piper opened Delarivier Manley's *The New Atalantis* at random.

> *She placed herself by the Duke. His eyes feasted them-*
> *selves upon her face, thence wandered over her snowy*
> *bosom, and saw the young swelling breasts just beginning*
> *to distinguish themselves, and ... gently heaved ....*

She quit reading.

In the Groverly Library, the display glowed and the *Book of Cures* rested unnoticed in the shadows of open, rare and famous volumes. The sealed cover leaned against a bronze stand at the rear of the display, next to the sliding door of the locked case.

CHAPTER 12

Goats bleated below in the nearest field, their inquisitive noses facing the morning breeze. Lily's body was limp, her shoulders sagging against the back of the rocker. The night had dawdled impossibly into morning, leaving her eyes dry and scratchy.

She looked out the window, then noticed a book on the desk. When she found Katherine Mansfield's *Leves Amores* in the anthology, she read to the jasmine.

> *Even the green vine upon the bed curtains wreathed itself into strange chaplets and garlands, twined round us in a leafy embrace, held us with a thousand clinging tendrils.*

A thump startled her. "Who's there?"

The door cracked open. "Only me, Aggie, with a pot of tea. I thought you'd be up. Or almost up. I have morning nourishment. Cumin seeds in tea give energy and peace." Aggie poured steaming hot liquid into cups from Griffo's cupboard.

Lily held her teacup to her breast. "Do you know the Chinese poet Lotung? 'When I drink tea, the cool breath of Heaven rises in my sleeves, and blows my cares away.'"

"Lily, you talk like the books you carry around with you. And I have gypsy ancestors who might have talked like that, so even though I know no Chinese poets, we are more alike than you think." Aggie's form melted into a well-used bamboo chair. "I wait for the cup to warm my stiff hands. You wait for it to warm your heart."

"Here we are. Two women inhaling the aroma of amber

liquor," mused Lily. "The color of pale ponds in foreign lands."

"See there? You paint pictures and I tell you to sip the heat slowly to avoid a burnt tongue."

Slowly, they brought their bodies into the morning.

For Lily, the minutes rolled over and under, the empty teacup resting warm against her body. "I'm taking a trip back to Groverly today to see some old books. To tie up a thread hanging over my heart. But I'll be back by tonight."

"And I'd stay longer to visit now, but there's work to do. Like a sign to take down from the mailbox. We'll talk over tea again later." Aggie closed the door.

Lily put on her dark blue pants suit with matching pinstripe blouse and drove to Groverly. Along the way, she entertained herself watching seeds blow in fits and flurries through the crop rows, flying away on nature's propellers, wings and parachutes. Hungry birds dipped down to snatch them up, then disappeared to colonize other ditches, fields and slopes. On the outskirts of the city, the wind wailed through the pines like a wounded animal, rattling the corners of houses, playing games on lawns, sending leaves and twigs tumbling across the street. And then she was near the library and the smell of the sea washed over her.

She parked the bookmobile and hurried up the flagstone steps, past the marquee that announced the new exhibit of antique books. Resting her hand on the polished bronze door handle, she centered herself before she entered her old haunt. A crowd of people milled around the lobby and she rushed past them into the hallway that led to her cubicle. The space once hers was empty, but the supplies still waited in place for someone to use them. She tucked a chewed pencil with the library logo into her tan leather handbag, then added a little pot of congealed library paste. She snapped the purse jaws shut on her souvenirs.

She paused before she threaded her way through the visitors waiting to reach the antique book display. Groups of people stared into the case at volumes locked safely behind glass, studying the condensed history of printing, illustrated with a variety of typesetting, bindings, and paper types. When she saw President Humphrey with his fancy cane and Director Trummel in her turquoise suit approaching, she slipped behind the marble column.

Mr. Humphrey gestured to the crowd, then turned to Ms. Trummel. "What a great exhibit. A literary coup for our library, I'd say."

"Thank you." She smoothed her upswept hairdo.

"Don't know why, but I assumed it was Lily's idea."

"The show was my inspiration. I did order Lily to find it."

"Then I commend you." He made his way around the crowd, tapping with his cane.

Lily clenched her jaw. She watched the two drift down the hall toward the conference room for the monthly meeting of the board. She knew what she must do, but first, the beautiful, old books.

She took her turn inching forward as the visitors crowded around the display, commenting on ornately illustrated manuscripts, pointing at pages with unusual formatting. She noticed that all the books were open, except for one sealed book in the back row.

Suddenly her eyes widened. Her heart sailed. She almost shouted because the *Book of Cures* was there, in the case. When she'd arranged the tour, she'd read the list of scheduled titles chosen to travel. That book was not among them. Somehow, this extraordinary manuscript had found its way into the display. Entranced, she wedged herself forward to put her hand on the glass, to view the volume as closely as possible. The book radiated in the florescent light. If only she could touch it, even once, through thin, white gloves.

She felt an impatient nudge behind her and moved aside, then walked deliberately toward the boardroom. The outside wind intoned a cadence with each step.

She marched into the conference room, dragging the condensed aura of old pages and library paste with her, and took the open seat next to President Humphrey. She leaned over. "Since this is a meeting open to the public, I decided to attend. I hope to have some time to address the board."

"I could give you a brief moment."

She watched the board, a dozen well-dressed people, come in the private side door that led directly into the conference room. They entered without seeing any books at all, a privilege she didn't understand, since the special entrance meant they missed the idea that formed the institution.

The president's gavel knocked on the table for attention. "Time to begin." He stood and glanced at Lily. "You all remember Ms. McFae. She's assisted several of our library directors for longer than I recall." He leaned on his cane. "In years past, Ms. McFae has exemplified the very word "librarian." Helpful. Knowledgeable. Quiet and prompt. She's here to give us her proper goodbye." He sat down.

She rose. Releasing her fingers from her bulky purse, she gazed into the faces of the assembled members she knew. She cleared her throat to chase away her fear of public speaking, but her voice still evoked the soft timbre of a broken bird.

"Mr. President. Members of the Board. We are fortunate to be in this great place. It was Alexander Smith who said, 'I go into my library, and all history unrolls before me.' A library is an institution that connects our civilization, tied together in its own way by Melvil Dewey's system. Bringing order from chaos, where the world's offering of knowledge and imagination is numbered, put into place and made available to all. Life is rarely so well organized. Particularly my own."

Mr. Humphrey touched her elbow.

Her voice picked up speed and volume. "Before I leave, I want to say how grateful I am that through the years, I was given the opportunity to offer thousands of books to our community." She raced on, looking at Ms. Trummel. "I'll miss the arrival of new volumes overlapping old, the sense of literary decades passing. Miss it all more than I can express. As Jorge Luis Borges said, "I have always imagined that Paradise will be a kind of library.""

The president interrupted, "Thank you, Ms. McFae."

But she would not be stopped. "Truth be told, I didn't want to go. I was asked to leave my books, my irreplaceable friends. In the end, I was fired. I'll miss the people who work here. And those who come into this building to learn. Or find escape from reality. Even those who enter to get away from the cold." Her voice cracked. Her eyes welled. "It's been … uh …." She tried to compose her face. "It's been enough. But it is true, change happens."

President Humphrey cut short her faltering. "We wish you well, in spite of everything." He rose and shook her hand. "Now, we need to discuss next year's computer bids. Let me show you out by way of the private exit, so you can conveniently be on your way." Taking her arm, he escorted her to the door that led directly outside. "Good luck and goodbye, Ms. McFae."

Lily paused. The pearl of a tear rolled down. "Sometimes, life sucks. I believe that would be attributed to 'anonymous.'"

The pearls on her cheek multiplied into strands and the door latch sealed her exile.

She stood outside the closed door and continued the speech she'd intended to give. "No librarian is a stereotype. And I'm not the boring person you think I am. I'm not only pale and prompt and forgettable, but a woman with my own secrets of nonconformity. Beneath my dark suit, you would be surprised at the extraordinary tattoos. They would simply amaze you."

The heavy wooden panels of the door stood mute. The full force of the wind dried the regret that coursed down her cheeks.

In the cool, antiseptic setting of a Groverly clinic, Piper waited for the doctor's touch. She dreaded medical appointments and set her teeth together when he approached, looming over her, reaching for her exposed breast. His hand encircled her flesh. His words were soft and comforting, but she didn't listen as his cool hand gently kneaded, then increased the pressure. She stopped thinking. His fingers probed her vulnerability as she stayed frozen through his examination.

When the doctor was finished, he said. "Yes, you were right. There seems to be a lump."

She bowed her head. "Okay. And now?"

"Next step, a mammogram. Call the office to schedule it. Your birth control prescription is waiting at the desk, but I suggest you wait with the pills until we get this sorted out."

She bit her lip. She wanted to ask another question, but the door was closing. As she stepped down from the exam table, she put a hand down to steady herself.

Late in the day, the man slipped into the library, lost in a crowd of nursing home elderly who'd come to see the special display of old books. He separated himself from the group using walkers to wander near a far stack dedicated to engineering. Browsing away the time, he moved casually among the back shelves. If someone came near, he'd place his hand on a volume and withdraw it, then return it, once he was alone again.

When the man's watch indicated closing time, he moved down the hall with the dwindling number of visitors. After the corridor was empty, he slipped inside the utility closet, wedging his body against a cart filled with brooms and mops that smelled of pine oil. Once he sensed the library was empty, he crept to the bottom of the basement stairs near the furnace. Above him, he heard the noise of squealing wheels and clanging pail that signaled a janitor's cart roving the corridors. He listened to the workman's soft humming and imagined the wide dust mop sweeping up and down the terra cotta tile halls. When footsteps approached the top of the stairs, the intruder barely breathed. Silently, he stepped back further into the darkness. Finally, the janitor and his sounds faded away and the place was silent. The man inhaled deeply and climbed the stairs to settle on the floor of nearby stacks.

As Lily drove back to Nolan, she replayed her library farewell. She was glad she'd mentioned Melvil Dewey, the man who published the Dewey Decimal System in the United States in the late1800's. She marveled at its invention, a four-page pamphlet that expanded into multiple volumes as the years went by. She gave a big sigh over the new ways of categorizing books now discussed, debated, and utilized.

As she lay in bed that night, her face softened with thoughts of Argentinian Jorge Luis Borges, famed poet, essayist and short story author. She was partial to him because he'd worked as a librarian, so he deserved mentioning.

As she nodded off, she thought of the Scottish poet Alexander Smith, who'd written, "To be occasionally quoted is the only fame I care for."

CHAPTER 13

Quiet. Dark, dead quiet. The three a.m. kind of quiet that fell like fine dust between the spaces of the bookshelves at the Main Branch of the Groverly Library. The man moved from the stacks into the corridor. Like an errant moth, his flashlight beam flitted from wall to wall. No one heard his footsteps echo down the hall.

Scritch. Scratch. He took out a pointed tool and jimmied the newsbox in the lobby, then snapped the lid shut. Minus one newspaper. He'd researched the special glass case that featured antique books and he was confident of his skill. Briefly his light flickered on the aged volumes, then he moved behind the unit. *Scritch. Scritch. Scritch.* A few fumbles later, the back of the case swung open and his gloved hand darted into the display. One red covered manuscript disappeared from the rear of the exhibit before the door fell softly into place again. His shadowy form folded the newspaper around the stolen object before he tightened the screws back into position. Then, the darkness of the back stacks absorbed him once more and he sat silently on the floor, the *Book of Cures* tucked safely inside his shirt.

The next morning, he listened for early library workers to arrive and settle in their places. When the first patrons chattered in the corridors, he slipped out of the stack and quietly joined those who browsed the popular display of best sellers. He worked his way to the nearest exit, left the building and hurried toward his car, parked one block over.

Safe in his room, the man laid the parcel on the desk. Unwrapping the newspaper bundle, he examined the loosened red wax seal. He pulled on the gloves he'd saved from his library visit and his fingertip traced the seal's impression of a leaf, now broken. His heart beat as he opened the book. Its brittle pages were covered with outlines and drawings. He puzzled over unfamiliar symbols and a language he couldn't read. Eerie with the darkened patina of age, the inked line map showed a garden of seven beds, surrounded by animal sheds and other buildings, but his interest lay primarily in plants and ways to use them. He could only guess that some of the writing involved the cures.

When he reached the end cover, he saw the sealed parchment pocket. A line of sweat formed along his hairline. His mind raced. Tapping at the bulk within, he guessed that the long hidden remedies might lay folded under the second seal. A broken seal, however, might lead the pharmaceutical company to suspect that the recipes were not real and the authenticity of the book questioned. No need to lose a million bucks being overeager.

The warm air closed in. One drop of sweat and then another landed next to the manuscript. Afraid he'd drip on the pages and damage them, he closed the book, wrapped the package, tied it with twine and placed it in the desk drawer.

A tall man with an athletic frame strode into the Main Branch Library. He wore an oxford shirt, navy blazer and khaki trousers and his classic profile with graying hair at the temples gave him a distinguished look. Three men filed in behind him.

In the lobby, the elegant old man waved his cane at the visitors. "I'm Humphrey, Board President. So grateful you came quickly. This is Library Director Trummel and Global Tour Representative Durand."

The tall man held out his hand to Humphrey. "Detective Hughbert Jamison of the Groverly Police, in charge of major theft." He gestured behind him. "The forensic team."

"We've closed the library and set up in the conference room," Humphrey said.

"First, show us the display case where the book was stolen. We'll start there."

President Humphrey, Director Trummel, the tour rep and the

detective marched down the hallway, with the police team following.

At the empty display case, Detective Jamison tapped on the glass and frowned. "All the books are gone. What happened? I thought only one had disappeared."

Tour Rep Durand stepped forward. "It was critical that we pack the exhibit up and ship it off to our next destination. And so we did. The transportation was ready and is waiting for me now at the airport. The most important thing for you to understand is that the stolen book was not part of the tour. The Global Antiquarian Society knows nothing about it. Nothing at all."

"That's a twist. Tell me how the theft was discovered," the detective said.

"We met this morning in front of the display to pack it up, so it could go on to the next city. This was only a brief stop," Director Trummel said.

"When I saw the exhibit, I noticed something wrong," the rep said. "There was an empty holder in the back row."

"I unlocked the case right away, and took out the bronze stand." Ms. Trummel stepped forward. "The tour representative was here the night I arranged the books and he was present when we set the alarm. He was here when we unset it this morning."

"That is true," the rep said.

"I don't understand how the deuce this could happen." President Humphrey looked squarely at the library director.

"I don't know either. I followed established procedure, but somehow the *Book of Cures* is gone."

"When I notified our headquarters and the insurance company, I found out the book wasn't even part of our tour." The rep started to move away. "I hope I can be on my way now."

"Wait a minute, sir," the detective said. "A few more questions. What book is missing?"

"It's called the *Book of Cures*. There was a packing list," Ms. Trummel said, "but in this case, there was also a small separate sheet concerning the book and its title. The representative was present to direct the process."

Durand frowned. "I was worried about the condition of our books after traveling, and didn't direct my attention to checking off the number of volumes. But the society is certain it is not one of our books and we have no interest in retrieving it. Here is my card. I really must be off."

The detective exchanged the card for one of his own. "You may go, but leave the tour itinerary. I'll be in touch."

"Nice to have met you. Good luck," said Durand.

Jamison consulted the forensic team and gave instructions for fingerprinting. He ordered a search of the premises and parking lot.

"Okay, now I'd like everyone in the building to proceed to the conference room."

When they were assembled, Jamison introduced himself to the employees gathered around the big oak table. He produced a recorder. "So you know, I will be taping the information I receive today. The most puzzling thing is that the Global Antiquarian Society and its representative do not know anything about the stolen book. Any ideas?"

President Humphrey pointed to the library director. "Ms. Trummel will speak for the library, since she set up the display. What thoughts do you have, Ms. Trummel?"

"I haven't the faintest notion about any of it," she said.

The detective stared at her. "Could the book have been taken the day before, or did it disappear in the night?"

"Anything's possible." She pulled a handkerchief from her pocket and dabbed at her nose. "Once the display was in place, everyone resumed a regular schedule."

"Was there special interest in this particular tour? Or this particular book?"

"It was a successful short stay. If it had been scheduled for a longer time, it might have rivaled the famous comic book tour from last summer. I'm unaware of anyone who called about the missing volume."

"What can you tell me about the book? Was there anything at all unusual about it?"

Ms. Trummel dabbed at her lashes. "Only that the form required the book be shown closed. It was a sealed book with a red cover. Naturally, we wouldn't break the seal."

"Where was it positioned in the case?"

She closed her eyes. "In the back row."

President Humphrey tapped his cane on the floor. "The library director and I walked by yesterday and noted the crowd numbers. I'm sure the book was there at that time."

"Anyone else wish to comment?" Jamison said. "Or remember anything else?" He waited for a response, but no one spoke. "Then may I ask if you've noticed any suspicious characters around lately?"

"No more than usual," Ms. Trummel mumbled.

"We called the police and our lawyer immediately." President Humphrey produced a paper from his suit pocket. "In consultation with our lawyer, we prepared a statement for the media."

The detective directed his gaze at the board president. "From your first phone call, we started preliminary work. We're fingerprinting the case, and we'll check the prints against all employees. In the past, libraries didn't always report such thefts, because of bad publicity, but now, there's a global network set up to earmark the sale of rare books. That's usually how the cases are solved. From what I can tell, the time of theft cannot be determined. Not even the date, because no one remembers exactly when the book left its position. Is that correct?" He waited.

Director Trummel sniffled into her handkerchief.

"Unfortunately, that seems to be the case," Humphrey said. "The press release we sent out to the media offers a reward for information. Also it mentions our Special Collections Room."

Ms. Trummel stepped forward. "It does so because we have an encyclopedia in that room that refers to the *Book of Cures*. It's in an article about the Jardin Estate in Alsace. One of the library personnel was talking about it in the lunch room."

Detective Jamison looked at the library director. "After this meeting, I would like to be escorted to that room." He nodded to the group. "We will track down the missing book and find out who owns it. This could be global, or a local matter. At any rate, I will post information about the stolen book on the international databases as well as notify surrounding law enforcement. Any suspected criminals will be kept under surveillance and the thief will ultimately be apprehended. Now, let me see that encyclopedia."

He followed Director Trummel through the hallway to the Special Collections Room and did a quick tour of the stacks. "Anybody ever try to steal one of these?"

"No. Someone is always present when a patron studies any of the volumes here."

"Which book would bring the highest price?"

Gloves in place, Ms. Trummel pulled out *Unexplained Ancient Mysteries, Volume II.* "I have no idea. Here's the encyclopedia."

"Tell me who was talking about it."

"I can't remember. I wasn't paying too much attention to the conversation. Let me see." She scanned the index, then flipped through the book. "This is not good. That page you wanted to read has almost been cut out of the book, but it is still in place. Be very careful."

"Can you make me a copy of the article to take with me? How could someone damage your book?"

"I have no idea."

"Well, who checked it out last?"

"No one is allowed to remove any of these books from the premises and we keep a record of those who view it."

"And that log is where?"

She pulled open the desk drawer. "Right here, but don't get too excited. The page from the encyclopedia could have been damaged some time ago. We have no way of knowing."

He checked the names of people who'd viewed the encyclopedia in recent weeks. The signatures were tangled scribbles and it appeared someone had brushed a dirty hand over the lot.

"What do you think?" he asked. "Is that Lillian Newcastle? C. or G. Vorhees? Maybe Z. Vinlies. And this looks like Marxie Muntor? Maybe Sam Martar. Then B. Ralshow or Ruheu or R. Rustrauv." He pulled an evidence bag from his briefcase. "I will need to take the log book, so I can work through the hen scratching. The location scrawls looked like Nawler or Nawlie. I suppose that's Nolan. The log will be returned."

"Take it. We'll start a new log book. Return it when you're through."

"Who uses this room?"

"Ordinary people. No different from anyone else coming

to the library. Teachers and college students use the facility for research. But no one seems to stay long."

"I'll wait up front for the copy of the article." He handed her a card. "If you think of anything else, I'll be at work at my desk."

At the station, Jamison assigned his sergeant the job of checking out the Global Antiquarian Society and their representative, so he could concentrate on the Jardin family and the *Book of Cures*. He pored over the encyclopedia article on the Alsatian estate before he scanned the pages of the log book. There wasn't much activity in the Special Collections Room before the illegible scrawls began. He set the technological wheels revolving on the scribbled names, and the Internet whizzed off to retrieve information. Gradually, from a process of cross-checking and elimination, the illegible names in the guest book emerged. Llewellyn Blanding from Neubland Pharmaceutical, outside Groverly. The others were residents of Nolan. Griffo Verkie from the Verkie Goat Farm. The proprietors of the Used Stuff Store, Maxine and Sax Morton. Finally, Boris Ratchov, manager of the Emporium. Five possible suspects for a start.

He found a judge on the library board who issued a short term warrant for probable cause on the guest book signees. The detective pushed through the necessary requisitions for initial surveillance on those officially under suspicion, including taps on business and cell phones.

His Internet research revealed the recent death of Duke Quincy and the name, Duke Remy, the son now in charge. The detective checked overseas time, found the number for the Jardin Estates and dialed. "This is Detective Hugh Jamison, from the Groverly California Police, calling from the United States. I wish to speak to Duke Remy of Jardin."

"This is he."

"It seems your father died recently and suddenly."

"Yes, he was a very old man. Our family physician made the judgment that it was a natural death. Why do you wish to know?"

"I'm in charge of a case involving a stolen book. An old volume entitled the *Book of Cures* was taken from a library tour in the States. We believe that book belongs to your family."

"We have such a book, but we've kept it locked up for hundreds of years."

"It appears your book was part of a rare book tour sponsored by the Global Antiquarian Society in Strasbourg."

"I don't see how ...."

"This was a very old sealed book, entitled the *Book of Cures* that was displayed in a California library and disappeared. Are you sure your book is not missing?"

"It couldn't be." Duke Remy dropped the phone, ran to the storage cave and dialed the combination. The vault door creaked open. The shelf where the book belonged was empty. Empty. Saved for centuries, the Jardin garden manuscript had somehow crossed the ocean to America to a California library and was now missing. "Great God in heaven," he whispered.

The wind chattered against squares of window glass in the man's room. He curled into a breathy ball of heat on the firm mattress. He could almost hear the buzzing created by rumors of the stolen manuscript. The sound must stretch to the far corners of the earth by now. He'd decided to stay close. It seemed more sensible than running. His sensitive nostrils quivered. Was his connection to the book traceable? How could he know for sure?

If, for any reason, the authorities found proof of his travels that he might have overlooked.... If some scrap of evidence or fingerprint appeared.... If the police showed up at his door unannounced... if... if... if....

Turning from side to side, sweating on the sheets, he considered better places to hide the book. In case of a search, he needed a hiding spot away from his presence. A safe haven. Somewhere no one cared about or ever looked. Suddenly, he knew where it was. An unlikely place so out-of-the way that authorities would never search there for a valuable masterpiece.

A push of reckless wind curled around the goat pen, grazed the farmhouse and deposited dust on every surface. In her bed, Aggie heard the garbage lid clatter, the tin cover unhinged from its place by the backdoor. When her eyelids refused to stay shut, she got up and fixed some tranquility juice, an age-old gypsy remedy for relaxation: one lettuce head boiled in salt water.

She gulped down a big glass of warm lettuce juice.

Jamison researched cases of book theft. In addition to stealing and selling for profit, there were those who pilfered for the beauty of the volume. Those who cut out important pages. Those who stole to increase the price of their own collections. He shook his head when he read that as far back as 600 BC people stole written works and thefts were combated with warnings, like:

> *Whosoever shall carry off this tablet or shall inscribe his name on it side by side with mine own may Ashur and Belit overthrow him in wrath and anger and may they destroy his name and posterity.*

CHAPTER 14

Detective Jamison's next phase of the investigation started with Neubland Pharmaceuticals on the outskirts of Groverly. He took one of the company tours and followed the pretty, young guide who led the group through the antiseptic facility, the office spaces, big warehouse, and shipping areas. She paused to let the group peek through an inside window overlooking the research lab.

"What's the most promising new drug now on the table?" Jamison asked.

"I've heard rumors about our lab studying the properties of something called monkshood."

"Exactly what does that do?" he said.

"I don't know. It's all confidential. They don't give that kind of information to tour guides."

On his way out, he stopped by the reception area and asked for the card of a Neubland salesman named Llewellyn Blanding.

Back at his desk, he looked up monkshood and whistled, then studied the list of people from the library log book who'd asked to see the article that mentioned the *Book of Cures*. He picked one and dialed the goat farm.

A woman answered. "This is Aggie."

"Is Griffo Verkie there?"

"No."

"May I ask where he is?"

"No notion. Some suppertime he'll show up when he's hungry enough. Who is this?"

"Just a friend. Wanting to talk. I'll call back later."

Jamison stopped by the chief's office with an idea. "I'd like to take this case on the road. Several suspicious names have popped up, all near or in Nolan. Let's see what I can discover."

After his plan was approved, he grabbed a disguise in the locker/equipment room of the police station, and put on an old T-shirt and jeans, a baseball cap and sunglasses. The wheels of his unmarked car whirled off toward Nolan. Turning off a highway exit, he braked at his first stop, the Emporium.

"With you in a minute," a voice called.

His hand slipped under the front counter and pasted on a tiny listening device. Then, he strolled through the store and ended his survey by picking through the rental DVDs.

A husky guy sauntered out of the office. "I'm Boris, the owner. Can I help you?"

Jamison held up the DVD *Curious Yellow.* "I could be curious, since yellow's my favorite color."

"It's not in color though. It's an old, subtitled Swedish classic in black and white. Cash or debit?"

"I heard about it years ago. That'll be cash. I was looking around. I don't see any books."

"You don't see them because I don't carry any. Just DVDs."

The detective drove into Nolan, past tidy homes, little shops and a bright orange bookmobile parked at the town square. When he saw the Used Stuff Store, he pulled in.

The woman at the register greeted him. "Hello, can I help you find something useful?"

"Just passing through." He poked around used kitchenware.

"I'm Maxine. What do you need?"

"Just browsing." He perused the crammed bookshelves. "You ever get any valuable, old books? I'm a collector, of sorts."

She shook her head. "If we thought any book was valuable, we'd sell it ourselves to a dealer in Groverly."

"Guess I'll take this book of poetry, *Cowboys & Wild, Wild Things.*" As he waited for his change, he pasted the bug underneath the counter.

He drove out into country sunshine, past the goat farm, but didn't stop.

Rocking on the porch, Aggie watched the car slow down as it drove by the farm. A few minutes later, she watched it go by in the opposite direction. There was no reason to wonder or worry about it, but in true gypsy fashion, she did both.

Since Hugh Jamison's schedule was light, he checked into Motel 5 to give himself a temporary stopover in Nolan. Later that evening, he installed the voice activated taping equipment in the bushes outside the Emporium. He traveled on to hide similar equipment behind the batches of foxglove at the Used Stuff entrance.

Shifts of Neubland lab workers crushed dried leaves, smashed stems and collected the sticky fluid of monkshood. They separated petal from stamen from pistil. They made elaborate charts and kept meticulous records as they tested poisonous levels. Multiplying. Fortifying.

CHAPTER 15

"Open the windows for the daily airing, Sax," Maxine ordered. "And don't forget to unlock the front door."

"Yeah, before the crowd breaks through the gate." Sax wended his way through the old furniture. He pulled up the shade, cracked open the door and called out, "The Morton Used Stuff Store is now officially open for business. Oh, hello, Piper."

Maxine smirked. "See, I told you. A customer."

"Morning, Sax, I'm looking for a little reading lamp." Piper's step was lively as she moved toward him.

"Lamps to your left. All sizes and shapes."

"Hey Sax, did you hear any more about that book worth a million?" she whispered.

"You know about that?" he said.

"Only what I heard at the Emporium that day, but I was curious. I found out some books are really worth that much."

"That guy was drunk. I never heard anything else about it."

Maxine crooked her finger at Sax. "Let's get started since today's the day we get ready for the annual sale. If that's okay with you, of course."

"Selling off the remains of the remains. Sure."

The owners walked the aisles, noting the overflow of dusty bargains, ticketing crusty bake ware, run down shoes, snagged sweaters and stacks of magazines. Knick-knacks, trinkets, gewgaws, and bric-a-brac crammed on top of, around, and behind the furniture. Everything got tagged.

Maxine took a thick marker and made a big lettered sign for

the book sale and propped the huge placard up next to the coffee table. "Books 50¢ each."

"I'll help you clear off the top layer of grime." Maxine grabbed two feather dusters and handed one to Sax.

He bowed and smirked. "I am so grateful for your assistance, dear sister."

"You're a clod." Maxine turned to whisk away at a needy shelf of pottery owls.

In the midst of their dusting, Boris walked in. "Busy, busy, huh?"

Maxine looked up. "Too much stuff everywhere means no space for more."

"So for pete's sake, buy something, will you?" Sax said.

"Don't need anything, but I'll look around." Boris reached into his pocket. "I brought over these sleeping pills from the Emporium." He handed the packet to Maxine, "Sax said you had bouts of insomnia. Matter of fact, I do too."

"Well, thanks." She slipped them in her pocket. "I'll try them."

Boris winked at Piper. "You find any of those naughty books you wanted?"

She blushed. "I might have." She paid five dollars for a half-price lamp and left.

"I'm looking for something irresistible." Boris worked his way from back to front, poking around, opening drawers, sitting on overstuffed chairs. When his extensive tour was over, he called out from the front door, "Sorry, couldn't find a thing. And Maxine, you're cordially invited to the Emporium for our dagger throws. Sax enjoys them."

Sax hurried after Boris and caught him by the arm. "C'mon, Boris, why'd you have to ask my sister to join us?"

Boris looked him in the eye. "Just being neighborly, that's all."

Customers popped in throughout the day, including Llewellyn Blanding, who browsed a while, then paused by the rickety shelf unit propped against the back wall. He examined the items on display: moldy books, boxes of rusty bolts, broken hinges, chipped dinnerware, and tatty neckties. He picked up a damaged glass and showed it to a shopper. "Do you think someone would pay good money for any items on these shelves?"

The shopper shook his head and moved away.

Llewellyn ambled up to the register and leaned toward Maxine. "You ever think of selling out-of-date pharmaceuticals here? I know the right people and could make the arrangements."

Maxine nodded toward the customers nearby. "Now is not the time to discuss it. Come back after the sale. Anything is possible." She shooed him out the door.

Even Griffo stopped by to examine the used books in back, before he approached Maxine at the register. "I own several interesting old books myself. I could be persuaded to sell, if you're interested."

"Maybe later, Griffo. But not while we're up to our ears getting rid of things."

Word of the sale filtered through Nolan, and the cash register rang up sales throughout the day. During a lull, Maxine sought out Sax, "What did Boris mean, about the daggers?"

Sax gave her an annoyed look. "Our pastime at the Emporium. You wouldn't be interested."

"Of course, I would. Sounds dangerous. Sounds like fun."

Sometime during that day, a hand carefully pushed a newspaper-wrapped package under the old storage shelves along the back wall. A corner of the package wrapping caught the jagged wooden edge on the bottom of the case, but only a small bit tore. Just a hint of shaggy newsprint peeked out from the edge of the bottom shelf board. The old stuffed chair and the coffee table close to the unit, piled high with outdated magazines and sheet music, disguised the situation.

Piper blew through the open gate of the goat farm and rattled the back screen. "Hey Aggie, is Lily around? I thought we could organize Griffo's old books and check them for erotica."

"Come on in. She's off doing errands in Groverly, but I don't see why we couldn't look."

"You worried about Griffo leaving? Being a relative and all."

"I'm used to it. He's gone more than he's here and when he's here, he's mostly trouble. You and Lily are closer to me than Griffo. In a way, you're family. Sit." Aggie pointed to a chair. "I was reading something special."

"Looking for erotica?"

"No, it's a letter left by a wandering gypsy. It was written hundreds of years ago and translated by someone in my family. My relatives saved it because the traveling man was also a Romani and his words sing out to me."

"Is it a love letter?"

"Not really." With a slow, reverent gesture, she picked up a small scrap of disintegrating pressed fiber and showed it to Piper. "This is all that's left of the original in German, but the translation is saved. I can read it to you ...

> *Here I be - sorry old man adrift - knowing that some died from my herbal trials at the Jardin Castle. Most patients were near death before taking my cures, so who is to say the reason they passed. And some times I worked miracles. Some day the secrets of healing will be uncovered in plant souls humming quietly in the ground. Witness the garlic and onions that nourish our bodies.*

Piper scooted her chair closer. "Oh, I love onions."
Aggie read on:

> *Methinks the tea recipe frightened the duchess more than my failures. I give it to you my friends. But with this warning – mix the tea of love only after a SIGN from above. Know that any who ignore this message will be cursed. Z the Healer*

"Oh, Aggie, a tea of love. What does it taste like?"

"I've never made it. The healers in my family were afraid of its power."

Piper nodded. "Are you a healer too?"

"Only in small ways." She closed the book. "The things in my book are for family only. So do not talk about this to others, except Lily. When she is back, I'll share it with her too."

"You have my word, but can I ask you something, since you're a healer?"

Aggie nodded. "Healer of sorts. Small sorts."

Piper took a breath. "If a woman has a serious disease, what happens if she gets pregnant?"

"Oh dear girl, are you sick? Are you pregnant?"

"No, no, I'm asking for a friend of mine."

"I don't know what to say. If your friend is expecting, it would be a question for a doctor. In Groverly, there are many who could help her. Has she seen anyone?"

"Oh, she's not pregnant now, but she wants to know. In a way, she's afraid of the answer."

"All I can tell you is be there for your friend, in every way you can." Aggie patted Piper's hand. "Should we go now and look at Griffo's books?"

"Somehow, Aggie, I'm out of the mood."

Detective Jamison assembled the library employees and board members in the conference room for another session. "A few more questions, if you please." He laid the file down on the table.

They waited with impassive faces.

"To begin, did any employees report in sick on the day you noticed the book missing, or the day before?" He scanned the group, carefully noting their faces.

"No one," the library director said.

His eyes drilled into those of his audience. "Then as I requested, is every board member and every employee present today who was in the library the day the book disappeared? Let me add, also the days before."

"Yes," Director Trummel said. "Everyone's here." A strange look passed over her face. "Except of course, my ex-assistant. The day of the book display she gave the board her unique version of a farewell, but she was let go before the tour opened." She shook her head. "Such a regrettable appearance."

"I don't believe this information came up before." The detective rubbed his chin. "Why didn't anyone mention it? Who is she?"

"In all the excitement, apparently we didn't think of it," the Board President said. "Her name is Lily McFae." His fingers tapped the papers in front of him. "Reliable. Never absent or tardy. Intelligent, quiet, reserved. Due to certain circumstances, we let her go."

"Exactly why?"

The director narrowed her eyes. "She was fired for extreme insubordination to me. Come to think of it, she was the person who talked about that encyclopedia."

The detective gave her a stern look. He shuffled his notes. "Anyone speak to her since that day?"

Ms. Trummel blinked rapidly. "I would guess not. She didn't mix in much. A plain woman. With a drab existence, I'm sure. She was let go simply because she broke the rules. That was it."

"I will certainly check on her." He stalked out of the room, mumbling, "motive... motive."

When Detective Jamison called the phone number listed for Lily McFae, he heard the message about a disconnected line. After a few phone calls, he found a judge to give him a warrant to search her home in Groverly and left to visit the fired librarian. When he checked her mailbox, it was empty. When he knocked on her cottage door, she didn't answer, even after his fist pounded with authority. He twisted the knob. Locked.

"I have a search warrant, Ms. McFae," he called through the crack. In the back, he found another locked door. "This is H. Jamison, Groverly Police Investigation Department. I need to speak to you. I am about to enter your property."

He peeked under the welcome mat and ran his finger over the flat top of the lamppost. Not until he lifted the book-shaped foot scraper did he find the key. As the back door creaked open, a wall of emptiness hit him, the feeling of vacancy.

He moved through at a steady pace. A tidy-looking place. Lights not functioning. No milk in the refrigerator. Water turned off. No sign of cooking. Clean bathroom. No toothbrush. Seated at the desk, he noticed the newspaper. An article about the butterfly population was circled with red ink.

The second red lines on the page made him scratch his ear, the underlined heading that announced the dates of the antique book tour at the Groverly Library. "So, you were interested in the exhibit and now, you're gone. And so is the book." Underneath the paper, he found her checkbook on top of paid bill stubs.

As he revisited each room, he noted that all bookcases stood empty. She'd skipped out, a librarian taking her books with her, leaving the soundless ghosts of missing books lingering on the bare shelves. He put the newspaper and checkbook into evidence bags and called for experts to powder the place for fingerprints.

Neighbors contributed little information on her habits or whereabouts, only that she'd kept to herself. They described her as an average woman without special characteristics. There was nothing to remember or report. He went to the post office, took a number, and waited his turn.

After displaying his badge and showing the proper paperwork, he asked for her mail.

"All I know is that Lily McFae's mail is on hold," the clerk said. "She should be coming back to her place within a month."

"Not necessarily. Some folks disappear for good."

"Matter of fact, she did leave an odd note." The clerk brought out the yellow form. "Do you think she meant suicide?"

The detective read the neat lettering on the bottom of the official card.

> *If you wonder why I left, it's because people should care more about books. Now, I do what I can. If others ask where I've gone, tell them destination unknown.*
>
> *Sincerely, L. M.*

The detective frowned. "I have no idea. One thing about Lily McFae. She's not as forgettable as some people think. I find her perplexing."

On a hunt for books containing a whiff of erotica, Lily entered the Used Stuff Store and approached the woman at the register. "Hello, I'm Lily McFae."

"I remember you. You talked about books at our store. I'm Maxine, the manager."

Lily blushed. "Sorry, I didn't remember you. I was nervous

that day. Anyway, now I own a bookmobile and I'm in the market for some special books."

"Then you've come to the right place. Lots of them near the back, all special in their own way."

Lily took a circuitous route, making her way through the dining sets and nudging a coffee table to reach the tall bookshelves. She took her time examining the titles, but no gems appeared.

She returned to the register. "I'm interested in more unusual books."

"Unusual is our forte, old books on most every subject. If nothing appeals today, then another time, perhaps we can deal. I'm quite a reader and collector myself."

"I'll keep that in mind."

She sat in her bookmobile for ten minutes before she made the decision to drive to the Emporium. Freed from employment constraints, she could get another tattoo on any part of her body. If she wished. And today, with feelings welling up, she wished.

Inside the Emporium, a dusty herbal smell filtered through the air. She stopped at the DVD display, where two men lounged in the preview area, intent on watching trailers of seduction scenes.

Lily sighed. "Is Boris around?"

The men glanced up. Sax turned and pointed toward the office, then his head swiveled back to the action.

A deep voice called out, "If you're a salesman, I'm not interested."

"I'm not selling. I'm buying. An old customer, wondering if I can get a tattoo without an appointment."

"With you in a sec. Put your name on the log by the register and get changed if you need to expose any unusual body parts. I'll meet you behind the purple drapes."

Lily signed in and went to the drab dressing room. She put on the clean, folded hospital gown, but kept on her jeans. Shuddering in anticipation, she thought about tattoos. For her, the markings fell between dreaded vice and tingling pleasure, a gesture of defiance toward her non-eventful life. She drew aside the purple drape and took a chair. Paraphernalia that belonged to the executor of upcoming pain gave her pause. The same photos of huge tattoos still covered the walls. In contrast, her own designs seemed a fragile piece of symbolism.

Boris stepped into the room wearing immaculate scrubs. "Look who's here. Ms. McFae. It has been awhile."

She blushed. "I've decided I want one more."

He brandished a bottle of denatured alcohol, then sprayed a light mist over the equipment.

"I remember you told me in the library that you wouldn't be back. But it's hard to stop sending those inked messages, isn't it? All my customers, blue collar guys, gang members, business types, lady professionals share the same urge. A human foible. Doesn't matter whether it's vanity or culture, one-upsmanship, even spiritual, my indelible work stamps an identity on the body as solidly as dental x-rays."

"After my surgery was one thing. This is something else. I'm sure this will be the end of it. I left the library and have my own bookmobile now. My plan is to travel to other places. Spread my love of reading."

"And what design will illustrate this voyage?"

"I've sketched it out. It stands for books now lost to me, including one I'll probably never open."

"And where does the tat go?" He studied the picture she drew for him.

She pointed to the top of her shoulder.

He nodded. "By the way, I could use some ready cash. Can you pay in advance? Two hours time should do it, since you know the drill." He grinned. "I plan to dash off soon as we're through."

"I could do that." She handed over the bills, then cradled her purse against her side. "I'm ready." She let the top of the gown slide down a few inches in back to allow space for the markings.

The needle buzzed and she clenched her teeth as the tips plunged into the beginning of the design. She endured the stings in silence, without twitching. As the process continued, she puckered her lips tighter and tighter, taking deeper breaths each time Boris blotted away the blood.

"Whoa!" Her cry accompanied the needles that danced along her skin, the surface now altered, traced with blood and ink. "I need a few deep breaths." She imagined the black outline, the shape of book spines emerging. Needle pinpoints ripped through tender surface layers as her hands clutched at her purse.

"Okay, go ahead," she said.

He wiped the picture clean with his antiseptic cloth and resumed his work. "I'm ready to apply the color, if you're up to it. What shades do you want?"

"Mixed colors, but give the middle one a scarlet binding." Her voice was faint.

"Relax. Close your eyes. Think of something wonderful."

She concentrated on the *Book of Cures*. The mystery of its contents. She allowed her eyelids to droop. With great effort, Lily remained immobile as the needles moved in and moved out, drilling in tandem through her epidermal layer. The pain deepened.

"Ow!" She winced and her purse fell to the floor.

"Sorry for the discomfort. I'll put your bag behind the desk by the front register." He leaned over and picked it up. "Take a rest."

In a minute, he was back. "Not much left to do. You know you're the only customer I have who's a global expert on tattooing. Tell me about it. It'll take your mind off the needles while I finish up."

"Global is a stretch. It was New Guinea and I taught there, ate taro, hunted for cuckoo eggs and watched the ritual tattooing of young women before they married. Buttocks, legs, faces, nape of necks and breasts marked to signify betrothal." She clenched her teeth. "I guess that's what made me realize the symbolism of tattoos."

"Yes, indeed. You're doing fine and you'll be happy to hear I'm almost done."

"Just a librarian without a job, taking old books out on the road to spread a love of reading."

Boris gave the final swipe of antiseptic. "Finished and if I say so, beautifully done." He gave her a mirror and held another one up behind her."

"That's exactly right," she murmured.

"I'll put on the bandage. You're paid in full and the changing room's open."

She dressed carefully and retrieved her purse from Boris at the front desk.

He handed her a receipt. "I'm sure you'll be well rewarded for your special literary project. Old books are highly regarded in today's marketplace."

"That's the truth. And now, it's my new business."

"Good luck, wherever you end up. Hey guys, hustle on out of here. I've got to go. I'm late."

Lily glanced at the men entranced in another promo. Intent on nude bodies, they didn't notice a clothed woman at all. But she was used to being unnoticed.

Aggie struggled into the Cut & Curl, toting a heavy bag. "Lily's not back yet, but I brought some of Griffo's books into town for us to check out for the book club."

"Let me help." Piper took the bag. "We can look through them in the waiting area."

Aggie spread the books out on the magazine table. "Here's one called *The Pirate and the Princess*." Sound inviting?"

"What about *One Thousand and Two Nights*? "Piper opened it at random and read, "*and after we had waited a while till the wind was favorable, we spread our sails*. What's that mean?"

"You think 'spreading our sails' stands for something else?"

"Who knows?" Piper opened to a dog-eared page in a different book. "What about this one by Charles Darwin? *Among the captive girls taken in the same engagement, there were two very pretty Spanish ones, who had been carried away by the Indians*." She flipped through the book. "But most of the rest talks about lizards and birds' eggs and snakes."

"I guess we should wait for Lily. We don't know enough to do this." Aggie stacked the books and glanced out the window. "Oh, here comes Freddie."

Piper dashed off toward the back door. "I can't talk to him. You handle it."

"What do I say?"

"Make something up." She disappeared.

The front door opened and Fred came in. "Hey, Aggie. How goes it?" His eyes scanned the room. "Where's Piper?"

"She left me here, working on book club stuff. We're almost

ready to start. You ever read *Voyage of the Beagle*?"

Fred stood by the front door. "Naw, but we have Jaxon, our mutt." His face looked grim. "Do you and Piper talk much about stuff other than books?"

"Not too often."

"Here's the thing. We don't either. I don't suppose you know why she's acting so different."

"I don't mix in."

"Well, tell her I stopped by. I'm getting awful tired of waiting for that talk." He clomped out.

A few minutes later, Piper opened the storage room door and peeked around the corner.

Behind the foxglove plants of Used Stuff, the voice activated recording units quit humming after Lily's conversation with Maxine. But no one listened to Ms. McFae inquire about "unusual kinds of books" or Maxine's words about "doing business." Not yet.

Under the blackberry bushes outside the Emporium, the tape also started and stopped as programmed. The owner Ratchov spoke to the same woman about "a special literary project" followed by "highly regarded old books." Their conversation stayed imbedded on the spool of tape, to be heard another day.

When Lily walked past the mildewed books on the Used Stuff throwaway shelves, her shoe brushed against the torn newsprint, but fate gave not the slightest quiver of magical coincidence. The *Book of Cures* lay wrapped in disguise. The inked pictures of lovage and yarrow, the labels marked "poison" under monkshood, foxglove and belladonna, lay unnoticed on the dusty floor.

Sometime later, a hand checked to make sure the package at Used Stuff was still in place.

CHAPTER 16

The woman skittered through the mall in low wedge heels, wearing tinted aviator glasses and a blonde wig peeking out from under a big, felt hat. Nestled in the side compartment of her purse, she possessed someone else's credit card. She'd traveled to a newly opened mall away from home, where no one would know her or care. With no payback consequences, she could indulge her weakness for free money until the account maxed out.

She gravitated to an upscale boutique, with a window filled with the luxury of silk and the texture of fine linen. Inside the store, her fingers caressed the cloth, drawing the sensual experience out as long as possible, her form of shopper's foreplay. She tried on selections of the most expensive ensembles and chose two outfits of imported fabrics.

The emerald green suit skimmed her slim figure. "I'll wear it and take this too." She put on a hat with a pheasant feather, setting it at a jaunty angle. "Each shopping trip is a new start in life, right?"

The clerk folded the other outfit into tissue paper. "Could be."

She dug in her purse and presented the credit card. "Here you are."

"Thank you, Ms. McFae."

With one transaction, she'd baptized her new name. As she walked along, window shopping, her large bags dragged from the weight of newly credited purchases. The wrappings whispered to her with each step. Packets of extra buttons, twists of colored thread, instructions to dry clean, awaited her unpacking pleasure.

The woman in green sped off from the mall toward Groverly. In a deep valley surrounded by rocky inclines, she spotted the Arts and Crafts Fair. Sunlight bounced off the sign, *Griffo's Rare Gems & Jewels*. His display shimmered outside the painted gypsy wagon. She slowed and parked to decide whether to go forward. Pulling out her cell phone, she tried to place a call, but the signal did not go through.

She drove into the courtyard, stopped in front of the wagon, and got out of the car. A prickling ran down her arms. Approaching the display, she adjusted her sunglasses and pulled down her feathered hat. With a casual air, she examined the jewels hanging by threads in the open window. Her voice was light and high. "What beautiful sapphires. That's my birthstone."

Griffo Verkie stood with arms folded over his paisley vest. "My sapphires reflect the blue heavens, but they also come in rainbow colors. Other shades are very unusual." He reached inside his vest for a soft, gray cloth. "Exceptional gems. Yellow, pink, orange, purple. How much do you wish to spend?"

"I buy what pleases me." She was glad she wore the new, expensive suit. The drooping pheasant feather off the back of her hat suggested a person of taste and means. "Do you accept credit cards?" She watched him appraise her worth and noticed his jewelry did not have price tags.

He nodded and unfurled the cloth. His voice rose and fell seductively. "Of course, these are spirit birthstones, a custom dating back to the 1700's. And the most magnificent of all are the sapphires, the rarest of elements heated in the depths of the ground, crystallized by great pressure."

Teasing, he let the sunrays reflect off a purple ring. When the woman reached to examine it, he moved back, so it could not be touched. "Did you know the Persians believed that sapphire was a chip from the pedestal that balanced the earth? This one comes from the oldest mine in Ceylon. For that reason, it is not cheap."

He pointed to his glimmering array of jewelry. "But there are prices for everyone, ranging from twenty dollars to eight thousand. You look somewhat familiar. Have you purchased from me before?"

"No, I'm only passing through this area." She pointed to the deep purple sapphire. "That's the one that interests me."

He placed the ring on her finger, nudging it gently in place. "What excellent taste you have, my most expensive jewel. The cut reveals its elegance. Move your hand and watch the light dance across the surface. Imagine this stone, born deep in the earth, rising to the surface in a violent avalanche. Arriving in this country. Coming to me. Waiting for you."

"I'll take it." She opened her purse and brought out a credit card. "Here you are."

Griffo took the card and turned away.

She watched him insert it in the square white plastic cube.

"Because of the amount, I need to make a call," he said.

She edged back a few steps, car keys in hand, ready to bolt, if necessary. She shifted her weight as he poked in a number.

He tried the number again, then slammed his cell phone shut. "Can't get through. I'll call again in a few minutes."

She looked at her watch. "But I can't stay. I'm late as it is. And I don't believe I'll be this way again."

Griffo shrugged. "Wait. Wait. Let me think." He looked down at the machine. "Everything is ready to go. And I hear the sapphire calling to you. Okay, sign here."

The ring glittered on her hand. With a swift gesture, the woman wrote "Lily McFae."

"May the stone of your birth ease the yearnings of your heart," Griffo called out as she left.

Her mind raced. She'd done it, the transfiguration of restrictive cocoon to butterfly. Metamorphose. Transformation. Transmutation. Wham.

On her way down Main Street, Lily noticed the gas gauge on her bookmobile read empty. She braked for the service station and saw the handsome attendant wave from the garage window.

"Everyone's friendly in this town," she murmured and waved back. She read the sign that said to pay inside after pumping. Monitoring the rolling dollar amount on the pump, she stopped at $87, grabbed her purse and went in. "Not your most fuel efficient vehicle." She opened her billfold. "Darn, I seem to have used up most of my cash."

"I accept most cards, ma'am," he said.

The empty slot in her billfold gaped. Her credit card was missing from its usual pocket. "Oh drat, my card's not here either." Her fingers scrambled through the wallet again. "I know I had it."

Her knees locked tight when she couldn't find her checkbook. She remembered writing checks at the desk in her cottage, paying all the bills before she left home. In her hurry to escape from her life there, she must have forgotten it.

"What seems to be the problem?" the attendant said.

She squeezed her hands together. "My check book's at home and my credit card's gone. Lost. Maybe stolen."

"Keep calm. Let's figure this out. I'm Fred."

"I know I had it, but it's disappeared." Lily rifled through the side pockets of her purse again. She dumped some change and a few dollars on the counter. "This is all I have. I've been paying cash for most things along the way."

"You'd better report it."

"Where do I do that?"

"Here, use my phone."

Lily unfolded the typed list of necessary phone numbers for utilities, credit cards, etc. in her billfold. She listened carefully to the voice on the other end of the line and answered the identity questions. "The last time I used the card? To gas up in Groverly, before I left town."

"Would that be Larry's Service Station?"

"Correct."

"Did you use the card at Burkley's Imported Elegance?"

"Definitely not. Did someone find my card and use it? What do I do now?"

"If someone else used it, the matter goes to the fraud division. Now that you've reported it missing, your card will be cancelled out."

"How soon does that happen?"

"Immediately."

"How could someone do that to me?"

"If it's any consolation, you're not alone. Millions and millions of dollars in credit card fraud are processed every day."

"But how do they track the person who took my card?"

"Maybe the person will use it again and that will help the authorities. But there's no profile of an identity thief. Could be a man or woman. Young or old. Rich. Poor. All kinds of backgrounds."

"Creates an unusual person-to-person relationship, doesn't it?" Lily put her purse back in order.

"You'll be reissued a card with a new number."

"But I'm traveling."

"Give us a temporary address, soon as you can. Our mailing to you will contain a compilation of stores and purchases. After you receive it, mark any you have not made and return it immediately."

She let the phone fall softly on the cradle and turned to Fred. "Now, here's the big question. What do I do about paying for the gas?" She eyed the girly calendar decorating the wall. "I have an idea. We could engage in barter."

Fred frowned. "I'd rather not be left holding the bag on this one. Particularly since you're not a regular customer." He rubbed his ear. "What exactly do you mean, barter?"

"Follow me for a way out of this predicament." She beckoned for him to follow her and waved him inside the bookmobile. "Look at my wide choice of reading material. You take the ones you want, until my debt is paid in full."

"I don't know. I wouldn't call myself a reader."

"You might be surprised."

Fred pulled out a book on geology. "Looks too, uh, different. Got any about cars?"

"How about this?" Lily removed *The Body Beautiful: Automobiles.* "A collector's item featuring famous photographers." She uncovered a two-page spread that featured the curve of a Rolls Royce fender.

"Hmm." Fred noted the well-lit shape of the fender and quickly leafed through the book. "You know, barter might work. How do I know how much this book is worth?"

"Price in pencil, inside cover."

Fred turned another page and sighed. "Been watching too much TV alone anyway."

"There's a matching book you might wish to consider." Lily reached for *The Body Beautiful: Painter's Models*. "It's the companion volume with works by famous artists. A Venus or two. Some famous nudes by de Goya. Titian. Manet."

Fred looked at a photo that featured other well-lit curves. "Tell you what, I'll take these two books in exchange for the bill. That should do it. And don't worry, ma'am. Stolen IDs happen all the time."

"I keep getting this picture in my mind. Someone pretending to be me."

"Don't think of it like that. Here I am, looking right at you."

"The right to be Lily McFae was about the only thing I had left."

Fred hopped down the step of the bookmobile. "Hey, I know who you are now, the book club lady. It was my wife Piper who invited you to town."

She blushed. "She's a very nice person. Enjoy the books." She sat down in the driver's seat and twisted the key in the ignition.

Mortified, she drove out of town, whizzing along the gravel road on her way to the goat farm. Why hadn't she remembered that Fred was Piper's husband? And she'd asked him to barter for gas. What would Piper think?

Whoop. Whoop. Whoop. A siren slit a wide swath through the country air.

"Unbelievable to be stopped like this on a country lane." She glanced at the speedometer. It verified her lead foot had been bearing down. She eased off the pedal and pulled over to the side, ready to confront the kind of patrolman who searched out speedsters on rarely used roadways.

She lowered the window. "I seem to have lost sight of the speed limit."

"Ripping right along there, lady. Trying for a spot at the time trials?" The sheriff tossed her a grim glance.

Lily smiled. "I blame it on your smooth roads and splendid scenery. The miles zip by before you know it."

The sheriff's face was impassive. "This vehicle used to be a rock star rig or something?"

"Not quite. I carry books, not musical instruments."

He pulled out his pad. "I need your driver's license and registration. Are you in the habit of riding through life like a tornado, Miss? Mrs.?"

"My name is Lily McFae."

"Oh yeah, now I recognize you, the library lady who came to town about a book club. I stood in the back of Used Stuff the day you talked. Keeping the peace."

"And you did an excellent job. No riots over books that day." She flipped open her billfold. "Oh dear, not my day. My driver's license is missing, but I have the registration." She reached into the glove compartment for her travel packet of documents.

"Anything else with your current address and phone?"

"My insurance card has that information." She removed it from the travel packet and looked through her billfold again. "More good news. My library card." She handed the items over.

He walked around the vehicle. "Maybe I'm being overly protective of this town, but without a license and since you're not from here, follow me back for the ticket. Turn around and we'll drive to the office. I'll check your vehicle registration on the computer. If things pan out, you pay the fine. Away you go."

Lily hunched her shoulders at the mention of an escort and a fine. "Is there any way I can move forward to another place for this procedure? It's embarrassing. I know people in your town."

"Sorry, lady, my office is in Nolan. I'll write out the ticket quick as I can."

The sheriff kept the speedometer at a steady thirty-five miles an hour. Every so often, he gave the siren a whirl.

She was grateful for an empty Main Street. Braking gently, she stopped behind the patrol car.

He came up to the window. "Stay put. Back soon." He strode into his office and came back in a few minutes. "Ran your registration. It matched your name and address on the insurance card.

The sheriff whipped out his official pad and tore off the ticket. "Here's the damage. On the back road, it's twenty dollars. You sure you're only toting books. No contraband?"

"Only lots of reading material. I'm happy to show you."

"You carry any detective stories?"

"Blood and guts or cozies? My assortment runs from Agatha Christie to Raymond Chandler, Mickey Spillane to *Sherlock Holmes.* They're toward the back. Want a tour?" Lily walked through the bookmobile and opened the rear door.

The sheriff stepped in and suddenly nosed down into her boxed pots of plants. "And just what would you be growing, lady?"

"Old fashioned garden herbs. For decorative purposes only." She broke off a leaf of lovage and offered it to the sheriff. He smelled it and tossed it aside.

Smiling, she pointed at a shelf of books. "See, detective stories, right there. You didn't say the kind of story you favored."

"Uh, shoot 'em up, blow 'em up, I guess."

"How about this one?" Lily opened it at random and read aloud.

> *Rocky McRoney shoved the gun muzzle deep inside the rotten scum's heavy bathrobe. He pushed it against the velour, close to the gambler's heart. Ka-bloom! One shot. The furry fabric melted together in a blob of red.*

The sheriff took the book from her, flipped back to the beginning and read to himself. In a minute, he peered over the top of the page. "Anyone can check these out, or what?"

Lily nodded. "You sign up for library privileges with this form." She pulled out a pad. "There's a $10 membership fee. Then you pay three dollars to rent each book. Keep it for one week, renew for another three dollars, if you aren't finished. I also buy and sell used books. I plan to stay in town as long as business is good. When I leave, if you feel you haven't received your money's worth of literature, we'll talk about it."

"Tell you what, where's the signup sheet? I have my eye on a few of these."

Lily found a pen. "First, I need some information, something with your current address and phone. How about your driver's license and another form of ID, like a library or insurance card."

The sheriff grinned. "I get it, lady, I get it." He completed the form and handed over his identification, along with twenty-five dollars. "I got four books. Keep the change. Hope you'll stay awhile. I might turn into a reader."

She handed back the twenty dollar bill. "For the ticket," she said. "Can I ask a favor? Would you keep quiet about escorting me back to town? I'd hate to embarrass the book club ladies."

"Sure thing, I don't want to embarrass them either."

Lily went to the front to readjust the due date before stamping the numbers on the book slip. She watched the sheriff walk past the other shelves, studying book titles.

He turned around. "Since you're in the book business, you hear anything about a *Book of Cures,* something like that?"

Lily gazed at him. "I believe it's part of a rare book tour. Why do you ask?"

He hopped out of the bookmobile. "It was stolen from the Groverly Library. Authorities are beating the bushes for it. You being a book lady, I thought you might have your ear to the ground and know something."

Something shifted inside her body. "I didn't know it was missing. I've been traveling."

He walked around the outside of the bookmobile and yelled back, "It says something about a frigate. What the hell's a frigate?"

She knew he'd read the quotation printed on the back of the bookmobile. She said, "Look it up and pin the crime on Emily Dickinson." She murmured to herself, "There is no frigate like a book."

Lily clenched her fists over the painful knowledge that someone had stolen the *Book of Cures.* She looked down at the gravel carried in on his shoes, picked up the fragments and tucked them in her pocket.

She waited until he drove away, then parked the bookmobile in the square and opened up for business.

The man looked behind him before checking under the old bookcase at Used Stuff. He wanted to make sure the package was still in place. Satisfied, he gave the coffee table a little shove to rest it against the bottom of the unit. As he walked to the front, he decided to ease off. Too much hanging around that rickety unit might cause suspicion.

Griffo parked his roadster down the country road and waited by the bushes near the farm. After Aggie drove off toward town to deliver goat milk, he dashed into the kitchen and rounded up bread, cheese, and elderberry jam. On his way out, he grabbed her old family book, ready to convert gypsy history into quick cash.

Aggie noticed a change in the kitchen the minute she entered. A patch of sunlight drew her eyes to the blank space on the counter. The place where she kept the family book. Her body vibrated, alternating between burning anger and sick sadness. She knew who'd taken it. Who else?

CHAPTER 17

Red welts clustered together, forming a mass that attacked Griffo's nerve endings. He patted and scratched, but it didn't help. He rubbed his body gently, then more firmly. The harder his fingers pushed, the more his skin reacted. He sat on the bench in the vardo, holding Aggie's remedy book. Even though it was rumpled, wrinkled and darkened by age, somewhere in the book he'd find the remedy. He glossed over German and French recipes, before locating the cure for itching, luckily translated into English. Next, he'd find the ingredients. He tore out the page and left it on the table, then drove to a nearby field, where he picked a few pods of milkweed.

Stepping inside the Emporium, he stopped at the bins. Boris waved from the other side, where he talked to an exceptionally tall customer.

Griffo raised his hand in a salute and called over, "I need a pinch of some herbs. Mint and thyme. Basil."

"Feel free to forage. Maybe I have them, maybe not."

The tall man unfurled a large poster. "Can I paste this on the Emporium window?"

"Go for it," Boris said.

"The circus is passing through your town on the way to Groverly and we're a little shorthanded." He laughed and held up his large palms. "We lost a couple acts, so we're hiring. If anyone loves the traveling life, the circus is the answer."

Griffo rushed over to help with the poster, holding an edge in position. "If you're hiring, I do anything and everything."

"We're looking for a stripteasing snake charmer and a sword swallower. Our two acts ran off together."

"Then, this is your lucky day. I'm a wizard with snakes." Griffo moved his hand slowly up and down his itchy throat. "And I've done a fair amount of swallowing."

"Here's my card. I'm the manager. You have your own serpent?"

"Not right now, but I have a cape. I'm Griffo, the Magnificent."

Boris chuckled. "Yeah, that's what I always call him."

"The last charmer left her snake. You could borrow it, I guess, but a sword swallower needs his own blade. Who wants to swallow a sword that's been down someone else's throat?"

"You'll hear from me." Griffo raised his hand in a wavy salute. "Count on it."

The circus manager left, and Boris headed into the office.

Griffo tagged along behind him. "I need one spoonful of sage, basil, mint and thyme. Can you deduct it from my picketing pay?"

"I can do that. Take a handful of each. Use the envelopes next to the herbs."

Griffo didn't move. "And it looks like I need a sword."

"Your pay won't cover that."

"Look, my wallet's thinner than usual, but I've got an idea." He produced Aggie's book. "This is filled with gypsy remedies. Amazing stuff written in other languages, with lots of them translated into English. Think of colorful vardos rolling through the European countryside. Nomads cooking up potions and salves." Griffo plopped the book down on the counter. "I'm willing to swap these valuable recipes for a sword. You could package the remedies with bags of your old herbs. It would be worth pure gold."

Boris wiped his face with a handkerchief and let the book fall open. The language was indecipherable, but he sounded out the words. Cevapcici. Romani zumi. Djuvech. Corbast pasulj. After studying a few pages, he copied down a remedy written in English for swollen ankles, then stuck the book next to the yellow pads. "I'll keep it for now. Do you have your eye on something in my collection?"

Griffo eyed the weaponry. "I need a suggestion."

Boris touched the hilt of a drab sword. "Can you control your gag reflex?"

Griffo ran a finger along the serrated edge of a shiny blade with a jeweled handle. The tiny cut oozed blood.

The storeowner laid down the plainer version of cutlery. "Wait a minute, this is what you want. Straight as a ruler. Thin as a dime. Dull as a dunce. Here's the arrangement. From your first circus salary, I'm paid in full, or I push the sword down your throat personally. In addition to the recipe book, I need your watch as a deposit. I hold your things until the debt is paid. We'll handle the agreement at the front desk. Follow me and I'll write it down at the register."

"Right behind you." Griffo removed his watch and handed it over.

Boris placed it in a plastic bag and put the contract on the counter. "So we have a deal on the valuable book. Sign the paper, while I wrap your treasure. Newspaper okay?"

"Yeah, great idea. Disguises the value." When the knife was wrapped, Griffo grabbed the papered sword and flew out the door to his next stop, the Used Stuff Store to look for books on snake charmers and sword swallowing.

The tape in the bushes rolled merrily forward, saving the Emporium conversation that mentioned "valuable book" and "treasure" and "disguises the value."

At dawn, the song of a nightingale wafted through the open kitchen window. Aggie picked up the poetry anthology she'd taken at the Used Stuff meeting about starting a book club. She read a poem by Christina Rossetti.

> *I shall not see the shadows,*
> *I shall not feel the rain;*
> *I shall not hear the nightingale*
> *Sing on as if in pain;*

"Oh, Cim." She leaned against the sink, her knees aching.

A noise at the door made her jump and Lily stood at the screen. "I'm up way too early, I know, but I forgot to unpack my plants. You okay?"

"Just tired. I spent the night worrying about Griffo stealing my family book. By the time I drink a cup of tea, the sun will have found its way up and I'll revive."

"Maybe he'll be back soon. I'll get the plants."

"You're an unusual person, Lily, with a traveling garden."

"Not really. Just a few starts from heirloom seeds. I unpacked my clothes, but forgot the seedlings."

"Water will perk them right up and the sun will find them. Put them on the windowsill in your room."

"That's exactly what I'll do." Lily left to carry the box of drooping herbs to the garage.

Aggie hobbled out to examine Lily's plants before she took them upstairs. "Our minds travel together." She went into the garden and picked a few leaves. "See, your plants match mine. Mint. Lovage. This one's agrimony, but my crop browned out this year."

"Feel free to take mine, if you want," Lily said.

"And here's belladonna. Some call it Sleeping Nightshade. You do know it's deadly."

Lily pointed to another pot. "So is monkshood. Right?"

"Yes, it's dangerous. The story goes that gypsy women sipped tiny bits of it to become accustomed to its poison. Then after a night of passion, they'd offer it to their partners and they'd die."

Lily smiled. "Not too useful, if any of them wanted a second romantic evening."

"Always use gloves with the handling."

"You know, the same is true with rare books."

Aggie's eyes moved from the plants to Lily's face. "How strange that we grow the same poisons. Mine are for tradition. What about yours? Are you sure you aren't part gypsy?"

"It's curiosity. And a historical mystery. The seed package plainly said 'not for consumption.' I have one more pot in the bookmobile. It looks like my garden will fit perfectly on the sill."

The sun threw more light on the two women. Aggie wandered

into her garden to weed and Lily retrieved the last herb, tucked it in the corner of the box and hauled the plants up to her room.

Chipping sparrows flitted nearby. After she'd arranged her pots on the sill, she called down, "What do you think?"

Aggie looked up to admire her boarder's window garden and shrieked. "Lily, that last plant. I know it by the strange-shaped leaves. I've seen pictures. But never the real, growing thing."

Lily lifted the pot. "This one? It's my favorite."

Aggie struggled up the steps and burst into the room. "My stars! It's a lively plant. See the elf ears. You wonderful woman. You've brought magic to my farm." She nestled her nose into the heart of the green shoots. "I have a recipe that calls for it, but I've never had the leaves."

"Then take some. It's my healthiest survivor."

Aggie collapsed in the rocking chair, puffed her cheeks and slowly blew out a stream of air. "Oh, dear, nice lady. You have turned from a book woman into a gypsy sign."

Lily knelt beside her. "Are you feeling okay?"

"I stood underneath your window and looked up at the pots. Just as the healer wrote. A sign from above." Aggie jumped up and limped to the door. "I will make my recipe, but I need time to make sure it's the thing to do. First, the milk deliveries in town. Then, if I feel it's right, I'll stir up a some tea for book club. Who knows? It may heal my joints."

Lily reached for her iPad. "Maybe it's the weather that brings on your arthritis."

"Or age. If you'd rather plant your herbs in a corner of my garden, please do. The soil is rich and nourishing. They'll catch hold like wildfire."

Aggie left to sterilize jars for the goat milk and while she worked, sang a gypsy incantation to her departed mother, grand-mothers and aunts.

> *You called forth the earth. You called forth the rocks.*
> *The sun rose and the sun descended.*
> *The moon shone down and winds, they sang.*
> *Ancestors, I honor you. Great and good ancestors,*
> *I honor you.*

Her knees weakened from the prospect of mixing up the magical tea. She'd waited so long for this moment, yet she felt distracted. The obligation of customers expecting milk orders hung over her. The mixing and sipping of the tea should not be rushed. Afterward, she might want to dance or sleep or run through the goat pastures. It must be a moment with no time limits. She waited for the milk processing to be done, packed up the orders, and left for town.

First stop, Morton's Used Stuff. Aggie parked and took three jars inside. "Hello, you two." She nodded at Sax and Max, seated side by side at the register. "The usual delivery."

"Mind taking the milk upstairs today?" Maxine asked.

"And when you come down, you'll find plenty of bargains." Sax gestured with both hands to the store overflow.

"I'll be right back." Aggie moved up the stairs to the apartment.

"Great markdowns," Maxine called up. "Do take a look. Furniture, dishes, books half-price. Sax and I are headed to the office to check on the accounting, if I can get him interested in our bookkeeping practices."

In a few moments, Aggie made her way down the stairs and stopped outside the office door. "I'll see if I can find a surprise for the book club," she said, and headed for the back shelves. Her eyes skimmed the selections, looking for suggestive titles. She slumped into the cushions of the old armchair to skim through a possible volume. Pushing the coffee table aside, she made room to stretch out her aching knees. Before she sat down, she wrinkled her nose at the smell of three mildewed books on the throwaway shelves. The tiniest bit of newsprint poked out from underneath the bottom shelf and she pulled it out. It looked like an X-rated book, wrapped up in newspaper, to hide naughty words. Not a plain brown wrapper, but a covering that might hide erotica.

She folded back a corner of the paper to see what was hidden beneath. A red background peeked through the opening.

"Oh my," she sighed and undid the package. Inside she found the *Book of Cures*. The red wax seal on the cover was broken. With a delicate touch, she opened the book and saw page after page written in French with some words that matched her family book remedies. There were red-inked drawings of pens for goats, sheep and chickens, next to a circular plan for a garden.

She gasped in surprise. Garden beds in a spoke pattern matched the plot Camlo had built for her. She looked closer at the faint drawings of familiar plants. Rows of vegetables like parsnips, cabbage, radish and onions. And herbs: lovage, yarrow, gypsywort, dragoncello, monkshood, foxglove, belladonna. The similarities of one old garden to another made her swollen fingers ache.

At the back of the book, a pocket was sealed with another patch of wax. Something about the fragile paper and the strength of the second seal made her shiver. She folded the newspaper around the book.

On her trip to the cash register, holding the package to her breast, she saw Sax trudging out the door.

She called into the office, "Maxine, are all the books the same price? I found an old one I like, but it might cost more. Do you want to take a look?"

"Don't need to," the voice wafted back. "Every book's the same, marked down from a dollar. That's 55¢, including tax. Just leave your money on the counter. Thanks, Aggie."

She reached into her blue macramé change purse, placed five dimes and one nickel next to the cash register, took one of the free bookmarks, and breezed through her next two deliveries to hurry back to the farm.

She carried the book into her bedroom. Waves of excitement, followed by caution, crept over her. The lively leaves had needed a sign. She was certain she'd received one. Should she wait for a signal to read the book more carefully, before sharing it with book club? Should it be a time filled with candlelight and invocations? That seemed more respectful. She taped the free bookmark to the newsprint and put the package away.

It rested in her closet next to the samovar. She set the tambourine on top to keep any of the book's secrets from flying away. "I am old enough and wise enough to wait and let the book reveal itself to me more slowly."

Still, her whole being tingled at the thoughts of the magic dropped down upon her since joining the book club. After her husband's death, she'd met two women, totally unlike herself and found acceptance. Now she'd been blessed twice in one day. First, the leaves of lively. Then, the *Book of Cures.*

Cousin Vladislov often said, "Treat your luck well and it will never leave you."

✑

In the bookmobile, Lily sat entranced by the global weather report on her iPad, possibly an example of the chaos theory. According to the Total Ozone Mapping Spectrometer, the cosmos stirred up dust in Chad, making it the dustiest place on earth. Strong winds funneled around the eastern slopes of the Tibesti Mountains, blasting minute pieces of earth and clay out of West Africa. The movement drifted over the Atlantic toward the Americas. A few bits of dust, a drift of wind, and you could end up with something big.

When a young man entered her bookmobile, she flipped off the screen. "Hi, come on in."

He approached her slowly. "My name's Anton Judd. Jeremy from the Hopper is my uncle."

"Do you like to read, Anton?"

"Yes, I just graduated from college in Groverly and the newspaper there hired me as a reporter. When I told my uncle I needed an idea for a feature, he suggested your bookmobile."

Lily perked up. "Well then, let me give you the grand tour."

"Can I record you?" he asked.

"Of course, to keep the facts straight." She led Anton through the stacks, telling him about the Dewey Decimal system and showing him how it worked. She pulled out some of her favorite classics, but decided against opening up the closet of erotica.

"Where'd you get the idea?" he asked.

"It was simple. Books are my life. What could be better than spreading the love of books?"

He snapped some pictures. "It should make a good feature. Sign the release, and I'm off to write my first newspaper story."

✑

In the kitchen, a cold breeze washed against Aggie's cheek. She stepped back and looked at the tightly shut window. A shadow seemed to pass by and she crept up to the glass to peer out. Was someone watching her? But there was no one. She remembered the words of Aunt Florista written in the family book, "In the hour of success can be sown your destruction." Underneath it, the caution went, "To keep good luck, turn sideways in the wind." Aggie sashayed sideways out of the room.

Minnesota Fiddler, a middle age woman wearing gray sweats and a matching windbreaker limped out of the Groverly Prison after serving six months for reckless driving and road rage. Her more serious arrest for the burglary of a coin collection did not result in a conviction. The police were unable to find the loot. "My good fortune," she murmured, hopping on a city bus.

CHAPTER 18

Griffo walked up the crest of the hill to find a place out of the dead zone that surrounded the Arts and Crafts Fair. He spoke the credit card number of Lily McFae slowly into his cell phone.

"Please hold," the voice said.

Griffo shielded his eyes against a rolling wave of dust and waited until another voice came on the line. "Am I speaking to Griffo of *Griffo's Rare Gems and Jewels*?"

"Yeah, but speak up," he said. "The connection's bad."

"Your most recent charge came from a card reported stolen and it's now over the credit limit. I will pass this purchase of eight thousand dollars from your store over to the Fraud Department. You indicate the sale was made to Lily McFae. Is that correct?"

Griffo wheezed. "Yeah."

"Will you be able to describe the person who bought the item in question?"

Only a shadowy image of Lily McFae emerged before him. "Tall, but not so tall. Big sunglasses. Hair maybe light brown. I don't know. She wore a green hat with a feather and a skirt with a jacket of some kind."

"Hold on, the description is not for me. The authorities may ask you later, if they arrest a suspect. Unfortunately, that's unlikely, but sometimes it helps to refresh the memory as soon as possible."

Griffo tried to regain the air just sucked out of him. "Damn blast it. How long before the person who owned the stolen card pays for the purchase and I get my money?"

"They don't. Insurance takes care of it. You will be contacted on the procedure for filing a claim. When a card is reported stolen, the customer is reissued a different card."

"What if that someone says it's stolen, but it's not?"

"That is not our experience."

"Then your experience is different than mine." He snorted. "I need my money now."

"We apologize for any inconvenience... proper forms must be... someone will contact you as soon as...."

As the voice cut out, the wind whipped dust into Griffo's eyes. "I need immediate retribution," he growled.

"I ... your sale. But the ... filed and you will ... ask ... patience...."

"Patience is not something I abide," he yelled. "I will deal with this thieving woman personally. I can spot a grifter a mile away. She has the jewel, dammit and I think she just told you the card was stolen." Griffo snapped down the cell phone receiver just as his hat flew off his head.

His boots skidded as he chased his Homburg down the hill. He grabbed it and locked himself in the wagon. Pouring down a slug of slivovitz, he let the clear plum brandy warm his gullet. He'd been screwed by a clever swindler and her name was Lily McFae. Using his own form of gypsy justice, he would find her and get even.

His anger incited his itches. Spots demanding attention puffed everywhere in unreachable places. He lit the camp stove inside the vardo. From the page he'd taken from Aggie's book, he began to stir together a batch of calming lotion. He grabbed vinegar from the cupboard and poured it into a pan, then added minced sage, basil, mint, thyme and a few fibers of milkweed. Once the mixture was warmed, he poured in oatmeal and stirred to thicken. Vinegar fumes crept into hidden spaces, filling empty fake jewel boxes and cubbyholes behind the desk and bed. He followed the words of the remedy to the letter.

> *Warm ingredients gently over flame. Do not scorch. Read incantation and burn. Add ashes and cool. Smooth on skin and leave overnight to dry. Wash off by morning light.*

He moaned the words,

Spirits of ancient herbs and healing. In the secret places
of day and night, make my itches dissolve, never to re-
turn. Be gone, be gone, all itchiness from the universe.

Then, he wadded the chant into a ball and threw it in the cast iron frying pan. Fire from his lit match gobbled the paper and reduced it to ash. Scraping out the flaky bits with a dented spoon, he slowly added it to the congealing mixture in the saucepan. After the potion cooled, Griffo lit a candle and rubbed the green paste over itchy body parts until the pan was empty.

His misery subsided, replaced by revenge. He imagined McFae's body sprawled flat on the ground, feather askew, her green hat crushed by his boot. To toast his revenge, he threw down a few more jiggers of brandy and mentally stripped the sapphire ring from her finger.

Slowly turning the pages of his book of spells, Griffo sought a chant specific for his enemy. When he found it, he intoned the curse three times. His voice crackled with anger.

Hass, Zorro, feel my anger each morrow. May the dark-
ness overcome your soul. And your heart made of coal.
Hass Zorro, feel my revenge each morrow.

Now all he needed to do was find Lily McFae. Surprise would be on his side. She wouldn't see him coming.

When Aggie smelled wild carrots, even though they were not blooming in the fields, she knew for certain. The scent that blew through the murky air signaled that this minute, her magical tea time could begin. She collected ingredients from the herbal bunches in the garage, then picked a few leaves from Lily's plant. Clutching them tightly, she dashed through the dust devils to the kitchen. Even though the book was gone, she knew the recipe by heart and recalled the exact order and amounts with ease. Her hands were steady as she assembled the necessary herbs before her.

She bowed her head over the small, green leaves and whispered,

*Wise women of the past, please look kindly on what I
am about to create from these lively leaves, sent to me
with a sign from above. And so I begin, listening to the
earth's great voice, shouting outside my door.*

The wind roared outside the window. Dust blew through the
cracks. Stirring, sprinkling, she measured and poured until she
had recreated the healer's "Feel Good Tea of Love." The bent
teaspoon trembled as she brought it to her mouth.

Her mind zigzagged. An unfamiliar taste attacked her
tongue. Her body shook. "Sastipe," she sang out. "Sastipe. To
your health." And clapped her hands above her shoulders. A
crescendo of music streamed down through the centuries from
hand-carved violins. The melody came from the depths of long
forgotten Romany forests and touched her soul. A beautiful, mysterious feeling enveloped her. She felt good, oh, so good.

In a gypsy forest, wolves howled. Foxes purred.

In gypsy heaven, ancestors danced. Clouds turned to lace.

In a gypsy kitchen, Aggie reveled in life's sensuality and intensity. She'd tapped on a new and tantalizing doorway. And danced
through its opening.

CHAPTER 19

Lily parked the bookmobile outside the Cut & Curl. She examined the books on the closet shelves that housed her worn collection of erotica. She pulled out a deep brown cover with gilt lettering, *Venus in India*. She opened it, turning thin pages of passion that awaited willing readers. She gathered other books and stacked them in a column on the table.

Dipping and turning, she tangoed through the dust to the beauty shop entrance, carrying *Venus in India*. She noticed the pulled blinds. When she rattled the doorknob, it resisted. The door was locked. Coughing from dust, she tapped on the windowpane.

Piper cracked open the door. "Come in. What a crummy day. I locked the door because I didn't want customers bothering us."

The farm pickup pulled up, and Piper helped Aggie struggle in with a large brown paper bag.

Lily brushed off her jeans and put down the book. "Did you know that dust blown from the deserts of western China takes less than two weeks to circle the globe before it comes to rest atop the French Alps?"

Piper's eyebrows went up. "Should we be worried?"

"Maybe. I get the feeling there's something in the air, besides dust," Lily said.

"And I had a premonition the other day that someone was curious about me, just a car driving by slowly." Aggie shook her head. "But we must deal with that another day."

Someone knocked on the salon glass and Piper peeked out the door. "Sorry, I'm closed today." Piper turned to the book club members. "How about that? Customers when you don't want them."

Aggie took a mason jar out of the sack, then her old teapot and three little teacups. "Today, we sit down, nice ladies, and mark the beginning of drinking lively tea for our refreshment. Prepare yourselves." She poured green liquid into the teapot, then into the cups.

"This ancient gypsy recipe was passed down from a special healer. Its most magical ingredient comes from our friend, Lily. I warn you, it is best to sip slowly for the most pleasure." She rose and lifted her cup in the air. "Let this ancestral tea flow gently down the chalpa mum." She sipped. "Sastipe. To your health."

"Sastipe." As the taste of the tea met Lily's taste buds, she couldn't keep herself from jumping up.

Piper sipped. Eyes wide, she sat frozen in place.

Aggie watched the women and grinned.

"Good grief, that's uh, refreshing." Lily walked to the window blinds to hear the sparrows twittering operatic arias behind the slats. "Uh, stimulating. Uh, intense."

"Cool, cool, cool, cool color." Piper rolled a drop around her tongue, then closed her eyes and giggled. "This stuff curls my insides."

Suddenly the wind died down and Lily could hear gears shifting inside her body. "Provocative, that's it. A provocative taste. Exactly." She moved a slat to peek out. On the other side of the glass, an explosion of sensuous butterfly wings moved up and down, up and down. Like a man and woman in an ultimate embrace. "Ah, Eros," she shouted, "And Aphrodite too."

As each club member took a second sip, the world snapped into sharp focus. Electric currents jolted the air, and each woman felt like she'd placed a wet finger into a socket. Flashing arcs shook them down to the tendons of their ankles. They sighed with twitchy satisfaction and dissolved into themselves.

Aggie dreamed of dancing with her beloved in the moonlight, their nude bodies rhythmic to the beating of their hearts.

Piper savored the flavor of her tea, intent on Freddie's hands caressing her throat, her arms, her legs and the rest of her body.

Lily sank down to pull herself together as her thoughts dwelled on a man's throat. Tan and smooth. Lips bending to find hers. She tipped her head to see if it would help her focus. "Aggie, is your tea, by chance, high in alcoholic content? Or drug related?"

Aggie chuckled. "No. No. Only herbal. Serve hot or cold. And enjoy."

"This tea makes me think now might be the time to explore the literary delights of erotica. I say we adjourn to the bookmobile where we can lock ourselves away, surrounded by literary temptations." Lily grabbed the book she'd brought and handed it to Piper. "If you carry this, I can get the door."

Piper giggled. "I'm for that. I can't stop thinking about men and their ... bodies, and what they do with them." She giggled again. "Aggie, don't forget the magic teapot."

Lily led the stumbling members to the van. She opened the door and took the book from Piper. "Let's begin with some Charles Devereaux. This is *Venus in India.*"

"All right then, Charlie." Piper grabbed the edge of her chair. "Hit me."

As Lily read, their eyes widened and they fidgeted back and forth.

> *Pressing her swelling bosom to mine, and letting me*
> *pull her to me until our bodies seemed to form one, not*
> *denying me the thigh I took between mine.*

"Hold it." Piper stood up. "Splash me some more tea, please." Aggie poured.

Lily pointed to the stack of reading material on the table. "You can see I have classics with intriguing passages waiting for you. *The London Journals of James Boswell, Mansfield Park, The Handmaid's Tale, A Spy in the House of Love, The Wide Sargasso Sea.*"

The room was spinning around Lily's head. "The closet is filled with books from my own collection and others I just bought recently. I lost the Groverly Library. So what? It's only a building, right? What about more important things, like romance? In the night, I drown myself in the game of why. Why am I alone? Why no husband? No lover? Why are there no dark-haired men to kiss me senseless? 'Would I could be with you.' But who, I keep asking?"

"Men came into your library, didn't they?" Piper asked. "Didn't you meet anyone there?"

"I suppose men stood before me, hoping to find a like-minded friend and I opened the door to knowledge, quoting poetry and prose, then pointed them off to the library shelves." She covered her mouth with her hand. "Forgive me for fussing over supposes."

Aggie put down her tea and rose. "Isn't that why we're together, besides the reading? To prattle of this and that, to talk about ourselves and our troubles, our loves and passions?" She twirled and her full skirt spiraled. "The power of the tea makes me remember. And loosens my tongue enough to tell you of a wondrous night with my husband. On a beach. Before we married." Her face flushed, her skirt tangled in a twist of color. "There was a summer moon sending out humid vapors and we lay down on the sand for love, then ran into the lake after." She stopped dancing. "And bound ourselves together again in the water. Later on the beach, the wind brushed past and dried our bodies. We stayed all night curled together on a ripped old quilt, listening to the music of lapping waves." Aggie stopped. "So hard to describe. It makes me dizzy to remember."

"You did pretty well." Lily leaned back.

"Afterward, I asked Cim if we would sleep in moonlight after we wed?"

Piper looked down. "Or make love according to schedule? On weekends. Is that the way with most couples? I thought I'd find the answer to that in erotic books."

"He said we'd fallen into each other's hearts so deeply that we'd always find love under the stars."

"And did you?" asked Lily.

"We loved wildly and well, but mostly on our bedsprings. Like most others, I suppose."

"But you have the memory." Piper downed the last drop of tea in her cup.

"Painted in moonlight," Lily said. "Wait a minute, I know an author who agrees." She found a book, located a passage and handed it to the old woman. "By anonymous."

Aggie pulled the book close, her eyes adjusting to the print.

> *O would I were the salt sea-wind*
> *And you upon the beach*
> *Would bare your breast and let me blow*
> *Upon your heart I reach.*

Piper lightly touched the buttons of her shirtwaist. "Would bare your breast. Yes."

Aggie put down the book and did the same, her hand on her ample bosom. "Your heart I reach. Yes," she murmured. "Yes."

Lily lightly touched her own chest, then reached for the volume on Aggie's lap. "Translated from the Greek by F. A. Wright, from *Erotica: Women's Writings from Sappho to Margaret Atwood.* Think of it. A poet more than two thousand years ago wrote about the same emotions you and your husband discovered on your own sandy beach. Which only proves love is eternal."

Aggie chuckled. "We were young. We thought we were the only ones to make love in such places."

Lily closed the book. "There are as many images of love as there are couples, I guess. Sappho said, *Love shook my heart like the wind on the mountain rushing over the oak trees.* That was from a Greek lyric poet from the Isle of Lesbos in 500 BC."

"And love is exactly that way, isn't it?" Piper said. "Different, but the same. Love is love."

Aggie stroked her chin. "You know, in our family we did not say the word at all. A hug said love. A smile. A wink. But never the word. It was that way for many gypsies, who thought if the word was spoken, it might destroy the feeling."

Lily nodded. "All kinds of people following their own ways of loving. It's to be honored."

Aggie and Piper nodded.

As the wind kicked up again and the club members imbibed their magical tea, they talked on. They stitched themselves into a long and winding scarf, wound together in a knitting and purling of sexual longing and remembering.

Finally, Piper rose and paced the bookshelves. "Can I check out something erotic to take home to read?"

"Yes, indeed. That's a good sign for the club." Lily got up and stretched, then looked in the erotica book closet.

Aggie wobbled to her feet. "I should leave too, but I feel too tumbly to drive. I told you, I worry lately that someone watches me. Would the sheriff arrest me for driving under the influence of tea?"

Piper examined her candy-pink nails. "Maybe we all need a minute to recover before we go home. Or did you just say that, Aggie?"

"I can't remember." She touched Piper's arm. "About your friend, Piper? How is she?"

"Oh, getting along okay, I guess."

"We've shared some secrets and some tea." Lily shook her head. "Who knows? Next time, you may even decide to read a book and discuss it. Like a traditional book club." Her face broke into a smile. "But who cares if you're traditional? You're the nicest ladies I know."

"Here's to the tea and the way it makes us feel," Aggie said.

"To our lives." Piper folded her hands and bowed her head. "Our decisions."

"Getting to know each other," Lily added. "And the joys of books read together. The meaning of our book club."

They sat back down awhile before coming back to the real world.

"We could meet tomorrow to decide what to read." Piper grinned. "But will there be tea?"

"If my friend supplies leaves, I'll stir some up." Aggie gathered up the empty teapot and cups.

Lily stood by the closet door, books in hand. "Yes, use my plant and take some reading with you. Piper, try *Boswell's London Journals*. For you, Aggie, Anais Nin. Browse through *A Spy in the House of Love*. She's known as one of the finest authors of female erotica."

"There won't be much time to read before tomorrow," Aggie said.

"Just scan to see if the writing style appeals to you. And since you brought up the short amount of time, here's a book of haiku. Few words, big thoughts. I'm going to stay here awhile until I plummet back to earth."

"You know the way home." Aggie packed the books with her tea things. "And your room is still there."

"Funny." Piper giggled. "I feel funny. Wacky and wonderful. It's been awhile since I felt like that."

Lily watched the two women disappear into the dust. Exhausted from the emotion of the session, she sank to the floor. As her thoughts cleared, her mind went to the Groverly Library. Although she missed the books that filled the city library, she knew they didn't miss her. She'd engaged in a one-sided literary relationship that was now over. On her knees, she reached for *The Venus in India* and found imaginary delight in words that danced across the pages … "ardor"…"delicious"…"hard"…"denying of the thigh"… "hand that glided swiftly."

She still didn't feel stable enough to drive the bookmobile home. Fighting the remains of blowing grit from China, she walked the two miles to the goat farm. Never mind that the present explosion of world dust was filled with heavy metals, fungi, bacteria and viruses unfurling about her. Never mind that such things could cause an impact on living things, on oceans and continents far away. The effect of magic tea and the words of Devereaux rang in her ears and kept her from worrying about incidentals. She half expected a man to appear out of a dust cloud and wrap her in his arms. Although she was too preoccupied to notice, somewhere along the way, thinking of hands and thighs and dark-haired men, a smooth rock slipped through a tiny hole in her pocket and fell to the ground.

As she walked past rectangles of fenced fields, the wind faded. The silhouettes of the barn and garage loomed ahead. Drawing closer, she saw the white shapes of goats sleeping outside, many of them snuggled together on the picnic table Aggie provided for their climbing enjoyment. Still filled with emotion, she picked a twig of elderberry as she glided up the driveway. In the calm eye of her personal hurricane, Lily took her potted plants, dropped to her knees and transplanted her herbs into Aggie's garden.

In her bedroom, Aggie hovered over the flat package and tuned into the universe. She sniffed at the open window. No scent of wild carrot. She listened for distant violins or voices of ancestors and waited for earthly vibrations. But the wind had died down and offered only silence. So, instead of opening the package, she opened the book of haikus. Her eyes fell on the sparse words of Seifu Enomoto.

> *Rumbles from the rocks –*
> *cherry blossoms in the moonlight*
> *far from the world of men.*

She gazed out the window. The mention of blossoms reminded her of Camlo's flowering plum. And Camlo was far from the world of men. She picked up the book by Anais Nin and read into the middle of the night, sighing when the author wrote of men and their capes.

Piper read James Boswell, in his own words, *strutting up and down, considering myself a valiant man who could gratify a lady's loving desires five times a night.* And she grimaced when she read that afterward, he contracted gonorrhea, asked for (and got) his two guineas back.

CHAPTER 20

In his Groverly office, Detective Jamison checked the hot line for rare books to see if there were any rumors about a stolen book belonging to the Jardin family. The experts he'd contacted verified that book theft cases were usually solved when a sale was in progress. All he had were names on a log from the library's Special Collections Room, people who might be suspected of stealing the book, who might be waiting for the opportunity to cash in.

Plus Lily McFae, in charge of that special room, the person who'd arranged the book exhibit. Her straightforward face stared at him from the duplicate driver's license he'd ordered.

The sergeant stood in the doorway. "As requested, I've collected and listened to the tapes from the bugs at the Emporium and the Used Stuff Store in Nolan."

"Give me a rundown."

"As you know, Boris Ratchov deals in X-rated DVD rentals, tattoos, herbal products and antique swords. He's been operating the store for about a year and a half, after a death in the family, but it looks legitimate. The Used Stuff Store in Nolan is just as it appears, a second hand shop. The brother and sister who run it have been in business there for a number of years. Their parents owned it and they inherited." The sergeant handed over the transcripts.

"You'll have some questions, though, about conversations with a certain Lily McFae. With Ratchov, it concerns 'a transaction' and 'highly regarded old books.' With Maxine Morton, it's also about books."

"I see." The detective drummed his fingers on the desk. "As a matter of fact, she is also under investigation." He remembered her sudden departure.

"Another conversation of interest was Ratchov's conversation with a man named Griffo Verkie. They talked about 'a treasure' and 'a book.' Verkie lives a couple miles outside Nolan on a goat farm."

"From what I know, he's not in residence at the moment. Leave the tapes."

The detective listened to the latest cell phone taps, including an excited call from Griffo, regarding the stolen credit card of Lily McFae.

On the tapes, he heard Boris at the Emporium with Lily and then, Maxine talking to Lily at Used Stuff. Damnable woman. Her shadow passed across several areas of concern. The Neubland salesman was not included in any conversations.

The detective needed to know more about all of them, but he noted several of the conversations included Boris.

Dressed in khakis and a cotton shirt, Hugh Jamison returned to the Emporium in Nolan. He ignored the X-rated DVD display and sifted through a bin of imported twig tea packets. "Boris, is it?"

"Yep, that's me."

He leaned down to sniff some aging star anise. "Strong odor, that. You know, I keep hearing interesting things about your shop."

"What do you mean?" Boris asked.

"Your store, it's off the beaten path and there's that certain herbal smell in the air." Jamison lowered his voice, "I was hoping to score a little smokeable herb, if you know what I mean?"

"Sorry. Today, I can rent you a hot movie or give you a tattoo." Boris squinted his eyes and his cheek scar stood out. "But who knows about next week? You know, with my contacts up north."

"I didn't think you were a small town kind of guy. Where you from?"

"Do we know each other?"

Jamison shook his head. "No, just heard talk about you."

Boris stacked DVDs. "I'm from lots of places. Just call me a traveler."

"Then call me a collector. I've also heard you dabble in other valuables."

Boris's face lit up. "Who knows what lurks behind my doors and drapes?" He pointed to the curtain on the tattoo room. Or what I might be selling?"

"Since I can't make a score today, any rare books?"

Boris turned away. "Sorry, nothing to offer there. Totally out of my area of interest. But stop back in a few days if you're still interested in the pot."

The detective stood by the cash register and let his hand slip under the edge of the counter to check on the bug, still firmly attached. He sidestepped a display of dried alfalfa bags on his way to the door.

"Let's just say that on the chance you find a supply, or hear of someone who'd help me find a certain book, I'll come back. There's considerable money involved, so perhaps a rare volume will show up."

The muscles around Boris's mouth tightened ever so slightly. "Your chances are slim there. Not even a book store in town. What does that tell you?"

"One never knows." The detective nodded and left.

In the salon, Piper's eyes were glued to the pages of Boswell.

"I went to Louisa's in full expectation of consummate bliss…"

She drank deeply from her coffee mug and sighed over the words, *"slipped into bed and was immediately clasped in her snowy arms and pressed to her milk-white bosom."*

The words cut deep as the writing intensified her craving for Freddie. She tried to think of an excuse to stop by the garage, get a hug and start a conversation, but couldn't think of a way to start that first sentence. Erotica wasn't helping her state of mind, just magnifying it.

She put down the book and decided to clear out her mom's boxes in the storage room. The one marked "very personal" had always tempted her. Today, she cut the tape, folded open the cardboard top and pulled out familiar clothes. Wild print scarves, out-of-style blouses and peasant skirts. A slinky jersey and some slingback pumps her mom wore when she went out on Saturday night. Piper took the lid off an empty perfume bottle and breathed in. The scent turned her into a little girl again, curled up in her mom's arms, inhaling the heavy fragrance that made her drowsy. She sighed and looked in the bottom of the box. A long, narrow package was all that was left. She pulled out the sealed box still in original wrapping and read the label.

> *ECSTACY VIBRATOR. Does not only what, but when a lady wishes. Settings, high, low and in between for added control. Pulsing RPM's to guide your waiting body to indescribable pleasure.*

She wrinkled her nose and slowly tore off the cellophane. Cautiously, she opened the top and took out the slender stick modeled from nature. She read the print on the box. Waterproof. Seven multi-speeds for personal massage. Batteries not included. She reached up to the supply shelf and after inserting double AA's, listened to the soft low hum of the stick, a throaty noise of something familiar. "Oh, that's weird. It sounds just like my blender." Bit by bit, she ripped up the packaging. Grabbing the vibrator, she marched from the storage room and tossed it in the waste basket. Even with only the handle sticking out from the crumpled papers, its prominence disturbed her. She lifted it with care and set it in the drawer, hidden among the curling irons.

The phone ring startled her, and she was surprised to hear Aggie.

"It's me and I'm at odds out here on the farm. Maybe it's too soon, but I think it's time to meet. I'm coming into town. Want to join me at the bookmobile?"

"Be there with bells on."

✥

Lily sat reading in the seating area. She looked up when the door opened and Piper and Aggie appeared. "Oh, come in, come in.

I'm so glad to see you. I wanted to tell you there may be a story about the bookmobile in *The Groverly Gazette.* A young reporter interviewed me, but we'll see if the story makes the paper. I didn't give your names or mention the club."

Aggie carried in a bag with tea supplies. "A story may bring you more book renters."

Piper flopped down. "Yeah, publicity's a good thing."

Aggie arranged the cups on the table. "I have another surprise for us at home, but it's not for today. When the time is right, I'll bring it." She poured. "It's a book I found at Used Stuff, more for pleasure than erotica."

Once more, the fizzy green liquid set them free. One. Two. Whee.

Aggie gestured toward the flower in her buttonhole. "I wore this monarda today as a flower of love. Cim planted our yard with beds of them, so the monarchs would visit whenever they passed through. Mostly, the flowers attract bees. That's why some call the monarda by another name, bee balm."

"Freddie never brought me flowers, but he gave me a pack of wildflower seeds once. Gas company sent them out free. Still, that should count for something. He's really a good guy." Her voice cracked. "I wonder if I'm being fair."

"Men flourish like determined seeds inside our minds, don't they?" Aggie refilled everyone's cup.

"And so hard to weed out." Piper rubbed her temple.

The three women drank their green potion in silence, reeling inside from the tea.

"Yes. Men." Suddenly, Lily stood up and moved to the closet. "I have a flower story too, about a serious romance I had with a man who never brought me flowers. When I finally mentioned it, he brought me a bouquet of red roses on my birthday. I set the vase on the kitchen table, so we'd see it at breakfast. The next morning after a very, uh, torrid evening, I went into the kitchen to make coffee. On the table, where there'd been red roses, now there were white ones. I almost cried. He came up behind me and whispered in my ear, "You waited so long for me to bring you a bouquet, I thought you deserved a miracle."

Piper gave a huge sigh. "Oh, that's the most romantic thing."

"A gypsy would say, that's real magic," Aggie said. "What happened to him?"

"He was transferred overseas and we lost touch. Ladies, I have a reminder. You haven't picked a book to read yet." Lily brought out volumes to set before them. "Here are some others to consider. Did you have a chance to read anything from the books I lent you?"

Aggie shook her head. "Not really."

Piper nodded. "Just a page or two. That Boswell guy's kind of a skunk."

"Then, browse through these."

"Why don't you read us a spicy selection of something? And if we like it, that will be the book we choose," Piper said.

Lily let her forefinger play along the covers. She stopped at a deep maroon book with a filigree design. "Let's try *Candide*, a classic among classics. I'll read a random selection and you decide yes or no." She paged through and then stopped.

"What's it about?" Piper asked.

"It's a series of adventures of several people. In this part, women have been captured by pirates. I'll read something in the middle." The women leaned forward when she read, *"they were immediately stripped stark naked, my mother, our ladies in waiting —"*

"Whoa, did you say stripped?" Piper said. "I'm going to pretend her mother wasn't there."

"I believe she said 'stark' too," added Aggie.

Lily drank a sip of lively liquid. "Yes, the very words, stripped stark naked."

"Let's take a minute to think about that." Aggie finished her tea. In the stillness of her mind, she pressed against Camlo's hard body. Naked, under the moonlight, she felt him strong against her. "I might need at least two minutes," she said.

Piper poured herself another dram and imagined Freddie slipping the silky teddy over her head and tossing it to the floor. "Yeah, at least two."

Lily daydreamed of meeting a man in the library. But then it turned into a sailing ship. And his coat was rough against her exposed skin. A man whose name she didn't even know.

After a while, she picked up the book. "Now, let me continue,

'It was wonderful how quickly these gentlemen can strip people; but what surprised me more, was that they put their fingers—'"

"Wait. Wait," Aggie said.

Lily stopped.

Aggie sighed. "I'm not sure about hearing the exact where-fores of where the men looked next."

Lily's voice was low. "Oh, it just goes on to say -

'They wanted to make sure we had not hidden any diamonds there.'"

Piper giggled. "Blush to tell you, but been there, done that, without the jewelry. Boy, sorry ladies, this tea makes me really chatty."

"Let me read on." And Lily continued with the passage, with her listeners thinking of the men in their lives. Instead of fol-lowing along with Voltaire, they thought of eyes crinkled with laughter, chiseled noses and tender fingers, tan muscled arms, firm abdomens, tight buns.

The session left them satisfied with recollections. Smiles played at the corners of their mouths. And as erotic triggers swept through their veins, their cares and wrinkles disappeared.

"Aggie, your tea exhilarates." Lily stretched her arms and waved them above her head.

"I need to move." Piper leapt up. "What say we adjourn to the Hopper? There'll be real men to watch there. Good looking, drinking men. We'll pick our book next time."

"Well, okeydokey." Aggie bounced up from her seat. "But I don't watch men much. Haven't in a long while."

"Hold on a minute." Lily grabbed another book and her half-full cup of tea. "While we study the males on tap, we can analyze erotica from a different point of view."

The women tripped out of the bookmobile and into the bar. They gravitated to a table in back. As they settled in, they lis-tened to the cable weatherman give his report on the huge bar TV screen.

"In India, purple rain is falling from the sky. In other parts of the world, downpours are reported in shades of scarlet, green, yellow, brown and black. What causes these colors? Scientists maintain it's the presence of sand, pollen, dust, soot or other impurities."

Aggie sighed. "Gypsies would say this rain of many colors is meant to reveal the mysteries of the universe."

"And those who value knowledge and imagination might say that all opinions are possible." Lily noticed a tall man enter and sit in a far corner. Their eyes locked. He wore a brown tweed jacket. She imagined the touch of his hand. His body close. She shook her head as her stomach flipped over. His mesmerizing stare caught her again and held her. Made her forget to breathe.

Piper waved at Jeremy, and he hustled up for their drink order. "Ms. McFae, did you see my nephew's story on your bookmobile?"

"Not yet."

"I'll get you a copy." He looked at Piper. "What'll you have? I saw you waving."

"Oh, just waving hello. This is an unofficial meeting of the Erotica Book Club. Oops, shouldn't have mentioned that." She looked around. "Too bad Freddie isn't here. He's my most sexy guy. But you know, Jeremy, you're not half bad."

"Had a few already, Piper?" The bartender smiled, then worked his way through the tables.

"Good rear quarters." Aggie grinned. "I believe I'm getting the hang of this. I deliver goat milk to Jeremy every week, and I never noticed his backside."

"Indeed, he appears to be a fine specimen of the masculine gender." Lily finished her cup of lively tea and her eyes strayed to the tall man in the corner. His face was tanned. His dark hair with a touch of gray was cropped neatly around his ears. When he looked her way, she blushed and his mouth turned up at the corners. She picked up the book she'd brought along. She picked up the book she brought along and stroked the cover.

Piper cleared her throat. "There's something I've been dying to ask you two." Her voice rang out. "What do you know about vibrators?"

Lily looked over at the next table. Sax had stopped talking to hear the answer to the question. Boris adjusted his chair and Maxine smirked.

Aggie knocked on the table three times. "Gypsies vibrate enough on their own."

"As do librarians, to the surprise of some, so I'm not much help either, but I could look it up for you." She opened the book she'd carried in and ruffled through the pages. "I brought *Pride and Prejudice* by Jane Austen."

"So what's Jane got to say for herself?" Piper said.

Lily gave a fleeting look toward the profile of the man she'd been watching. He was standing still, and the image of his lithe, attractive frame thumped against her midsection. "She says that *to be fond of dancing was a certain step towards falling in love.* Think of couples dancing, the rhythmic coupling to music."

"Coupling, that's a good way to put it." Piper gazed at the bar crowd.

Another glance at the tall fellow made Lily weak inside. "She also says *A lady's imagination is very rapid; it jumps from admiration to love, from love to matrimony in a moment.*" Does that sound right?"

"For some women, I guess the answer would be yes." Piper said. "I wanted to get married."

Aggie winked and grinned. "Oh, there are gypsies I've known that took their time deciding."

"Well I say, cheers to all those dancers falling in love." Piper jiggled her shoulders. "Dancing can be very sexy."

One table over, Sax inched closer. Lily gave a little wave toward him, and he waved back. She smiled at the strange bulbous flower tattooed on his inner arm, a work of art obviously handcrafted by Boris.

Lily watched the stranger start toward them, then turn and walk out of the bar. "Anyone else feel overheated?"

"Oh no, I feel very and most fine." Aggie waved at someone on the other side of the bar.

Piper wiggled in her chair. "Too bad we can't go dancing. I feel like swaying and moving and loving someone who shall be nameless."

"I haven't been this warm in a long time." Lily fanned her face with the book. "Did you see that good looking man watching us?"

"I didn't notice," Piper said. "I was thinking of my favorite fella, who's not here. He could raise my thermostat a few notches. Actually, now that you say it, I believe there are quite a few guys watching us. Maybe more men are interested because now we're lots better looking."

"Do you think that's true?" Aggie looked carefully around the room.

"Buy you pretty ladies a beer?" Boris held up his mug.

"No thanks, we are sufficiently fortified with tea." Piper lifted her cup. "And feeling f-f-f-fantastic."

Earlier, Hugh Jamison had put down the phone, after hearing the goat farm tap and the women's arrangement to meet at the book-mobile. "It's time," Aggie had said. Time for what, he wondered and left for the town square in time to see two women enter the bookmobile. Not long after, three women left and entered the Hopper.

Following them, he noted that one woman closely resembled the driver's license photo of the ex-librarian, but was much prettier, with wisps of auburn hair framing her face. She looked younger, wearing jeans and a bright pullover. The stern Lily McFae on the official driver's document did not seem to be present. A likely guess was that the two were related. Sisters? Cousins?

No question, he'd enjoyed the scene of her reading at the bar, her graceful hands and lively, dark eyes. When his body tightened in a healthy reaction, he'd ordered another tap to study her, this person who elicited a response that got him flustered. He'd started toward the table to question the group and then stopped. It was not the way he usually went about business. Generally, he needed more information and a quiet place to pursue detailed questioning. Besides, the librarian wasn't with them. He'd glanced toward the pretty woman one more time before he left, troubled by his confused feelings.

The middle-age woman in a gray windbreaker limped into the office of the Groverly automobile auction house and leaned on the counter. "Maybe you can help me. I'm trying to find an orange bookmobile you auctioned off for the county. You happen to know where it is."

The clerk grinned. "Oh yeah, I remember that vehicle. A woman bought it."

"Wonder if she'd sell it back to me. Can you give me her name and address?"

"Guess I could, since it's a matter of public record. Save you a trip to the court house." He went to the files and came back in a few minutes. "Lily McFae lives here in the city. *The Groverly Gazette* just did a little feature on her and her bookmobile."

Griffo drove toward Nolan, hauling the vardo behind him. Bits of green salve covered his irritated expression. As the miles zoomed by, he plotted against the woman called Lily McFae. Whenever he thought about the purple sapphire scammed off him by the lady in green, he boiled over. It was the first time he'd been bested by anyone, let alone a woman.

Hugh compiled the information on his conversation with Boris about the sale of pot, including the grassy, earthy smell of the Emporium. The report also added a report on Boris's phone talks with book theft suspects. He carefully worded his search warrant request for the store.

Before he turned off his computer, he double-checked for any sign of a relative for Lily McFae. None existed. As past experience proved, sometimes relations appeared out of nowhere.

CHAPTER 21

Boris bowed to his restless past. Through the years, his cop antenna had saved him jail time. Bong! The stranger who'd stopped by with several questions rang the gong big time. The decision to take a break from Nolan came easy. As Boris often did, he'd pick up and leave the status quo, seeking a better quo. Sometimes he returned. Sometimes not.

He packed clothes, a sleeping bag, and all the money from the cash drawer. In a quick move, he pulled the shades, flipped off the neon sign and locked the doors. His swords were hidden in the storage room wrapped in muslin, but his favorite daggers nested in the glove compartment of his delivery van.

Heading down a side road, his van passed several trailers pulling elaborate, painted units. One displayed monkeys flying across the outside panel. Another featured macaws and balloons, followed by a unit that showed the picture of a sword swallower, hilt touched to his lips, posed next to a beautiful snake charmer with a twisted serpent. The words, *Circus of Circumstance* scrolled across the top of each vehicle. Once he passed the entourage, he realized he'd become the leader of a small circus parade. To regain anonymity, he slowed down to let the vehicles overtake him, one by one, until he maintained a position at the rear. A few miles past Nolan, the vehicles turned into a pasture surrounded by a healthy stand of oak trees.

Boris gunned the engine and aimed straight for city life. There, he'd visit vintage shops, buy old items, create fake credentials for the pieces, and then sell them for a worthwhile profit. No one would bother him or get in his way. He'd disappear down the rabbit hole, until it was time to surface again at the Emporium. If that's what was most beneficial.

The drawn shades at the Emporium stopped Griffo, but not for long. Boris's vehicle was not on the premises. The neon was off and the door sign said "Temporarily Closed." He snuck around back and poked his tuning fork in the lock.

When the door creaked open, he called out, "Ratchov, you here? Aggie wants her book back and no smart guy tangles with a cross, old gypsy woman. Not even Griffo, the Magnificent."

Shadows from the DVD display cases fell across the room. The hollow sound of the place encouraged him to move quietly toward the night-light by the cash register.

"Ratchov, you anywhere?"

He flipped the light switch to look over the register area. No green book. He poked his head into the apartment. "Boris?" His eyes shifted over the area before he went into the office. There it was, leaning against a stack of yellow pads. He snatched it and ran out the back.

Later, when he drove to the farm hauling the gypsy wagon, he spotted the circus vehicles parked outside town, but first things first, he slipped Aggie's book into the farmhouse mailbox. Maybe her wrath would cool down, once her gypsy recipes were back. Since the pickup was gone from the yard, he sneaked inside the house and crept into her bedroom. Folded in the top drawer of the chest, he found the black cape. As the heavy garment settled on his shoulders, a warm energy swept through him. He felt justified. Since his uncle was gone, and his aunt hadn't burned the cape, it was only right it should pass on to a male family member.

At the circus parking area, he found a parking space for his decorated vardo, nudging it in between two other brightly colored vehicles. Adjusting his cape, he stopped at the trailer marked "Office," and thumped on the window. The *yip yip* of a dog sounded through the panel and a short man opened the door.

Griffo looked down at him. "Here I am, your new snake

charmer and sword swallower."

"You talked to the manager?"

"Yes sir, he invited me to join the circus as Griffo, the Magnificent." He flashed a white card. "He gave me this."

"What kind of guy knows how to do both those things?"

"A gypsy guy, that's who. I can do anything and everything. Gypsies have untapped talents you wouldn't believe."

"Then welcome, I guess. I've got something for you." He returned from the back of the trailer with a small cage. "Please, take this sulky rat snake out of here. It's driving my dog wacky."

Griffo stared at the tan serpent, with its smooth head and jagged light and dark stripes. It was folded into a plump curl. He swallowed hard and took the cage. "Where can I find the manager to discuss finances?"

"The guy in charge just left for town to get a haircut."

Griffo dropped the snake back at the vardo and covered the cage with a towel. To save on money, he trudged the few blocks into town. All the way there, his fingers rolled around the coins in his pocket, money he'd saved for something special. At the Hopper, he ordered a jigger of slivovitz and gulped it down. He breathed out. Aha! With plum brandy fizzing in his brain, the caped wonder bounded into Piper's salon with the black fabric billowing. "I have arrived," he crowed and turned a dramatic green-faced profile.

Piper stopped clipping and stared at him. "Heavens, Griffo. What are you doing?"

He rubbed at the remnants of green salve on his face before presenting the card to Piper's customer. "You might remember me. Aren't you the manager of the circus parked outside town?"

"I am."

"When we met at the Emporium, you said the circus needed a snake charmer, so I stopped at the circus and took possession of the reptile. Next, I'll polish up my sword swallowing routine. All we need to discuss is my cut."

"Okay, I like your costume and the patchy green disguise. But there's no exact cut, since the pay varies with the audience. The money comes out of the take." The circus manager reached out to touch the cape, then leaned back in the barber chair. "We're headed to Groverly in a few days for an engagement. We could try you out before that. Let me know when."

Piper resumed buzzing the clippers around her client's nape. "I'm almost done, sir."

"Perfecto." Griffo flapped his arms inside the cape. "But if I have two acts, I deserve double pay."

"You'll find that most of us do double duty."

"Okay, I'll wait for you outside. I left my vehicle at the circus parking lot." He waved his arms again like an erratic bat. "Make way for Griffo, the Magnificent." He flew out the door.

When Aggie caught the strong scent of lilies in the air, she tromped off to her bedroom. She took the newspaper-wrapped package from the closet and placed it on the dresser. The moment she set it down, a sun shaft split the air, marking the center of the paper. It was the sign she wanted, permission to show the book to her friends. She carried the treasure to the kitchen table, washed her hands and collapsed into a kitchen chair. Gently undoing the wrapper, she bowed her head and opened the cover. She examined the markings for a fowl pen next to an orchard, the orchard near a barn, and a healing room close to rows of growing medicinal herbs. This time she examined the pages more carefully.

Turning the page, she drew in a breath at the garden with its intricate herbal drawings next to animal dwellings. As she studied the book, she imagined onion and garlic sprouts mingling with the smell of feathers, earth and manure. Deeply scented green things of grace lived in the book, just as they'd lived in the plots of her family book and her own farm garden.

She knew only a little French and German, but from her family book translations, she figured rain water, laurel oil, and dung were possible antidotes for snake bites, coughs, and poison.

The back pocket stopped her with its suggestion of hidden things. Its tight seal signaled for her to wait until the three women were together. She packed candles for a ceremony at book club and rewrapped the book. "We will toast with lively tea and decide how and what to do. Send me forth, dear grandmothers."

She leaned the package against the inside of the goat milk

carryall, and with a heart light as whipped cream, set off on her milk deliveries.

Dreaming of a large ancient garden that matched her small one made the miles to town trip by. She stepped lightly into the Hopper. "Here you go, Jeremy." She set her carrier on the counter and waited for him to finish sweeping the floor.

"I'll be right with you. If you're in a hurry, leave me the usual two, and I'll put them in the cooler in a minute." He looked over at her. "Seems the whole town's talking about your book club meeting at the bar. Quite a change of scene from the farm, huh?"

"Coming to the bar was done on a whim. We usually meet in the bookmobile. You know, Ms. McFae, the librarian, stays with me at the farm." With care, Aggie pulled out the newspaper package so she could empty the carryall of its goat milk. "It's a good thing, the sharing of books."

Jeremy grinned. "Yeah, I noticed you readers had a fine meeting in back." He opened the register and took out some bills to pay her. "Say, Griffo stopped by a while ago. He was looking sharp in his fancy, black cape."

Her face crumbled. "Griffo? I don't believe it. That ratnik stole my dead husband's cape. My finest possession." She pocketed the money and grabbed the carrier. "Maybe I can catch him. It doesn't belong to him." She dashed outside.

Piper closed *Boswell's London Journal* when Jeremy walked in. "Give me a minute to clean up the station."

"I'm going for a crew cut today. Then I won't have to think about haircuts for a long time. I've got something for you." He spotted a sports magazine and set the newspaper-covered package he'd brought with him on the entry table.

"Sure thing. Be with you in a minute." She shoved Boswell in a drawer and bustled around, tidying up the station.

"All set." Piper waved the plastic cape like a toreador.

The electric razor chipped away his locks and afterward, Jeremy rubbed a hand over his neatly exposed scalp, soft and bristly as a baby brush.

"I like it." He paid the tab. "Gotta run."

When Piper put the sports magazine away, she noticed the ragged package Jeremy left on the table. She popped it in a plastic grocery bag for protection and put it next to the cash register. She'd drop it off at the Hopper later. Better yet, she'd take it to the gas station and ask Freddie to return it. It would be an excuse to talk. At home, all they did was avoid each other.

Aggie wove a basketweave pattern, up and down, back and forth, through the streets of Nolan, but she saw neither Griffo, nor his roadster. He'd disappeared, like a circle of smoke, carrying her family book and wearing the old cape of her dear, dead husband. Distracted by the image of Griffo in the haunted clothing, she fled to the farm. As suspected, the drawer in her bedroom chest was empty. He'd stolen the dark wrap that comforted her, that wrapped her in Camlo's soul. Nights would be colder now without it. A tremor passed through her.

Later, when she checked the mailbox, she found the family book. "But no cape." She strode back to the farmhouse, repeating over and over, "I do not forgive him. I will never forgive him."

When Aggie saw Lily sitting at the kitchen table, she waved the family book in the air. "The return of my beloved book. I know it was Griffo who took it, but he's still a thief. Scum on the pond, that nephew." She put a piece of mail on the kitchen table. "This came for you."

Lily ripped open the envelope to find a new plastic credit card engraved with her name. "Now I can stay longer. I can pay the rent."

Aggie threw up her hands. "You think this crazy gypsy lady takes credit cards? You pay in herbal leaves, not dollars."

With the vardo door locked, Griffo spun the thin sword around in the afternoon sunlight. Held so it caught the light, where the rust did not cling. He turned three times and stood erect. He straightened his neck to make a long line of his body and whispered to himself, "Open your gullet wide. Easy does it. Do not gag. Stay erect. Remember, do not gag. The cool metal will slide in and down. Smooth. Smooth as oil."

He did not breathe. As the metal touched his lips, his throat closed and refused the sword. Nausea swept over him, and he put the instrument away. He knew he could master the art of sword swallowing. Just not this minute.

There was always the snake. But when Griffo crooned to the serpent, when he sang funny tunes, when he put a yardstick inside the cage to pet it, he met with little success. Inspiration hit, and he sped off to the Used Stuff Store, to the book stacks in back. It took awhile, but he found a purchase that might solve his problem. He sidled up to Maxine at the register. "Does this book apply to animals and creepy crawly things?"

"Who knows? It might," she said, "since it's called *How to Be Charming, Ten Ways to Improve Your Personality*. At 50¢, you take your chances."

Griffo nodded and tucked the book under his arm. Back in the vardo, he read the first chapter heading, "Create a Pleasant Atmosphere." The creature stayed balled up in a corner of the cage. Leery, Griffo eyed the glint that came from the reptile's eyes. He threw some shaving lotion into the air and lit a candle. Since the snake had been abandoned by the stripper, maybe it was lonely. He came closer. Beady eyes stared him down, menacing and suspicious.

He crooned, "I think you miss your stripper friend. But now I'm here to keep you company." At the sound of his voice, the snake began writhing in its box. Griffo couldn't look away. The graceful movement of his cold-blooded guest captivated him, but the snake wasn't a friend yet. The creature held something back, something dangerous and tantalizing. Griffo was mesmerized.

"Watch this. I've got some moves too."

He took off his shoes and socks and waved them in front of the cage. He removed his shirt and swung it over his head. He swayed his bare arms to emulate the dance of the serpent. The gypsy's body undulated to and fro as a throbbing swept over him. As he pulled off his pants, he wondered, was he charming the snake or was it the other way around? The creature gazed at his captor, offering an intense degree of beadiness. Their eyes locked together in primordial rapture.

"Here I am, Griffo Verkie, the great gypsy. And I am pleased to meet you." Off came his boxers.

The snake twisted in the cage and buried its head. Then, suddenly it twitched and raised up. A forked tongue darted out. Griffo went weak from the sight of the fangs, afraid that poison would plume out into the air of the vardo and destroy him.

He sighed. Obviously the creature didn't find him all that charming at the moment.

When the phone tap on the Emporium went silent, Detective Jamison traveled to the store with the warrant in his pocket, to find the neon sign off, blinds closed, and door locked. He tapped firmly several times. After no answer, he plodded around back for a less noticeable place of entry. The door cracked open at his touch.

"Hello in there, coming in. Detective Hugh Jamison, with a warrant."

The unusual herbal smell still pervaded the store. He snapped on the lights. The metal birds were silent. There was no sound of conversation or TV. A quick walk through of the apartment, closet and bathroom revealed clothing and personal items missing. Boris was gone.

The detective returned to the store proper. Pacing up and down the rows of DVD rentals, moving on to the sparse herbal section, he looked for anything unusual, but everything appeared the way he remembered with the exception of a missing owner.

He peered behind the purple drape and found the tattoo area, but after a careful examination of photos: anchors, bridges, grand monuments, animals, birds, cold blooded creatures, and heartfelt words like "Mother" and "Sweetie," he saw no connection to the robbery.

Foraging through the storage area, his excitement flared, when he unwrapped swords clad in muslin and found one blade with a small speck that might be blood. Men's clothes, sports equipment, and a chess set didn't interest him, but in one corner, several pieces of expensive women's clothing hung on a make-shift rack. It could mean a woman lived or occasionally stayed on the premises. Did Ratchov have a special friend and conspirator in the theft? Was it Lily McFae? Thinking back to the conversation between Ratchov and Lily, Jamison recalled words like "confidentiality" and "rewards," which could apply to the sale of the antique book, or some other arrangement. Did Boris head up a group that included Griffo and the librarian? Or Sax and Maxine? Or the book club members?

He grimaced and left to continue his inspection. In the office, he spotted three blood-smeared fingerprints on the counter and made a note of their location. He looked around one more time and left. His visit to the Emporium had unearthed more questions than answers.

Back at the motel, he called the police station and ordered an evidence-gathering team for the Emporium, hoping to reveal if the woman in question was girlfriend, accomplice, or both. The blood spots on the counter and sword might indicate violence and a victim somewhere. Was it someone listed in the Groverly Special Collections log? Although Lily McFae's name wasn't in the book, more than the others, she'd had access to the encyclopedia.

In a few hours, police work proceeded at the Emporium. Detective Jamison and the team attempted to fit stray pieces together as they deconstructed the DVD section, herb shelves, tattoo enclosure, office with its sharp knife display, the apartment and storage area.

A review of customers showed that Maxine Morton had checked out several DVDs, with *Lust in the Dust*, her last rental return. Jamison ordered an expert to analyze the blood samples on the office counter and sword, as well as take fingerprints from various areas. All supplies on the herbal shelves were noted, digital photographs of the tattoo displays were snapped. Next, the swords were documented, in case any showed up stolen. When the police left, everything looked normal.

In Groverly, a desk officer typed customer names from store receipts into the computer. A click of the mouse sent off a silent searching with invisible twangings to data bases that captured multiple threads about identities, neighborhoods, addresses, telephone numbers, police records, financial reports and vital statistics. When the results were in, Jamison acknowledged he'd hit a blank wall. Not one sign of a rare book, sold or unsold. No victim. No missing persons. No bloody body. Not even any pot.

✄

Fred's pulse jumped when Piper put five gallons of gas in her car. He wiped his hands on a paper towel, waiting for her to come in. The photography book was open to a draped painting of the female form.

She walked into the station office with flushed cheeks. "I thought I'd stop by and see how things were going."

"Going great. Just great," he said. "How about at the salon?"

She laid the newspaper wrapped package on the counter and touched his tan arm below his rolled up sleeve. "Like always. Little slack now and then."

"What's that?" He picked up the package. "You bring me a present?"

"Uh, no. It belongs to Jeremy. I thought you'd see him at the Hopper before I do."

Fred thought her voice went soft when she said "Jeremy."

"So where'd you see him?"

"What do you mean, where? He came in for a haircut."

"What did you mean, I'd see him first? You think I turned to drink since you left our bedroom?"

Piper shook her head. "No, I meant that I don't get there often. Once with the book club members. You're the one known to drink a beer now and then, not me."

"Yeah, I heard about you and your cohorts and your tipsy time at the Hopper."

"Now wait a minute, we were only there about an hour, and we didn't even order anything. What are you talking about?"

Fred concentrated on the page of the half-clad woman. "I mean, from what I heard, you ladies had a high ole time. The town's buzzing about it."

He felt Piper's warm breath wash over his ear.

"Oh, forget it," she said, "I see you're reading something

inspirational. Not like the high-class stuff we enjoy at the Erotica Book Club. I'll leave Jeremy's package on the counter. Do with it what you want."

"Hey, wait just a minute. This book came from…." When Piper stomped off, he closed the book. "…your librarian friend. It was done by a guy named Goya. I thought you'd be interested."

He watched her car wheels spin on the pavement. She was incendiary, a flaming match. Did she feel too confined in a small town? Was he too damn boring for her? Was that why she'd joined a radical book club? Who knew what guys belonged to it? Hell's bells! He marched out and tossed Jeremy's package into the bed of his pickup truck.

With no information about the *Book of Cures* on the black market, Hugh Jamison pored over the suspects at hand.

He started with Lily McFae. Parents deceased. No mention of other relatives. After college she'd taught in New Guinea. He read documentation that covered several years of employment in the Groverly library system and the notice that she was let go. She'd received a recent speeding ticket a couple miles outside Nolan. A recent car wreck with information on her totaled vehicle was listed, followed by information about her purchase of a bookmobile owned by the next county. A story in *The Groverly Gazette* featured a photo of the exterior of the orange van, with an inside shot of the librarian's back as she returned a volume to the shelf. Because she'd been connected to the library's rare volume collection, had been fired, suddenly left town at the exact time of the theft, now owned a vehicle filled with old books, and had connections with other suspects, her name stayed high on the suspect list.

He examined the file of Boris Ratchov. No known live relatives, but a recently deceased uncle. No marriage license. No mention of a companion. A license for his vehicle appeared in order. His passport record revealed a life of travel and some close calls with international authorities. His credit rating exhibited shakiness, but his taxes were paid. He frequently closed up the Emporium.

The name of Griffo Verkie brought forth a few glitches. Complaints of illegal charity poker games. Complaints of overcharging as a taxi driver. Selling used books on a city sidewalk without a license. Use of other identities, but no convictions. No outstanding warrants. The license for his car was current. Hugh knew he'd left the goat farm recently, and although his whereabouts had been unknown for a while, his gypsy wagon had surfaced recently at a nearby craft fair, but apparently he'd moved on.

Max and Sax Morton inherited their store from deceased parents. The twins inherited matching trust funds. No arrests. Taxes paid. Recently, the Used Stuff Store had been closed for a brief time. This might have been unusual in Groverly, but appeared to happen regularly in Nolan.

Hugh's mind flew into orbit. Overseas, an old duke died and a family book disappeared. In the same time frame, the Emporium and the Used Stuff Store closed up temporarily. A gypsy wagon's wooden rims rolled away from the farm, about the time a bookmobile's tires sped away from Groverly. As far as he could see, the black market book world continued to spin round on its wobbly axis, with no sign of the antique book surfacing. All he could do was look for tie-ins and motivations.

Piper marched into the bookmobile, now parked in its usual spot at the town square. "Hey girl, get ready for a wild shopping spree. You're too serious."

Lily gave her an odd look. "What do you mean, serious? What about my birthday escapades? And for heaven's sake, I drive a bookmobile."

"Once a year doesn't count. And a form of transportation is not considered wild. It's necessary to get you from here to there."

"Well, since it's a slow day, guess I can close up shop."

"Then follow me to my car. We'll need the trunk."

Piper drove one block to Used Stuff and sauntered in, Lily a few steps behind her.

Maxine worked at the register and looked up at the prospect of customers. "Hey, you two, you're in luck. The half-price sale is almost over. Can I urge you to buy something? Anything?"

"Consider us serious book buyers." Piper headed for the book area.

"Best buy is the collection of Zane Grey. It's a beaut." Maxine glanced toward the back. "Histories. Geographies. Biographies. Novels. College books on all subjects. Five volumes of a medical encyclopedia. And remember, everything's half price."

"How much for the lot?" Piper asked.

Maxine dropped her pencil. "Uh, I'll make you a deal. Ten bucks should do it."

Lily stared at Piper. "You're buying all those books? Are you starting a home library, Piper?"

"No, the books are for you and your bookmobile." Piper put down a ten dollar bill and scurried to the back, with Maxine and Lily trailing behind.

Lily stood at the bookcase, a puzzled look on her face. "It's a great gift. I'm not used to presents and I don't know what to say."

"When I get an idea, I jump. You know, like starting a book club." Piper pulled volumes from the bottom shelf. "Besides, everyone in town gets the benefit from more books in your van."

"Let me help." Maxine grabbed empty cardboard cartons stacked against the wall. "You hand me the books, I'll box them up."

Lily joined in and in no time, they dismantled the shelves and the unit stood bare.

Piper gave Lily a hug. "From me to you, for getting the Erotica Book Club started."

Maxine grinned. "Erotica, huh? Maybe I should deliver the boxes to the club in person."

"Just a joke, forget it."

Pulling the boxes on a dolly, Maxine wheeled the load outside and they all joined in, stacking the books in the car trunk.

Piper started the engine. "Now we go sort this lot at the bookmobile. Who knows? Might find some sexy gems. Wouldn't that be fun?"

"Wait. Wait." Maxine ran up to the car, waving a stack of bookmarks. She handed them through the window to Lily. "You can put one of our promotional bookmarks in every book. "It says, 'Would I were' or something like that.'"

Lily ran her fingers through her wispy bangs. "Yes, indeed. 'Would I were.' And now quite happily, here I am. And off we go."

In Groverly, Minnesota Fiddler clicked away at one of the public computers at the library until she found the newspaper feature about Lily McFae and her orange bookmobile, now planted in Nolan, California.

Boris returned to the Emporium in the middle of the night. Worn out from the drive, he slipped in the side door of his dark apartment and flopped on top of the bed. Moonlight drifted in through the window as he stretched out and fell asleep.

CHAPTER 22

The next morning, Boris woke, still in his clothes. He stretched and opened the blinds, gazing at a morning fog that fell over Nolan. He looked around. The shade on the lamp by the chair tilted the wrong way. A quick inventory of the apartment revealed everything was almost in place, but he knew someone had been poking around his possessions. When he stormed into the store, he noticed things changed there too. Some of the DVDs not filed correctly. Bottles and jars of herbal products too neatly shelved. In the supply room, the wrapping on his swords looked slightly different. The office calendar hung crooked on its hook. Since nothing was missing, he was certain that it was the authorities who'd searched the place. He grinned. It was a waste of their official time. There was nothing to find here. Once he restored perfect order, he flipped on the neon sign to announce the store reopening.

Looking for any clues attached to the suspicious librarian, Detective Jamison visited the automobile auction house in Groverly and presented his credentials.

"What can you tell me about the purchase of a bookmobile recently by a Lily McFae? And give me the history of the vehicle, if you have it."

"Yes sir, I'll look that up immediately." The clerk left for a few minutes, then returned to present the detective with the purchase paperwork. "That gal made out like a real bandit on the deal.

Matter of fact, there was another inquiry on the bookmobile after the sale."

"Someone else wanted to buy it?"

"Yeah, a woman came in the other day."

"What was her name?"

"Don't know, but she planned to see if Ms. McFae wanted to sell it. The van came to us from the next county. On the vehicle history, it says it was previously owned by someone tried for burglary named Minnesota Fiddler. When she was convicted for road rage, the county confiscated it and used it as a bookmobile. Then, their new bookvan arrived and they hired us to auction off the old one."

Jamison examined the pages. "This is important. Did Ms. McFae know its history?"

"We don't get too historical around here. We disclose the background of the last owner, if asked, but that rarely happens. In the ad, it was described as a county bookmobile."

"Please give me a copy of this information. And what do you remember about the other woman who wanted to buy it?"

"Middle aged. Dressed casual. Oh yeah, she limped."

Back in his office, Jamison researched Ms. Fiddler. She had a limp. She'd been suspected of coin theft, but the coins were never found. She served a six months sentence on a driving conviction, had been recently released, but was no longer at her last address. He couldn't find any connection between McFae and Fiddler.

On his way home for an early lunch, Fred stocked up on his favorite groceries. Spam. Limburger cheese. Sardines. Salami. Crackers. A couple six packs of beer. The clerk put the items in paper bags and Fred loaded them into the bed of the pickup. The twenty pound bag of Jaxon's dog food ended up on top of Jeremy's plastic bag. Since Piper wasn't home, Fred took the groceries in and left unloading the rest until later. He sprawled on the sofa and chug-a-lugged a beer. Across the room, he saw the spider-web knit sweater she'd thrown over the back of an arm chair. She might be acting weird at the moment, and she might have taken to sleeping in the room down the hall, but she sure left fond frilly memories around the place. He closed his eyes and thought about the pretty girl in the see-through nightie who used to sleep next to him. Whose blond hair and pink streak made him happy and whose fair skin begged to be stroked.

Aggie got out of the pickup and trudged through the faint drizzle with one bottle of milk for Used Stuff. She waved at Sax trotting around the store removing sale tags, while Maxine, precise as a bank teller, sat at the register counting bills and stacking coins.

"Sorry I didn't get this order to you yesterday." Aggie held up the bottle.

"No problem. Put the milk upstairs today, will you?" Max glanced up, but kept flipping through the receipts. She called over to her brother. "I'm almost finished and things look good. Sales up. Stock down."

"In the retail round robin, that just means we start all over again," Sax said, "buying more second hand stuff."

Boris tumbled in, shaking off a few raindrops. "Hello, Morton family. I've been away on some buying trips. Don't know if you noticed."

Sax threw the sales tags in a wastebasket. "Don't think anyone was worried. You're the kind of guy who keeps moving."

Maxine smiled. "Now that our big sale's over, I'm ready to get out of town myself. If I could count on Sax to run the store while I was gone, I'd take a real vacation."

"I'd try to live up to your expectations, but I make no promises." Sax turned to Boris and grimaced. "You know, we did close up for a few days after I moved out. Trying to get things sorted out and guess what? No catastrophes occurred."

"Closing up is not so easy to do." Maxine shrugged. "And not good business."

Boris moved around the store. "Depends on how serious you are about a regular routine. Thought I'd stop in to see if Sax wanted anything from my storage area."

"No, whenever I come to throw the knives, I bring or take anything I need, but my favorite gear's at the motel. It's working out."

"Do you happen to know if anyone visited the Emporium while I was gone?"

"How would we know?" Maxine said.

Boris ran his hand over the top of a Victorian sideboard. "This one might really be worth something."

Sax glanced at the buffet. "I think Maxine had it appraised. Or did you?" He glared at her.

"Of course I did, dummy."

Boris grinned. "You two always sound so annoyed with each other. What's your problem? Is it about who does the most work? Or which one makes the most sales?"

Sax shook his head. "No quarrel on that one. The honor goes to Maxine. She sold every single book during our sale. In one shot. How about that?"

"With a few exceptions. Griffo bought a book the other day." She looked up to see Aggie coming down the stairs. "And you bought one too, huh?"

"I did, indeed." Aggie came over to the register.

"The craziest thing was Piper and Lily McFae stopped in and scooped up every book left for their explicit erotica reading club."

"I'll have you know, I'm in that club." Aggie's chin went up.

Boris laughed. "Oh, you gotta admit it, this town's full of odd-balls. Well, I'm off to pitch some daggers at the wall. Care to join me?" He pointed at Aggie. "Did you know she's a ringer?"

Maxine grabbed her purse and beckoned to Sax. "Come on. It's okay to take a short break once in a great while."

"I'm heading home." Aggie pointed outside at the weather. "I'll take a rain check."

Fog bathed the goat farm garden. Threaded through the original plants, Lily's herbs stretched their roots underground, tops catching up with their neighbors. She pulled weeds with abandon and the pile at her knees grew higher. It seemed like a familiar place with its design of beds splayed out from a central point. A tumbler in her brain snapped into place as she stared at the sunburst design of seven. Then she knew, it duplicated the one described in the library volume, *Unexplained Ancient Mysteries*.

Aggie pulled up the drive and parked. "Come into the house. My elbows say there's rain on the way."

Lily gathered the pile of weeds, let them fall in place on the compost pile, and headed for the kitchen door. She washed her hands and sat down. "Aggie, do you know your planting beds resemble a classic garden described in a very old, very special book?"

"Strange you say that." Aggie filled the kettle for tea. "My garden comes from a drawing in my very old and special family book."

"I meant the *Book of Cures*. It's a manuscript from Alsace, written a long time ago."

"My stars, you're a fortune teller. I have a book with that name too, though Cim never used it when he made my garden."

Lily shook her head. "That's impossible, Aggie. That old book is an ancient masterpiece. Maybe you have a reproduction. Where did you get it?"

"Used Stuff. Just the other day."

"I don't know about copies, but oddly enough, the original rare book is missing. May I see yours?"

"That was my surprise. I planned to bring it to book club, but Griffo took off wearing Cim's cape and I went all wonky. Running through town. Searching for him. The book went completely out of my head. Guess I left it in the goat milk carrier."

"Aggie, please, let me see it."

A fine drizzle fell as goats waited in clumps by the closed shed door. Aggie propped it open so the animals could come in from the damp, then fussed around the table that held the carrier.

Lily rubbed her hands together and shivered. "I don't see it."

"Because it's not here. I must have left the book at the Hopper. I took it out, so I wouldn't wrinkle it when I gave the milk jugs to Jeremy. Then he told me about Griffo, and I set off to find him. Don't worry. The book is wrapped up safe in newspaper. Soon as I get it back, I'll show you."

"The original was stolen while on tour. It's priceless."

"Not the same then, since mine cost two quarters. Used Stuff doesn't carry anything worth much by way of dollars."

"Probably not the one then, unless by some wild fluke, the

incredible happened." Lily paced around the goats. "The volume is rumored to contain medicinal secrets. I'll explain later. Right now, my brain is getting scrambled just thinking about it."

"Let's go back to the house and warm up."

The two hurried through the drizzle to the kitchen.

Aggie put the kettle on and brought out cups. "You lie down in your room, and I'll bring you ginger tea, with honey, lemon, and cayenne."

"Oh thanks, maybe later. Right now, a walk into town to see your garden book might clear my head. If I stop by the bar, can I tell Jeremy Judd it's okay for me to look at it?"

"Tell him to give it to you." Thunderous bass notes rumbled. "But I don't think you should go out with bad weather coming."

"I can't rest until I know for sure."

"If I can't talk you out of it, wear my raincoat and here's my bumbershoot to hold over your head. Be safe."

As the storm came clamoring down, Lily stood under Aggie's umbrella in front of the locked door of the Hopper. Taped to the window was a sign, "Out of town, funeral." She ran for the bookmobile to escape the downpour.

Her head ached from the possible nearness of the Jardin book. For the first time, she wanted to be alone instead of dealing with customers, but once open, she rented to a steady flow of book lovers, each with special requests.

A farmer chose Zane Grey. "When I can't work in the fields, I like to read."

"A great day for mysteries," said the feed store operator, "by Agatha."

"Nothing like putting the kids down for a nap and picking up a romance novel." The homemaker took two selections.

The coffee shop owner pored through the bookmobile's philosophy selections, and mused, "What's more satisfying than reading with rain drumming at the window?"

For the insurance salesman who shyly whispered his request, Lily quickly opened the closet door and checked out a book for him that described escapades with leather whips and studded collars.

"Can I help you?" Lily stopped to ask a woman in a gray

windbreaker, hovering near the back.

"No, just browsing. You have this bus long?"

Lily shrugged. "Not really."

"Are you interested in selling it?"

"No, I just purchased it."

The woman pointed to the closet. "What book did you get from in there for that guy?"

Lily glanced at her. "Just other reading material. Are you interested in something special?"

"Not today." The woman turned and left.

As Lily watched her limp through the square and disappear behind the pines, a queasy feeling in her stomach made her sit down. I'm getting paranoid, she thought, and not used to personal questions from people I don't know.

The crowd in the bookmobile thinned and eventually, she submitted to the demands of her aching head and closed up. When she tried to back the bookmobile from its parking spot, the tires dug into the muck, spinning in deeper and deeper. She surrendered and battled the weather on foot holding tight to Aggie's droopy umbrella.

Plodding down the country road, the obsession of the Jardin family book tightened its hold. Suppose it was real and she recovered it. Must she give it to the authorities immediately? Or could she keep it hidden, at least for a while? She struggled with her conscience over the temptation.

The farmhouse loomed dark, but she stopped by the kitchen and left a note.

> *Aggie, I plan to walk into town early tomorrow to see if Jeremy Judd is back from the funeral. It's important for me to see your book. Lily.*

The man in black stood alone inside Used Stuff. He looked around. The store was empty and dark as he headed toward the back. He gazed at the old storage unit used for castaways and flashed his light across the mildewed books and rusty bolts, cracked glasses and ragged ties. He knelt and looked underneath, then drew in a quick breath. He slapped his hand over his mouth to keep from screaming. Reaching far underneath the unit, his arm swiped the floor back and forth. He looked around and plowed through the old magazines, then sifted through the sheet music on the coffee table. Wiping away the sweat along his hairline, he took another look under the bottom shelf and rummaged through the magazines again. He nudged the bookcase away from the wall and found only mounds of dust. Collapsing on a nearby stool, he held back soft moans. He took off his baseball cap and pulled at his hair.

As his frenzy increased, he staggered toward the front, bumping into furniture. He pushed past a wobbly dinette set and almost fell, but caught his balance on the arm of a frayed velour chair. His silent intense anger made him dizzy as he struggled with the front door knob. Leaning against the frame, he almost fell out into the darkness. "Damn it," he muttered to the night sky. "Rat crap! Rat crap! Rat crap!"

That night, the weather cleared and the scent of lavender drifted in from the fields as books opened behind drawn shades in several Nolan houses. A western, a mystery, romance, philosophy, and whips-and-chains. The pages turned, whisking readers off to imagined lands.

The woman tugged at her gray windbreaker, then paused before the Motel 5 register. She signed in, writing down the name that matched her fake driver's license, Minnow Watson. Limping to her rental car, she drove to the spot in front of her room.

Time. Time. Time. It finally subdued the man's torment. He wrote names in a black notebook, people who might have stolen the *Book of Cures*, those who'd recently browsed or bought books at Used Stuff. He heaved a great sigh when he realized the suspects on his list weren't exactly sophisticated crooks with safes and bank vaults.

CHAPTER 23

The church bell chimed three a.m. in Nolan. The man stood at the door of the bookmobile, wearing a dark janitor's coverall and baseball cap. The first job would be the easiest one, he thought, with bookshelves arranged in Dewey Decimal order. With luck, the situation might be over.

The tip of his sharp instrument poked and scratched through the key opening. In a fluid movement, the man entered the rear door of the book van. His flashlight swept up and down the shelves before he started. From the top of each shelf to the bottom, he worked his way through the rows, examining every book before throwing it to the floor. Color and size eliminated several volumes, but each one was upended and tossed. He was excited when he found old books in the closet and took more time checking each one. When he finished examining all the books, his anger erupted and he hit the door with his fists, pounding until it hurt. Ripping a page from George Sand's *Lelia,* he threw it on top of a heap of books. Then, he scuttled out the door holding the book by Sand tight in his hand. He needed to take something away for his trouble.

The moon called to Aggie, a crescent carved from a pale apple. She inhaled the chilled lavender night and shuddered. The black cape was gone, no longer near to warm her bones. Still, she had the dust of her love close by. She unlocked the closet, pulled out the Mason jar from its storage place in the samovar and set it on the bed. Throwing a hand-woven shawl around her shoulders, she read haiku by the light of the bedside candle. Like Lily said, "few words," and tonight, Aggie found comfort in Basho.

> *Plum petals falling*
> *I look up… the sky,*
> *A clear crisp moon.*

The haiku sent its message. She thought of Camlo and the dying plum tree and how a writer in Japan, so many years ago, had sensed the pain of someone alone. Throwing off her shawl, she grabbed her tambourine and danced, circling the room in triple time rhythms, until she was exhausted. Then, she lay on the bed, clutching the jar of ashes.

The next morning, she found Lily's note and nodded. How well she knew the way the mind worked at problems of fixation or grief or worry, clutching you, never letting go. She watched the wind send pieces of monarda whirling, spinning, falling to the ground, making a blanket of red petals. She left the kitchen to pick bouquets of deep red flowers from blooming plants still intact. She carried vases, pots and glasses into the garage and made stacks of Griffo's books. With a big yank at the rusty hinges of the rear doors of the building, she created a drive-through. Once both openings were free, morning breezes floated through on the fragrance of monarda. Bunches of burgundy petals now topped each pile of books and a sweep of color exploded from front to back of the garage. She sighed in relief and returned to the house.

The Mason jar holding her husband's ashes was heavy in her hands as she returned to the garage and set it on the tall book stack in the center. She wore his fedora, but took it off, placing it on the makeshift altar next to the jar. Her slow steps moved around the book stacks.

"I'm sorry, dear heart, that this tribute is so late. Sorry I could not pay for a ground burial and turned your body into ashes. Alone, I lit candles, so you'd find your way and burned most of your things the gypsy way. But not your cape and hat." She stopped next to the jar of ashes. "Forgive me, I tried, but I could not set those two possessions afire. If the vardo and cape were here, they'd rise up in flames. I promise to deal with your hat when it is the right time to feed a bonfire."

Her feet dragged as she went to the kitchen. There she gathered ingredients for soup and pudding before she changed clothes and headed to town in a scarlet skirt and matching vest.

Early the next morning, Lily walked into town and found the sign still hanging in place. As she turned toward the bookmobile, she saw the gaping door. She raced to enter. "Dear God." Inside, her shriek reverberated against the empty shelves. Someone had desecrated her library, shoved the contents of every shelf to the floor. The mean carelessness toward the printed page, the ignorance of fragile bindings and roughness to thin paper, pulled her down next to the pitched words. She crumpled in a heap. Tears of frustration from a life refusing to go right spilled into her hands. She grabbed one of the scarves decorating the seating arrangement to wipe her face.

Surrounded by Dewey Decimal numbers gone astray, the librarian rocked back and forth, aching with shock from seeing her damaged books. Fiction and science and poetry and biography and reference, everything mixed into a sacrilegious literary muddle. The ripped out page of *Lelia* lay wrinkled on the carpet.

She found her bag and her fingers scuffled around to find the bookmobile keys. If she were hated this much in this town, she should leave. She hadn't planned to stay this long anyway.

"Oh, my dear, dead ancestors." Aggie stood at the door, still hanging open.

Piper appeared behind her. "Good grief, what happened?"

"Someone broke in," Lily whispered, "threw every volume to the floor."

Piper shook her head as she picked her way through the books. "What kind of creep does something like this?"

Aggie tiptoed after her. "When evil gathers round us, we must stay strong."

"'Some books are to be tasted, others to be swallowed, and some few to be chewed and digested.' Nowhere does Francis Bacon say, tossed in a heap on the floor." Lily bowed her head.

"I don't know what to do. The mess of the books. The mud on the carpet."

"Does someone want us to stop reading erotica?" Aggie whispered. "I told you, I feel someone's eyes watching us."

"You mean people are upset because we're reading naughty books?" Piper flopped down on the seat.

"But they aren't naughty and you aren't reading them. Not really." Lily stood up. "And those books have been judged suitable for a special category by learned people."

"But do people in town know that? Maybe some prude visited the van and saw the books. Oh my god, hope it wasn't Freddie." Piper shook her head. "No, he would never do anything like that. He hates messes."

"And Freddie hasn't ever stopped by the bookmobile."

"Thank heavens," Piper said.

"I've kept borderline books in the back closet, separate from the others. Since I left the library, no matter how hard I try to keep things together, my life keeps falling apart." Lily jangled the van keys. "I don't want to be watched. If someone in town despises me, because I'm a stranger or because I read sensual passages from old books, then I should pack up my few possessions and leave."

Aggie put her hand on Lily's arm. "If the town puts up with gypsies, like Griffo, why would they be upset with a lady and a van full of books?"

"Because I started The Erotica Book Club." Lily began stacking books. "It's a small town. The sound of it may unnerve people."

"Don't be silly. No one even knows the name of our club. It's a secret. I don't say it in front of other people." Piper wrinkled her nose. "Well, Maxine at the store that day. And maybe Freddie."

"And Jeremy Judd, that time at the Hopper." Aggie reached for the scarf on the floor and smoothed it back onto the seat back.

Piper flipped back her pink lock. "Mostly, I call it the book club. I think."

"With my customers, we only speak of goat milk and herbs," Aggie said. "Except I might have said the club name to Max and

Sax. And Boris was there too. He called us oddballs."

"I doubt he'd care about our books, with all his X-rated DVDs." Lily made another stack.

Piper picked up books in another part of the bookmobile. "Those guys in the bar were listening. They even hitched their chairs closer to hear the erotica you were reading."

"That was about dancing." Lily reached down for the torn piece of *Lelia*. She smoothed out the wrinkled paper. "I haven't found the book yet for this page. Maybe it was the one they didn't like."

"Do you want to be alone for a while?" Aggie asked.

"No, please don't go. You two make me feel better."

Piper looked at the mess. "Show us how to help you get this cleaned up."

"You put the books in groups. Fiction. Biographies. Reference. Ask me if you're unsure of the category. I'll install them in the appropriate places." Lily taped Dewey Decimal numbers on the shelves.

"I wish we knew something to make you feel better." Piper hunted and pecked through the jumble.

"You're doing fine." Lily took a pile of sorted books from Aggie. "If this mess was about reading, tell me what it does for the two of you. Or does it do anything at all?"

Piper looked for a minute at the candy-making book in her hand. "Mostly it's like a lemon drop melting in your mouth, like someone's thoughts slowly dripping down into your mind." She put her tongue to her lip. "Satisfying."

"Or is it like fishing? Casting a pole out. Reeling it in," Aggie said. "But for words."

"You two are a sure cure for a sad librarian." Lily slid books into their categories.

"What a bad day to leave the tea at the farm." Aggie stared at the pile by her feet. "I planned to have a celebration today for the three of us. With flowers and music and a bonfire to honor Cim. I was going to finally burn his hat, according to our custom. And we would eat together, like a family."

"Can't we still do it?" Lily moved quickly, filing more books into their slots.

"I've waited this long. Today is not the time for his ceremony. Let's wait until things get better. But we can eat together."

"I'll finish up. You've helped a lot." Lily held up a volume with loose pages. "Even though a few old books sustained minor injury, not many are damaged from the flinging and the mud. I guess I'm the one who needs time to recover."

"Come with me for a head massage and hair rinse. I think a tint called, "Maple Leaf Samba" would be life changing. You too, Aggie. I have a shade that conjures up a dark romantic night."

"I'm surprised I feel a hair rinse might be the right thing to do now," said Lily. "but it sound inviting. I'll start fresh tomorrow."

"I'll stay here to guard the books and read a bit before I go back to the farm," Aggie said. "Can you find me some of Christina Rossetti's poems?"

Lily pulled a volume from the shelf. "Here's a book with her work." She reached into her purse. "And my extra key to the bookmobile. Lock up when you leave. I'll see you at the farm."

Piper touched Lily's elbow. "We'll call the sheriff from the salon and tell him about the break-in. I don't know if he can do anything, but we'd better let him know."

Aggie called after them, "There'll be ox-tail soup and nut pudding at the farm later. Enough for all, since you can't make soup for one person. It was to be my celebration food."

The swarm of bees moved en masse, from farm to farm, sucking nectar from rows of lavender. Then they sped on, toward the strong scent of monarda that wafted aloft from the Verkie farm. The cloud of insects buzzed their way toward carmine blossoms of bee balm, intent on collecting liquid life they could deepen into mahogany honey.

Down the road from the farm, the man wearing coveralls and a baseball cap sat hunched in his sedan, clutching his volume of *Lelia.* He'd waited a long time for the farm pickup to pull out. Reasonably sure no one was home, he inched his car into the bushes a few yards from the farm mailbox.

CHAPTER 24

The elderberry bushes hid him as he sneaked up the farm driveway to the porch, then slipped through the unlocked door. Now, practiced at upheaval, he swooped through Aggie's rooms, following his search pattern of created havoc. In no time, he determined the book was not in the small farmhouse. He left his mark, a page torn from *Lelia*.

He dashed off to the farm garage. Through the open double doors, he saw the books, dozens and dozens of them stacked up, a jar of flowers atop each pile. "What kind of screwball stuff is this?" he mumbled. "Some gypsy curse?" Hundreds of red petals opened, warmed by the sunshine that heated the walls of the building, throwing out a strong, minty aroma to fill the space.

He grumbled as he lifted each flower container to examine the books underneath. Stopping frequently, he stayed alert for the sound of Aggie's pickup. Because of the quiet of the countryside, he could hear any vehicle approaching and whenever he heard a car engine, he grabbed the knife in his pocket. He'd already pulled it out three times, but the cars drove on by. Now, all he heard was the low refrain of insects humming in the direction of the garden. Sifting through the last stack, he shook his head and glanced outside.

A cloud of beating wings rushed toward the open garage doors in search of rich sweet nectar. Their sound flooded the air. The basso buzzing amped up louder and louder. In an instant, the thick mass of bees swept in to claim any red sweetness they could find.

"Crap. Bees. Shoo. Get away." His arms flailed back and forth at the horde of insects that hovered over his head. The waving motion only increased their anger as the swarm covered his baseball cap, bristling on his face and neck and arms and drilling into his skin.

He felt sharp stings. "Killer bees. Shoo! Shoo! Shoo!" He fled the garage and made it inside his car with only a few wounds. The thronging bees circled around his vehicle, but he was safe.

His trembling hand scratched through lines on his list. The *Book of Cures* hadn't been at the bookmobile and wasn't in the farmhouse or garage. After his stings healed, he'd be back to check the upstairs garage room rented by McFae. And next time, he'd wear a bee bonnet.

Aggie stayed safe in the bookmobile, lost in the words of Rossetti.

> *When I am dead, my dearest,*
> *Sing no sad songs for me;*
> *Plant thou no roses at my head,*
> *Nor shady cypress-tree:*
> *Be the green grass above me*
> *With showers and dewdrops wet;*
> *And if thou wilt, remember,*
> *And if thou wilt, forget.*

Thoughts of Camlo rushed through her mind. The printed words jumbled together and mixed with the features of his face. Now a flower tribute and a farewell to his hat waited for his ghost in the garage. She was glad the flowers were monarda, not roses, and not one cypress grew on the farm. But there was grass in abundance. She closed the book and locked the bookmobile.

When she walked into the farmhouse, she moaned at the mess. "That numbskull Griffo's been back." One item at a time, she put the rooms in order. "Looking for things that did not belong to him," she grumbled as she tidied up. "Things to steal from his aunt. Things to sell. Guess it's good I have so little." In the end, nothing seemed missing.

"Why can't he ask, instead of rampaging through drawers and

cupboards? He's cooked his duck now. I won't take him back. Ever." She picked up the torn book page and shook her head.

Not until she went to tend the goats, did she see the upset garage. "Oh Cim, what book could Griffo have wanted enough to ruin your memorial?" she cried. "I hope it wasn't *The Pirate and the Reluctant Lady.* Piper and I meant to return that one." In alarm, she grabbed the mason jar of ashes and the hat and put them back in her bedroom closet. Then she checked Lily's room and found it undisturbed.

In the pasture, the goats frolicked and the farm chores calmed her. Back in the kitchen, she stirred a steaming pot of soup and whipped up the pudding. She didn't call the sheriff. Her gypsy spirit whispered not to turn in a family member, even one so … Griffo.

A couple hours later, Lily and Piper slipped into the kitchen. "What can we do to help?"

"Everything's done. Soup's warming on the stove," Aggie said.

She carried the large pot to the table. "Dear ladies, I should tell you while I was in town, Griffo made a surprise visit. He scrambled up my possessions, looking for something in the house and garage, but he didn't go into your room, Lily. I checked. It's yet another reason the ceremony for my dear husband will be celebrated on a day filled with more love and light. While we share this food, let's forget today's troubles."

The book club members chatted, sipping rich ox-tail soup and telling stories. For a few brief moments, Lily's thoughts stayed with the desecrated bookmobile and the *Book of Cures* held captive at the Hopper, but soon she pushed those thoughts aside and relaxed into the camaraderie of the women and their childhood memories: growing up, no bra, first bra, first kiss, first love. Aggie told them of her travels with Cim. Lily mentioned her few male companions and Piper relived the beginnings of her high school romance with Freddie.

"So was I the only one who noticed the man at the Hopper?" Lily ate her last spoonful of soup. "Handsome. Tall. Tweedy jacket. He was watching me or maybe us, but then he left. I wonder who he was."

"Didn't see him." Piper got up and cleared the bowls. "Ask Jeremy. He'll know."

"Did it worry you, the watching?" Aggie dished up pudding, served it, and sat down. "Maybe he was a zebra finch in disguise, waiting for the rain. Or maybe his are the eyes that see us come and go. I still feel a shadow around us."

"I won't think about that." Piper took a bite. "This is special."

Lily looked into their faces. "It's the two of you who are special, although now that the bookmobile was invaded, I do still wonder what I'm doing here."

Aggie raised a finger. "You're here to show us that reading can change a person."

"How do you know that?" Piper said.

"Because in her book about a woman's many loves, Anais Nin talks about a man and a cape. Cim had a lovely cape, so it comforted me to read her words. Reading a poem by Rossetti brought me heart to heart with my departed and three words in one haiku took me to his very spirit. The reading was the reason I planned to honor him with red blossoms filling the garage."

"I didn't realize that," said Lily.

"Then Griffo ruined it, looking for something. But the flowers will stay in the garage until every petal falls. When Cim died, I had no proper gypsy funeral. I even went against tradition with his cremation. I couldn't get a loan for a different kind of burial. The banker didn't understand."

"Oh Aggie." Piper reached out to her.

"But now you see, some part of me is different because of words like, 'Plum petals falling.' And 'Sing no sad songs for me.' Something important inside me."

"Oh Aggie," Lily echoed.

"There is a plum tree dying in the garden. I've been waiting for it to blossom, but it may never fully leaf or bloom again. It was the haiku that comforted me and made me realize it was time to treasure the fallen petals, remember the beautiful parts. Not just a tree, but the time together that was Cim and me. And with Christina Rossetti's poetry, I will survive my grief, if I give it time."

She rose and took up the tambourine that rested on the counter. "After meeting you two women, life begins to grow full again. Tonight, you truly deserve the rhythms of the gypsy. I do three circles for the three of us." With a lilting, gentle motion, she danced around the table, touching each woman's shoulder with the jingly zils of the tambourine.

When Piper felt the touch, her hand went to her breast.

Lily wiped away a tiny tear. "Being with you and Piper makes it easier not to dwell on the damage to my library. Tomorrow for book club meeting, I'll find us a special quote."

Aggie hadn't realized her imaginary voyage into the poetic world of Rossetti had saved her from a confrontation with a person holding a sharp knife, the man who'd invaded the farm and destroyed her tribute. On the delayed trip home, the farm pickup had met the intruder's vehicle on the outskirts of town. She'd traveled north. He'd driven south.

As Lily walked to her garage room, stone after stone emptied out of the hole in her pocket. She was surprised at the way life suddenly overflowed with glorious connections. She believed it was called friendship.

Maxine Morton only had one dagger, but she rigged up a target in the apartment and spent her free time perfecting her aim. Starting off with an acceptable throw, she worked to increase her accuracy. After she was done with throwing practice, she'd polish the blade and take two Sweet Sleep pills to settle down for a deep slumber.

CHAPTER 25

The sign swayed in the breeze. *Open 7 a.m. to 7 p.m.* Fred trudged out to refuel the car at the full service pump.

The car window lowered. "Maybe you can help me. I'm trying to find a woman named Lily McFae."

Fred nodded at the male stranger. "She parks her bookmobile in the square. You can rent books from her."

"Does she have a relative living with her?"

"I wouldn't know about that."

"Does she meet there with other people in town?"

"Yeah, it's some kind of radical book club." Fred swabbed down the windshield, then circled the car to pinch the tire gauges and calibrate the pressures. He stopped at the open car window. "Uh, my wife belongs. Why are you interested in the lady?"

"I thought Ms. McFae was someone I knew from Groverly. By the way, if your wife is a member of that club, you may know the name of another young woman who belongs. Auburn hair, willowy, attractive."

"Not sure, but if you've seen the group, my wife's the drop-dead gorgeous blonde. I'm not exactly sure who else belongs."

"Does she sell things at the bookmobile?"

"Books. She rents, sells or barters them."

"Would you characterize the club as dangerous?"

"Knowing Piper, it's hard to believe it's radical about much of anything, but it must be interesting, because some of the guys at the bar said they might join. I plan to check out a meeting myself to find out what's going on, the radical part and the other men."

The man thanked Fred. "By the way, my name's Hugh Jamison. I'm a police detective." He flashed his badge.

"Uh oh." Fred watched the car drive away.

The man in the baseball cap checked the gas station. The pumps were busy and a vehicle rode high on the car lift, ready to be serviced. He moved up the block and watched Piper close up the salon and join Aggie in the bookmobile. After she disappeared inside, he turned around and drove to the Valerian house.

With a few wriggles of his metal tool, the man entered Piper and Fred's place. Following his usual method, he ripped everything apart. Scrambled the bedding. Emptied the closets. Yanked drawers out of chests. Threw magazines to the corners and left a shambles in his shadow. Though he sorted through objects in every room, he found no book with a red cover anywhere. He took the page torn from *Lelia* from his pocket and looked for a good place to toss it. It landed by the front door as he left.

Lily looked around the bookmobile, freshly tidied from front to back. It looked normal again. She opened up for customers and kept busy renting books to patrons. No one mentioned the break-in and she didn't bring it up.

When it was almost time for book club, she closed up and waited for Piper and Aggie to arrive. After a cup of tea, Lily stood up. "I promised you a quote last night and this morning I found one from the enlightened author, Voltaire. 'Let us read, and let us dance; these two amusements will never do any harm to the world.' The words seemed appropriate."

"Absolutely." Piper waved her newly painted lilac nails. "Although we could go dancing in the lavender fields to worry the farmers."

Aggie rubbed her brow "After what happened to the bookmobile, let's not cause a fuss."

"Then, for now, let's read," Lily said. "As usual, I have books to show you. *Mill on the Floss. Mrs. Dalloway. The Wide Sargasso Sea. Villette. Venus in India.*"

"How about something really racy today," Piper said.

Lily opened *Venus in India* and turned to a bookmarked passage. "Okay then, let's go.

> *She saw the mighty engine, its ponderous, well-shaped*
> *sack, and the forest out of which they grew, and knew that*
> *they were now all hers ....*

Shall I keep reading?"

Piper pulsated off the chair. "Oh, shoot, those words and the tea make me crave air and space. Anyone for a change of scene? Let's move to my house. Freddie's at the station. We'll have the run of the place. We can read and dance there."

They trooped outside and turned toward the Valerian house.

"Hey, wait a minute," Piper shouted. "No one's home and that guy's coming out of our house and getting in his car."

"Hop in the pickup," Aggie said.

They climbed in and Aggie gunned the engine.

"His car's turning down that side street." Lily grabbed the seat belt and latched it.

Piper waved her arm and shouted out the window, "Stop!"

"You. Intruder. You," Aggie yelled into the air, "You. Halt!"

"I couldn't see his face, but he had on coveralls and a cap," Piper said. "What do we do?"

"We catch him." Aggie raced the engine and honked the horn, ignoring stop signs, chasing after the dust cloud in the distance. Ahead, the sedan's tires squealed as the car headed toward the main highway.

"Are you used to driving this fast?" Lily said.

"Only this one time." Aggie honked the horn again.

Piper clutched the armrest. "Now I'm the one wondering who hates me enough to break in."

Aggie's pickup paused to find an entry spot among the steadily moving traffic on the multi-laned highway. Then, she plunged ahead and the pickup joined the tightly packed flow of vehicles. Truck horns blared at them.

Lily cried out. "There's his car, jammed in between two semis."

"No, he slipped through to the inside fast lane." Piper scowled. The pickup squeaked into the next lane, while trucks and

SUVs and busses barreled alongside, passing on either side.

"I'm trying to keep up." Aggie groaned. "I'm trying."

The pickup coughed.

"We're losing him." Piper held on for dear life. "Floor it."

"That's all it'll do," Aggie said. "We're outclassed."

"And falling farther and farther behind." Lily squinted, trying to spot the vehicle they were chasing.

Piper shrugged. "I don't think we'll catch him."

"You're right." At the next exit, Aggie turned back toward town.

"See if the sheriff's in his office, Piper," Lily said. "He could radio ahead and the highway patrol might catch him if we gave a description."

"Too late. He could turn off anywhere. I'll call the sheriff from home. Let's see how much damage he did. Too bad Jaxon was in the backyard, but then, he's not much of a watchdog."

They entered together, prepared for destruction, and found it. Piper surveyed the upturned furniture, the strewn clothing and discarded objects. Tears flooded down her cheeks when she reported the damage to the sheriff.

Aggie and Lily set about restoring order, while Piper catalogued personal possessions.

"Everything's accounted for." She picked up the torn page. "Except I don't know where this came from."

Lily studied it. "It's a page from the same book I found. From *Lelia*. See the heading on top."

Aggie snatched the paper. "There was one of these in the farmhouse when it was trashed." Piper pulled her bookmobile reading from under the guest room mattress. "Guess he didn't want my erotica, unless he didn't recognize it when he saw it."

"Not everyone does," Lily said. "And some see it where it's not."

Piper picked up the phone. "Guess I should call Freddie at the garage."

"That sounds private." Lily turned to leave.

Piper waved her lilac nails at them. "I'll see you guys later. You can hold my hand then."

Aggie and Lily slipped out the front door.

Piper poked in the gas station numbers. "So, Freddie, you'll probably hear about this soon enough, but I wanted to tell you myself. Someone broke into our house."

"Jeez, Piper. You okay? I'll close up and be right over."

"No. I'm all right. I wasn't here. The sheriff's on his way and afterward, he plans to stop by the gas station and give you a full report. He thinks it was a small time thief looking for easy cash. Or kids."

"What could anyone have wanted from our place?"

"Nothing, far as I can tell. Whoever did it, now knows we have nothing to steal."

"Maybe I should train Jaxon to bark, instead of training him not to. Hell, Piper, I'm coming home."

"You don't need to. It's unnecessary. The sheriff will give you all the details, and I have an appointment at the salon. I wanted to let you know before you heard about the break-in from someone else."

"Yeah, I get it. We'll talk about this sometime next year."

"I meant we could talk tonight."

"Yeah, sure. If you feel like it. Or if I do."

She tightened her lips. The phone line clicked.

Griffo tried. He really tried. When he brought the sword out from the corner of the vardo, held it to his lips, and smelled the rusty metal, his neck opening tightened into the size of a pinhole. Then, he'd stumble over to gag in the sink, afraid of slitting his own throat.

After each break-in, the man grabbed his pencil and crossed a name off his list. As he dwelled on the possibilities of who might possess the stolen book, another suspicion surfaced. Someone he hadn't considered before. Someone who might recognize the value of the book much more than any others on the list.

CHAPTER 26

In the heart of night, the man coasted into the back of the Used Stuff Store parking lot. He fumbled at the door working to open it before he sneaked inside. Flashlight in hand, he probed the office from top to bottom. He tiptoed into the sales area to examine rows of chests, sliding out drawers, neglecting to push them shut.

Quiet. Quiet. He checked hiding places in used desks for sale, French provincial, Danish modern, faux bamboo, regulation office types. He slipped with eel-like movements about the store as his slashing light played around different areas, highlighting corners, checking funky trunks, looking behind phonographs and on top of metal kitchen cabinets. He was barely discernible, barely there.

Except. Except for one time. In one unnerving moment, he could not control the bottom drawer of a classic sewing machine. It squealed with a penetrating vibration when he pulled it open. Its horrendous howl flew up and away, traveling up the stairwell to the upper reaches of the apartment, a sound curling around and around, making a noise to wake any occupant. The intruder held his breath for a moment, but heard nothing. All was silent in the upper reaches of the building.

Until along the far side of the room, on the apartment stairway, the third step from the bottom creaked with a footfall. The invader threw his intense flashlight beam in that direction.

It highlighted Maxine in a large lacy nightie, grasping the railing. Her droopy eyes faced the glare and she gasped for air. The sound of her heavy breathing reached him. Through streaks of moonlight penetrating the front windows, he realized she saw him, but knew he'd only be a blurry shadow of a man. Because of his baseball cap and goggles, she wouldn't be able to identify him. Her eyelids squinted at places the moonbeams revealed and her head swiveled toward the papers strewn by the cash register, next to sofa cushions gone askew, on to gaping drawers everywhere.

His voice was raspy. "Quick, go back upstairs and you won't get hurt. Just tell me where you hid the book?"

"Who are you, breaking in here? It's the middle of the night," she whispered. The stair squeaked again, as she continued down the last two steps and stumbled, bumping against an upended table, tripping over an errant footstool. "Damn it. What book are you talking about?"

She leaned against a hat rack that tipped, then crashed against a display of metal shelving. She stumbled again, ending up on her knees.

The man grabbed a rake from the ash can with the sign, "Garden Implements for Sale." He waved the long handle toward her, prongs close to her head. "Don't do anything dumb. Tell me where to find the book. The one wrapped in newspaper. The one under the shelving unit for throwaways. I need it now."

Maxine pulled herself up. "I honestly don't know what you're talking about."

"Oh, I think you found it, opened the package and recognized its enormous worth." The rake dipped above Maxine's head, threatening. "You realized you could secretly sell it for a million bucks."

"No. No. Listen." She clawed at the phone. "Just leave before I call the sheriff."

"Don't do that. I'm warning you." Like the arc of a rainbow, the end of the metal rake swung above her head as she swayed from side to side. The prongs moved closer and closer. Maneuvering to avoid the rake, she slipped again and went down. Crack went her skull, smacking hard against the refurbished pot-bellied stove marked "cheap $15."

He flashed his light and saw blood oozing onto the planked floor, the dark stain seeping into aged woodgrain. He rested the rake on the stove and the flashlight wavered over her still face. "Damn it," the man cried. "Coming down was a dumb move."

Maxine Morton didn't refute his remark. He realized she was unavailable for comment.

He knew she'd never wake up. In a trance, the intruder plowed through the store, checking overlooked pieces of furniture. He did the same upstairs. He turned on the lights and ransacked the apartment. By the time he left, he was certain the book was no longer on the premises.

When the sheriff answered the 911 call, he drove immediately to the Used Stuff Store. He nodded at Sax when the front door opened and patted his back when the sobbing began. The sheriff helped Sax to an old rocking chair, then moved a few brisk steps to the crime scene. Early light glowed ominously on Maxine's body. She was surrounded by violent destruction. He bent to examine her head.

The sheriff turned to Sax, "What can you tell me?"

Sax's voice was only a murmur. "Nothing except Maxine is dead. I found her this morning. Can I leave for my motel room to lie down?"

The sheriff nodded. "I'll be here surveying the damage. Doing what needs to be done." He wandered around the store, shaking his head, climbing over furniture.

Finally, he drove to Motel 5 and knocked on Sax's door.

Sax peered out through a crack before letting him in. "She's dead," he cried. "And while I was away, someone broke in here too. What's happening in this crazy world?" He fell on the bed, in the middle of tangled clothes and covers.

The sheriff observed the mess. Dresser doors hung open. Toothpaste, comb, razor and a string of personal care items trailed out from the bathroom door. He scratched his head. "Can you think of anything to help us solve this? Who might have wanted to hurt your sister? I'm so sorry about Max."

"I found this book page in my room." Sax produced a torn sheet from *Lelia*. "But I don't know what it means. I can't tell you anything." His voice broke. "I don't know what kind of monster hates us so much he'd do things like this."

The sheriff righted the chair and sat down. "A death is new, but breaking and entering in Nolan has turned into an epidemic. Your ripped up store and apartment are just the latest episodes. The Used Stuff cash draw still contains seventeen dollars, so it wasn't the money. Now, your motel room's upended too. Anything gone?"

Sax shook his head. "Nothing I can think of."

The sheriff grunted. "I dunno what to do. This is Nolan, for god's sake."

Back at Used Stuff, the sheriff was relieved when Hugh Jamison showed up to help with the investigation. The detective called Groverly and ordered a forensic team to take fingerprints and photos. After documentation of the body and a comprehensive inspection of the store's upheaval, arrangements were made for Maxine's remains to be removed.

"If it's murder, that's a big event for Nolan." The sheriff took his gun from his holster and wiped it on his pant leg.

It was a day for another big event in town. The full force of the butterfly migration washed past the outskirts, monarchs dropping from a powder-blue sky, drifting closer and closer to Main Street.

"See them dancing." Lily pointed at the butterflies as Aggie parked next to the bookmobile. They both saw Piper pacing back and forth in front of the van.

Lily jumped out of the pickup. "What's wrong?"

"You won't believe it," Piper's voice shook. "They found her body at the store."

Lily unlocked the door. "Whose body? What store?"

Piper rushed in and collapsed. "Maxine. Maxine Morton. Found dead at Used Stuff."

"Suddenly, a black cloud hangs over us," Aggie said. "And the town grows bleaker."

"Do you know what happened?" Lily moved slowly through the bookmobile, her eyes checking each shelf.

"I was on my way to open Cut & Curl when I saw the sheriff's car at Used Stuff. Folks outside were talking about how Maxine was hit on the head or pushed into a stove or something. And whoever did it really messed up the place."

"Do you think she was mixed up in something?" Lily said. "Like drugs?"

"Never in any trouble, far as I know." Piper's mouth quivered. "And we just bought all those books from her."

Lily stopped at the Zane Grey collection on the shelf. Her fingers brushed along the spines. "See, the Used Stuff sale books are with us right now."

Aggie sat and bowed her head. "So Maxine's presence lingers on the shelves of this very place. I said it before. Someone's after us and now, after others. A very evil person."

"A someone who broke into the bookmobile," Lily said.

"Into our house too."

"Maxine sold the cure book to me." Aggie rubbed her temple. "But come to think of it, she was in the office and didn't know that I bought it."

"What cure book?" Piper said.

"The one I bought at Used Stuff and left at the Hopper by mistake, chasing after Cim's cape. Lily thinks it's worth lots more than the two quarters I paid for it."

"A great deal more. If it was stolen from the library in Groverly, it's priceless." Lily stared at her books.

"If Maxine wanted that book back, she'd have asked. And I'd have given it. She was a longtime goat milk customer."

Piper quit nibbling on a fingernail and stood up. "Could it be the book I heard about, the one the drug salesman talked about at the Emporium? The one worth a million?"

"Who was in the store that day?" Lily asked.

"Boris and Griffo were both there. And Sax and maybe Maxine. I wasn't paying too much attention, and I don't remember the name of the company. I was nervous because I went there to buy some erotica."

"Suddenly there's a long list of crime in town." Lily moved to the front. "Maxine Morton's dead. The Used Stuff Store trashed. The bookmobile. Piper and Fred's place. And somehow, we're in the middle of it."

"Don't forget the farm. I thought that was Griffo," Aggie said, "but I found a torn page from that book too."

"I haven't seen Aggie's special book yet, but from the description, it might be the stolen one," Lily said. "I saw the exterior when it was part of the library exhibit."

Piper started pacing up and down the aisle. "But the crooks broke into our house. Freddie and I don't know about any book, unless it's connected to what I overheard at the Emporium that day. I'm scared."

Detective Jamison's car crawled past the bookmobile parked in the square. When he saw shadows of people moving inside through the back window, he pulled in and parked, nosing his vehicle close to the park's blooming bushes.

In a sudden rush, the colorful monarchs came from behind buildings, through alleyways and down hidden paths. Attracted by the invitation of flowers blooming in the square, the maze of bright fliers dipped down to feed. More butterflies floated through the town streets. Weaving wings clustering together, they created an advancing orange barricade. He watched as they hovered between his car and the bookmobile.

"What the hell. I'm being attacked by flutterers." Through the car window, he watched the flood of color move in mesmerizing rhythm. When they obscured the view, he ground his teeth. "Confound it." Ready to advance through the orange haze, he opened the car door and stood by his automobile.

Alarmed at the sound of a nearby car engine, the pitch of Piper's voice rose. "I heard a car pull up and I think it parked. Lock the door, quick."

"Just to be safe." Lily snapped the latch and looked out the window. "Oh my, look at that, a waving wall of orange wings."

"I believe monarchs are magical," said Aggie.

"Think of it. Thousands of amazing creatures migrating to our pines and eucalyptus." Lily leaned against a bookcase. "Nothing bad should happen when the butterflies arrive."

"Tell that to Maxine." Piper continued pacing up and down the van. "I don't see anyone coming, but I want things normal again. Know what? I'm driving into Groverly. I'll buy something pretty to cheer me up. Maybe stay at my cousin's for a day or two. When things go wrong, go shopping, I always say."

"Come on, when there's trouble, I say go home." Aggie grabbed Lily's arm. "We'll take the side road that passes the flower fields."

✖

When the bookmobile door opened, Jamison tried to see through the distraction. A blonde left and he waved his hand toward her, but the monarchs did not part. She ran across the square and unlocked the Cut & Curl. Through a pattern of wings, two other women left. One was older and the other one was the pretty woman from the Hopper. Her hair glinted in the sun and her step was quick and light. She drove off in the pickup with the older woman. The serious-faced person from the driver's license did not exit the bookmobile. To make certain, he scrambled through the wings and tried the door. It was locked. Damn. He shrugged over his stupid assumption. The attractive woman was not a long-lost relative. That was Lily. He'd been too intent on the driver's photo, relied too strongly on the description given at the library and by her neighbors. For whatever reason, he'd not been thinking straight and he knew better. Women change their attitude as well as their hair color and cut.

Perhaps because of the migration invasion, there was no traffic on Main Street. He noticed a woman in a gray hooded windbreaker sitting on the bench in the square. She was watching the bookmobile or watching the butterflies or watching him. For whatever reason, she was the first person from Nolan he'd seen stop to rest there.

He went to his room to conduct his daily global network search of recent rare book offerings. Online, the coroner's report on Maxine Morton blipped into his mailbox. Cause of death: accidental. The rushed autopsy showed a heavy dose of sleeping pills in her blood. It was determined she was groggy when she discovered the break-in, lost her balance and cracked her head on the iron stove. Whether she'd interrupted the intruder was not addressed.

Even though he might or might not accept the death as accidental, it didn't explain the rash of break-ins and vandalism in town. If the intruder had found the stolen book at Used Stuff, the crime wave in town might be ended.

Fred cleaned his pickup in front of the service station, deep in thought about the recent puzzling events in his life. When a car pulled up, he looked over and saw a woman using her credit card at the pump. He kept working.

"Hey, you there, you lived around here long?" she asked.

He turned. "Yup, all my life." He moved the big sack of dog food from the bed of the pickup and discovered the plastic bag Piper had left for him to return to Jeremy. He took it to the cab and looked at the take-out cartons on the passenger side. Opening the toolbox on the cab floor, he gently laid the package on top and closed the clasps, then took an armload of food cartons and dumped them in the garage trash.

The woman inserted the refill hose back in place and called out. "I'm interested in that bookmobile in the square. Has it been in town long?"

"Not too long. Why?"

"I might be in the market for a vehicle like that. Do you know what hours it's open?"

"Whenever the owner wants to open, I guess."

"So it's definitely a person who owns it, and it's not connected to the county in any way?"

He rubbed his chin. "I'm not sure. Are you some kind of cop?"

The woman pulled up her gray hood, and sped off.

Fred shrugged and drove off in the opposite direction to return the package to the Hopper. He planned to catch up on crime wave news. But the bar was shut tight.

The man dressed in dark coveralls slipped into Aggie's garden and went directly to the area that grew the herbs he needed. With a gloved hand, he pulled several leaves off some of the plants and broke off several stalks to make a bouquet. He stuffed the stolen herbs in a paper bag and left in a hurry.

Flat on a bed of small saws, the *Book of Cures* soaked up the weight of toolbox darkness. For thousands of years, surrounded by the aroma of wine, now the book moved from the odor of dry dog food to the scent of motor oil. In Fred's souped-up machine, the grumbly sound of the muffler vibrated the floor of the truck. The seal inside shook in time with the engine. Looser. A little looser.

In a morning filled with white clouds and sunshine, Aggie weeded the garden. She frowned over the lovage plant. Most of it was broken off. She worked her way down the rows. Suddenly, her hands began to shake. Someone had been there. Stripped the leaves off monkshood, foxglove, and belladonna plants. For some reason, this thief not only wanted lovage, but worse, needed poisons from her garden.

With the citizenry in shock, a black veil dropped over the town of Nolan. People gathered in knots, murmuring about the barrage of crime in town. They plodded through the streets with heavy hearts and heavy boots, suddenly suspicious of one another. At night, they locked their door. Stores closed. People carried weapons.

CHAPTER 27

Sax moved back to the apartment above the store. He lost interest in buying and selling old furniture. He packed up Maxine's
things and dropped them off at Salvation Army. When he found
a framed picture of her, he hung it near the store entrance and
bought one of Boris's windup caged birds to serenade his store
of discards and hand-me-downs. He scrubbed the floor plank
where she died and bleached it, but the spot didn't match, so he
threw a rag rug over it. Mornings, he threw the windows wide
open to air the store. He sat at the office desk and pushed chess
pieces around the board. Made plans. Made better ones.

When Boris offered him several sharp daggers for a good
price, he copied the Emporium setup, hanging the knives on a
golden cord that stretched across the new cork wall of the office.
Every day he cleaned the daggers until they shone, then attached
them back on the display hooks that wavered along the rope. To
pass the time, he practiced the art of the throw. It was only when
the tin bird sang that Sax relaxed, listening to the automatic melody, flicking knives at the big scrap piece of cork.

Aggie tapped on Lily's door. "If you want, I offer you another kind of ride to town. Why not borrow the farm's moped? It
would give you freedom to come and go at will."

"It sounds easier and cheaper. Show me how."

"Not so hard. Even I ride it."

Lily took a seat on the red motorbike, and under Aggie's

directions drove the moped around the yard, touring the fence line, making smaller and smaller circles in the drive.

"Hey." Lily hollered and parked. "I'll take a trial run to town and get the feel of it on the road. Maybe Jeremy's back from the funeral." She waved goodbye. "Maybe people are recovering from the shock of Maxine's departure."

"Sometimes the engine starts hard. Be careful not to flood it." Aggie gave a nod and watched the moped jounce down the country road toward town.

Within minutes, Griffo's roadster roared up and he stood wild-eyed before her. "On my way here, I saw someone riding my moped. Who the devil was that?"

"What do you mean?" Aggie went into the kitchen and took sudsy milk bottles from the sink. She rinsed them under cold water.

He pounded his fist on the table. "You sold my moped, didn't you?"

"Did you sell the black cape?" She carried the bottles to the big sterilizer in the pantry. "Did you take monkshood leaves from the garden and ruin my lovage?"

"I did not."

"Swear to me you did not."

"I didn't sell the cape, and I didn't take anything from the garden."

Arranging the bottles in the machine, she flipped the switch and moved back to the kitchen counter. "Now then, the moped belongs to the farm, not to you, and I lent it to someone. I had no notion when you'd be back. Or if. I only knew some scoundrel took the farm vardo. Pilfered my remedy book. And stole the cape of my dead husband. Also ransacked the farmhouse and garage. As far as the poison herbs, you are now forbidden to touch anything in the garden." She took crackers from the shelf.

"But I didn't ransack anything and yeah, taking the book was a mistake, but I returned it. The vardo I borrowed, and the cape you'll get back. You didn't burn them after Cim died." Griffo poked around the cupboards. "I always thought you'd give me the moped. Hey, I'm starving. How about a cheese sandwich?"

Aggie arranged leftover onion loaf on a cracked plate. "Can't you see I'm busy?"

He sat down at the table. "I've been thinking about moving back to my room. I could use a good night's sleep and some of your cooking."

"And you'd stay for how long?" She cut goat cheese squares for the center of the platter.

"I'm your nephew. Do I need to sign a lease?"

"No, you come and go like the weather and ruin things. That's why you're not welcome back and why someone else uses your room." Aggie pushed crumbs from the counter into her palm.

Griffo jumped from his chair. "Well, giving away my room evens the score for the book and the cape. Where did you find someone to rent that room in this crummy town?"

"The woman who started the book club is there."

"Tell her I want my room back. Tell her I plan to live there until the circus leaves for Groverly."

"I can't do that. Lily McFae is my friend and a real librarian."

Electricity sparked in Griffo's eyes. "Lily McFae? Was that who drove past on my moped? Is that the demon woman living in my room?"

"Watch your words. She's my guest."

"But that's the one who stole the sapphire ring from me. She's a crook."

"Quit rattling on. You don't know her. She's from the city. She wouldn't take anything from you."

"Forget it. Now I know where to find her. Talk about a gypsy sign. Auntie, you just handed over my purple ring on a platter of goat cheese." Griffo grabbed some crackers from the plate and flew out the door.

As Lily stood in front of the Hopper, excitement made her go limp. The sign was gone. She shifted her weight from one foot to the other to get her balance, then pushed open the door. The atmosphere of an empty bar hit her, the smell of yesterday's beer and peanuts. Rows of bottles stood in front of the long, be-speckled mirror. Bar stools waited for the day's customers and captain's chairs grouped around dark tables kept silent vigil for Happy Hour.

"What'll you have?" Jeremy Judd said.

"I'm Lily McFae, from the bookmobile."

"Yeah, I know. You gals are a dandy group."

Lily blushed. "Aggie told me she left a package here the other day and I'm here to retrieve it for her."

"Yeah, when I wiped off the bar, I noticed that package so I took it over to Cut & Curl. I thought Piper could return it to Aggie at your next book club meeting. You know, I might have forgotten to tell Piper about it."

"Yes, you did. Look, before I go, do you know the name of the tall gentleman wearing a tweed jacket the night we were here? He looked familiar."

"Don't believe I do."

"No problem, thanks anyway." She edged toward the entrance. "I'll go next door and check with Piper."

When Lily left the bar, she saw the woman in the gray windbreaker sitting on the bench in the square. She'd noticed most Nolan people didn't sit there. They just walked past it on their their way to the other side.

She hurried to the Cut & Curl, pushed open the door and smiled at Piper. "Oh, you're back from Groverly. I'm so glad."

Piper sprayed and rubbed at spots on the mirror. "Yeah, home again. Anything new and awful happen while I was away? Are you and Aggie okay?"

"We are. I'm here to pick up the package Jeremy left the other day. It was wrapped in newspaper."

"I did have it, but why do you want it?"

"Because it belongs to Aggie, not Jeremy. Under that newspaper is the book we were talking about."

"Darn it, I dropped the package off at the gas station. Told Freddie to return it to the Hopper."

"Okay, I'll get it from Freddie." She started for the door.

"Wait a minute, Lily, can you postpone that until after book club?" Piper put down her cleaning rag. "There's a secret I plan to tell you and Aggie at book club. It affects my marriage, about how to talk to Freddie. I need your opinion and Aggie's on how to say things right. Now I'm thinking, after book club, you and I could go to the garage together for the package. Then, you could take it to Aggie, but I'd stay and talk. It would mean a lot to me, you know, moral support from a friend to get me there. I keep trying to talk to him, but it doesn't work out. It means you'd have to wait for the package, but just for a little bit."

Lily blinked. "Certainly, I can do that. For a friend." And another stone slipped away.

☙

On achy knees, Aggie examined every plant in the garden. Only the lovage and monkshood had been noticeably harmed. She hobbled to the kitchen and wound a red ribbon around her wrist, then cut two more red lengths and put them aside.

☙

The man wearing the baseball cap watched Griffo drive away from the circus grounds in his roadster. It was hard to miss the gypsy wagon, even parked next to the circus animal trucks. With a few quick moves, he slipped in and dumped the gypsy's life on the floor. No red book cover beckoned from the corners. No historical treasure peeked out from under the breadbox. No recovery of a special book worth millions to the pharmaceutical industry. Only a snake in a cage covered with a towel. The snake was a big surprise.

CHAPTER 28

Lily watched the butterflies lingering in the park. On the bench, the woman in the gray windbreaker sat staring at the bookmobile.

When Piper and Aggie arrived, Lily asked if they knew the woman, but neither of them did. Lily shivered and brought out a stack of old books to entice the members.

Aggie unpacked the sack of tea things and unscrewed the lid to the Mason jar. "Today I brought the jug and cups, but forgot the teapot. I'm a bit rattled, but according to our tradition, we still will begin with tea." Pouring out of the jar, some of the tea splashed out of the cups.

"Oh, don't waste any of the precious stuff," said Lily.

"Sorry about that. Like I said, my nerves are jumpy." Aggie lifted her arm to show the red ribbon tied around her wrist. "I want you to match mine."

She tied a similar ribbon around the left wrist of each woman. "And I made sandwiches for each of you to eat later. All will be explained at the end of our meeting, but for now, enjoy your tea." She handed out the brown bags with sandwiches tucked inside.

Studying the two women, Lily wondered about the effects of the elixir. Their systems had adjusted to the qualities of the tea, and they didn't giggle as much anymore. She rarely wore her glasses and her face looked dewy-eyed in the mirror. Piper's blotchy complexion had turned to clear ivory. Aggie's fingers were barely swollen from arthritis, and she wore her braids down most of the time, letting them swing at her shoulders.

Lily tapped on her cup with a pencil. "Piper has something to say to us today. Go ahead and tell us what is on your mind."

"Let me get myself together. I'll talk later." Piper held out her cup and when it was brimming, took a big swallow.

Picking up a slim volume, Lily took the reins again. "We'll start with the reclusive life of Emily Dickinson. You've read her poetry, but it's good to know about the author."

She glanced at the women as she talked. Although they seemed to listen to details about the life of the famous poet, an air of distraction settled in. She guessed they were allowing their minds to wander along paths of their own separate thoughts.

She cleared her throat. "Now it's time to hear from you. I know you made a start early on, but let's begin again with "*Wild Nights – Wild Nights!*" Lily read the poem and closed the book. "Think about her words. We can start with the title."

"Something about the tea triggers waves inside me and makes the words spill from my mouth." Piper put down her cup. "I know exactly what kind of times she meant. Once during a thunderstorm, when Freddie and I laughed and thrashed and rolled and kissed and I'll spare the details, but when we were, you know, together, we got all wound up in the sheet and Freddie caught his toe in the bedding. When he tried to wiggle free, we rolled off the bed, all tangled up, and couldn't get unhitched. He was yelling to high heaven and I was laughing. We found out later, he broke his toe and was in real pain. He rented crutches in Groverly, so he could move around the garage. When anyone asked him what happened, he just said, 'Tripped and fell.' I'd say that was one wild night."

"And Emily Dickinson would probably agree." Lily picked through the stack of books. "A night of love passionate enough to break a body part. Perhaps we're ready to tackle something longer."

Aggie poured the last of the lovely, green liquid.

Lily held up *The Decameron*. "Have you ever wondered about the power of sex?"

"Gypsies sing songs of it." Aggie grabbed one of the scarves from the seat back, got up and waved it back and forth, creating a slow and flowing figure-eight. She sang words in a foreign tongue, moving back and forth to the rhythm. In a few minutes, she stopped and flipped her braid. "My song told of a passion so strong it disrupted the earth. Years back, after Cim and I had a wild night in the vardo, an earthquake was centered in Turkey. When we heard of it, we believed it was our fault. That together, we'd kicked up enough cosmic energy to travel across land and sea. Our passion that night measured four-point-five on the scale."

Piper took another scarf, got up and waved it around. "Well, once Freddie and I lasted till dawn. I never put it together, but the next day a quake measuring over six struck the border of Panama. That could have been us."

Lily rose. Her heart lifted at the sight of the bookmobile, alive with swirling color and energy. "If seismologists could track romantic foreplay on the Richter, they might develop a technology that would send out pre-tremor warnings." She reached for the third scarf and let it drift and fall in a soft wave motion.

Without a knock, the door handle turned and a tall man entered through the front entrance of the bookmobile. He stood on the step of the door well. "I'm Detective Hugh Jamison, here to talk to Ms. Lily McFae."

The scaves stilled, as the women plunked down in their seats.

Lily took a deep breath when she saw it was the attractive man from the Hopper. "I'm sorry, but we're in the middle of a book club meeting."

"But you are Lily McFae? Is that correct?"

"Of course, I am."

"Then I'll wait." He stepped up into the van, loose and casual.

Lily took in his blue oxford shirt, unbuttoned at the neck. She was intent on the imagined pulse of his throat. Her lymph nodes sent ecstatic messages to the tips of her toes. To calm herself, she reached for a book.

Piper returned her scarf to the seat back. She ruffled her curls. "This is a private club. Aggie and I were here first, and we're waiting for the reading. Couldn't you come back later?"

"No, I'll wait." He leaned against a bookshelf.

Lily paged through the book to find a passage. She threw him a look. "Then, let's make it interesting. I'll read aloud as usual and start here.

She, being hotter than wine than cool with chastity,
unreservedly undressed herself before Pericone … She had
never before known the horn with which men −"

"What in blazes are you reading?" He frowned.

Lily glanced up. "Boccaccio. *The Decameron.*"

He pulled out a badge. "Well, forget that. Since this is the radical book club, I'm here to ask about the subversive actions you're engaged in. Then we'll proceed to the crimes you may have committed. Ms. McFae? If you are in fact, Lily McFae."

His harsh words squashed her silvery sensations. "I beg your pardon. I am Lily McFae and this is not a Radical Book Club. It's The Erotica Book Club for Nice Ladies."

A puzzled look flashed across his face. "What?"

"Someone evidently misheard the name of our club," Piper said.

"We were looking for reading that's..." Aggie let the scarf in her hand fall gently to the floor.

"We were curious and I asked Lily to guide us toward some spicy reading." Piper looked down.

Lily turned the page. "Pardon me, while I go on, if I can recapture the moment.

…find and then lose and find again the hooded
little center that is her.

"Oh, this is ridiculous." His voice deepened. "Not Radical? but Erotica?" He stepped down into the well. "I'll leave and you go on with your meeting, listening to Boccaccio. By no stretch of the imagination am I finished with this. I have questions for you, Ms. McFae. And the rest of you too. Stay in town." The bookmobile door closed behind him.

"He said, 'stay in town.'" Aggie tugged at her braid. "Where would we go?"

"He had a badge." Piper wrinkled her brow. "Are we suspects of some kind?"

Lily put Boccaccio back in the closet. "I'm not sure, but we've had enough of *The Decameron* for now. We'll move on to something else. Piper, you had something to tell us?"

"After that man bursting in here, I'm too spooked to talk about anything personal. But I have a favor. My appointment book is crammed full, so could we meet tomorrow evening? I'll talk about that important thing then, I promise. And Lily, go see Freddie, if you want."

Lily nodded. "Aggie, you had something to talk about too."

"Not a good thing, but something I must tell you. Someone took monkshood and belladonna leaves of poison from my garden and broke off several stalks of lovage. I don't know who did it. Or what to do next. Except to ward off poison, I gave you the red ribbons that gypsies wear for protection."

"Oh Aggie, maybe an animal ate them." Piper played with her empty cup.

"No, I could tell. Some were stripped by hand. Others snapped off."

"Could it be Griffo?" Lily said.

"He swore not. But this is important. We must be careful. Eat and drink only the things you or I prepare. That's why I gave you the sandwich. When you get hungry, it is safe to eat."

"I don't want to think about that," Piper cried, "and I don't want to talk about it anymore. Too many things are happening too fast. Now someone's going to poison us? Who'd believe that?"

"We could ask the sheriff and find out." Lily fiddled with the red ribbon on her wrist.

Aggie reached down for the scarf she'd dropped earlier and arranged it on the seat back. "We can decide about that. For now, let's be cautious. And remain so as we go about our daily lives." She packed the cups and almost empty tea jar into a sack. "What else can we do?"

"Let me help you get your things to the pickup," Piper said. "Then I'll go to Cut & Curl for my next appointment. You're right, it can't hurt to be careful."

"We must stay in touch." Lily watched them go. She slowed her breath to stay calm.

After she tasted the last drop in her cup, she put the sandwich on a shelf in the closet.

To forget thoughts of poison, she revisited the appearance of the detective, his seductive throat, and perfectly shaped ears. She considered his eyes, and although his tone was harsh, the memory of his voice made the pit of her stomach waver.

As she locked the bookmobile and stepped outside, she noticed that the woman sitting in the square was gone. She sensed someone watched as she climbed on the moped and drove off toward the farm. Down the road, she heard noises and snapped her head around. No one was there. Later, she heard a vehicle behind her, but it did not pass. She kept twisting her body around, trying to figure out if she was officially under surveillance by the man who intrigued her, or some other dangerous person. The car moved closer. Her knees went weak. Her hands lost their grip on the steering wheel. As the vehicle neared, she almost drove into the ditch. She looked around again and saw the car turn into a driveway.

🌿

Under the dying plum tree, Aggie drank the remaining drops of lively tea and thought about the *Book of Cures*. If it were meant to be, the magical book would return. She went inside to the bedroom, locked the door, and unlocked the closet. She fondled the beat up fedora that rested on the top shelf, a hat still carrying the scent of a ghost she now called Cim.

That night in the dark, she wore only his hat. When the clouds parted, Aggie lit a candle to think about gypsy moon baths, known as taboo by many of her people. There were those who worried about the evil effect of falling asleep while gazing at the full moon. If her gypsy family cared about anything, it was taboos and legends and hauntings. She pulled the lace curtains aside and opened the window. Moonlight washed over her wrinkled body. She yearned to wrap herself in the stolen dark cape, but that was no longer possible.

She grabbed the tambourine on the dresser. Dancing around the room, metallic disks shaking, the old woman relived the bedroom shake-ups she'd experienced with her companion of more than fifty years. She raised her hands above her head and clapped, recalling heartbeats in tune with love's escapades. The clashing of their bodies. Fast. Tumultuous. Wild. Then gentle. Slow. Sweet. The tempo of past lovemaking shook her body like the quaking tambourine until she was exhausted.

"Cim and dear ancestors, keep me and my friends safe from monkshood," she whispered and put the fedora away. The flame gobbled up the candlewax. She climbed under three quilt coverlets. Her lids drooped and she found a few restful hours before it was time to wake and feed the goats.

Fred took the package out of the toolbox, glanced at the moon, and went into the Hopper. "I believe this belongs to you." He placed the plastic bag on the counter.

"Naw, belongs to Aggie," said Jeremy.

"Well, I got it from Piper and threw it in the bed of the truck. She thought it was yours. Luckily, the dog food kept it dry."

"I'll give it to Aggie next time she delivers milk." Jeremy put the package next to the bar's old issues of girlie magazines. The cover of the lightly clad figure on the top magazine grabbed his attention. "True classics never fade, do they?" Spreading the other magazines across the counter, he admired the golden girls and their poses.

"Gimme a Jack." Fred reached for a cover that featured a blonde beauty who flaunted her upper torso behind two crossed sledgehammers. "Make it a double, in honor of Piper."

"Yeah, that girl has advantages."

Fred set the jigger down and flipped through the pages. "Wow."

Jeremy held up a foldout. "Make that two wowzers."

A few customers overheard their comments and gathered around. Eventually each man grabbed a magazine of his own. Hoots echoed to the rafters as they compared tops and bottoms and backsides of semi-clad and non-clad models. They rooted through every dog-eared issue, seeking out old time favorites.

Even the plastic bag was checked and a corner of the newspaper ripped further to see if a special edition lurked inside the plain wrapper. With no female parts visible, they cast aside the newsprint package.

The men whiled away the hours with erotic commentaries of their own, telling stories filled with sexual humor and prowess, a literary seminar of the pool hall kind.

Later, alone in the bedroom, Fred leaned against the pillow with the dog nestled at his side. He buried his nose in the high school album he'd found on the bed stand. Piper's handwriting on the page stopped him cold.

> *I was here but now I'm gone. I've left this note to turn you on. Those who knew me knew me well, those who didn't go to h-e-double-hockey-sticks!!! Love, and xxx, Piper.*

"Always fun and always feisty," he said to Jaxon. Then he noticed that underneath she'd scrawled.

> *Hey Fred, I always knew I'd look back on the tears and that would make me laugh but I didn't know I'd look back on the laughs and it would make me cry.*

He didn't remember her writing that and wondered when she'd done it. And why. "Holy Christmas, I miss the way things used to be." Gradually his moans expanded to swamp the bedroom with melancholy and other expressions of personal activity. From his lazy, drinking mood, he thought of going to the spare room to nuzzle against her, but while he was planning the reunion, he dropped off.

The man in the moon looked down on Nolan.

Detective Jamison watched the woman in the gray windbreaker limp across main street to sit on the park bench. He meandered through the square. "Nice night," he said as he strolled by.

She looked up. "I guess, but I don't talk to strange men."

"Good decision." He walked on, but he'd seen her face and it matched the police photo. He could think of no reason to take her in for questioning. Minnesota Fiddler had the right to sit on a park bench in any town she chose. But he used her presence close to the bookmobile and his knowledge about the coin theft to requisition a search warrant for Lily's van.

He looked at his watch and headed to his motel room. When he dozed off, his fingers reached for the red-haired Lily. A horn sounded as his body covered hers and found her center…. He woke in a cold sweat, recalling the words from Boccaccio's *Decameron.* Reacting to an old classic was ridiculous, he told himself, and a fatal flaw for a member of the police department. He slid the image of the dream woman to the back of his brain and concentrated instead on the stern photo of the driver's license. He'd wait for her to make a mistake.

Piper lay in bed, worrying. Tomorrow, while she held her breath, an x-ray machine would squash her nicely rounded assets into pancakes. She thought of her love life with Freddie. The dating. The wedding. The sex. The earthquakes. She thought of someone mixing up poison to dust on her donuts or slip into her coffee. "Oh, Freddie, damn it, I need you." She crept to the master bedroom door and inched it open to enter, but his whistling and rasping snores sent her creeping back to the spare room.

Lily dreamed a long, erotic escapade about a shadowy figure who locked her away in a cell. He questioned her all through the night about poison, then moved close to touch her. At that point, she woke up with a start.

CHAPTER 29

Early the next day, Lily stopped by the gas station, filled up the moped, and went in the office to pay. "Piper told me she gave you a package. To deliver to Jeremy."

Fred put her money in the register. "But I dropped it off." He turned and smiled. "Hey, how are things working out for you?"

"Fine, far as I know."

"You sure everything's okay? A woman asked me some stuff about the bookmobile. And a man too. Thing is, he had a badge."

"I see." Lily gave a quick wave and scooted off to the Hopper. She stood at the door. The bar was empty, no one in sight.

"Hello," she called toward a back hallway.

"Just a minute," Jeremy hollered from the storage room.

She spied the girlie magazines on the corner of the bar. "Taverna erotica." She picked through a couple of them. On the bottom of the pile, the corner of her eye caught the look of newsprint. Peeking out from torn paper, she saw faded lettering against a scarlet background. It looked ancient. And authentic. In a flip of her hand, she slipped the package into her tote bag.

"Never mind," she yelled. Moving across the square, the walk to the bookmobile seemed endless. She remembered the book behind glass at the library, when she'd not been able to touch it. Now, through a crack in the universe, she possessed it. Unlocking the van, she entered, bolted the door behind her and collapsed next to the stacked books of erotica on the table.

She sat alone in the bookmobile and reverently removed the newspaper. She stared at the cover, memorizing the design. Then she opened the book.

"*I salute you, dear reader.*" That was the way the *Book of Cures* began. And the world stopped for Lily. As she absorbed the aged handwriting and drawings, she fell into a secret place of "once upon a time," a place interwoven with leafy greens and herbal fragrances. Her soul blossomed as she closed her eyes for one brief moment, grateful for the history, beauty and magic of the old pages.

The doorknob jiggled against the lock of the bookmobile. Someone was twisting it to enter. With a jerk, she rose and slipped the manuscript into her book bag under the driver's seat and unlatched the door. "Sorry. I'm not open yet. Straightening up."

The tall man stepped in to unnerve her again. "Let's start fresh. I'm Detective Hugh Jamison and I'm here to question you." He stared through the pupils of her brown eyes to the back of her skull.

She responded by gazing into his gray-green eyes, then blushed from last night's dreaming. She reached down to pick up one of the erotica books and carried it to the closet shelf.

"Consider the place now open for business," she murmured.

"I confess, for some time I've tracked your movements. A bookmobile taking off from Groverly to Nolan. If a butterfly flaps its wings, watch out for –"

"A hurricane." Her eyebrow lifted. "A typhoon in Saipan. Ice meteors in Spain."

"Interesting. Other than scientists, not many people are intrigued by the chaos theory."

"Oh, plenty others. Movie makers, novelists, library board presidents." She studied his throat taunting her above the yellow oxford cloth shirt. "And today you've blown across my doorstep. Was it some current from Madrid?" She couldn't look away.

He shrugged, then grinned, showing even white teeth. "Closer than that. I come to you from the Groverly Police Department, and my business of capital crime usually involves chaos in one form or another. I'm here to ask you about a stolen manuscript called the *Book of Cures*."

She slipped another book of erotica into the closet and checked her watch. "I see. I wish you'd made an appointment. I'm happy to discuss any subject with you, if it can be tomorrow. I have a very real commitment. Book club meets soon, and I'm in charge as usual. It might not seem critical to you, but I assure you, it's very important to the members. Piper has a problem, a serious one. And Aggie, hers is even worse and might affect us all. It's confidential, but if you'll wait until tomorrow, I'll give you as much time as you need. I may even ask for your help with Aggie's problem."

He moved closer and looked at her, never blinking. "I understand why the women might be enthusiastic about your readings, having heard a phrase or two of them myself, but I need to talk now." He produced his ID again. "Look, this is official. A rare book was stolen. It's a criminal matter." His voice was crisp. "I need to know your part in its disappearance. Two events collided. The book disappeared. You left town."

His intensity disturbed her. Her mind wavered when she looked at his long, tan fingers on the identification. A twist of fate was sucking her into its vacuum. First, possessing the *Book of Cures*. Then, a handsome stranger and the flash of his badge. Now, the possible confiscation of the book. Could the unread ancient book disappear that quickly from her grasp?

"Okay, this is a short account of what happened. For years, I worked at the Groverly Main Library as Assistant Librarian. Although I wrote the actual email that brought the tour, that book wasn't on the list sent by the Global Antiquarian Society. Also, I left town before the exhibit arrived to stay in Nolan. I did go back to the library to see the books on tour and to say my last goodbyes to the library, but I had no part in the theft. I was unaware that the book was missing when I left Groverly. I heard later that it disappeared."

He touched her arm. "Exactly how did you learn of the theft?"

Her eyes lifted to meet his look. "From the law. The sheriff here in town told me after he issued my speeding ticket. Go ahead and ask him."

"I need to find out who took the manuscript from the locked case and everything points to your involvement. Do you know anyone connected to this crime?"

She continued to gaze at him. "I do not. Truly, I don't."

"Were you upset when you were fired?"

"I was. I am, but it was my own fault. I got angry at the wrong time with the wrong person. And I walked away."

He took a step back. "Why did you mark the article about the book tour in the newspaper? I found it at your place. It ties you to the theft."

"You searched my home?"

"Yes, I was there to find out how you were connected to the disappearance of the book. To get a sense of you."

She flushed. "I marked it simply because I was the one who'd arranged that first stop at our library. My brief claim to fame. Then I was fired and drove off in my magical bookmobile."

"On your post office form, you wrote 'Now I do what I can. Destination unknown.' That's an odd thing to say."

"You are thorough, aren't you?"

"It's my job. Besides, you're an intriguing woman, uh, person of interest."

"I meant that I was taking my bookmobile on the road, and I didn't have an itinerary. What else would I mean?" She looked at her watch again. "Look, I really don't have time now. Pick a time and place for more questioning tomorrow. Ask whatever you want." She tipped her head back and smiled. Her white teeth gleamed. "I'll be available to you as long as you —"

"What?" A hint of a blush darkened his tan.

She moved closer to him. "As I said, ask me anything in depth tomorrow. Anywhere. Anytime. At the bookmobile. Or Aggie's. Or lock me in a cell at the sheriff's office. Meanwhile, I'll try to remember anything that might help you find the person who stole that book from the library. I'd like to know who took it, because revering and caring for old books was my career. I believe rare books are to be admired, not stolen."

He hesitated. "I have one more question. What do you know about Minnesota Fiddler?"

"Who's that?"

"Fiddler is the person who owned this vehicle before you."

"I don't think so. When I bought it at the auction, they said it was owned by the county and used as a bookmobile. The shelves were in place. It was all set to go."

"Did you find any secret compartment?"

"What on earth are you talking about?"

"I believe there is one, and I intend to find it. If I let you go now, I need to know where you'll go."

"I'll be in my room at Aggie's. With a few books to study for the meeting tonight."

"Technically we should wind this up now." His face was close to hers. Suddenly he turned away. "But I'll give you a few hours to come up with any clues about what happened. Think it over. And stay in town."

She reached for her bookbag and purse. "Why would I go away? The nice ladies would be extremely disappointed if I didn't show up for the meeting tonight."

"And what author have you chosen to read?"

With great care, she put two slim books inside the bag. "That's what I must decide in my rented room over the Verkie garage. Call Aggie to check on me. Or follow me, if you wish. That's what you've been doing, isn't it?"

He stepped near her and held out his hand. She shook it and sparks snapped. "Damn carpet," he said.

She watched the nape of his neck, his oxford shirt and trim khaki pants retreat from the bookmobile.

She needed time to untwist her body from her brain and while she was at it, examine the bookmobile to find its secret compartment, if there was one. Intrigued, she went about it methodically, looking under the driver's seat, in back of the glove compartment, checking for loose carpeting, peeking behind the shelving, and beneath the built-in seating. She was certain he'd tricked her, until she poked at the floorboard in the closet and detected a slight shift. She got the screwdriver from her driver's kit and wedged the board up. In a small well underneath, she saw a cardboard box and reached down to remove the lid.

Boom! Boom! The loud clap of gunfire sounded nearby. The lid dropped to the floor as she jumped up, clutching the open closet door for support. Outside, the town was silent. Holding her breath, she took a quick peek out the window and thought she saw a gray shadow move away, melting into the pines, but not a soul, not a vehicle, was in sight. Just parked cars and closed business doors.

From the edge of a cloud, an eerie light poured down on the town. A close rumbling noise sounded. She grabbed her purse and the bookbag and scrambled out of the bookmobile. Locking the van, she heard the rumble again and felt some relief when she realized it was thunder. But she didn't go back into the van. All she wanted was to get back to the safety of her room with her treasure, the *Book of Cures.*

Boom! The same sharp noise broke the air. An old, vegetable truck jerked its way down Main Street, backfiring. Her hand shook as she turned the moped key. The engine sputtered, and she heard footsteps behind her. Her hands flicked the key in the ignition, on, then off, then on again. When she gave a quick turn of her head, the area was clear. No sign of the detective or the woman from the bench. She clicked the key again, heard a rattle, followed by a purr. The moped engine started.

As the moped sputtered along at top speed down the country road, sounds of a car engine hummed far behind. Someone was there, but she refused to look back. Her heart pounded. The book bag bumped against her body, the thump of a stolen old book. If it was the woman in gray coming after her, did she have a weapon? Was she after the book? Lily felt helpless. All she could do was ride on. If it was the detective, he'd regard the historic document as evidence and take it away from her. That was his job, while she saw the book in some tenuous relationship with the Dewey Decimal System, where books are regarded as reading material accessible to others.

The road ahead was clear. The land rolled on and the wind from new storm clouds blew her back to the goat farm.

As she parked the moped by the garage, a car drove by. She was certain it was the detective, following to see that she kept her word. Tomorrow, she'd talk to him and bring up other worrisome things. About being followed. About the strange woman in the square. About Aggie's stolen leaves of poison.

She raced up the stairs to her room. She'd been given time. As a professional librarian and student of literature, she had an insignificant scrap of a few hours, in contrast to the thousands of years the volume had waited, hidden away. Somehow, this old manuscript had slid down through the centuries. Through fate, she'd caught it with open hands. Could a thoughtful police official like Hugh Jamison, understand her need to hold and read such a book? She had no idea.

Piper undressed and slipped into the open-fronted cotton garb. When told, she let one corner slide down, so the technician could fit her breast into the revolving mechanism. She held her breath as big metal plates squeezed and squashed her body parts. She endured another position, another picture, another view. Finally the mammogram was over. On the way home, she drove by the gas station, ready to talk to Freddie, but customers were lined up for the pumps, cars going out, coming in, going out.

At home, she closed the door to the lonely spare room to hide. Reaching under her bed for her book, she propped it up to read. But *Boswell's London Journal* did not comfort her.

> *I am surrounded with numbers of freehearted ladies of all kinds: from the splendid Madam at fifty guineas a night, down to the civil nymph with white thread stockings who tramps along the Strand and will resign her engaging person to your honour for a pint of wine and a shilling.*

Piper frowned. "Boswell, you're a jerk."

She wanted Freddie home. She wanted to be in his arms, but he was busy running his business. She'd have to wait until he closed up and came home.

Griffo's roadster roared in as Aggie pulled clothes from the line. She refused to face him, but spoke out clearly. "I remind you again. Return the cape and the vardo."

"I need the cape for my performance in Groverly," he said. "After that, I'll have money to buy my own. And the vardo's close by, parked in a field with the circus vans."

"Another thing is important for me to know. On an oath of Rom, did you take any plant leaves from the garden?"

"No, cross my gypsy heart." His fingers moved across his chest. "But I'd sure appreciate some food from the kitchen."

"On an oath of my own gypsy heart." She signed her bosom. "You will be forever sorry if you use any poisonous plants from my garden. And you never told me what you were after, ripping apart the house and my flower tribute to Cim in the garage."

"What's that supposed to mean?"

"Not that you'd tell me anyway. I've decided. I don't want you living here anymore."

"Then I need my clothes. Is your tenant in my room?"

"Don't bother her. Your clothes are clean and folded in the basket by the back door. Were you going to ask her for money or try and sell her something illegal?"

"Why would you think that?" Griffo sneered. "She's the thief."

"Go. Go now." Aggie waved him away. "You're trouble, plain and simple." She rushed inside, put the basket of his clothes outside the kitchen door and turned the lock.

Detective Jamison admitted it to himself. He was attracted to Lily McFae's obvious intelligence and quiet spirit, but he wasn't a fool. He'd thrown her a long length of proverbial rope, to give her time and space to contact Boris. So far, his two main suspects had ignored each other. And now another piece joined the puzzle. A new face was in town. Minnesota Fiddler.

The search warrant for the bookmobile came through, with permission for Jamison to check for one stolen book as well as hidden coins. He decided to conduct an immediate inspection without Ms. McFae or Ms. Fiddler present. Although he knocked, he was reasonably sure no one was inside, since he'd followed Lily to the goat farm and didn't expect her back. If she went anywhere, it would be the Emporium. When his door thumps went predictably unanswered, he adjusted the simple lock on the front entry of the bookmobile and entered. The blinds were drawn. The place was dim. He started at the first stacks, using his flashlight to immerse himself in the librarian's literature. He checked every volume, up, down, and sideways. *Birds of South America.* May Sarton's *Journal of a Solitude.* Each book went back in its slot after he examined it. *How Things Work. The Life of Robert Louis Stevenson. The Notebooks of Camus. Three Lives* by Gertrude Stein. When he got to the back, he noticed the open closet door with more books in place. He checked the titles, but no stolen *Book of Cures* appeared. His beam flashed downward on a piece of wooden flooring propped along the wall. A cardboard lid leaned sideways against it.

"Hey, pay dirt." He moved the cover and stared at the shoe-box nestled inside a hollow floor space. Something glinted inside, and he flashed his light directly on the contents. "Gotcha," he said, taking time to put on gloves before removing the cardboard box. Enclosed in hard plastic containers, the old coins gleamed. He lifted out one container at a time to study the collection of Double Eagles, old colonial issues, and Indian Heads. "Damn, looks like they're in mint condition." He returned the lid to the box, laid the floor covering back, closed the closet door, and left the bookmobile with his prize.

From his trunk, he selected a large evidence bag and slipped in the shoebox of coins. Snap, he locked the bookmobile, then drove to the police property room in Groverly. On the way, he issued an all-points bulletin for Minnesota Fiddler.

A cyclone in Mozambique and a twister in Limassol heralded a mild change of weather in Nolan. Light breezes swirled around horse farms. Haystacks poked up like medieval hats. The wind picked up speed and with its witch's broom, hurried along any fallen leaves, fanning the fate of Lily McFae.

CHAPTER 30

At the farm, Lily stopped by the kitchen to see Aggie. "I might be a little late getting to the meeting tonight. There's something I need to do. Go ahead without me. I'll use the moped."

"Do you want some mint tea? Or a radish sandwich?" Aggie puttered around the room. "It's safe. I just ate."

"No, I don't think so. I'll be in my room."

She carried up the bookbag and made sure to lock the door. She sat on the bed, a pen and notebook beside her, the package on her lap. Her meeting with Hugh Jamison was set for tomorrow, light years away. As the barometric pressure shot up outside the window, so did her excitement. She felt no guilt. Billions of earth dwellers weighed in with opinions on crime and punishment every day, everyone judging matters from self-interest. Each personal world turned on its own axis. Just like all the others, she deserved a point of view. Sometimes the earthly marble reflected the dark side of humanity. Other times, the light. And she was halfway in-between. Holding a stolen book she'd not stolen in her white gloved hands.

The once taped bookmark from Used Stuff hung loose on the newsprint. She smiled.

> *Oh would that I were where I would be, there would I be where I am not.*

Leaning against the crumpled pillow, she drew a breath with the first page, translating the French.

Thanks be, our herbs and vegetables follow the whims of nature with blessings from above. Our humble garden is depicted for special eyes and pure hearts to appreciate.

With a delicate touch, her fingers turned the pages, paper old as mountains, binding fragile as a cuckoo egg. The seven beds of a garden radiated from a center. Graceful drawings of medieval herbs were familiar from the seeds ordered from the Jardin Estate.

She concentrated on each word, each illustration, each simple remedy for common illnesses, jotting down notes. At the back, a sealed pocket promised another mystery to be revealed, but some inner force kept her from opening it. She wanted to copy more things down, but the clock moved relentlessly, marking time before the evening meeting of the book club. At every gathering of the three, the bond that linked them together grew stronger. Lily closed the manuscript. Instead of racing through the book, she'd wait until afterward to resume this pleasure. Later, alone in this tranquil space, she'd forego sleep to decipher the depths of the book and learn its secrets. The manuscript was hers alone until tomorrow. She prepared for book club.

Meanwhile, Llewellyn relaxed in the last row of the Neubland annual meeting. He watched his brother update the group of forty shareholders, who attended the power point presentation on the latest R&D projects.

Elcott Blanding dripped confidence at the podium. "I have exciting news about Neubland that will change our fortunes forever. We're diligently at work on new formulas for cancer and heart disease."

After a burst of applause from the audience, he continued, "In this revolutionary new venture, we're basing our laboratory work on ancient cures. In more than one way, we pursue the use of herbs from old European gardens."

A young board member raised a hand and when not recognized, stood up. "Sorry to interrupt, but isn't that contrary to the image of Neubland representing the most modern technology? Why put money into old remedies?"

One glance at his notes and Elcott clipped off his reply. "Think of belladonna. Extractions from its roots and leaves are used in small doses as diuretics and sedatives. Atropine, which dilates the eye, is also an extract. And foxglove flourished in old gardens. From its dried leaves came digitalis, the cardiac stimulant."

"Tell them about the experiments for an aphrodisiac." Llewellyn spoke with enthusiasm.

Elcott threw him a dirty look. "I was saving that for my surprise ending. However, now that you bring it up, it's a remedy that might apply not only to Alzheimer's, but to an extended vibrant sexual life. An updated version of products available today, but for both sexes."

The group clapped with enthusiasm.

"Naturally, we'd have first shot at the new drug," the voice of an old board member called out.

"Naturally," Elcott responded. "I'll put your name right after mine."

"Don't forget me." Llewellyn's cell phone chimed.

His brother glared at him from the stage. "You know perfectly well, no calls during the meeting."

"Sorry. Sorry." Llewellyn dashed into the hall to answer his phone. "Hello, this is Lew Blanding."

The voice was clear. "This concerns a certain book."

Lew's stomach flipped. "I've been waiting for you to call." He heard bird song twittering in the background. "Do you have the book? When do we meet? Elcott's given me the okay to proceed with this project."

"First of all, has Neubland come up with the money?"

"I have it ready to go. When can we get this done?"

"The authorities are still nosing around, but soon."

"Reach me on my cell anytime. Day or night."

The moment Llewellyn hung up, he raced to his brother's office. He waited for the meeting to end, pacing about the room.

Elcott marched in, his face stern with annoyance. "You're a distraction, Lew. You've got to get your act together."

"As a matter of fact, I've done just that. That phone call concerned the stolen *Book of Cures*. My contact asked if we had the million dollars and I said yes."

"Well, keep my name out of this transaction, will you? And be careful. The reputation of Neubland is at stake. You know how to get in touch with him?"

"I know where to find him."

One flip of the large framed company logo behind the presidential desk revealed the safe. Elcott reached under his credenza for a leather briefcase, then jotted something on a slip of paper. He unlocked the safe and loaded stacks of bills into the open case until it was full. "Here's a classy carrier. The rest is up to you."

"I can do this. Trust me." Llewellyn left the premises. The lines of worry etching his forehead eased as he drove off on the sales route he knew so well. For the first time, he controlled the situation. The difference: a briefcase filled with cash. Without even touching the money, it lit up his world.

He raced to Nolan, tires skimming the pavement, and jolted to a stop at the Emporium. The neon sign was off and the picketer was absent. He got out and tried the door. It was locked. The words, "Temporarily Closed," made a dent in Llewellyn's mind as he peered in the windows, pounded on the door, and shook the handle. His violent oaths spiraled through the parking lot. Boris was gone.

After a stop at the liquor store, Llewellyn pulled into Motel 5 to rent a room.

"With our low rates, we're all booked up with circus folks, eager to sleep in king size beds," the clerk said. "We even got a detective from Groverly renting space."

"Really, I didn't know about any circus. I planned on a quick stop at the Emporium, but it's closed."

"That guy comes and goes, but he shows up eventually."

Unnerved at the thought of a detective nosing around, Llewellyn zoomed off to the Groverly suburb closest to Nolan and pulled into the parking lot of the largest hotel. Before he registered, he dropped by the bar, downed a vodka martini, and purchased a bottle. Back in the lobby, he filled out the hotel registration form, signing his name as "Larry Newsome" and reconfigured the numbers on his license plate. He paid cash for three days, then drove the car into the hotel underground parking. He held the new briefcase close to his body, stopping often to look back. Entering his room at the rear of the hotel, he double-locked the door and poured himself a tall drink. Without ceremony, he opened the new Neubland briefcase to count the money. "One thousand, two thousand," he chortled. When he got to $200,000, the money was all counted. A big problem loomed ahead, not enough money to buy the book. The note at the bottom of the case said, "our down payment." It was too late to back out now. After a few drinks, things looked brighter. If the cures were real, Elcott would come up with the rest of the funds. Neubland would deal.

He'd wait in this room quietly, until Boris arrived back in Nolan. As soon as he got the phone call, the deal would go down. Vodka would help until it did.

In the gypsy vardo, Griffo got ready for his revenge on Lily Mc-Fae. He went over to the cage and whispered to the snake. "I will share with you how it will happen, my friend. I will be stealthy. And swift. Grab her finger. Snatch the ring. What's mine is mine."

The snake hissed and twisted in its enclosure. Griffo hissed back. "Someday I may turn into your prince of magnificence, but there's no time to be charming tonight." He picked up a gunny-sack in the corner. "Wish me luck, buddy."

He started his mission near the outskirts of town, at the row of streetlights that welcomed visitors to Nolan. From the pile of rocks on the seat of the roadster, he grabbed a hefty stone and got out of the vehicle. A perfect throw and shattered glass fell to the ground. He smashed the next globe and the next, until he'd snuffed out the lamps that lit the way to town. It was darkness he wanted for any vehicle entering this way.

In the gypsy vardo, Griffo got ready for his revenge on Lily Mc-

Detective Jamison noticed the woman in the windbreaker sitting on the park bench again. He reached for his cell and told the sheriff about Minnesota Fiddler, the confiscated coins, and the bookmobile.

"I'd appreciate you stopping by the square to see what she's up to, and follow her if she leaves. I don't want to lose track of her and it's possible she'll contact Boris or others in town. I'm betting she'll enter the bookmobile to get the coins when there's no one there. I'd follow through on this, but I have another appointment."

After his call, he stopped by the Hopper and watched the bookmobile from the bar window, while folks chattered of this and that. He ordered a beer, took a swig from his mug, and nodded to the bartender.

Jeremy came over. "Hey, mister-wearing-the-brown-tweed jacket, were you in here the night the book club met in back?"

"In fact, I was."

"Well, the book club lady asked about you. She wanted to know your name."

"Did she, indeed? I'm Hugh Jamison. I was wondering about her too. In fact, I just met her. Did she say why she wanted to know?"

"Aw, guess she figured you were cute."

"Hm, don't know about that," he mumbled, then gestured out the window. "Have you noticed that woman hanging around the square?"

"Matter of fact, I have," Jeremy said. "I don't know who she is, but it's not a good idea, hanging around outside a bar night and day."

Hugh watched the light play through the amber liquid in his mug. "I keep hearing about a local book club. What's the deal?"

The bartender grinned. "It started when Ms. McFae came to town."

"How often they get together?"

"I think whenever they're in the mood. Might be at the book-mobile, beauty salon, or the back of my bar. Guess that's why they call it Erratic, A Book Club."

Hugh smiled. "I wonder how many members there are."

"Far as I know, only Piper from the Cut & Curl and Aggie from the goat farm. Kind of a different mix of women, ages and backgrounds, but you never know what brings people together."

"According to my business, it's often crime," Jamison said.

"Aggie's a good old gypsy woman. Sells goat milk in town. Has an interesting garden of herbs and such. Lots of raised beds arranged in some circular pattern. I've never seen it myself."

Hughbert's mug landed on the counter with a clunk. "How did she arrive at that particular design?"

Jeremy leaned in. "I can tell you that. Aggie's husband finished it before he died. I think the idea came from some old book of Aggie's. Griffo was in here talking about it one day."

"Well, I read an article in an encyclopedia that described a garden like that, and I'd be interested in seeing her book." Hugh swirled the beer around.

"If you're headed that way, I've got a package for her." The bartender reached under the pile of magazines at the end of the bar. He frowned and sorted through the stack. "It was here. Fred dropped it by. Damn, that thing keeps disappearing. Oh, well. You ready for another beer?"

"Nope, one's my limit tonight."

The TV weatherman began, "Intense weather dominates the globe. High winds from the outer bands of cyclone Cilla have gusted across Fiji. Heavy rains washed across Madagascar, and there's flash flooding in South Asia. If you look at the map, a roiling path has whipped across the ocean to the States and is aiming directly at California. To the highlighted spot right here." He pointed at Groverly and the surrounding area.

As Hugh sat on the barstool, his mind wandered off into his own chaos theory, imagining the book stolen from a castle, riding an Alsatian wind storm, lifted across an ocean, landing in a corner of this little town. It didn't make sense, but here he was, waiting for something to wash in on Nolan's beach of crime, bringing him the culprit and the book. And wondering if Lily McFae would wash in with it.

Outside, darkened skies sent the barometer skyrocketing. He looked at his watch. "I have an appointment to keep."

He was on time for his surveillance of the book club meeting. The woman in the windbreaker was gone and Lily McFae was late. Aggie and Piper arrived as a few drops fell from the sky. He continued his stakeout of the bookmobile, checking his watch regularly. The leader of the Erotica Book Club did not appear. He gritted his teeth as the rain soaked through his jacket. He'd been conned by a librarian.

Lily caressed the manuscript, its exquisite...historic...mesmerizing...pages. She rewrapped it with care and placed it in her tote bag, then grabbed her notes for tonight's discussion. She tucked them inside one of the two books she'd taken from the bookmobile to guard her prize. Since she had room, she put her scissors and repair kit in the outside pocket of the bag so she could fix the few books damaged by the break-in. With everything securely packed, she lifted it over her shoulder.

She glanced at the dark sky, with its low layers of thick woolly clouds. The farmhouse yard light beamed as she climbed on the moped and left the farm.

With the wind scooping along her back, she drove carefully along the graveled edge of the road. Even then, the moped wobbled, but the book rested securely under her wing.

The threatening weather made Lily wonder about her choice of transportation. She looked over her shoulder. Far down the road, car lights glimmered, creeping up behind her in the night. Raindrops went splat against her back, then drummed down hard. She slowed up to control the movement of skidding wheels. Ahead toward town, the road loomed black. The string of broken streetlamps stood like pinched out candles, marking the miles before the houses started. Kids with rocks, she thought, practicing some rite of passage, smashing lights for those who wished to see. Perhaps the same rambunctious kids who'd attacked the bookmobile in rebellion over book reports. Were there simple answers to the questions that worried the three women? Had they become a paranoid book club?

The bright eyes of the car flared up behind her and lit up the bushes, edging closer to her little moped. She thought of the detective following her, or was it someone else? Her nerves kicked in when she realized the car was bearing down faster and faster, aiming straight at her back. She swerved farther to the side of the road as the car engine roared, ready to rear-end her. Barely braking, she leapt off and fell, just before the front of the vehicle smashed into the moped. Pieces of metal flew into the ditch. Wobbly and disoriented, she dodged the scraps of falling red parts.

"Are you Lily McFae?" A rough voice came out of the night.

"Are you crazy?" She struggled to regain her equilibrium. "And yes, I'm Ms. McFae. Who are you?"

"I'm the SOB you swindled."

"Is that you, Fred? You mean the barter? I can pay for the gas now."

A dark figure approached.

"Is it Jeremy? Jeremy Judd? I'm sorry I took Aggie's book from the Hopper, but she said I could. Wait, are you the woman on the bench?"

"I want my sapphire back."

"Sapphire? I don't have a sapphire." Lily was on her knees. "You must mean someone else."

His presence, an enormous shadow, hovered over her.

Instinct made her reach for the scissors in her library kit. "I've got a weapon. Get away from me."

"No weapons, if you know what good for you."

She flashed the scissors. Then a sack covered her head and a rock smashed through the rough cloth hitting her temple.

With the rain pelting down, the bag covered her mouth and gagged her. She couldn't see, only smelled garlic mixed with rain. Someone grabbed one hand, then the other and shoved her down. Slowly, like a pebble sinking to the bottom of a pond, she fell in slow motion into the mud. Dark pain, more intense than the night, pulled at her as she collapsed into a suffocating black hole.

Her mind whisked off into oblivion. And the wind wailed over her still form.

In the bushes outside the farm, the man wearing the bee keeper bonnet watched the old woman come out the door and drive toward town. Then he waited for the lights to go out in the room over the garage. When he saw Lily leave, he crept up the stairs to the room overhead. He picked the lock to enter and turned on the light to set off another one of his intensive, destructive searches for the *Book of Cures*. In a flurry, he removed all objects from their resting places, scattering them to the far corners of the room. Finally, he realized the object he sought was not there. He left his signature page and departed in the rain.

🌿

The flashlight moved across Lily's hands, then streamed briefly inside the sack to light up her face. Griffo pulled off the sack to see her better and muttered, "Dammit, you look different." Then, he scurried back to his roadster and drove toward the goat farm, in time to see a car pulling out of the drive. Aggie must have got a ride to her meeting, he thought.

Griffo parked his car next to the garage, ran through the rain, and climbed the stairway to the landing. He turned the knob. She'd locked the door, but it didn't matter. He bounded down the stairs and scrambled up the drainpipe. Leaning on the ledge, he shoved the window open and climbed inside. He flipped on the light. Puzzled, he saw piles of clothing and blankets scattered everywhere. Desk and bureau doors gaped open. Sweeping his arm under the bed, he created a hill of dust. He whipped through the woman's few possessions on the floor. Clothes, papers, books.

"No jewelry. No damn ring." He squatted on the floor for a minute, then unlocked the door and fled into the damp night.

🌿

In the old hand game, it's rock smashes scissors. Tonight, that was the way it worked out for Lily McFae.

🌿

The detective ducked into his car parked across the square to check his telephone messages. He gave a low whistle, when he heard the conversation on Llewellyn Blanding's phone tap: "book," "money," "soon." He put a BOLO out for Blanding's car and ordered officers not to intercept, but follow and notify him immediately.

CHAPTER 31

"Damn it, time's run out." Detective Jamison stormed into the van. "Where is she? Ms. McFae?"

"We don't know and we're worried," Piper said. "Even if gale force winds rocked this place, it wouldn't keep her from the club meeting."

Aggie gathered the cups. "I have an extra key, so we came in for our tea and waited for her. She said she might be a late."

"So we waited and are still waiting." Piper looked out the window. "And now, worrying a lot."

"Listen to me, I'm the detective investigating her. I'm in charge of finding a valuable book stolen from the library where she worked. If you know where to find her, tell me. For your own sakes, do not protect her."

"But we don't know where she is." Aggie put the near empty tea jar in the sack.

Piper scowled. "And we don't have any stolen book."

"I'm staying at Motel 5. Contact me there or on my cell immediately, if you hear anything." He handed Piper his card.

"We'll do that," Piper said. "We should go home now."

Aggie dangled a key. "I have this legally. Lily gave me the spare in case of emergencies. So many strange things happening in our town. Can I lock up?"

"Give me the key and I'll do it. You two can leave."

After the two women left, the detective scoured the area around the bookmobile. Rain soaked through his tweed jacket, but he had no time to change. He checked the tap on her phone again, as well as on the other suspects. When nothing came up, he issued an all-points bulletin for Lily McFae, a red-haired woman driving a red moped. He called the sheriff and asked him to find a deputy to watch for Minnesota Fiddler, so the sheriff could stand guard at the Emporium. Staring at his hands, he sighed. She'd slipped through his fingers.

Aggie and Piper drove back to the goat farm, through waves of heavy rain, retracing Lily's route to the meeting.

Piper rattled on, "Be careful driving, Aggie. The road is slick. We don't want to get stuck. Oh, I hope she isn't sick. Or had an accident on the moped."

The pickup inched along. "I hope she's not involved in that big book theft."

"And we can talk to her before the detective does. Look, there. What's that?" Piper pointed to bits of red metal on the gravel.

"Could … it…?" Aggie jerked the pickup to a stop with the headlights focused on a body in the ditch.

The women raced over and took the sack from her head. Aggie searched for a pulse. "There's a faint throb."

"Thank God." Piper pulled out her cell phone and called an ambulance. "Who did that to her?"

"Oh, Lily, Lily, what happened?" Aggie covered the still form with her rain coat.

The women moaned and prayed and slogged about in the mud. Occasionally, one of them would lightly pat Lily and whisper, "We're here and we won't leave you. Why was your head covered?"

When the ambulance arrived, the two attendants lifted Lily onto a stretcher and slid it into the vehicle.

Piper scooped up the muddy carryall from the ground. She reached in her pocket for her flashlight key chain and peeked inside. "Books, a newspaper, and her wallet. Thank heavens, her billfold wasn't stolen."

"You ride with her in the ambulance to emergency. I'll follow in the pickup," Aggie said.

Lily lay flat on her back, with Piper holding her hand. "Can't you wake up, Lily? Hurry back and open your eyes. We'll talk."

The face stayed carved in granite.

In the Groverly Hospital Emergency Room, Piper took charge at the desk. She pulled Lily's medical card from her bill-fold, located identification and discovered a home address in Groverly. Piper filled out the registration forms as best she could and wrote down her own name in the space for nearest relative, listing herself as cousin. Aggie stayed with Lily until the nurse rolled the patient through coded double doors and pointed the women to a nearby area.

They sat with other worried people in the waiting room, a circle of concern filled with uncertainty. Piper prayed, letting her invisible thoughts rise to the roof of the hospital and slip through the insulation and cracks, sending continuous threads toward the sky. Aggie sent messages and fervent requests to her ancestors.

The doctor approached them. "Are you relatives of Ms. McFae?"

"A close, close friend," Aggie said "Her landlady too."

Piper stepped closer. "I'm a cousin. Her closest relative."

"I can give you a small amount of information. She's in a coma, with head contusions and bruises on her hand. On the plus side, no broken bones. We'll do more tests, keep a watch on her, and monitor her progress. That's all we have now. Can you tell me anything about what happened that might be helpful?"

"It was a moped accident outside Nolan. Someone attacked her." Aggie rolled her hands together. "The moped was crashed to bits."

The doctor studied the chart. "I'll leave it to you to notify any other relatives of her condition. There's nothing you can do tonight. She'll be resting. Come visit her tomorrow."

"We'll do whatever we can." Aggie inched backward.

Piper shook rain off the canvas carryall. "We'll see if we can fig-ure out what happened, and then I'll clean the mud off her bag."

The two women plodded toward the lobby.

"Why did you say you were her cousin?" Aggie looked puzzled.

"So we could get medical information about her. If you aren't related, they can't tell you anything."

Aggie nodded. "There's a saying, 'A gypsy has three truths. One for you. One for me. A third for himself.' See, now you've become an honorary gypsy."

Piper took her arm.

Evidence of chaos continued its path around the globe.

Currents crawled through the ocean.

Water dripped from faucets.

Blood flowed through blue vessels.

Hearts beat out simple songs.

Things set in motion progressed according to the laws of physics, and hummed a tune. Do re mi fa. So there.

CHAPTER 32

The two club women trudged up the creaky staircase to Lily's room above the garage. At the top, Aggie flung open the door.

"Good grief, I know this look. The person watching us has attacked again." Aggie stumbled toward the curtains flapping at the open window. She pushed down the sash with a thump.

"What a disaster." Piper looked at the open dresser drawers. "Not her housekeeping, for sure." She picked up a sweater. "Everything strewn around. You're right. It looks like my place after the break-in. Like you said. The same person."

Aggie foraged through the clothes on the closet floor. "And he comes closer and closer." She hung up shirts and slacks and skirts. "And now Lily has been hurt."

Piper leaned over to pick up a leaflet. "Look, it's about monarchs. I'll take it to the hospital. Lily loves butterflies." She stacked books by the bedside. "What about this? A flyer about the *Book of Cures.* I'll take that too."

Aggie turned the wastebasket right side up. "Griffo had a red flyer too. Did you get one?"

"I don't know. Freddie handles the mail at home." Piper pulled out her phone. "I'll call the sheriff. Darn, we shouldn't touch the rest of her things. Except maybe pick up her underwear."

"Someone plans to poison us and we're warned not to leave. Someone breaking in all over town. Then Lily is attacked." Aggie paced around the room, murmuring, "Dear ancestors of the forest, protect us from evil. Protect us from poison. Protect us from darkness and burlap sacks. Keep us safe."

In ten minutes, a siren wailed its loud song down the road, then arrived at the farm. They ran to the top of the stairs to meet the sheriff.

"This is downright scary," Piper said. "Someone crashed into Lily."

Aggie added, "Someone put a bag over her head."

The sheriff marched through the door. "Don't worry. I'm here now. And more help is on the way."

"We did tidy up some," Piper said. "Probably shouldn't have done that."

The sheriff nodded. "Don't worry about it."

Detective Jamison arrived and shook off his wet coat. "You two, sit on the bed." He poked around Lily's dislodged furniture and belongings and finally turned to the sheriff. "What can you tell me?"

"My deputy is watching the Emporium," the sheriff said. "And I deputized Fred to keep an eye out for the lady in gray. I'll take over as soon as I can."

"But what happened to the librarian?" Jamison checked the rain on the window sill.

The sheriff turned to him. "I got the 911 that Ms. McFae had an accident driving Aggie's moped into town. Someone smashed her little vehicle to kingdom come and attacked her. About the state of this room, not sure. These two cleaned it up some before I got here. I'd say someone was after her valuables. She's in the hospital."

"I don't think Lily had much to steal," Aggie said.

"Which hospital?" Jamison gripped the bedpost.

The sheriff stopped sorting objects. "The closest one, Groverly General."

The detective came over to the women. "I'm taking over. Aggie, let Piper walk you over to the farmhouse and lock the door. Piper, I'll drive you home after I make some calls."

"I'd feel better staying with Aggie."

"Okay, that's fine." Jamison turned to the sheriff. "Keep the deputy at the Emporium. Let Fred go home and you watch the bookmobile. I'll contact you after I check on Ms. McFae's condition. With the bookmobile closed, Minnesota Fiddler has the perfect window of opportunity to retrieve her stash."

✑

Back in the vardo, Griffo took a slug of slivovitz and pulled out the sword. He was able to slip it down an inch into his throat before his hand shook. He pulled out the blade and threw it down. "Things are goin' hellova caddywompus." He yanked off the cage cover.

The snake hissed at him, and he rattled the cage.

"She didn't have the ring and it wasn't in my room. The craziest part was, she didn't even look the same."

His nerves rampaged through his body and he bounced from one wall to the other, batting at the cabinets until he was worn out. He opened the vardo door, turned around three times and rubbed his rabbit's foot, then slumped down on the mattress.

The snake coiled in its enclosure, ready to strike.

Griffo got up to kneel before the cage. He crooned to the serpent, "Why don't you like me?"

The tattooed lady stood at the open door. "I like you fine."

His head swiveled around, and he took in her colorful, design-covered body. "Wow, don't you look great. I'm Griffo. Do you know anyone who knows anything about this snarly snake?"

"Matter of fact, I do. I'll tell you a secret about working with your little buddy. Learned it from my friend, the stripping snake charmer."

✑

Early the next morning, Aggie and Piper waited outside the hospital room for the doctor to finish his examination.

"Can we see her?" Piper walked up to the physician, catching him before he moved on.

"Only for a few minutes. She's still in a coma. We're watching her carefully."

"Is there anything we can do?" Aggie said.

"Talk quietly to her when you're there," the doctor said. "The sound of familiar voices can be beneficial to someone in her condition.

When Aggie and Piper entered Lily's room, they saw the nurse fussing around the monitoring equipment.

She smiled at them as she checked the drip tube. "I'm so glad she has family with her. She must be an interesting woman with such glorious tattoos."

Aggie shrugged.

Piper stared.

"I have to answer a call, but I'll be right back. Remember to talk quietly."

The two women waited for the nurse to leave.

"What did she mean?" Piper hovered at Lily's bed. "I never saw any tattoos."

Aggie moved to the other side. "I have no notion."

"Dare we look?"

Aggie smoothed a wrinkle in the cover. "Better not to."

"A temptation, though." Piper leaned over the still form.

"We just hold her hand and talk," Aggie said, "like the doctor said."

"Do you think the tattoos were a secret she might have told us?" Piper put her mouth close to Lily and whispered. "I've got the bag of books you had last night. The mud on the outside dried, and I brushed it off." She placed the tote bag on the bottom shelf of the nightstand. "Almost good as new."

"We brought reading from your room. It's here, waiting for you." Aggie set two books on top of the stand. This old book of poetry and – oh, wait, I'll put this one about classic erotica in the drawer for when you wake up."

The patient was silent. So were the visitors.

Aggie went to the window to gaze out. "It's hard to keep talking when she can't answer."

"Maybe I'll read to her about the butterflies. That might make her happy." Piper pulled out the leaflet she'd found in Lily's room. "*Studies show that chemicals sprayed on corn crops might affect the plant pollen and might blow on milkweed plants nearby. When monarch butterflies feed on the milkweed...* Oh dear, it would be poisonous. That's not a cheery thought."

There was no sign that Lily heard their voices, but when butterflies were mentioned, the yellow and green spikes of the monitor moved up an increment. On another machine, little white blips drew out a miniature mountain range, up and down, then up a bit further. The nurse floated in.

"I wonder what she's thinking." Aggie said.

The nurse checked the machines. "Wish we knew. We scan the brain and take pictures. Doctors interpret all the blips and stimuli racing around inside. Some day we may know more about what goes on inside the head of a coma patient."

"What do you think?" Aggie asked.

"Only that technology can't chase down our thoughts yet. Maybe that's a good thing. Our ideas still belong to us alone. The world is round. Or flat. We think what we choose."

"And through closed eyelids, the world's as thin as an insect wing." Aggie murmured. "Mama Nanninski once said that."

"Exactly. All is not as it appears." The nurse straightened the blankets. "If I were you two, I'd go home and rest. Come back this afternoon. I don't expect anything to happen for a while."

At Cut & Curl, Piper answered the phone and winced at the notification. Her Groverly doctor's office was calling. "This is Piper Valerian."

"Mrs. Valerian, I've examined your mammogram and after checking the results, I believe the next step is to schedule a routine biopsy. It's not a difficult procedure, and it gives us the answers we need. I can put you through to scheduling now, so you can set a date."

"I need a little time to think," she said.

"Be sure and call the office to set up a date. Try not to worry. It's not a long procedure."

"Okay." She hung up and crumpled into the barber chair. She felt her body go numb.

If Lily wanted to say something, she couldn't, even though she tried. Words about butterflies fluttered through her head, about symbiosis and biodiversity. Pesticides blowing on plants endangering monarchs. About caterpillars half the normal size, after feeding on leaves dusted with poisonous pollen. Then, dying. Words. More words. Sad words.

In her mind, laser beams bounced back and forth as she plowed her way through fields of corn, searching for interconnected strings between men and women and other species. She thought she heard a butterfly struggling to break free of its cocoon, working its way toward the light and the leaves. Like an insect fighting to break the threads that held it tightly inside its silken womb, Lily struggled to break the cords that bound her to the bedding.

Shift after shift, the hospital caregivers intruded with necessary body pokes and prods. Lily kept busy, breathing in and breathing out. Outside her hospital window, the universe poured its explained and unexplained events down the funnel of time. Fronts passed. Stars came out.

Minnesota Fiddler grabbed an ale at the Hopper. "Sleepy little town you've got here. It's surprising you guys have your own bookmobile. But it doesn't seem to be open much of the time."

"Yeah," Jeremy polished glasses behind the counter. "The librarian had an accident. Now that she's in the hospital, it's closed."

"That's too bad." The corners of Fiddler's mouth twitched.

CHAPTER 33

At the Groverly Hospital, Detective Jamison presented his credentials to the doctor and explained his purpose. At first the physician denied the request, then relented, as long as a nurse was present and the visit was brief. The detective opened the blinds and turned up all the lights to watch the patient's expressions.

"Ms. Lily McFae, can you hear me? It's Detective Hugh Jamison. There's something I need to say." He lightly touched her hand. "In case you're fooling the doctor. And me. I want you aware of your situation."

Lily's face was a mask, without wrinkle or emotion.

"I'm not sure you should say anything that might disturb the patient," the nurse said.

"It will only be a few sentences. If she's in a coma, she won't understand."

"And you must understand that I will be keeping a close eye on her machines."

He looked at Lily. "If evidence is found that you're connected with the theft of the *Book of Cures*, you may be taken into custody."

The patient did not budge, but the pulse in her vein bobbled at the sound of his soft, calm voice.

"I see a small signal. It might be the start of distress. I'm sure the lights should not be so high." The nurse snapped off the lamp and turned the dimmer to low.

"Sorry, but she's under suspicion in a stolen book theft. In addition, I have questions about more serious crimes committed in connection with the theft. And about her accident." He turned to the patient. "Things will go easier for you if you can provide information that results in the return of the volume, or any information about the death of Maxine Morton. And I need to know about your attack."

The nurse checked the machines. "Look here, her blood pressure's up. I suggest you stop now, because I need to notify the doctor."

He touched Lily's hand. "I understand. It looks like she has nothing to say today. Get well soon. Damn it."

Kicked out of the hospital, he started for Nolan and the bookmobile stakeout.

He pulled in, parked, and found the sheriff in an unmarked car. "You've had a big day. I'll finish the watch tonight."

"If you're sure, I'll take off." The sheriff started the car and waved goodbye.

Although Hugh's least favorite thing was surveillance, he'd made the positive ID of Fiddler in the square, found the coins, and felt a responsibility to join in the stakeout. When he re-parked between two cars in front of the Hopper, he had a clear view of the bookmobile.

After the bar closed and the cars left, he moved his vehicle next to an SUV that shielded his presence. A couple hours later, he spotted a shadow limping through the middle of the square. Now and then, the form disappeared in the trees, but the person moved steadily toward the bookmobile. The figure stopped at the rear door for a few minutes, hovered over the knob, then disappeared inside. Jamison checked to make sure his gun and handcuffs were ready. It wouldn't take long for the intruder to check the loose floorboard. He counted to ten. Sliding out of his car, he ran to the bookmobile door and yanked it open. "Hands up. Stop whatever you're doing right now. I'm an officer of the law and my weapon is drawn." He flashed a light at the intruder. The woman in the windbreaker turned, her mouth open. She put her hands over her head. "Hey man, where'd you come from?" The closet door hung ajar and the floorboard was removed. A backpack lay at her feet.

"Never mind. What's your name?"

"Uh, Minnow Watson."

"Not to be confused with Minnesota Fiddler, I expect. You're under arrest for breaking and entering this vehicle. Now, hands behind your back."

"Look Mister, give me a break, huh? I was hungry. Thought there'd be food in here."

"I don't think so." He snapped on the cuffs. "What else were you looking for?"

The woman shrugged "Uh, I left, ahh, I left my book."

"And you expected to find it under the floorboard of the closet?"

"There's nothing inside, but old books and cleaning things. I looked inside that compartment. It's empty. You can't prove I took a thing."

"Maybe because I confiscated the items you wanted to reclaim, gold coins stolen from a family in Groverly. Unfortunately, they were not recovered in time for your trial, but we now have fingerprints. Get moving, Ms. Fiddler. You're going to Groverly to be processed." The detective marched her out the bookmobile, locked the vehicle, and led her to his car.

In her hospital room, Lily was deeply involved in an imagined interrogation. Under a bright light bulb, a man named Hugh pressed her hand and threw impossible questions her direction, pinning her down, not believing anything she said about a book. The brilliance of the lamp sent out heat to warm her blood. The filament glowed hot and white. The heated particles vibrated. Shafts of energy headed straight for the pupils of her eyes. If she could open her lids, the light would enter and she'd see him and the color of his shirt. She'd look into his face and speak.

But her eyes stayed glued shut. Her dream hand tried to reach her breast, but her body disappeared. The back of his tweed coat faded away, and the scene slowly dissolved to black.

Aggie came by the next afternoon. She peeked around the corner to see a nurse taking Lily's pulse and temperature, checking her blood pressure and smoothing her bed.

One soft step and then another, she tiptoed in. "I was with Lily when she came in. Can I stay a few minutes?"

"Yes, but her condition remains the same. I'll be next door," the nurse said.

Aggie waited until they were alone. She bent over her friend and whispered, "Forgive me, Lily, but I need to talk to someone who won't think I've lost my rocks, or is that marbles? Anyway, you're the chosen one."

Brow smooth, hands folded, the patient rested peacefully.

"It's about the way I act when I'm alone. I don't think it's what other people do. Since Cim died, I've gone all achy inside. I feel his ghost, and it scares me, yet consoles me too."

She took Lily's hand and gave it a gentle squeeze. "From the day he died, life without him left me cold. The first night after he passed, a sorrow appeared to me, like his ghost wearing the shape of his heavy, winter cape. I was supposed to have burned it, but I wore it on my shoulders night and day for weeks. A cape so heavy, it pulled me down, but it kept me from freezing. Later, I only wore it at night, and when I tried to stop, to fold it up and store it away, I couldn't. Now, I'm still haunted by a vision of Cim. And since you can't hear me, I'll whisper his name, Camlo. My dear Camlo."

Aggie watched a fly buzz at the glass, its thin antennae beating against the window.

"I keep his ashes in a jar I've hidden inside my samovar. When I hear the shutters rattle in the night, I think his ghost has come back for his cape and his ashes and I'm chilled to the marrow from the aching. Sometimes, I hold the jar and dance in the night. It's a secret craziness. But now, Griffo has stolen the cape and oh, Lily, I am so cold." Aggie crushed her face down into the covers of the hospital bed. "I don't know what to do."

When Lily trembled, Aggie pulled the covers up. "You must get well, dear friend. Coma's not a good thing. Still, it made your ear an easy place to tell my troubles. And we didn't even talk about the stolen leaves of poison."

As Aggie bent down to touch Lily's warm forehead, peace and resolve coursed through her old gypsy veins, and she felt rays of heat flow outward, warming the sadness inside her. Saying the words, letting them out, worked like balm for her soul. The feeling stayed with her all the way to the farm.

The first thing she did was gather kindling, a rake and a broom and place them near the plum tree. Then, unlocking her bedroom closet door, she reached for the fedora and put it on her head. With great tenderness and tears, she took down the samovar and lifted out the Mason jar of chunky dust. Inside that glass jar rested the spirit of Camlo. It was a vessel filled with happy times and problems of their life together, a bond that tied them in a gypsy love knot. Gliding with steady steps, she carried the jar of ashes to the garden. The rake scratched away at the dirt around the plum tree as she murmured sweet, private words and gently scattered the remains. Then she moved the soil back in place.

Near the garden, she chose a spot and lit a match. The felt hat burned with a smoke that swirled, and she let the strong smell envelope her. When the fire was done, she swept up the ashes from the fedora and sprinkled them under the plum tree. "That is as far as I go today," she said. "When next I see Griffo, we will burn the vardo, like our ancestors did. Then it is finished. Your body gone, but mine still here to always remember."

On her way back to the kitchen, she noticed sprigs of mint poking through the cracks of the stone walkway. She stood absolutely still and felt the burn of the sun on her skin. The corners of her heart melted and uncurled.

Griffo pulled into the Emporium and appeared at the door. He saw Boris unpacking DVDs and strolled over. "I've been waiting for you to come back and open up, because I need a favor."

"Of course you do." Boris kept working.

"I'd like to park my vardo in your parking lot. I almost parked it here while you were gone, but thought that might upset you."

"I meant to ask you, do you know anything about someone visiting this place while I was out of town? Did you break in?"

Griffo nodded. "I did come by to get Aggie's book. She needed it back, but that took only a few minutes. Lots of odd things happening around town, break-ins and worse. Did you hear about Maxine's death?"

"Yeah, damn shame. And the librarian's accident."

Griffo nodded. "What do you say to my parking here? I could be your watchman."

"I don't know. I'll think about it."

"Hey, we're friends. You rented me the sword. And I could do a practice act in your parking lot for the town. I'm up to an inch and a half on the sword and the adrenaline of an audience might shove it right down my gullet."

Boris filed the last DVD. "Okay, but I never know how long I'll stay. I might plan to leave again for a while, but if your show happened when the store was open, I'd get customers out of it."

The Erotica Book Club for Nice Ladies moved its meetings to the hospital with Aggie and Piper taking turns holding Lily's hand.

"Today I brought safe sandwiches to eat. And tea." Aggie brought out paper cups and poured. "We could toast to Lily. To her good health returning and to both of us remaining safe."

Piper lifted her drink. "To us."

A nurse scurried into the room. "I came to change the bedding."

"Can we stay? We've come from Nolan for our book club meeting."

The nurse nodded. "I'll do it later, but I need to check the machines."

Piper brought out a book. "I thought I'd read aloud, like Lily used to read to us."

"Go right ahead. Don't mind me." The nurse went about her work.

"*The New Atalantis.* It's kind of suggestive." Piper hesitated.

"Better yet," the nurse said.

"By Delarivier Manley." Her voice was low.

> *He drew her gently to him, drank her tears with his kisses, sucked her sighs and gave her by that dangerous commerce new and unfelt desires.*

"It's okay to keep reading." The nurse charted Lily's pulse and temperature and adjusted her fluid intake.

"I wonder what the author means by 'dangerous commerce,'" Piper said.

"I don't know, but don't stop now." The nurse looked at her watch and went to the door. In a minute, she came back in and sat down. "I'm on a break. Would you mind if I listened?"

"That would be okay." Piper read on, and soon another nurse slipped into the room.

> *...she closed her eyes with languishing delight! Delivered up the possession of her lips and breath to the amorous invader; returned his eager grasps and, in a word, gave her whole person into his arms in meltings full of delight!*

A disembodied voice filtered through the transom. "Visiting hours are now over."

Doves called to duty, the nurses left with white flutterings, except for the first one who asked, "Exactly how does someone join your book club?"

Piper smiled. "I guess Aggie and I could vote for hospital meetings with additional members. All in favor?" She held up her hand.

Aggie raised hers.

Piper gave a quick glance at Lily's hand. She thought she saw one finger move. "Next time, we'll talk about the amorous invader."

Aggie shrugged. "Without Lily, this gypsy and this beautician may stumble and stray a bit."

"I don't think our patient cares about that," the nurse said.

For Lily, when the chatter stopped, the machines plodded on. Body unmoving, eyes closed, she heard words. Something about languishing delight. Lips, grasps, and meltings. But she couldn't reach out.

Piper stood by the doctor, waiting for his report.

"Things progress slowly, nothing to worry about. I wonder if it's too tiring for you and Aggie, staying with the patient, all through every day and every evening. You look worn out," the doctor said. "Are there other friends to stop by?"

Piper thought a minute. "If I passed word around town, there are people who knew her from the bookmobile."

"Let's try a few visits from others. Only during regular hours, only talking quietly, not staying long. The nurse will monitor Lily's vital signs to make sure everything's okay."

"Great idea," Piper said. "I'll tell a few people."

The news of Lily McFae's accident threw Fred Valerian for a loop. He downed a quick beer at the Hopper and considered visiting the hospital. One more beer and he found himself outside Room 3, carrying the photography books.

"I can let you stay a few minutes," the nurse said.

"I won't stay long."

"I'll be down the hall, but I'll look in to check."

Fred pulled a chair next to the bedside. "Ms. McFae, I came to tell you I'm sorry you're here."

He opened the top book. "When you stopped to gas up the moped, I should have said how satisfied I was with our barter. I enjoy the car book a lot. And the model book too, matter of fact. All those beautiful bodies. You had me pegged. The fenders of a Rolls Royce, man." He leaned closer. "But you know, the shape of curvy things makes me think about the shape of other curvy things and how they're missed."

Lily lay still as a discharged battery.

Fred held up a page toward her. "I know you can't hear me or see me, but here's a '27 Chrysler. With a rumble seat. I wanted to show you." He came close to Lily's ear and whispered, "And tell you about my married life with Piper. I don't have anyone else to tell how I work my butt off at the station, but zone out at home. I suppose that bores her." He flushed and put the book back on his lap. "Are you sure you can't hear me?"

Her mouth was sealed shut.

"Piper and I are not so close of late. She probably told you at a club meeting how she moved into the guest room." He opened the other book. "But I have something to run past you. If I tell her these books came from you, wouldn't she see we have something in common? Maybe I'd become a more interesting guy."

Her chin tilted half an inch.

He buried his nose in a photographic spread. "Wow, look at that great rack. If you were awake, it'd knock your socks off." He quickly turned the page. "Well, maybe not, but it reminds me of Piper. She's got such great – hey, never mind. Tell you what, when you open your eyes, I'll treat your bookmobile to a full tank of gas." Fred closed the book and whispered. "But one thing for sure, Piper has the greatest duo in town."

Lily's mind moved to his words, but her lips couldn't speak. The image of Fred dissolved, and the focus changed to the pink and white curves of a woman's body with words skipping out from *Upon the Nipples of Julia's Breast.*

> *A red rose peeping through a white?*
> *Or else a cherry (double graced)*
> *Within a lily? Centre placed?*

The tender, erotic words of the poet flowed like a sorrowful river through her mind. The man named Hugh leaned to kiss the red rose. To nibble at the cherry, let his long tan fingers pluck a lily. But instead of her breasts, he found a flat field of flowers and greenery and birds.

One word, soft as the flesh he described, formed on her lips. Unfortunately, there was no one there to hear her whisper "Herrick." The machine jumped with increased brain activity and made a few little beeps.

Inside her head, an age old question surfaced: If there is no one in the forest, does the falling tree make a sound? If there is no one in a room to hear a whisper, has it actually happened? Do machines count?

Small scenes of the countryside filled the Verkie farm yard. Goat tails whisked. Leaves wobbled. Lizards slid from under rocks. Bird feathers ruffled. Gnats whizzed by. And a beetle sneezed.

❧

Detective Jamison's car shot down the road toward the Verkie Farm. He saw the owner sitting on her porch and drove in.

"What a nice place. Do you remember me, Detective Jamison?" He presented his badge.

"Yes, and I'm Aggie."

"I have a few questions for you. Only a few."

"Go ahead."

"To begin, are you acquainted with Boris Ratchov?"

"A while back, I stopped by the Emporium to see if he wanted to carry goat milk from my farm. He didn't."

"Does your nephew Griffo know him?"

"He did temporary work there for a while, but Griffo's not living at the farm now. You could track him down and ask him."

"In town, I heard your garden is a copy of one on the Jardin Estate in Alsace."

"But it's not. Mine is a tribute to ancestors, taken from my family book."

"Would you let me see your book?"

"It's in the kitchen. I don't show it to people. But since you have a badge, I'll show you. Follow me."

At the table, he paged through Aggie's gypsy remedies. "Not much in English."

"Some in German, lots in French. Some recipes in Romany, but it's mostly a spoken language. For forty years in Central Europe, my people were not allowed to speak in their native tongue. The language was not written down, but secretly passed on. See there, the page where an ancestor drew a picture of the plot my husband used for my garden. It has the names of the herbs I grow."

He looked closely at the faded writing on the page. "Does it say monkshood? Have you sold any of that to Neubland Pharmaceuticals?"

"I don't know that company and I wouldn't sell them that herb." She pointed to a page. "Here are the names of plants with poison. Ones that are dangerous to eat. They are separated from the other herbs in my garden, so no mistake will be made. I cook like an old gypsy, like Romas did for centuries, with things I grow. But I never use those."

"Did Lily McFae spend much time reading your book?"

"My book is private, used only by me. Only a few things in English anyway. Only because I do not want trouble do I show it to you."

"So again, about your connection to this fellow Ratchov."

"There is none. But I knew his uncle."

"Okay then, can I take a close look at your garden?"

"Follow me." She led him to the plot and watched him bend over to examine a plant. "Someone took some of my herbs recently, without asking. Go ahead, take some dill, if you want. Will this take long? I have goats to tend."

He moved on to a far bed. "Is this one parsley? I don't garden."

She started toward him. "I'd stay away from there. Beware of those plants. That's monkshood and belladonna. Foxglove, too."

He moved away from the bed. "Tell me about monkshood."

"Some say it came from the saliva of a mad dog."

"And you grow it?"

"For sentiment only. Never used."

"You're some sentimental lady, Mrs. Verkie, growing poison in your garden."

"I'm a transplanted gypsy, and the plants were grown by my people."

"And how did they use the poisons?"

"They didn't. They were grown because of tradition." Aggie picked some tips of feathery green. "It's dill and it's safe to eat."

He brushed it against his nose. "I must ask. Do you have the stolen *Book of Cures*?"

"On my gypsy oath, I do not have it." She crossed herself.

"Are you sure you did not get that book from Boris or Lily?"

She stared at him. "I did not." She turned on her heel and left the garden.

He followed behind. "I expect we'll talk later, after Lily regains consciousness. Stay close by. Thank you for the dill."

In his car, Jamison wrote Aggie's name in his notepad, followed by the words "garden" and "poisons." On his cell phone, he called for an officer to shadow Mrs. Verkie.

☙

Worry about the biopsy kept Piper awake all night and pushed her to the beauty shop earlier than usual. She yawned and turned the key to open up the salon. Inside, she twisted open the blinds. In the slatted light, next to the barber chair, stood a stranger. He wore coveralls, goggles and a baseball cap. Magazines were scattered over the linoleum. The floor was littered with broken jars and bottles. The intruder's hand rummaged in the drawer of clippers.

"What are you doing here?" she yelled. "What do you want?"

"Can't you guess?" the low voice said.

"If you're the same man who ripped up the house, you know my stuff isn't worth scoot."

"I came for the *Book of Cures*, the one you took from the Used Stuff Store. It has a red cover."

"All the books I bought there went to the bookmobile. Every single one." She leaned against the counter as her knees turned to liquid.

"It's gotta be somewhere." The man yanked open another drawer and pulled out a straight edge barber's razor.

In that instant, Piper reached in the drawer for her own weapon and clutched a handle tight. He grabbed her with one arm, strong enough to hold her against his body. She felt the scrape of the razor against her face, the metal cool and rigid. She could imagine it slicing into her skin.

His voice was harsh. "Tell me where you hid the damn cure book."

She struggled against his hold, feeling faint. "I don't know anything about it. Let me go."

She closed her eyes and tried to breathe.

Splat. Her eyes sprang open and she saw a sparrow had collided with the front window. "Look, the eye of the sparrow," she shouted. She looked down at the handle in her hand attached to the vibrator and hit the intruder on the head with it, whacking him over and over with the instrument. As he jerked away, the razor slashed the side of her face. Blood slid down her cheek, falling bright red on her pink blouse.

Free from his grasp, she rushed for the door, turned from the side of the salon, and ran into the alley. She fell bleeding through the delivery entrance of the Hopper next door.

When she came to, the sheriff was holding a towel to her cheek. The white cloth turned red as he pressed down to stem the flow. "You're all right, Piper. Tell me what you remember."

Dazed, she looked around. "Freddie likes to sing the hymn, *His Eye is On the Sparrow,* but he wasn't around, and the sparrow was. Then it flew away. So did the intruder, I guess."

"Who was it?" the sheriff asked.

Her voice was weak. "I didn't recognize him, but he wore a janitor suit and goggles and a baseball cap. It looked like the same guy who left our house after he trashed it. He asked if I had a book of cures and I said no."

"If it's about that stolen book, the detective will want to talk to you. But let's get you fixed up first."

Siren blaring, the sheriff hustled Piper to the emergency ward at the Groverly Hospital and stayed by her side until a technician arrived to clean up the cut.

"The recommendation is for you to stay here overnight," the sheriff said. "I can notify Fred, or you can."

"I will. And I need to call Aggie. Listen, you don't have to stay."

"I'll contact her for you when I'm back in Nolan, okay?" He slipped out the door.

The emergency doctor came in and his examination found the cut to be superficial. The wound was treated and bandaged. "The sheriff told me about the attack. A person can go into shock after an assault like that. To be safe, I recommend you stay overnight, so we know there is no concussion or other injuries from your fall."

When Piper was admitted, she asked to stay in the empty hospital bed next to her cousin, Lily McFae, and the nurse arranged it. Piper wondered if the hospital would keep the two of them safe from the intruder. She tried to call Fred at the garage, but the line was busy. When her meal was delivered, she picked at it and rearranged it, but did not eat.

Afterward, she tried to call Fred again, but the garage line was tied up. She didn't feel up to explaining her situation with a phone message.

❧

Aggie talked to the sheriff and joined him at Cut & Curl to sort out the mess from the break-in. After he collected evidence, she swept and cleaned until the place looked presentable.

Then, she drove to Groverly General to see Piper. During the trip, she noticed a tan car behind her pickup. When she drove faster, the vehicle hung in place. When she slowed down, so did her shadow. In the hospital lot, the same sedan parked a few rows over. Inside the lobby, the driver disappeared behind the potted plants.

"Bah, begone." She snapped her newly limber fingers in his direction, but his back was turned.

She slipped into the dim hospital room and sat next to Piper's bed. "I'm glad you could be near Lily after you were hurt. Can I turn up the lights to see you better?"

"She rests better in the dark."

Aggie opened the blinds. "Just a little light on things. Does Freddie know you're here or is this room a dim place to hide, if you want to cry?"

"I tried to phone him, but the call didn't go through."

"Except for the bandage and puffy eyes, you look fine. I straightened the shop, so your place is neat and tidy again. The cash register money is at the sheriff's office. Sixty-eight dollars. Does that sound right?"

"Yes, about that. Oh, Aggie, you saw the shambles. That man cut my cheek because he wanted a book about cures. He thought I had it."

"All this trouble about a book I might have bought from Used Stuff that I don't have anymore. We're caught in the clutches of a devil and we don't know who he is." She sat down next to the bed. "I didn't tell you the detective came to the farm and asked about Boris Ratchov and Lily. He thought I got the book from one of them. I told him that I didn't have it. That was an honest answer. Everything I said was truthful. Even about my garden."

"The guy who cut my cheek was certain I knew where it was. I think he disguised his voice."

When Piper looked up, the doctor she'd seen about the lump in her breast stood in the doorway. "Piper, I saw your name on admissions." He held up a paper and glanced at Aggie. "I need a few minutes to go over this form with my patient."

"That's fine. I'm going to a grocery to buy us something safe to eat." Aggie ambled out the door.

Piper looked at the paper with the word, "biopsy" on top.

"Will you sign this?" he said. "We didn't hear from you and then, your name appeared on the patient list here. You're about to be discharged because the cut on your cheek isn't serious."

"I couldn't decide what to do."

"Here's the thing. You're here now, and I can make the arrangements for the biopsy. I asked and they'll squeeze you in. The procedure doesn't take long."

"I'm just not sure yet."

"Well, think about it. Even small surgeries are up to the patient, but I strongly recommend you go ahead. I'll leave the paperwork."

As soon as he left, Piper threw off the covers and rushed over to Lily. She stayed, holding tight to her hand until the nurse came in.

"It's time for Lily's bath and she might prefer privacy." The nurse pulled the separation curtain after Piper went back to her bed. "I'm glad she has a relative staying with her. I'm a strong believer in hand-holding."

"I'm her only relative and best friend. We're incredibly close." Piper grabbed a notepad from her purse. "I love her tattoos."

"It was an amazing thing to do after a total mastectomy, covering her chest with that beautiful artwork. Butterflies and birds. Flowers and greenery. So intricate. I've never seen anything like it."

"I know. I know." Piper wrote down the descriptions. "Yeah, amazing. Her total mastectomy."

"Of the two, it's my favorite, although the one with the books on her shoulder is nice too. Green and red and yellow books, all in a row."

"Yes, nice, very nice." The words spun in Piper's head as she wrote them down.

After the nurse left, Piper sat down by Lily's bed and put her mouth near Lily's ear. "You don't know it, but you may have changed my life. You and your amazing chest."

The patient waited, motionless.

"Because the reason I moved out of our bedroom was the secret I planned to tell at book club. About finding a lump in my breast. A while ago, the doctor told me I need a biopsy, and I've been afraid to do it." Piper's voice broke. "I'm afraid of what Freddie will think about my body, if I lose part of it. He always says I have the best figure in town. And on top of that, he wants to have a baby, and how could I do that if …." Tears dampened the hand on the blanket that covered Lily's chest. "But you've been through it. Lost both of them. If only I'd told you, or you'd told me." Piper sighed. "I needed someone to understand. Now I know that you'll be there for me. And I'll get through this."

Piper signed the authorization and rang for the nurse. "Soon as possible, I'd like to go ahead."

When the nurse left, Piper went to Lily's bed. "You helped me decide." With two light taps, she patted Lily's chest. "I'll call Freddie, once I screw up my nerve. I promise."

Lily's head gave a most vague nod in her most vague world.

They remained together, letting the hospital move about its business.

A nurse poked her head into the room. "Piper, they'll expect you upstairs for the procedure in an hour. Afterward, you'll be released once your body signs are stable. Detective Jamison is waiting to see you. Do you want to talk to him? The doctor can put him off."

"No, I'll do it," Piper said. "I need the distraction."

"He's down the hall."

Piper grabbed a hospital robe and lightly kissed Lily's forehead. "Soon as we can, Aggie and I will find that darn book."

Lily felt the light pressure of lips on her brow. She worked hard to come back when the tears fell on her hand. The word "biopsy" shuddered against the poetry that sang inside her.

> *Or seen rich rubies blushing through,*
> *A pure smooth pearl, and orient too?*
> *So like to this, may all the rest,*
> *In each neat niplet of her breast.*

"Robert Herrick, seventeenth century," slipped from Lily's barely moving lips, but no one was around, except the machines. Once again, they blipped a little higher.

Piper managed a quivering smile as Hugh Jamison laid his ID on the desk and punched the cassette button to record her answers.

"As you know, I'm the detective investigating the theft of the *Book of Cures* from the Groverly Library. We met briefly during your book club meeting. Do you feel up to a few questions?"

Piper nodded.

"The doctor said this conversation should be voluntary, so stop me if you wish and we can do it later. I'll try not to tax you."

She played with her chipped nails. "Go ahead. I have nothing to hide."

"Do you know who the intruder was in your shop? Did he look familiar?"

"I have no idea who he was, but I suspect he was the man who robbed our house. The man we chased after, Aggie and Lily and me. I told the sheriff that he wore the same clothes and goggles. A baseball cap."

"I have that report. Was anything taken from your shop?"

"I haven't been back to check, but he jumbled everything up, broke bottles, spilled stuff. Aggie cleaned up the mess and the sheriff counted the money. The guy said he wanted a certain book."

"Exactly what did he say about this book?"

"Something about wanting a book with a red cover from Used Stuff. A while back, I bought the whole lot, and Lily and I took them to the bookmobile. I told him that. We carried them in and sorted them. They were just old books."

"Do you remember any red-covered book from Used Stuff?"

"No, I don't think any were red."

"Did you see Lily McFae with any book that color? In the bookmobile? Or at Aggie's farm? Or anywhere else?"

"No, never."

"Are you personally in possession of any book about cures? Or any very old book?"

"I have the journal of someone named Boswell with a gray cover. It's from the bookmobile. You can see it later, if you want."

"Do you know a man named Boris Ratchov?"

"He's the owner of the Emporium, but he's not a friend. I went to his store to buy some potpourri."

"What do you know about Lily McFae?"

"She came to Nolan a while back to help us start a book club. You can check with the Groverly Main Library. When they fired her, she drove here to start a book club and stayed on."

"Did she ever mention Minnesota Fiddler?"

"Minnesota who? No, I've heard of Minnesota Fats, but we never talked about him."

He grimaced. "After your injury, you were assigned to her hospital room? Do you know anything about her accident?"

"She's a friend, and I thought she'd appreciate having me there. I don't know who attacked her."

"Think carefully before you answer. Are there any signs that she's out of her coma, just not ready to visit with the police?"

"Look, she just lays there. Not talking to anyone." Piper took a few deep breaths. "I've tried to talk to her, but she doesn't answer. Is that about it? I'm having a biopsy, you know."

"That's all for now, Mrs. Valerian. Good luck with that."

She looked at the clock, then hurried off to find Aggie in the hospital lounge. "I only have a few minutes, but I want to tell you something. About Lily." She produced her notes. "I know what her tattoos look like."

Aggie bent over to see the words on the page. "How did you

find out, Piper? Did you see them?"

"I was there for her bath and the nurse was talking behind the drape. About butterflies and flowers and birds totally covering the mastectomy scars on her chest."

"And Lily never told us."

Piper flipped the paper and pointed. "The problem might be the second tattoo on her shoulder. A red book drawn on her shoulder in a row of different colored books."

Aggie put her hand to her mouth. "Oh dear, whatever does that mean?"

"We need to talk to her."

Piper heard her name called over the system. "Listen, I'm due upstairs for my medical thing."

"I'll wait," Aggie said.

Piper swallowed. "It shouldn't take too long."

From across the hall, Jamison watched the two suspects, Aggie and Piper. He couldn't hear their soft voices, but he noted how intensely they examined Piper's notebook. In spite of the fact that they gave off an impression of nice ladies, their brows, their expressions, their gestures signaled trouble, perhaps something illegal. He wanted to look at Piper's notepad, but it would be secured by the hospital during her procedure, and he didn't have the authority to see it without any real evidence. He found the police officer assigned to follow Aggie and signaled for him to resume the order when she left.

At the nurse's station, he checked on Lily McFae's progress.

"Sir, the patient remains in a coma, with slight signs of improvement."

He laid a document on the counter. "This is the required paperwork for the police to get the blood type of Lily McFae."

"I will need to get approval." The nurse bustled away.

When he received her blood type, he nodded.

With the doctor's permission, a few Nolan townspeople stopped by Groverly General Hospital to visit Lily. Three homemakers.

A farmer. The coffee shop owner. Feed store clerk. Salesman. The sheriff. Word filtered through town that since Lily couldn't hear, she wouldn't repeat stories whispered in the dim confessional of Room 3. Visitors were free to tell their troubles in her ear. The nurse noted that Lily's blood pressure stayed even and the doctor decided the visits could continue.

The detective heard from the sheriff's office that Griffo's vardo was now located at the Emporium. He was anxious to meet him: Aggie's nephew, Boris's employee, previous resident of Lily's garage room, one-time seller of old books. He was one of the missing faces at the time the book disappeared.

Griffo stuck a finger in the back of the cage and gingerly felt the snake. The scales were dry and cool. As his performance drew closer, Griffo found he could no longer spit and his skin erupted with more bumps. The only part of his act that Griffo liked was whipping the black cape around.

CHAPTER 34

In her rearview mirror, Aggie watched the tan car behind her, following along the miles from the Groverly Hospital to Nolan to the Valerian house. She didn't tell Piper. Why worry a friend with a bandage across her cheek?

After she dropped Piper at home, Aggie drove to the farm and pulled in the driveway. The car behind her picked up speed, then disappeared. Hurrying inside, she locked the doors. Her heart thumped as she sat by the window, waiting for an evil visitor. She only had a few old gypsy curses and the goats to protect her.

After an hour drifted by, she mixed up a small batch of lively potion, poured it in a teacup and crept into the garden to sit on the railroad tie under the plum tree.

She looked down at the earth now mixed with Camlo's ashes. "Oh, dear heart, when I drink gypsy tea, I remember our days together and it eases the troubles that brew around me now." She took a tiny sip, then poured the rest over the spot where she'd spread his remains. "May you be at peace."

The liquid seeped into the ground, dampening the top roots of the plum tree.

⚘

Detective Jamison stopped at the vardo in the Emporium parking lot. He tapped on the door and listened, then called out, "This is an official visit. May I come in?" He poked his head in the door.

Griffo stood by the little stove burner in back. "If need be."

"You are Griffo Verkie?" The detective stepped inside and presented his ID.

"That's my name, yes."

"Will you answer a few questions?"

Griffo nodded and sat on the hand-painted bench. "As if I had a choice."

The detective sat down next to him. "Mr. Verkie, recently you had dealings with Boris Ratchov and purchased an item."

"Yes, the sword, but it's more like a rental."

"I'm not referring to a sword."

"You mean the herbs?"

"Not even close."

"What then?"

"I refer to the stolen volume called the *Book of Cures.*"

"Man, you're totally off base. I didn't buy anything like that. Bought a few herbs in his shop and lent him Aggie's recipes. If that's the book you mean, talk to her, not me. I did buy a book at Used Stuff." He reached behind him. "About how to be charming. I'd like my 50¢ back."

The detective took the book, rippled through the pages, then set it down. "Did Ratchov give you permission to park here?"

"He did."

The detective leaned forward. "Where can I find him?"

"I don't know. He comes and goes."

"Do you know Llewellyn Blanding from Neubland Pharmaceuticals?"

"Doesn't sound familiar."

"Do you have anything in your possession to sell to Neubland?"

"You can see I have very few possessions."

"But you have a record of arrests. Will you come with me for further questioning?"

"I'd rather not."

"It won't take long. I need a blood sample. Bloody fingerprints were found on the Emporium counter. I want to know if they're yours or belong to a possible victim."

Griffo chuckled. "Boris, Sax and I formed a knife throwing club. Sealed it in blood with fingerprints. There is no victim."

"So you'll give us a sample of your blood?"

"Tell you what, I'll do it. I can spare a drop or two to prove I'm innocent of anything you care to invent."

The detective led Griffo away. Under thorough questioning at the station, the gypsy offered no vital information about the book or any of the other suspects. After the technician poked Griffo with the needle and extracted rich, red fluid from his veins, the woozy gypsy fainted. When he recovered, he was released.

Jamison studied the first results of the blood samples taken from the Emporium counter. He had no blood type record for Boris Ratchov, Sax Morton, Aggie Verkie, Piper Valerian, or the Neubland salesman, but he now knew that Griffo Verkie matched one of the prints. And Lily McFae didn't.

Piper knocked on the kitchen farm door and waited for Aggie to unlock it and let her in.

"Here I am, banged up and bandaged, but doing pretty well."

"Quick, come in and sit down." Aggie heated up the kettle. "Did you see anyone sneaking around out there?"

"No, is someone bothering you?"

"A car follows me wherever I go and I don't know what to do. It started after the detective stopped to see my garden and family book." Aggie snapped the latch on the door, then went to the cupboard and got out teacups and a knob of ginger.

Piper shook her head. "Let's face it. We're drowning in trouble. I need to talk to you."

"Is Lily okay?"

"Yes, I want to tell you something that I told Lily in the hospital." Piper took a deep breath. "A while back, I found a lump here." She put her hand on her blouse pocket and closed her eyes.

"Oh, my," Aggie said.

"That's the reason I moved into the spare room. Freddie loves my breasts and I didn't want him to find a lump while we were making love. They were a big part of our coupling, you know."

"Oh, come here." Arms open, Aggie folded Piper into the scent of rutabagas. "You haven't told him?"

Piper shook her head. "I tried, but it hasn't worked out."

"How serious? The lump."

"Don't know yet. But it meant so much when I knew Lily went through the same thing. I don't know anyone else who's been through it, and here she's had a double mastectomy."

"What do you do next?"

"They did a biopsy at the hospital and I'll hear soon. I wanted to tell you, to hear the words aloud, to practice for when I tell Freddie." Piper paced around the kitchen. "But now that I've said it, I don't want to talk about it anymore."

"Are you sure?"

"After I find out the results, we'll talk. Today, I need distractions."

"Then let's put our brains together and get the book back. We have homemade rutabaga potage for energy and strength." Aggie put bowls on the table.

"If we find the book, maybe it will clear Lily." Piper peeked under the pulled shade. "Why do you think you're being followed?"

Aggie poured two cups of ginger tea from the teapot. "Because there's a tan car behind me, wherever I go. Always tan. I can't see the driver's face, but it must be evil. Go ahead, sit and eat."

Piper took a sip. "Mmm, ginger. On the plus side, now that we've all been ransacked, that part is probably over."

"But being poisoned is something new."

"And spooky. Maybe the car is your imagination. Let's go see Freddie to get the book. That's where I left it, although there's a chance Lily picked it up. Maybe Fred and I can talk, if there aren't customers."

After they finished their soup and tea, they drove in Aggie's pickup toward town.

In a quick gesture, Aggie pointed with her thumb. "Look in the rear view mirror. Tan car behind us."

"Okay, I believe you now."

The gas station fuel pumps were empty when the farm pickup pulled in.

"That tan car's parked half a block behind us," Aggie said.

"After we get the package, we'll hightail it over to the sheriff's office and report it."

"I suppose we should." Aggie took two bottles of goat milk into the station and Piper followed, a few steps behind.

"Milk delivery, Fred. The usual. I'll put them in the cooler."

He took money to pay for the milk from the register and glanced up. "Good grief, Piper. What happened to your cheek? " He walked over and touched her bandage. "You're hurt."

Her hand laid gently his arm. "I'm all right, Freddie, honest."

Aggie put the money in her pocket. "I came to pick up the newspaper package Piper thought belonged to Jeremy. It belongs to me."

"But it's at the Hopper. Piper said to take it there, so I did." He stared at her bandage. "You must have been in an accident. What happened?"

Piper gave his arm a squeeze.

The hose bell rang as a semi-truck pulled in, followed by another bell and a station wagon at the service pump. A sedan waited in the wings.

"It's long and complicated. I tried to call you from the hospital, but the line was always busy. Now you've got customers who need gas. Basically, someone broke into the salon, but I'll tell you more later. I'm doing okay." Piper's mouth quivered. "I mean it, Freddie, I really do." She rushed out the door.

Outside, Aggie caught up with her. "Are you sure you don't want to stay?"

"No, let's go to the Hopper and see if the book's there. Then we'll go to the sheriff. And later, visit Lily. If we talk to her about the book, it might trigger something in her mind. If the book goes back to where it belongs, when Lily comes to, it won't matter."

"She might be innocent of stealing it, you know." Aggie frowned. "And you're putting off meeting with Fred."

"You're right. I don't know why it's so hard. No one in our family ever talked about big, bad things. We just moved past them, hoping the trouble would go away."

They sneaked backward glances along the way, watching the tan sedan following behind.

At the Hopper, Aggie stood next to the bar, and Piper perched on a stool, while Jeremy filled a tray of four dark brews for a table of bikers in back.

When he came back, Aggie motioned for him to come over. "I left a newspaper-wrapped package the other day and I'm here for it. It got misplaced, then Freddie brought it over."

"Yeah, that package came and went and came back to me. The funny thing is, I can't find it now. When it turns up, I'll let you know."

His words stunned Aggie. "It's very important." She turned to Piper. "Well then, let's go see the sheriff about the tan car."

Jeremy looked at his watch. "You won't find him in his office. Because of all the looniness going on, he patrols the county twice a day, looking for troublemakers."

Piper grabbed Aggie's arm. "Then we'll check on Lily."

Nerves amped up, they drove the thirty miles to the Groverly Hospital, with the tan sedan trailing behind.

"I'll park next to the door," Aggie said, "and we'll run in."

When no one came in after them, Piper stopped at the main desk to ask how to get her biopsy report.

The receptionist nodded. "Check with your doctor to see if you can pick up the results here."

Piper called her doctor and received the okay to get a copy of the report, if she'd be willing to wait about an hour.

The two women strolled over to the hospital door, looking for the tan car. Aggie thought she saw it in a back row, but couldn't tell if the driver was still inside. They decided to visit Lily and wait out the situation.

Piper paced the room. "When I get the report, I could open it here with you and Lily. If I know the results, it might be easier to tell Freddie."

Aggie shook her head. "It's important for you to tell him first. A married life belongs to two people, not to women in a club." She fingered the scarlet ribbon around her wrist. "Gypsies say, 'If your tears need to be dried, go to the one who holds your kerchief. When you need love, go to the love you know best.'"

They sat in Lily's room, not talking, aware of minutes crawling by.

Eventually, Piper checked her watch and stood up. "Okay, that's it. I'm going down to get the results, good or bad."

"I'm coming with you."

After Piper signed for the sealed biopsy envelope, before she could change her mind, she made the call to Freddie. She turned to Aggie with tears welling in her eyes. "Freddie says he knows what's wrong. He'll be there waiting for me at Cut & Curl."

Aggie rose and patted Piper's shoulder. "You're doing the right thing."

Clutching the envelope, Piper rushed for the door and started out into the sunshine.

"Better wait for me. I'm your driver," called Aggie. "I'll drop you off."

All the way to Nolan, Aggie sang gypsy songs. "The music of good fortune," she said. "Sing along. 'Kavoursnik. Kavoursnik. Tra La La. La. La La. Kalomp. Kallah.'"

"Not only do I not know the melodies, I don't understand the words, but keep singing."

Freddie waited outside the salon and Piper ran up to him to give him a quick hug.

Inside, Fred flopped into the barber chair. "I didn't wait for you to tell me what happened to your cheek. I talked to the sheriff about your accident, which was not exactly an accident. Jeez, Piper, what's going on? Is some criminal after you? I was trying to track you down, then got your call."

"I'm glad you came, Freddie, but this is not about my cheek." Piper flipped the sign on the door to "Closed" and shut the blinds. "It's a more personal matter."

He looked grim. "If it's not about that, before you even start, I think I know what you're going to say. And I don't want a divorce. I couldn't take it."

Her lips twitched. "Divorce? Of course not. It's more of a health thing, Freddie. I'm sorry, but it's something I should have told you right away. It's the reason I moved into the guest room." Piper slowly undid her blouse buttons to show a bandage instead of a lace bra. "Then I was too scared. And then I was afraid to get pregnant, if I didn't know what it was."

"Well, what's wrong?"

"I found a lump in my breast, and I had a biopsy." She held up the sealed envelope. "Here are the results. It will tell whether I need a lumpectomy or mastectomy or not."

"Jeez." Stunned, he stared at her. "Jeez."

"The decision will be up to me, but I know how much you like my figure. I've been putting it off, figuring out what to do if it's cancer. How to tell you."

He got up and wandered over to the closed blinds. Piper turned her back and buttoned up her blouse.

"You've knocked the wind right out of me. I don't know what to say." He plunked down in the closest reception chair. "I'm no good with words, Piper. You know that. And now you've turned everything upside down."

"Take your time." Piper opened the window, then buzzed around the room, dusting cabinets and furniture. The scent of lemon oil filled the room.

Absently, he picked up Piper's book and read to himself. "Hey, this doesn't looks like radical politics. It's more like sex stuff." He turned the page. "Why are you reading this?"

She shook out the dust cloth at him. "It's for book club."

"That doesn't make sense. It's about some guy's god-like vigour. Is god-like vigour what I think? What kind of club reads things like that?"

Piper grabbed *Boswell's London Journal* out of his hands. "My book club ladies, that's who. Besides, you and I are in the middle of a talk."

"But why do you want to read something like this?" He reached for it. "Is our sex life too dull? Is that it?"

She moved toward him and opened the book. "The book shows the pleasure people feel with one another." Her voice was soft as she read.

> *The friendly curtain of darkness concealed our blushes.*
> *My bounding blood beat quick and high alarms.*

She stopped reading and put one hand on Fred's shirt. Her body moved closer to his, so the bandage on her face nuzzled his cheek.

His arms went around her and the book fell to the floor. "Jeez, Piper. I don't think well under pressure. You know it always takes time for me to absorb bad news."

"I know. It took me some time to get through it too."

Dust speckles moved in through the screen and waltzed

through the air in three-quarter time.

"You smell like furniture polish," Fred mumbled.

"I'm sorry."

"Oh, I like it."

Her fingers fondled the nape of his neck, rubbing the bristle of his hairline.

His voice sounded edgy. "You've been gone such a long time, and I missed you so much. Where you been, darlin'?"

"Right here, Freddie. Cuttin' and trimmin'. And in the spare room at home, worrying the nights away."

Inch by inch, they tiptoed toward the old couch in the storage area. Clinging together, they dropped into mohair cushions, squashing the throw pillows, making the springs squeak.

"I don't suppose that author wrote any other books like that?" Fred asked much later.

"His name is James Boswell, but he's kind of a jerk," Piper sighed. "I'm so sorry. I should have told you about the lump."

"Don't you know by now, hon, that I don't give a damn whether you have one nose or two, one breast or none? I love you. All the time. Every single minute."

Outside, butterflies did pirouettes to celebrate the tender, nearby loving. Hundreds of wings beat the air in golden rhythms. Eventually, Piper remembered the envelope and opened it. One word leapt from the page, "Benign."

The butterflies stopped mid-air and waited for the couple to fall into each other's arms again. Then, the beating wings danced on, a fluttering circle of time moving around the front of Cut & Curl.

CHAPTER 35

Lily McFae. Condition – stable with increased machine activity.

Aggie leaned over Lily's hospital bed. "I know you can't hear, but Piper has good news."

The patient lay peacefully under her waffle-weave blanket.

A smile played on Piper's face. "I can say my meeting with Freddie was delicious and complete. We talked about the lump, and I should have trusted him." She played with the loosening adhesive tape on her cheek. "And the test result was benign. How about that?"

"I called the sheriff about the tan car following me," Aggie said. "He told me, 'Nothing to worry bout.' Hah! We thought it might help, if I told you what I saw inside the garden book." Aggie pulled a chair up to the bed. "So this is what comes back to me. Inside the red cover is a drawing of a garden that looks like mine."

The hospital machine spiked up.

"The same things grew there, planted in the same places, even down to the poisonous herbs. Foxglove. Monkshood. Belladonna."

Piper held the flyer. "And we brought you this red leaflet." Aggie and Piper read together:

Alsatian Heirloom Seeds for Sale
Poisonous and Nonpoisonous
For Decorative Use Only
From the Medieval Garden of the Jardin Estates

Lily opened her eyes and said, "home of the hidden, sealed *Book of Cures.*"

Aggie's mouth dropped open. "Dear lady, you're awake."

Lily squinched up her face. "It's so bright in here. It hurts my eyes."

Piper ran to the window, twisted the rod to close the blinds, and rushed back to the hospital bed. She hit the call button several times for the nurse.

Lily fluttered her eyelids. "My throat is dry, but I think I finally caught up on my sleep."

"That's one way to do it." Piper laughed. "The doctor called it a coma."

"Well, I feel very rested." Lily's eyes focused. "And very weak. Where's Hugh Jamison? He was here, I think."

First, the nurse and then, the doctor arrived.

Piper and Aggie waited outside the room during the examination. Finally, the nurse bustled out and gave them a thumbs-up.

The doctor came through the door and walked over. "She's asking for you both. Stay only a few minutes."

They rushed in and stood by her bedside, waiting for words to come. But there were happy tears instead.

Lily's voice trembled. "I can't remember what happened."

Piper took her hand. "The moped slipped in the mud, and you crashed. We found you when you didn't show up at our meeting."

"Was someone following me?"

Aggie gave Piper a long look and turned back to Lily. "No one knows for sure. Maybe you'll remember later." She smoothed the coverlet. "We had book club meetings at your bedside."

"And some of the nurses listened to our readings."

"And things happened. Special things," Aggie said. "I talked to you about Cim and you listened. Afterward, I was able to burn his fedora and spread his ashes in our garden."

The patient opened her mouth, but nothing came out.

Piper moved closer and told Lily about the lump in her breast and all the details of getting back with Freddie.

Lily nodded. "A lump can scare a person senseless. I know."

"That's the thing. You were with me when I needed you. I heard about your tattoos from the nurse."

Lily's hand went to her breast. "My mastectomy. A secret I planned to tell, about losing my breasts and decorating the empty spaces with beautiful things."

Piper smiled. "While you were in a coma, we talked to you, and worked out our problems."

"I should start a therapy practice." Lily gave a feeble smile. "All the rocks fell out of my pockets."

"I don't know what you mean, but if there are holes, I'll stitch them up," Aggie said.

"I'd like to see your faces. Open the blinds a little."

"Can you talk to us about the tattoo on your shoulder?" Piper asked. "Or would you rather not?"

"Oh, that's a symbol for all the special books lost to me at the library. And the special book that went on tour."

Piper took a deep breath. "Here's the thing you should know. That stolen book's still missing, and the detective thinks you took it, or we did."

Lily frowned. "I might have had that book for a while. Or did Aggie have it? So many things are running through my head, it's blurry."

"The nurse said you need to rest. Don't worry. We'll talk about all this, later." Aggie closed the blind again and ushered Piper out.

Later in the day, Detective Jamison intercepted the doctor. "I hope to have a few words with your patient. The nurse said she's out of her coma." He produced his identification again. "Official business."

"Let me check to see how she's doing. She might be too confused to speak to you. Wait in the reception area."

After further tests and examinations, the doctor found the detective. "She can see you, but I'll remain in the room. Don't make the visit a long one."

"Agreed." The detective slipped into the room and sat next to the bed. "I do keep telling you my name, but that's protocol. I'm

Detective Hughbert Jamison, of the Groverly Police." He took her hand. "And this is an official conversation."

She looked at his hand on hers. "I remember you."

He let her fingers go. "Let me begin by telling you about a thief named Minnesota Fiddler, who owned your bookmobile, before the county did. She used the secret compartment in the closet to hide a stolen collection of coins."

"I remember the closet. After you told me about a secret place, I found it, but then I heard gunshots and left."

"I was able to retrieve the coins and then arrest her when she was caught trying to remove them from her hiding place. She's in custody. There's no evidence that you were involved. All this happened while you were in the hospital."

"Congratulations, I guess."

"But now, I need you to recall our brief discussion about the *Book of Cures*. How you and the book disappeared from the Groverly Main Library at the same time. This is a serious and unsolved crime, so I need to question you further. Do you know who stole the book?"

"Wait a minute," the doctor said. "Is this now a police inquiry?"

Lily blinked. "No, it's all right, but my mind's so fuzzy, I don't know if I can help."

"I must tell you, your name keeps coming up in various ways. I'm interested in information about Boris Ratchov, Griffo Verkie, Llewellyn Blanding, and the other members of the book club."

"Can you ask one question at a time?"

"Of course. I didn't mean to rush you. What about Griffo?"

"He's Aggie's nephew, but I've never met him."

"Where did you meet Boris Ratchov?"

"At the Emporium. He did my tattoos." She reached up to her shoulder and at her touch, her gown slipped down to reveal the top of her markings.

"Is that a red book tattooed on your shoulder?"

She put her hand up to adjust the gown. "There's also a green and a yellow one. That tattoo represents the many books of my career, all kinds and colors of books as a long time librarian."

"Do you think someone hit you and the moped intentionally?"

"Someone was following behind me. I thought it was you.

Then everything went black." Her voice wavered. "I'm sorry, but I do feel dizzy. And nauseous. I'll need some time to remember what happened and when. Things are still hazy."

"I'll leave now and we'll talk more when you're up to it." He touched her hand and sought her eyes for a quick glance. Then he followed the doctor, who snapped the door shut.

The doctor turned to him. "Since my patient's blood pressure shot up again. Let's eliminate your visits until she's fully recovered. She'll rebound soon enough, now that she's out of her coma. Time will clear her head, and she'll be able to provide the answers you require."

"Will you notify me when I can see her again?" The detective scanned his notes.

"Depending on various health issues, she may be released soon. I'll contact you when it happens."

With sunshine flooding through the blinds again, Lily sucked on ice chips, sipped broth, and drank mint tea. After a series of tests and a few steps, she felt alert enough to read. She reviewed the material on her nightstand. Then she opened her tote bag and saw the torn newspaper package.

She smiled. In this sudden way… unexpected… unheralded… unsung, but in all its scarlet splendor, the *Book of Cures* appeared again.

"Incredible," she murmured. Her machine charting bounded up as memories flooded back of holding and reading the manuscript in her room above Aggie's garage. The promise of a *Book of Cures* was real. She remembered pages filled with drawings of the estate, the flowers and herbs.

The nurse stopped in to check her vitals, and Lily hid the book under the blanket. She worked to find her normal body tempo. "I'm just excited to be out of the coma," she said. "Resting will soon calm me down."

To make sure she'd be alone, she asked the nurse to close the blinds and permit no visitors. Lily willed her body to relax and turned on the bedside light. Reverting to habit, she removed the cotton gloves from the library kit in the carryall before she unwrapped the newspaper.

Through thin finger protectors, Lily stroked the book that meant so much to her. Gradually, she moved through the pages, caught up in elaborate inked images of vegetables and herbs grown in a strange Alsatian garden. She murmured the names, and admired the delicate drawings.

When she got to the end, she saw the loose seal on the back pocket. Her hands shook as the seal cracked open.

A few days ago, she'd asked fate to give her a few more hours with the book. Now, releasing the dusty scent of time, she slid the thin papers from the back pocket and unfolded them. Faded ink, once blood-red, left pale marks, like ragged threads on a bleached antique carpet. She breathed in and out lightly to keep the spell alive. The book reached back hundreds of years, telling its forgotten tale of herbal mysteries. Of a castle. A duchess. A healer.

Her mind went spinning as she slowly deciphered the French remedies. For the heart and diseases of the blood. For tremors. For growths. Lily noted the ingredients. The volume markings were lost on the brittle paper, no longer visible to the naked eye, but the herbal names remained. Dried lovage blossom. Healing potion of yarrow. Oil of dragoncello. Recalling Aggie's listing of dangerous herbs, Lily's hand wavered over other names scrawled on the crumbly-edged paper. Words that still dripped with poison. Heart of foxglove. Crushed monkshood. Fluid of belladonna root. In many ways the healer foresaw the medical applications of poisons. Vaccines and medications gleaned from questionable herbs now used around the globe.

One recipe turned her head dizzy. A tea for memory and invigoration. For love. With five ingredients, marked safe to consume. And lively was the last herb listed. Though Aggie never told her the recipe, Lily had stood in the kitchen while the green liquid was mixed together for book club. She saw Aggie lay the ingredients on the kitchen counter, and although Lily couldn't read the proportions in the book, the herbal names corresponded.

The fact that she'd sipped one of the ancient remedies in the book made her feel faint. She put the manuscript away to recover her equilibrium. It was time to gather her strength and recover. And then what? She folded up the thin pages and put them back where she'd found them.

During visiting hours, one by one, those who'd talked to Lily when she was in the coma, were allowed to visit again, to tell her about their enjoyment of reading. With each person, Lily gained strength. The farmer expounded on frontier adventure. The coffee shop owner discussed the philosophy of Nietzsche. The feed store clerk revealed "whodunit" in his mystery. Several women whispered favorite passages from romance novels. The insurance salesman only smiled and made a gesture to simulate the cracking of a whip. Each person mentioned the benefit of a bookmobile in Nolan, and no one referred to their whispered secrets. Lily felt better and better, fed by short conversations with her book patrons in Nolan.

When visiting time was over, nurses in crisp uniforms trod up and down the halls on soft-soled shoes, chasing out late-stayers.

Once they were gone, Lily renewed her soul with the magic of the the scarlet-covered manuscript.

Back in his room, Hugh waited for the doctor to contact him about Lily. Before any arrests could be made, he needed the next call to go through to Llewellyn Blanding's cell phone, with information on the sale of the book. Unfortunately at this point, the salesman and his car were missing.

Griffo bought an ice chest and heavy gloves. He put in a supply of sardines and drank a snifter of fish oil from the cans each day.

At Used Stuff, Sax swept the floor and dusted the furniture daily. He wound up the caged bird and listened to its tinny music, while he practiced knife throwing, per Boris's instructions. Focus. Grip. Angle. Release.

Boris stayed busy too, relentlessly hitting the bulls-eye with his golden dagger. He studied maps and made plans, finally deciding it was time to change things up.

Behind bars, Minnesota Fiddler stared out at a bleak and cruel world.

CHAPTER 36

In Lily's hospital room, Piper reached into her purse and brought out her simulated eau de cologne. "My mother's favorite. To rub on our elbows." She uncapped the large container and the intense vapors of pseudo *Evening in Paris* escaped the captivity of the blue bottle to flood the room.

"Against my better judgment, we've decided to watch Griffo perform," Aggie said.

"It's a big deal. He'll perform at the Emporium parking lot," Piper added.

"We'll drop by afterward and describe every single minute. I can't see Griffo turning into a snake charmer and swallowing a sword." Aggie sighed. "He's no good with animals or sharp things."

"Everyone in town's going. You bring your own seating so the hardware store is sold out of lawn chairs." Piper rubbed cologne on the back of her knees.

Lily looked over at the bedside books. "I'll keep busy reading. And when you come back, I have a nice surprise."

"I have one too," Aggie said. "Griffo offered all his used books to the bookmobile, but Piper and I studied them. No erotica."

Lily sat up. "Don't be too sure."

"We'd better leave, or we'll miss the show." Piper stood up and motioned to Aggie.

"Have a good time." Lily moved to the edge of the bed and rang the bell.

When the nurse arrived, she helped Lily dress in street clothes.

"Bet you're happy to go home," said the nurse. "It's the high point of any stay."

"I'm glad it's quiet." Lily slipped on her shoes. "I don't need any more excitement."

"We'll finish up your walking exercises." She fiddled with the room thermostat. "I turned up the heat in your room. If you're too warm, I'll adjust it."

Lily practiced walking up and down the halls with the nurse, then did a solid turn without help and returned to her bed. There she rested, immersing herself in her favorite reading material, the book that belonged in an Alsatian castle. She expected Hugh Jamison to question her soon. With a shrug, she wrapped up the book. "Goodbye, old friend. I'm the one who has read all your secret remedies and now they should be returned to your family." She slipped the book into her bedside drawer.

Lying on top of the covers, Lily waited for Aggie and Piper to re-appear. She was free to go as soon as the clubwomen returned. Waiting out that stretch of time, she picked up the red flyer and read it again. Then she used it as a marker for her favorite passage in the book of poetry. It was one of her oldest books, its cover flimsy with pages near falling out, a book destined for repair. She felt tired and when the temperature hiked up a few degrees, it sent her drifting off. The slim volume fell to her lap.

Griffo narrowed his eyes to look out of the vardo and frowned at the sight of clouds building in the east. He saw Aggie and Piper in ringside seats at the Emporium parking lot. In back of them, at least sixty folks had hauled in chairs to form uneven rows for a view of his performance in front of a card table.

Taking a few deep breaths, he carried out the covered cage and sack of necessary items. His stately walk to the other end of the lot attracted attention. He put the cage on the table and swirled his black cape. "This is a day you'll long remember. The first performance of Griffo, the Magnificent."

The crowd offered a few welcoming claps.

He reached under the table into the large sack."

Pulling out a musical instrument, he played minor notes on

a Zambezi flute. "I am preparing," he said. "Watch closely." He whipped off the cover of the cage and slowly opened the door to reveal a big dozing rat snake, curled in the corner.

The crowd gasped. He pushed the flute inside the enclosure near the snake's head, and played, shifting the instrument across the cage in a wide motion. The snake seemed reluctant to participate, until the end of the flute tickled its tail. The crowd roared.

The serpent twitched and roused enough to follow the flute, back and forth. The audience clapped as the snake swayed to the music. Griffo now knew serpents couldn't hear the same frequencies as humans. They reacted instead, to the wide movement of the flute. The snake unwound from its coil and began to react more quickly.

Suddenly, he pulled the flute out of the cage and closed the door. His cape undulated as the audience applauded wildly.

"Thank you. Thank you," he shouted and twirled around in his black cloak. He was grateful for the tattooed lady's advice to keep the snake in an iced cooler all night and all morning, so the creature would be well chilled and only interested in thawing out. It was the reason he kept the song short.

Lightning flashed as he turned aside to do a quick read-through of the swallowing directions. Then he set the cape billowing and faced the expectant audience.

"Prepare yourselves for the most dangerous, most exciting part of my act, the swallowing of the sword. I am soon to travel the world, and my official debut performance will be with the circus in Groverly, two days hence."

He waved the sword with a broad gesture. "Feel free to applaud as I endeavor to slip this dangerously sharp instrument down through my body." Coated with sardine oil, the narrow slice of metal hovering over his head, aimed straight for his throat. The crowd roared the moment the sword touched his lips. He felt numb and weak.

He heard Aggie's voice fading away. "He's fainting. The dumb gypsy is fainting."

Far off in the distance, someone said, "Call for an ambulance."

Groggy, he felt someone shaking him. "Wake up, Griffo." He opened his eyes and saw the sheriff.

"Who cares if you swallowed the sword." It was Aggie's voice.

His lids fluttered. "I'm sorry, Auntie. I didn't mean to do it."

"Fiddlesticks, I'll wager plenty other performers panic the first time."

Griffo shook his head. "I meant I'm sorry about the librarian."

"What do you mean?" the sheriff said.

"I ran her down and hit her, because I thought she stole my ring." His voice cracked. "I didn't mean to hit her so hard."

"You did that?" Aggie shouted. "How could you?"

"Looks like I'll be taking Griffo in for questioning," the sheriff said. "I'll get some handcuffs. Sorry about that, Aggie."

The woman in the green-feathered hat pushed open the exterior doors of Groverly Hospital. The halls were empty and quiet as she walked the corridor, looking for Lily McFae's room. Since everyone in Nolan knew the number, it didn't take long to find it.

She slipped into Room 3 and saw the patient napping peacefully with a book on her chest. Quietly, the visitor in emerald green came close to read the title of the book resting on the patient's body, but she didn't touch it. Bending down to reach Lily's bookbag on the bottom shelf of the bedside stand, she bumped her hat against the lamp. After she looked inside the bag, she inched open the bedside table drawer.

The room temperature hiked up another degree and the hospital ventilation system bumped into operation. A rush of cool air brushed across Lily's cheek. She woke with a start and saw a woman wearing a green-feathered hat gone slightly askew. When the woman reached up to fix it, her flowing sleeve fell downward and displayed the bulbous tattoo on her forearm. Then, her arm came down, and she grabbed the newspaper wrapped package from the open drawer.

"Wait." Lily's voice quavered. "I know you. Give that book back. It's not yours." Alarmed, she sat up and punched the call buzzer. "Stop now, you're a marked man." The figure stopped at the door of Room 3. A gleam of metal flashed. A dagger cut through the cool, antiseptic air, directed toward Lily's heart. In a quick reflex gesture, she lifted the old book on her lap to protect the tattoos that decorated her torso. The cover fell off and yellowed, old pages were exposed.

Slooop. The dagger pierced the Table of Contents. Stabbed the Foreword. And plunged into the poem called *Wild Nights – Wild Nights!* Poetry saved Lily that day. The printed words penned long ago by Emily Dickinson stopped the knife cold.

Lily gasped. Her body shook as the intruder disappeared.

"I know you. I know you," her voice shouted out toward the hall. Pulling herself together, she realized that she'd lost the treasured book.

※

Llewellyn's cell phone rang.

A voice said, "This is the call you've been expecting. I have the book in front of me."

The salesman blinked as he heard tinny trills of bird song fill the line. "When do we meet?"

"You have the money?"

"I do."

"Then we meet now, before the storm hits. Come to the Used Stuff Store in Nolan."

"Not the Emporium? That works better because I'm your salesman. No suspicion, see."

"Not there. I repeat, come to the Used Stuff Store. Make it quick or I'll deal with someone else."

※

Lily waited at the door of the hospital lobby. She reminded the receptionist, "Don't forget to tell the detective or the sheriff that it's an emergency. Extremely urgent. Get to the Used Stuff Store ASAP."

As she walked out of the hospital, Aggie and Piper drove up. "Quick. I'm officially released and we have somewhere to go in a hurry," Lily's voice quavered.

"Like home." Piper opened the truck door and took the bookbag from Lily. "You shouldn't be carrying."

"I'm on the trail of the stolen book. Are you game?"

"I'm up for it." Piper pulled Lily into the pickup.

Aggie pushed on the gas pedal and they roared off.

"We follow the book to Sax and the Used Stuff Store. I'll bring you up to date on the way," Lily said.

"We'll do the same," Aggie raced the engine to a big crack of thunder. "That's the sound of big weather."

The sky opened and the windshield wipers swished back and forth as they drove through a sudden downpour.

"I had the *Book of Cures*," Lily said, "in my hospital room."

"What do you mean?" Piper gave her an odd look.

"The stolen book everyone wants, it was there. I found it in my bookbag."

"Are you sure? You know, you were confused when you came to." Aggie reached over and turned the windshield wipers down a notch. "We're driving so fast, we're almost out of the storm."

"The book was real. I touched it. I read it. It was there. Then someone took it."

"Who?" Piper asked.

"The woman with the green hat. I saw her. But she was Sax dressed as a woman and he threw a knife at me."

"Are you sure this isn't part of your coma?" Piper said.

"I know it was Sax. He had the flower coming out of a bulb tattooed on his forearm. When his arm flashed from under his green sleeve, I recognized it. Believe me."

Aggie sighed. "Maybe we should talk about something else. Like about Griffo. He was the one who hit you and sent you into the coma. He thought you'd stolen a ring from him. Now he'll go to jail. He's a stain on the family name."

Lily's throat felt dry. "One thing at a time. I'll deal with Griffo later. We're almost there."

Aggie swerved to avoid a fallen branch. "Are you sure we should do this?"

When Detective Jamison got to the hospital, he discovered Lily had been released. "Damn it, why didn't the doctor tell me? Why didn't you hold her?"

"The physician called the motel number you left, but there was no answer, so he left a message that she was being discharged. We had no reason to keep her."

"You said Ms. McFae left word of her whereabouts."

"She said it was urgent to get to the Used Stuff Store, quick as you can." The nurse handed the book to the detective. "And she left this for you."

He saw the point of the dagger cutting into the pages. "Did she mention who did this?"

The nurse shook her head. "She only said, 'Extremely urgent.'"

His cell phone buzzed, and he listened to the tape of Llewellyn's conversation about buying the book. He dashed off to his car and phoned the sheriff to head for the Used Stuff Store immediately.

On the grounds of the Jardin Estate, the scent of newly planted lovage and yarrow washed over the vineyard and drifted down the hillside.

At the goat farm, pink and white blossoms clouded the corner of the garden. The plum tree branches, once leafless and lifeless, now bloomed in profusion.

In Nolan, behind the Used Stuff Store, strange and powerful currents from Mozambique arrived after a long trip across the ocean, just as a sparrow poked a twig into the downspout and a butterfly circled, in anticipation of random circumstance.

Inside the Used Stuff office, the lady in green arranged a bouquet of lovage, then poured the liquid she'd concocted from stolen leaves of poison into the silver flask. If things did not go as planned, the tea would be waiting, next to two matching cups and a newspaper covered package. In readiness for the client, she unlocked the front door, then moved back to the office.

Llewellyn walked into Used Stuff and looked around at the usual display of old furniture and odd memorabilia. He didn't see anyone.

"Back here," a voice called from the office.

CHAPTER 37

Out of breath and a bit wobbly, Llewellyn arrived at the office doorway. "I'm here. With a case stuffed with money. Out of vodka, but I'm here. Even with a tornado about to touch ground." Rain dripped from his hat onto his briefcase.

"Come on in," the soft voice said.

The salesman saw the woman in green. "Who are you, ma'am? Damn it, where's Boris?" He stumbled into the room.

"Never mind him. I realize you've been drinking, but listen up." He touched the newspaper package. "Here it is. It's the two of us who will make the deal. Now let's see the payment."

"Okay, but first, the book. If it's the real thing, I show you the funds." He patted his bulging valise. "Instructions from Elcott."

Waves of giddiness swept through them as they sensed the book's mysteries about to unfold. The secrets. The ancient cures. One volume between two people standing face to face, a few breaths away from intriguing remedies for a trio of the world's most deadly diseases.

Attracted by the inviting aroma of lovage, a monarch flitted through the window and settled on the petite bouquet.

Llewellyn's hand twitched. He eyed the package. "You say the book is under that newspaper. How do I know that?"

The woman in green peeled down some newsprint to reveal the scarlet cover. "Now let's see some cash."

Llewellyn unlatched the briefcase and stacked bills on the table. "Just a few, to match the glimpse that I got from under that torn paper. I need to open the book."

He reached for the package. Like a steel paperweight, the woman's fist pounded down, holding the packet in place.

Llewellyn waved some bills under her nose. "Here. Grab a handful, grab two. This part of the payment will be yours, soon as you unwrap the book. I look through it and if it looks right, you take the money in the briefcase. I take the book to our experts who tell us if the cures are real. If they are, one million dollars goes to you. And Elcott gives me a bonus."

"That was not the deal. I asked for a million, and I need to count what you brought before we proceed. This deal may not work out. Others will be interested in the book."

"This is a legitimate down payment, lady. You must see Elcott's position. The company can't buy the cures without checking them out. That will take time."

The woman in green reached for the flask. "I see. Well, if I have to indulge you, then you must do the same. Before we proceed, we will seal this new arrangement with a toast of lovage tea. To prove we trust each other, I've mixed up my favorite refreshment." She poured liquid into the two cups. "And just for you, I loaded it with vodka."

The wind kicked up, sending a wild burst of air through the window. Sprigs of lovage and hundred dollar bills swirled around the room.

"Wait, the money's flying away." Llewellyn ran toward the window. "I'll close it."

"You do that. I'll pick up the cash." The woman shoved some bills into an empty drawer.

The salesman's hand tugged on the window sash. A loud chirping startled him and he stuck his head outside. "Hey, birdie, what the hell? It's a damn sparrow, building a nest in your drainpipe. With this big rain, it'll clog up and overflow."

He leaned out to wiggle the nest free. "I can fix that easy." When the drainpipe shook, he put his other hand on the gold cord to steady himself, pulling on the rope that held three daggers.

Underneath the rope, the figure in green leaned over, distracted by a hundred dollar bill under a fallen twig of lovage. At the same moment, the orange-winged butterfly fluttered from its perch to land on top of the sprig.

"How the hell did that thing get in here?" She stood to swat at the butterfly.

"I've almost got your drain problem fixed." Llewellyn leaned further out to disengage the nest. The cord that held the daggers wobbled as it supported his weight. The end wall fasteners that held the rope shook and the daggers danced.

The woman reached down again to retrieve the last fallen bill.

A sparrow's third eyelid winked, a butterfly antenna tremored, and the hooks attached to the end of the cord gave way. The whole arrangement crashed, the row of daggers slipping down, a sudden descent of gleaming points. Down. Down. Down. Sharp blades falling straight as bullets.

A scream pierced the room. Knives cut straight through the fabric of the emerald shirt and jabbed deeply into the bent over back. The fallen daggers stuck deep into flesh. Blood trickled from the wounds.

Llewellyn turned. "My god, what happened?"

The voice from the floor yelled in pain. "I don't know how you did it, but I've been stabbed. Call an ambulance."

Llewellyn moved, but he did not reach for the daggers or the phone. Instead he grabbed for the newspaper package and ripped it open to reveal the manuscript. "Holy Toledo, I've got it." He pulled it to his chest, while sheets of rain rushed through the window.

The store bell rang, and the damp, nice ladies of The Erotica Book Club rushed in to hear the racket coming from the Used Stuff business office. They stood at the office door, staring.

"Hold everything. We're here." Piper held up her purse. "And we're armed."

"Help me, someone. Help," a voice called out from the floor. "This guy tried to kill me."

"I did not," Llewellyn yelled. "I lost my balance. This is an invasion of privacy. He'll have you women arrested. Back, all of you. Get out of this office. Get out of this store. It's closed. This person and I are conducting a business transaction."

The figure in green groaned.

The ladies of the Erotic Book Club moved around the table to view the body, now leaking streams of blood, daggers sticking out of a ripped green shirt.

Piper stared at the salesman. "I know him. He's the guy at the Emporium who talked about the book worth a million, the drug salesman. Guess I better call an ambulance for the lady." She pulled out her phone.

"I didn't stab her, I swear," Llewellyn cried.

Lily bent down. "She's a he and he's a thief." She pulled off the wig. "I told you. See, it's Sax."

Llewellyn clutched the *Book of Cures* to his chest. "It was an accident."

She approached him. "But you do have the stolen book in your possession."

"Yes, but I'm an innocent bystander." He pointed at Sax. "The book belongs to her. I mean him. I was invited here to take a look at it and drink some tea. Some lovage tea." Llewellyn set the book on the counter. "See, here's my cup." He swallowed it down.

"Don't believe him." Sax lifted his head. "That's Llewellyn Blanding from Neubland Pharmaceuticals. He was here to buy the damn book and he knew it was stolen. Look at the money in his briefcase. I'm not alone in this. Call a doctor, will you? I'm in serious pain." His head dropped down as he moaned.

Llewellyn staggered and swooned on the floor next to Sax. "What kind of cheap vodka was in that tea, anyway?" He stared out through a gauzy gaze. "Yes, I'm Llewellyn Blanding. Call a Neubland Lab doctor."

Aggie sniffed at the cup and bent to touch Llewellyn's cool skin. "I doubt he'll make it. It smells of lovage, but underneath, there's an odor of monkshood. That is pure poison stolen from someone's garden." She closed her eyes. "Probably mine."

Sax lay immobile, still bleeding.

Aggie stood over him. "I remember when you came dressed as a woman and wanted to buy monkshood." She thought of the daggers hanging from a golden rope at the Emporium, now repeated at Used Stuff. Staring at the knife points stuck in his deep green shirt, she mumbled, "When you couldn't buy it, you came back to my garden and stole the poisonous leaves, didn't you? You get what you give, Sax."

Piper and Aggie hovered over the wounded men. Lily wrapped the book back in its newsprint protector. She felt her adrenalin evaporating and sat down in the desk chair.

"I hear sirens." Piper ran to the window. "Red lights are spinning."

"Thank heavens, they're here," Aggie said.

Detective Jamison, the sheriff, and the ambulance pulled up at Used Stuff and the group dashed into the crime scene. They stared in wonder.

"The culprits are down and out." Aggie pointed to Sax and Llewellyn.

"You ladies responsible for this?" the sheriff asked.

"Only in part," Piper said.

"I'm Detective Jamison of the Groverly Police." He aimed his badge downward, toward the two men on the floor.

Aggie spied the ring on Sax's hand. "Look, he wears a purple sapphire. It belongs to Griffo. He told me someone stole it, but he thought it was Lily."

Detective Jamison motioned to the ambulance attendants. "Take these men to the Groverly hospital. They don't look so good." He turned to the sheriff. "If they revive, we'll question them as soon as possible. The three club women will come with me to give statements. And I'll take custody of the book which I assume is the cause of all this mayhem." He looked at the package. "Is that it?"

Lily nodded and stood up. "I'm glad you made it. When we got here, Sax was bleeding on the floor, and the Blanding fellow had the stolen book." Her hand rested on the newspaper package. "It was Sax who threw the dagger at me in the hospital. I recognized him and we came here to get the book back. We weren't expecting violence."

"I don't expect you were." Jamison stood nose to nose with Lily. "I got your message."

"The damaged book and the blade?"

"You had a close call, Lily ... ah, Ms. McFae."

The close, rainy smell of the detective's body made her ankles shake. "I'd better sit down again."

"Take as much time as you need," he said. "It's hard to believe that a woman just out of the hospital and her cohorts could tie up a crime scene so neatly. I'll have a tough time explaining that."

Piper gripped her hands together. "The salesman drank the tea Sax gave him and then he fell over."

"Those two men accused each other of the crime," Aggie said. "We heard them."

Lily held up the wrapped package. "Now it's yours."

He took the book from her. "Thanks for guarding this."

"Please handle with extreme care. It's hundreds of years old."

"Of course, and it will be delivered to the Jardin family. By me personally."

"You should use gloves when you touch it, you know."

Before the full force of the storm hit, the sparrow retrieved the dropped sticks that had fallen from the nest and the butterfly left the scene.

At the goat farm, the women gathered around the returned gypsy wagon and lit candles. The decorated vardo was parked at the end of the driveway roundabout, away from the farm buildings. Aggie explained the gypsy custom of burning the owner's vehicle after he died. Following tradition, she lit a match and threw it into the kindling under the wagon. The women watched the flames consume the remnants of Aggie's traveling life with her husband.

Sax recovered from his dagger wounds, and underwent psychological testing. Judged sane, he was tried for the murder of Llewellyn Blanding and convicted with life imprisonment, no parole. The stack of evidence against him pointed to breaking and entering, theft and credit card fraud, but he maintained to the end that Maxine's death was accidental. That case was never tried, nor did the Jardin family wish to pursue the death of Duke Quincy.

Sax spent hours boasting to the police, talking about his criminal maneuvering. "I wanted to be the twin who got big things done. Maxine said I couldn't plan a fishing trip. But I created an intricate plan. It was the chess game of my life." Sax smiled. "I wanted to be the talk of the town. And I am."

He wore a lacy blouse that matched his sister's to the trial and entered his cell carrying a copy of *Lelia,* written by the French woman Amantine Lucile Aurore Dupin, the cross-dresser famous for writing under the male name, George Sand.

The Neubland lawyers denied any knowledge of the activities of their salesman, Llewellyn Blanding. He was buried unceremoniously, and Elcott recommended the company cancel all research on herbs grown during medieval times. The scientists destroyed the experimentation reports and threw the seeds into the dumpster, the contents of which were hauled to the nearest landfill in quick order.

Behind security doors at R&D, computers spewed out new formulas, using infinite variations on up-to-date ingredients. Employees in white coats hovered over flasks and Petrie dishes, studying previous trial remedies for persistent health situations that troubled world occupants: itching, allergies, and indigestion.

Griffo prepared to serve his jail sentence for attacking Lily. From his cell, as reimbursement for goat farm debt, Griffo gave Aggie the gems to resell to a well-known distributor of facsimile jewelry. He also promised that when he was released, he'd seek other relatives to visit.

A sign went up in Nolan. "Used Stuff Store. For Sale."

Once the excitement blew over, Boris packed up his fancy knife collection and tattoo equipment to move on to greener pastures. Soon, another sign appeared in town. "Emporium. For Sale."

CHAPTER 38

Blossoms perfumed the air outside the bookmobile. Inside, a silver stream of light shot through the window, like a river of energy connecting the women assembled there. Lily looked at Aggie and Piper, who waited for the next meeting of The Erotica Book Club to begin. Surrounded by books and friends, the women relaxed in their circle of friendship.

Piper beamed. "Ladies, you'll be happy to know Freddie and I talked a good deal about me being afraid to tell him about the lump. And lots more personal things too. Like we're thinking of having a baby."

"Oh, my dear," Aggie said. "How wonderful."

"That's really exciting." Lily hugged her friend.

Piper's eyebrow lifted. "So, tell us about the detective."

Lily frowned. "I haven't heard from him."

"Then I guess we talk about books," Aggie said.

Piper waved her hand. "I'm proud to say, I started *The Lustful Memoirs of a Young and Passionate Girl,* and I'll pass it on to Aggie soon as I'm done."

"And eventually, we might discuss it." Aggie poured liquid green ambrosia.

Camaraderie clinked with the cups. In the magic of book club tea, they were alive and beautiful and filled with billowing thoughts of bodily delights.

The door opened and there was a quick flutter of orange wings. When Lily looked up, she saw Hugh Jamison leaning tall and friendly in the well. The butterfly flew past him.

"Is it safe to come in? Anyone reading something to make my ears burn?" He laughed and the women laughed too. Closing the door with a gentle touch, he moved to the librarian's side.

Lily glowed from tea and desire. "I'm happy to see you." Everything else faded away.

"We just finished our refreshment, detective." Aggie pulled Piper toward the door.

Piper grabbed her purse. "Like Aggie said, we're leaving."

Hugh escorted the two women out. "Call me Hugh. I came to invite Lily to accompany me to Alsace to return the *Book of Cures*."

Aggie waved goodbye. "There is one cup of tea left for him."

Lily shimmered in the light. She gazed into his eyes, his gray-green eyes.

Their hands touched. He took the tiny cup. The traveling electric current from the touch of their hands blew out the circuits at Nolan Consolidated Electric.

Hugh took a quick swig and the lively potion was gone. "Isn't the book by Lorenz in the last row? I meant to check it out."

He drew her to the back of the bookmobile, to the open closet door. His face was a page length away. She leaned forward until only a paragraph separated them, then a sentence, a word and then, a letter. He kissed her. "I've been thinking of doing that for some time. Did we ever finish our discussion of chaos?"

"The flap of wings." She touched his throat and her nerve points tingled.

"The speed of winds." He stepped down into the door well and flipped the lock.

"Fractals like the edge of ferns." She pulled the shades down over the front and back windows and rushed back to his arms, her feet skimming over the carpet.

Their bodies zapped together as he kissed her again. "Lily McFae, you fascinate me."

The errant butterfly quivered and it landed on the cover of *Candide*. Pieces of clothing floated to the floor. His hand traced the tattoos where her breasts once were. "You are so beautiful. I knew you would be," he said. "Every part of you."

"I'm so glad you found me."

"I followed the butterfly trail and you provided the chaos." He kissed her ear. "Would you read to me? All night long. Or right now, if you want." He kissed her ear.

"Are you familiar with *Venus in India*? It's quite explicit."

"Don't let that stop you."

She took his hand. "It tells of 'transparent pajamas, of raging and throbbing.'"

"Better read it to me quick then, lady."

"Dickinson's poem is shorter. *Wild Night – Wild Nights!*"

"Then that's the one. Did anyone ever write about wild first encounters in a bookmobile?"

"Not as far as I know."

He lifted her to entwine them together near erotic novels and poems and essays. Sweet *Sonnets from the Portuguese* by Elizabeth Barrett Browning. And wild tales of Boccaccio's *The Decameron*.

In all kinds of places, the colored rain nourished seeds of lively dropped by wandering sparrows. In the landfill near Neubland Pharmaceuticals, along with other medieval herbs, leaves like elf ears appeared amidst composting debris. Next to Lily's mailbox in Groverly, seeds of the same plant waited for the sun and rain. And in the garden of the Jardin Estate, the seeds continued to renew their story.

Eventually the electric power was fixed at Nolan Utility, but not for a long time. The transformers kept blowing out from strange currents that disrupted the machinery as the couple engaged in pent up passion. Eagerly. Ecstatically. Erotically.

Sampling of Books Found in
Lily's Bookmobile Closet

As Lily told the book club members, "There are varying degrees of heat found in selections of erotica."

Austen, Jane, *Pride and Prejudice*

Boccaccio, *The Decameron*

Boswell, James, *The London Journals of Boswell*

Bronte, Charlotte, *Villette*

Browning, Elizabeth, *Sonnets from the Portuguese*

Casanova, *The History of My Life*

Devereaux, Charles, *Venus in India*

Eliot, George, *Mill on the Floss*

Grove Press, *Lustful Memoirs of a Young, Passionate Girl*

Lawrence, D. H., *Lady Chatterley's Lover*

Mangeul, Alberto, editor, *The Second Gates of Paradise*

Manley, Delarivier, *The New Atalantis*

Nin, Anais, *The Delta of Venus, A Spy in the House of Love*

Rhys, Jean. *The Wide Sargasso Sea*

Sand, George, *Lelia*

Voltaire, *Candide*

Woolf, Virginia, *Mrs. Dalloway*

Wright, F. A., editor, *Erotica: Women's Writings from Sappho to Margaret Atwood*

Book Club Discussion Guide

1. Which book club member did you like the most and why? Do you know women with similar characteristics? Lily, lonely and out-of-work; Aggie, a grieving widow, unsure of her position in the community; or Piper, the young salon owner with a health problem who looked for unusual ways to help her through a difficult time in her marriage?

2. Discuss the age differences and backgrounds of the three women. If you have friends of varying ages, what drew you together? Did the book club members form a family?

3. How is communication a real problem for each of the three women? Is it a familiar difficulty in our culture? Did the tea make it easier for the women to tell their personal stories or would it have happened anyway?

4. Lily reveals her deep feelings about libraries and books. What is your favorite thing about books? About libraries? About librarians? Have you visited a bookmobile?

5. Have you been touched by cancer or know cancer survivors? How did cancer affect the women?

6. How did the poetry of Emily Dickinson save Lily? How did reading Christina Rossetti's poems help Aggie escape danger? What about a sparrow saving Piper and the hymn she remembered her husband singing? Have you ever thought about how one simple thing can change events or lives?

7. What interested you about – Boris, Griffo, Sax, Llewellyn. How were the relationships of the two sets of siblings different or the same? Llewellyn and Elcott. Maxine and Sax. Do people ignored by family members or others find ways to strike back?

8. Did you guess who stole the *Book of Cures?* Discuss the murder of the duke and the salesman? Do you think psychological problems can cause people to commit such serious crimes?

9. Would you like to visit the Jardin Estate? Have you been to Europe or visited a chateau? Have you lived in a small town or know others who do? What is appealing about such places? Have you shopped in a place that reminded you of the Empori-

um? Or the Used Stuff Store?

10. Do you garden? Grow herbs? How have you used them? Do you believe in the healing powers of herbs? Discuss the use of herbal remedies by family, others, or in different cultures.

11. Would you like to sip some of Aggie's tea? The herb named lively is fictional. It's important to know that these mixes are not intended to be used by readers. Herbal use is dependent on health issues, specific knowledge, and exact ingredient amounts. Some herbs are poisonous. Others have serious effects.

12. Discuss the quirky components of the story, the whimsical or offbeat elements. For example: Gypsies. Goat farms. Collectible knives and daggers. A personal bookmobile. Small town stores closing up for any reason. Tattoos. Do you have a tattoo or know anyone who does?

13. Have you seen or heard about the monarch butterfly migration?

14. Do you have any experience or connection with rare books? Have you heard about book thefts from libraries and private collections?

15. Have you heard of the chaos theory? Did you sense how impending weather – the butterfly effect – was an undercurrent?

16. Are you curious about erotica? By chance, have you read or considered reading *The Tropic of Cancer, Lady Chatterley's Lover* or *Fifty Shades of Grey*? Other books of erotica? Are you interested in checking out any of the classics listed in the back? Were you surprised at the famous authors whose writing can be found in an anthology of erotica?

17. Or are you happy to read other books and not spend time on this genre? That's one of the greatest things about reading and book clubs. There are enough books available for every taste.

Meet the Author

How would you describe your novel?

Women's fiction/nontraditional cozy mystery. It began as a cozy mystery with realistic characters and plot. Paraphrasing Tom Robbins, "Truth above realism," the truth of the quirky characters sent the novel careening off center. It's also been called literary fantasy, with its use of nature, weather, and chance.

Are you a naughty or nice lady?

I'm mostly a nice lady, but one filled with curiosity, the kind who reads some of everything, even classical erotica. I've met lots of women just as curious. When I decided to write this book, I asked a clerk at a Tucson, AZ bookstore for classic erotica. She made several recommendations and I left with a large stack of books. I was surprised at the authors included.

Are any of the characters from real life?

There's a starting point for characters, then it turns into a free-wheeling process. Lily's character evolved from a librarian friend of mine and her tattoos came from a woman at a Crone meeting, crone meaning wise woman, not hag. She revealed a beautiful tattooed butterfly on her back. Piper came from my mom's friend in Wagner SD who owned a small beauty shop. Aggie blossomed from my grandmother's vegetable and herb garden on a small Nebraska farm. Gypsies wandered into the small town where I grew up. Despite my parents warning to stay away, I was fascinated and snuck off to their camp to watch their activities.

What themes run through your novel?

I've made many friends through past and present book clubs, and one storyline looks at the way friendships develop among different kinds of women. The mystery evolved from an old art book my designer daughter brought home from the University of Iowa and left in our library. Totally intrigued by the illustrations of a medieval garden, I knew I'd write about it one day. A collective of Mexican/American women writers called Sowing the Seeds inspired herbal cures passed on by family members. Dealing with cancer and grief comes from my mother's, my friends', and my own experience.

Where does the book take place?

The California location is based on a car trip Bob and I took, traveling toward the Pacific Ocean. As we drove along, monarch butterflies surrounded us, a surreal experience I never forgot. On that back road, I found thousands of magical migrating butterflies, or maybe, they found me.

What is your writing background?

I met my husband, Bob, at Creighton University in Omaha, NE. Both of us studied Radio, TV, Communications. After we married, I was writer/producer for our film/video production company and Bob was cinema/videographer, editor and pilot. We traveled the country on interesting projects for large and small companies, received Clio and other national recognition. When we moved to Arizona, I began writing essays, short stories, and memoir pieces and was published in twenty anthologies. I taught writing classes through the U of AZ Writing Works Center, wrote and produced videos for women, and ran workshops encouraging women to write their stories. I've published a creative non-fiction, two nature essay books, poetry and a novel.

What were your most exciting career moments?

I had an essay chosen for the anthology *The Art of Living, A Practical Guide to Being Alive.* Before it was published by Editorial Kairos in Spain, the British editor emailed the names of everyone in the book to the selected authors. I almost fell off my computer chair when I read: The Dalai Lama, Mikhail Gorbachev, Desmond Tutu, Deepak Chopra, Mario Vargas Llosa. A similar high point came when I was published in the anthology *What Wildness Is This, Women Write the Southwest,* with my nature essay appearing alongside the words of Barbara Kingsolver, Terry Tempest Williams, and Susan Tweit. My *Wise Women Video Series* is archived in Harvard University's Museum on the History of Women in America. *The Desert Eternal* was a 2008 Southwest Book of the Year, and *The Legend of Brook Hollow,* was selected as 2012 top nature book by NLAPW in Washington D.C.

What about your personal life?

Bob and I live in Omaha, NE, by a secret pond, visited by mink, Great Blue Heron, grebes, foxes, and other lurking wildlife.

ACKNOWLEDGMENTS

My lasting gratitude to Bob, Jami, Fae, Valerie, and Judd for their support. Special thanks to Kira Gale for perspective, Jamison Design for book design, Margaret Lukas and Carol Weber for editing, and Omaha/Tucson bookstores and Tucson/Omaha librarians. Heartfelt thanks to the band of women who encouraged me through the many versions, the real world and online readers and friends in Tucson, Omaha, and other parts of the country.